A Novel

Sifted *as* Wheat

A Novel

Sifted *as* Wheat

Frank G. Wheeler

Trusted Books
A Division of Deep River Books

Trusted Books is an imprint of Deep River Books. The views expressed or implied in this work are those of the author. To learn more about Deep River Books, go online to www.DeepRiverBooks.com.

ISBN 13: 978-1-63269-054-8
Library of Congress Catalog Card Number: 2013903278

This book is dedicated with love and gratitude to Susan, my wife of 43 years, for her faithfulness to and love for God and for me; also, to our children, Deborah and Cynthia; sons-in-law, Steven and Richard; and grandchildren, Robbie, Jonathan, Steven, Caroline, Gregory, and Jeffrey.

Thank you to the following for their advice and suggestions:
David Tuttle, Robert Hewey,
Arthur Amirault, Tom O'Connell
Ron Thimot, and David Withe.

In loving memory of, and in tribute to, author Frank G. Wheeler (1945–2010).

"But blessed is the man who trusts in the Lord, whose confidence is in him. He will be like a tree planted by the water that sends out its roots by the stream. It does not fear when heat comes; its leaves are always green. It has no worries in a year of drought and never fails to bear fruit." Jeremiah 17:7 NIV

—Susan Wheeler
March, 2013

CONTENTS

Part Two: New England

Part Three: Vietnam

Part Four: Home

Job

Rejoice! Oh my soul, though wearied with time.
Rejoice! For soon thy God's face to see.
Before Him all joy is thine,
From dust to glory thy reward to be.

But once, this upright, righteous soul
Sought death o'er treasure in its misery,
Cursing the day when the womb brought forth
This body of flesh for such sorrows to see.

In the presence of Holiness, the Accuser was asked,
"Hast thou considered My servant, who from his birth,
Hath feared Me and evil scorned?
One more righteous treads not this earth."

The Accuser with arrogant pride spewed forth,
"Thy servant, Job, he fears for naught.
All he is and has is encompassed by Thee.
Blessing upon blessing from Thy hands wrought.

"Thy servant will curse Thee to Thy face
If Thou put forth Thy hand to touch all he hath."
"Then test him, for all he hath is in thy power.
But touch him not, or know My wrath."

"Oh, how on that day my soul was cursed.
The Accuser, Destroyer, in fullness of fury,
Servants, livestock, did plunder, did consume.
And all sons and daughters I did bury.

"Thou, my soul, buried thyself in the dust of earth,
To worship, even in torment and strife.
Naked thou came, naked to return.
Bless Thou, my soul, the Giver and Taker of life."

Again before Omnipotence the Accuser stood.
"Consider My servant, who remaineth guilt free,
Whose soul, without cause, was ravaged and plundered,
Yet held fast, held firm his integrity."

"All a man hath he will give for his life,"
The Accuser relentlessly pursued the chase.
"Put forth Thine hand, touch bone and flesh,
This soul will curse Thee to Thy face."

"Permission I give thee to smite this soul,
Thy hand to restrain short of his life."
So Satan went forth, the attack to pursue,
Bringing suffering to add grief upon grief.

"My God! My God! Such pain to endure.
'Curse God and die,' a wife's foolish word.
Only good, no evil, from God's hand to receive?
No! My lips will sin not against my Lord."

I longed for the grave, where master and prince
And earth's kings and counselors rest together.
Where prisoners and slaves, the oppressed of this earth,
Hear not the voice of their oppressor.

"Why, O God, was I not stillborn,
That day of joy in its dawn cursed?
My sighs like a raging torrent flow.
Thine arrows, O Lord, my soul have pierced.

"Bring comfort, O God, destroy this life,
This wind of wearisome nights.
My grief, heavier than the sand of the sea,
Yearns for a grave without breath, without light.

"My torment is made grievous all the more
By miserable comforters with 'wise' counsel unsought.
'Thy tests and trials from sin are birthed.
Confess, repent, or God's mercy thou will know not.'"

Out of the whirlwind came this piercing charge:
"Dark counsel from words without knowledge I abhor.
Now, like a man, gird up thy loins.
A question I ask of thee, thine answer to be pure.

"Where was thy soul when earth's foundation I laid,
Or made the clouds, or restrained the sea?
Who gave thee wisdom, or understanding to thine heart?
Answer this question, where were thee?"

"I am vile, I am shamed, Thou hast proven this true.
Once I spoke, now I will not answer.
My mouth o'er flows without understanding.
I will not, cannot, proceed further."

"Then behold Behemoth, with tail as a cedar.
And Leviathan, from whose mouth goeth forth fire.
O, my child, tested and tried,
Love Me, trust Me alone, your heart's desire."

"I know Thou, God, art almighty in power,
No thought can be withheld from Thee.
I uttered that which I understood not,
Things too wonderful, too lofty to see.

"I have heard of Thee by the hearing of the ear,
But now mine eye hath seen.
In dust, in ashes, my soul repents
Loathing, abhorring this life unclean.

"Now old, and weary, and full of days,
My soul no longer oppressed.
With sons and daughters, servants and wealth
My latter end more, by double, blessed.

"Though He slay me, I will trust Him,
For my redeemer liveth, full of grace.
He upon this earth will stand.
All eyes to behold my Sovereign's face.

"When death's sting o'er takes me and breath denies,
And this worm in the grave decays,
In my flesh one day I will behold
My Lord, my God, the Ancient of Days."

—Frank G. Wheeler, 2008

PART ONE

KANSAS

Chapter 1

The Nightmare

March 5, 1954

Jeremy stood in the field. He was alone—more alone than he had ever felt before. Unharvested wheat surrounded him, and a starless, moonless sky stretched overhead. Thunder exploded over his head like a cannon. Rain began to fall, pelting his face like shotgun pellets. Lightning crackled, slicing the night sky open. It struck the wheat to the right and left of him, and in an instant everything was ablaze.

Run! his mind screamed. He tried, but his legs felt like cement. Then, through the sound of the thunder, a mournful bellow in the distance reached his ears. Fear gripped his mind. *Bessy?*

He pushed his cement-weighted legs toward the barn. "Bessy!" he screamed. He could just make out the face of his cow, a face that pleaded for help. *I'm close now*, he thought. He reached out to comfort her, but the barn doors slammed shut. Another mournful bellow echoed from inside.

"Bessy!" he yelled again.

The sounds faded, and darkness closed in around him.

"Jeremy!" a voice said beside him.

"I have to save her!" Jeremy cried. His heart raced.

"Jeremy! Wake up."

Jeremy slowly blinked his eyes open as he returned to reality. His mother set on the bed, gently shaking him.

"You're having a nightmare." She pulled her sweat-soaked son close to her.

Jeremy's breathing was labored and heavy, and his body shook in his mother's arms. Tears streamed down his face. He allowed his mother to hold him for several more seconds.

An overhead light snapped on. Jeremy squinted in the brightness.

"A nightmare, Virginia?" Roger asked as he approached the bed. Grandma Martel was close behind.

Virginia nodded in his direction, and then turned back to her son. "It's okay now," she said softly. She rocked him and stroked his wet hair. "It was just a nightmare."

Grandma went to the window and pulled it shut. The sill was soaked. Lightning lit up the horizon, and a final rumbling of thunder sounded in the distance.

Roger sat on the edge of the bed and rubbed a hand through Jeremy's thick blond hair. "You're soaked," he said. "Better get changed out of those pajamas."

Virginia pulled the top of the pajamas over Jeremy's head as Grandma searched in the bureau for a dry replacement.

"I was trying to run, but I couldn't, Pa," Jeremy said. "It was like I was running in slow motion. Bessy needed me, and I could tell that she was in so much pain. But I couldn't run fast enough."

Roger looked at his wife, and then back to his son. "Jeremy, Bessy's … Bessy's gone."

"Gone?"

"Bessy died three years ago. Remember? You were just four at the time."

Grandma handed the fresh pajama top to Jeremy. He pulled it over his head and sighed deeply. "It seemed so real," he said in a whisper.

Grandma's authoritative voice broke in. "Okay, Virginia, you get yourself back to bed now. You and that young'un you're carrying need all the rest you can get. And Roger, that rooster will be crowing in a couple of hours. So scoot, the both of you. I'll stay here with Jeremy 'til he gets back to sleep."

Virginia began to protest, but Roger interrupted her. "My dear," he said, "it's useless to argue with the boss. Let's get back to bed."

Virginia nodded, kissed her son's forehead, and slowly left the room. Roger snapped the overhead light off on his way out and began to pull the door closed.

"Roger," Grandma said, "leave the door open a crack so we get just a bit of the hall light. Thank you." She turned the sweat-soaked pillow over.

Jeremy lay back and folded his arms above his head. Grandma tucked in the blanket and sat on the edge of the bed. Jeremy could barely see her face in the dark. "That was quite a nightmare you had," she said.

"I was so scared, Grandma. The thunder and lightning, and the fires, and Bessy moaning."

"Well, you try to get back to sleep now. When you wake up, I'll make you your favorite buttermilk pancakes. How does that sound?" She could just make out his smile in the sliver of light that penetrated the room.

"Grandma?" Jeremy said after a pause.

"What, child?"

"Why did God let Bessy die?"

She stopped for a moment, surprised by the question after all these years. "To be honest, I don't really know," she said. "You really loved her, didn't you?" She stroked his matted hair and felt him nod. "I do know life is filled with blessings, but it also has moments that teach us lessons—hard lessons that prepare us."

Jeremy rolled to his side and lifted up on one elbow. "Prepare us for what?"

She paused again. "Well, perhaps Bessy's death was one of those hard lessons that teach us to simply trust Him. Have I ever told you about a man in the Bible named Job?"

"I don't think so." Jeremy lay back and folded his hands behind his head again.

"Well, Job lived many, many years ago ..."

Grandma began telling the story, but it wasn't long before her grandson's soft, deep breathing told her it would have to wait for another day.

Chapter 2

Love at First Sight

March 13, 1954

Jeremiah Elias Martel sat on the farmhouse porch in one of Grandpa's oversized rocking chairs. His blue eyes were fixed on the sky, watching the thunderstorm approaching from the west. Pa had told him that Kansas was the blue-ribbon state for thunder and lightning storms, and the town of Groveland had certainly seen its fair share this year.

Pa had also told Jeremy that he could judge how far away the storm was by counting the seconds between the thunderclaps and the lightning—every five seconds was equal to one mile. When Jeremy first saw the storm, he was able to count to nearly thirty. His last count was three seconds.

The rain, gentle and peaceful only moments before, now came down in a deluge. A flash of lightning blasted the afternoon darkness into a split-second of brighter-than-daylight. Jeremy, nearly jumping out of his skin at the voluminous blast that followed, unconsciously clamped his hands over his ears and squeezed his eyes tight. A nervous giggle escaped from his lips as he slowly opened his eyes. Every muscle in his body tensed in anticipation of the next explosion, hands at the ready.

"One thousand one, one thousand …" *Boom!* His hands returned to his ears, and his eyes squeezed shut again. A giggle. Jeremy was enjoying every minute of being scared. "One thousand one, one thousand two, one thousand three, one thousand four …" *Boom!*

The sound of the squeaky hinges on the screen door caught Jeremy's attention. He turned to see his father stepping out from the living room on to the porch. "May I join you, son?"

Jeremy smiled and nodded. "It's moving fast, Pa."

Roger sat, put the sole of his foot up on the railing, and pushed back until the chair was resting on just its rear legs. He placed his hands behind his head and interlaced his fingers. Jeremy returned to his counting.

Father and son sat quietly for several moments, listening to the sounds of the storm as it moved eastward. The rain fell softly now. Rivulets flowed down the barn roof into gutters that channeled it into a barrel on the ground.

Jeremy broke the silence. "We gonna have a good crop this year, Pa?"

"Well, right now it looks like it."

"Pa?" Jeremy's voice had a pleading softness to it.

"Yes?" said his father. The crow's feet in the corner of his blue-green eyes revealed the beginning of a smile. He had heard this plea before and knew what was coming. He had also heard Grandma talking with Jeremy on how best to "approach her son," as she put it, about the topic. "Be direct on with your pa, child," she had said. "He don't cotton to people beating around the bush."

"Well, I was talking with Sylvester at school just this morning," Jeremy continued, "and he said Buster's litter is about ready to be weaned. Pa, can I have one?" He had been watching the last of the storm drift off along the horizon, but now he turned to look at his dad to plead his case. "Pleeease!"

His dad paused, put his foot down from the railing, and leaned forward in his chair. His forearms now rested on the arms of the chair. "But we've already got two dogs, Patch and Sooty," he said. "What do we need with another?"

"But they're old and, well … they're not mine. Not really. I'll take real good care of the pup. You and Ma won't have to do a thing. I'll wash him and feed him and housebreak him and —"

"You know, son," Roger smiled, "that sounds just like the arguments I gave my father when I was about your age and wanted a dog. When I got one, all my promises lasted about a week."

Jeremy thought about this for a moment. He had not expected to hear anything from his pa but a yes or a no. That's what he had always been given in the past when he had asked for something. "No, I mean it, Pa," he said. "I'm almost seven—at least, I will be in two months—and I'm a lot more responsible now."

"Oh, really?" Pa raised his bushy eyebrows. "What about those *C*s and *D*s I saw on your last report card? Seems to me a responsible son would be working harder on his education than that."

Jeremy felt that he was losing ground. "Can we … negotiate?"

Roger looked at Jeremy and burst into a laugh. "Where on earth did you learn such a big word?"

"I heard you and Ma talking about whether you should paint or wallpaper the empty room for when the baby's born. 'Painting is cheaper,' you said, but Ma said, 'Wallpapering would be prettier.' Then you said, 'Babies don't need expensive pretty walls, they just need clean walls,' and Ma said, 'Let's negotiate.' And then you said, 'There's nothing to negotiate,' and Ma said …"

"Whoa, slow down. I remember what I said. How is it you remember every bit of that conversation but can't remember eight plus seven? Tell you what—you learn your addition facts by the end of the school year, and we'll look into getting you a dog."

"But it will be too late by then," Jeremy said. Now his plea was desperate. "Sylvester said all them German shepherd pups will be gone by week's end."

"So, what do you have to 'negotiate' with me to get my yes?"

Jeremy bit his lower lip and fixed his gaze on a piece of chipped, gray paint on the porch ceiling. He hadn't thought that far ahead, but now he realized he needed to come up with something quick.

Roger could see the wheels turning in his boy's mind.

"I promise I'll paint this whole porch during summer break!" he blurted.

"And feed the animal, clean him, and housebreak him?"

Jeremy bobbed his head like a dribbled basketball. "Promise!" he said, crossing his heart with an X.

"Well, I'll tell you this, Jeremy. I think you're going to grow up to be a businessman the way you negotiate. You've made an offer that's hard to refuse."

Jeremy's eyes went saucer-wide as he realized what his father had just said. "Really, Pa? I can get my own dog?"

"Yup," Pa nodded. "Tomorrow being Saturday and all, we can go over to Pearson's farm first thing in the morning to take a look at that litter. That's *after* chores and breakfast are done, mind you. I met Ira Pearson in town a few days ago at Harvey's Hardware Store, and he said you could have your pick, no charge, just because you've been such a good friend to Sylvester."

"Pa, I'll keep every promise I made, and I'll help take care of my new brother …"

"Or sister …"

"Or sister, and …"

Roger Martel sat back and rocked in his chair. The crow's feet were more pronounced around his eyes as he listened to his son rattle off more promises than a hayloft could hold.

"Hey, wait a minute," Jeremy said as the realization of his pa's words began to sink in. "You were going to take me to get a pup tomorrow anyway?"

"Oops! Did I forget to mention that?" Roger said as he rose to his feet. "And after that, we can drive to Harvey's and pick up a couple gallons of gray paint."

"No fair!" Jeremy complained. He squirmed out of the oversized rocker and chased his pa into the barn.

Jeremy did not need a rooster or alarm clock to wake him the next morning. He was up before sunrise, milking cows, gathering eggs, and putting slop in the trough for the two pigs. At about seven o'clock, he and his father heard the call for breakfast.

"Food's on the table, and it's getting cold, you two," Grandma called toward the barnyard.

"Coming!" Roger yelled back. He tossed one last pitchfork—full of hay—into the cows' stalls.

Grandma and Virginia were seated at the table, waiting patiently for the two men of the household to arrive. After washing up at the sink, Roger took his place at the head of the table. "Let's give thanks," he said. The four held hands as Roger said grace. The blessing was no longer than usual on this day, but for Jeremy it seemed to last an eternity.

Jeremy loved Grandma's cooking. His mother shared the responsibility, but now that she was in her third month of pregnancy, she willingly yielded more of the cooking duties to her mother-in-law. Grandma loved to cook—it was her passion. Whenever participants in the county fair bake-off learned that Grandma Martel had entered one of her rhubarb or cherry pies, they knew the best they could hope for was second place.

Jeremy's plate was piled high with scrambled eggs, crispy bacon cooked just the way he liked it, and a stack of flapjacks soaking in maple syrup. But on this day, Jeremy barely tasted the food. He could not wolf down the meal fast enough.

"Jeremy, slow down!" his mother scolded gently. "You'd think you had someplace important to go this morning." Virginia winked at her husband. "After breakfast maybe you should go up to your room and practice those addition facts, hmm?"

Jeremy stopped chewing, his mouth stuffed with egg, and looked at his dad. A shocked expression bordering on panic came over his face.

"Well, dear, perhaps we can put that off 'til later," his father said. "We men do have some important business to tend to after breakfast. Right, son?"

Jeremy looked at his mother and nodded so fiercely that some of the egg fell from his mouth into his lap.

"And just what might this vital business be?" Mother teased.

"Pa said I could get a dog today from the Pearson's!" Jeremy blurted. More egg fell from his mouth.

"Ah, yes, I do remember hearing that you negotiated some such deal. Do you have a name picked out yet?"

"Uh huh," he said through another mouthful. "Shep. You know, for shepherd."

"What a great name," Grandma said. "It sounds like you've put a lot of thought into this."

"Almost all my life." There were smiles all around the table.

Roger leaned his chair back and patted his stomach. "Well, Grandma, once again, that was a great feast, but I think I'm done."

Done? That was all Jeremy needed to hear. In an instant, he was out of his chair and tugging on his dad's shirt. He didn't want to waste any more time with small talk. "Let's go, Pa," he said.

Roger pushed his chair back from the table and stood to his feet. "Be back in a bit, ladies," he said. "Seems we have some urgent business to take care of."

Roger drove about a mile down the road and then slowed the pickup to turn left over a culvert. He entered the Pearson's graveled driveway and slowly made his way up to the farmhouse. Free-roaming chickens scattered for safety as he pulled into a spot near the front porch. Before Roger could turn off the motor, Jeremy was out of the truck, running toward the front door.

Thelma Pearson opened the door on the third knock. Felicia and April, Sylvester's three-year-old twin sisters, clinged to her apron. "Jeremy, we've been expecting you," she said. She stepped aside and invited him in, holding the door open a moment longer for Roger to catch up. "How is Virginia doing?" she asked as she closed the door.

Jeremy stood at his father's side and looked up into his face, trying to make eye contact. Impatience was written all over his body. He began pulling at his dad's pant leg.

"Jeremy, don't be rude," Roger gently scolded. "Virginia's doing just fine. She's due sometime around the end of September. She's been having some morning problems, though."

"That should pass in a while," Thelma replied. "If there's any way I can help, just give me a call. You know I'll be right there."

Jeremy's eyes widened, and he pressed his lips together in frustration. He was beginning to think this conversation was deliberately intended to make him suffer all the longer.

"Thank, you, Thelma," said Roger. "Now, I'm thinking that if I don't get this boy here to that litter of pups, he'll 'bout explode."

"I think you're right," she said. "He's acting like he has ants in his pants." She looked down into the boy's anguished face. "They are in the barn, Jeremy. Go ahead and make your way out there. I've got something cooking on the stove I need to tend to."

Roger gave him the nod, and Jeremy darted toward the door of the house. He sprinted down the porch steps, almost losing his balance on the loose gravel in the driveway, and ran through the open barn door. Sylvester was sitting on the hay-strewn floor, leaning against a bail of hay next to where Buster was lying. Two of her pups were cradled in Sylvester's lap, and the other four jostled for position at their mother's teats.

"Hey, hog breath," Sylvester said.

"Hey, pond scum." They had been best friends since first grade, and that was all the conversation needed for now. Jeremy moved a bit closer, but not too close. This wasn't the first time he had seen a litter of pups, but it was the first time he would get to choose one from that litter.

Jeremy lay down on his belly a few feet away and rested his chin on folded arms. Sylvester put down the two pups he was holding and limped over to Jeremy. He lay down beside him, mimicking his friend's position.

The two pups squeezed into the mix of sucking siblings, pushing one of their brothers out of the way. The pup tried to get back in and grab onto a teat, but he was not the biggest or the strongest. After a few minutes with no luck, he backed away, turned and stared straight into Jeremy's face. His head tipped ever so slightly to the left, his curiosity overtaking his hunger for the moment. Then he began to puppy-walk toward Jeremy, stumbled over his own paws, stood up again, and shook unsteadily. He tried again, stumbled again, and stood shaking unsteadily again.

It took three tries, but the pup finally reached Jeremy and began licking his nose with his sponge-like, saliva-covered tongue. Jeremy, keeping his lips pinched tight to keep out the yuck, began to giggle. This only seemed to encourage the licking machine, and the pup now went for the full-face licks. Jeremy's giggling became a full-fledged laugh, and the puppy's tongue went right into his gaping mouth.

Roger stood at the entrance to the barn and watched the scene unfold. He wanted to tell his son that this particular pup might not be the right choice, as it seemed to be the runt of the litter. Perhaps one of the others would make a more acceptable farm dog. But Roger did not want to interfere.

Jeremy sat up, lifted the pup and hugged it to his chest. The pup squirmed in his arms and stretched his neck upward to take more swipes at Jeremy's delicious chin.

"So," Roger said, making his presence known. "I guess you've made your choice."

"Ain't he grand, Pa?"

"He truly is, son. Shall we thank Sylvester and Mrs. Pearson for their generosity and take Shep home?"

"His name isn't Shep. It's Shakey."

Roger nodded his approval of Shakey, the newest Martel.

Chapter 3

From the Heart

March 14, 1954, 6:00 AM

"Jeremy, wake up," his mother said, shaking him gently. "It's Sunday. Time to get ready for church."

Jeremy groaned and rolled over. "Not today, Ma. I'm so tired." He pulled the covers up over his head. Virginia yanked them down and poked him in the side.

"Ouch!" cried Jeremy, now wide awake. "That hurt!" He sat up in his bed.

"Too tired?" said Virginia. "What's this 'too tired' nonsense? Get yourself out of bed and get dressed. Breakfast will be ready in twenty minutes."

"Aw, Ma, can't I just sleep in this once?"

"No, Jeremy. 'Once' has too many relatives, like 'Twice' and 'Thrice.' You know that we all go to church on Sundays. Now get moving!" She gave him a stern look as she left the room.

Jeremy stretched and yawned, kicked off the covers, and sat on the edge of his bed. He reached down, lifted Shakey out of his cardboard box bedding, and hugged the pup. He was immediately rewarded with another wet, slobbering lick to the face. Jeremy laughed and set the pup down. He got dressed, and the pair headed for the kitchen.

An hour later, the Martel family was walking into the small Baptist church at the center of town. They were a bit late this week. This was unusual for the Martels, as Grandma believed it was a sin to arrive late to God's house. However, with Virginia's morning sickness, it couldn't be helped.

As they entered, they saw Pastor Sterling was already seated on the raised platform at the front the sanctuary. His eyes were closed prayerfully, and his face was lifted toward heaven. He stroked his graying beard as he waited, patiently, for the organist to play the last few bars of "The Old Rugged Cross." The Martels would have to say their hellos and do their greetings after the service.

Deacon Stanley met Roger and greeted him with a hearty handshake and a contagious smile. He ushered the Martels to their usual unpadded wood bench pew and handed each a bulletin of the service's order of worship. He gave Jeremy's blond hair a ritual tousle as he left, which made Jeremy smile. If the deacon hadn't done this, Jeremy would have wondered if something were wrong or if the old deacon didn't like him any more.

Pastor Sterling nodded to Addy Stanley, the organist, who then struck the first notes of the prelude, "Make Me a Blessing." Addy was hard of hearing, and she played the organ accordingly. She had been doing this for so many years that people no longer paid attention to the volume, except maybe visitors, who were few and far between.

Pastor Sterling stood to his feet, giving the cue for the congregation to rise. The parishioners picked up their hymn books—though most already knew by heart all the songs—and began flipping to the page listed on a sign at the front of the sanctuary. Pastor Sterling waited a moment with his hymnal in his left hand, and then began waving his right before the parishioners, doing his best choir-directing imitation. Without further announcement, everyone began to sing.

Jeremy looked around for his friend, Sylvester. Sylvester had a left foot that was nearly three inches shorter than his right, and he needed special shoes so he wouldn't limp. Some of the other kids found this strange, but it never bothered Jeremy—he just plain liked Sylvester. He spotted him two rows back on the other side of the aisle, sitting with his mother, brothers, and sisters. The two made eye contact, and

Jeremy smiled. Sylvester stared back cross-eyed at Jeremy, and then stuck out his tongue and touched his nose with it. Jeremy was about to return the favor when he felt the hand of his pa on the top of his head. He quickly did an about-face.

The hymn ended, but the congregation remained standing. Pastor Sterling gripped both sides of the pulpit, leaned slightly forward into his praying pose, and paused for a moment. The congregation, with their heads now bowed and their eyes closed, went silent. Their pastor was not a shouter, and the people had to strain to hear his words as he began.

"Lord, we gather here in Your name to bring You worship. Worship from our lips."

"Amen," a few people quietly whispered throughout the congregation.

"Worship from our hearts."

"Amen."

"Worship from our souls."

"Amen."

Jeremy opened his eyes to slits and looked over at Grandma. Not many people in this old conservative Baptist church raised their hands, but Grandma had come from a Pentecostal background before marrying Grandpa, and now both of her thick, fleshy arms were raised toward heaven.

"And worship from our pocket books," Pastor Sterling continued.

"Amen."

"This we pray in the name of Your dear Son, Jesus. Amen."

"Amen," the people said, raising their heads.

"Dear friends," Pastor Sterling continued, "please be seated."

As the congregation sat, Jeremy, sitting at the center aisle end of the pew, was pleased to find a rather tall parishioner seated directly in front of him, blocking the view of the pastor. He searched the bookrack attached to the front pew in front of him and found a stubby pencil without an eraser. He took it out and began drawing stick figures of him and Shakey in the margins of the church bulletin.

The pastor continued to conduct the service as he had done for the last twenty-four years: announcements of church events and upcoming weddings, births, and illnesses (for which he paused to pray); a request for volunteers to help plan this year's Sunday school picnic; the offering; and the doxology. Finally, he began his sermon.

"Today's text is from the book of John," Pastor Sterling said. Jeremy tuned him out and starting drawing the cardboard box in which Shakey slept.

He heard several members of the congregation murmur among themselves. He looked around and noticed it came from some of the older, crinkle-faced parishioners in the back. He leaned to his right, coming out of hiding, and stuck his head into the aisle for a better view.

Pastor Sterling had stepped away from the pulpit and was now walking down the center aisle. In silence, he began stopping at every pew and looking piercingly into each pair of eyes he found, first to his left and then to his right. Some made eye contact, while others, feeling uncomfortable, looked quickly away.

Jeremy couldn't take his gaze off of his pastor. Something was about to happen. He felt it. He began to lick his lips, noticing how dry they had become.

The pastor was two rows away … then one … and then he stood at the end of Jeremy's pew. Jeremy sat up straight and looked into the eyes of his pastor. He was surprised to find that those eyes glistened. *Tears?* he thought. *Why?*

Pastor Sterling looked to the far end of Jeremy's pew, and then slowly moved his gaze person by person, until at last he stared down at Jeremy. Jeremy never flinched. As he looked up into his pastor's face, he saw a tear release from its perch, tracing a path along his creviced cheek before it disappeared into his thick beard.

Pastor Sterling moved to the next pew. Jeremy let out a breath and followed the man with his eyes, as did the rest of the congregation. When the pastor reached the back of the church, he pulled a handkerchief from his back pocket and used it to wipe his eyes. He noisily blew his nose, and then stuffed the handkerchief into his back pocket. After pausing a moment, he turned and strode to the front of the sanctuary. He walked at a quicker pace, but he did not mount the stairs to return to the pulpit.

"My loved ones," he said when he had reached the front steps, "you are my joy. I have tried to serve you faithfully these many years." Heads nodded in affirmation, and some voices spoke out their approval. For many in the congregation, this man was the only pastor they had ever known. He was a part of their lives, just like any family member—a brother to some, a father to others, and dearly loved by all.

"I have been warmly received in all your homes," Pastor Sterling continued. "When my dear wife, Helen, passed into the arms of her Lord and Savior these five years ago, you came beside me and comforted me and loved me."

The congregation grew deathly silent. They knew their pastor was about to make an important statement, but none of them had any clue as to what it might be.

"But I fear I have failed you."

The silence was broken. Some members spoke out in protest, while others looked at one another with questioning looks.

Pastor Sterling raised his hands, quickly silencing the congregation. "Please, hear me out," he said. "There is a reason I walked the aisle today. There is a reason I looked into each person's eyes. I have been your pastor for twenty-four years, and I recognize every face in this room."

"But that's a good thing, isn't it, pastor?" someone sitting behind Jeremy called out. Jeremy turned to see who it was but got the hand on the head again.

"Yes … and no," Pastor Sterling replied. "I have married some of you and watched the children come from those unions." Roger and Virginia looked at each other. He took hold of her hand, and they smiled at the memories.

"I have also buried some of your loved ones." Grandma removed a handkerchief from her pocketbook and pressed it against her eyes.

"But I have failed you because I did not look into a single new face here today. I have not looked into the face of a new member, or even of a visitor, in far too long. And I have failed you because … because I have not been faithful to declare God's Word with power." The pastor stopped and cleared his throat before continuing.

"The Scripture says the gospel is the power of God unto salvation. The proof of that power is in the fruit, but I did not look into the eyes of one new person here today that represents that fruit. I have not been used to lead new souls to Christ for too long now. I have preached on the sin of greed, the sin of adultery, and the sin proclaimed in each of the Ten Commandments. I have preached on loving your neighbor, the gifts of teaching, and preaching, and service. I have preached on worship and faithfulness and tithing. But I have too seldom proclaimed the gospel of salvation with power. If I had, we would have seen the fruit. I confess this to you, and I ask for your forgiveness."

The people were speechless. No one, not even the deacons, knew how to respond.

"Let me be clear," Pastor Sterling went on. "I am not trying to make anyone feel guilty. This week I spent many hours on my knees in prayer, asking for the Lord's forgiveness. I asked him to give me just the right words for this morning, and God, in His graciousness, has laid on my heart what I have said to you today. He has laid it on my heart to proclaim His gospel today in all its simplicity. That simplicity is that He loves you and me with an unconditional love."

I've heard this before in Sunday School, Jeremy thought. He went back to drawing his stick figures.

"But sin creates a wall that keeps His love from having the result He desires: that each and every one of us become a part of His forever family."

I've heard this too, Jeremy thought. But, an image of a time he had lied popped into his mind. Then he remembered another time he cheated on a spelling test. *Never told anyone about that, not even Sylvester,* he said to himself. He had received a 100-percent on the test—the only 100-percent he had ever gotten. Ma and Pa had been so proud. Strangely, he remembered not feeling good about it.

Jeremy smiled at the stick figures he had drawn. One was of Shakey with elephant-sized ears and clown-sized feet.

"If I do not allow Jesus to be the one to pay the price for the sins I have committed against this holy God," Pastor Sterling said, raising his voice, "then *I am accountable to pay it for myself.*"

Those words struck a nerve in Jeremy. *Pay it for myself?* he thought. He now understood his pastor's tears. *They were for me. Maybe they were for others as well, but they were definitely for me.* He knew what sin was—he didn't have to be some grownup who studied deeply about such things. He had lied and cheated and stolen and … well, he knew that his heart was not right with this God he had heard about all of his short, six-going-on-seven years.

After this, Jeremy heard only bits and pieces of the sermon until Pastor Sterling again began to raise his voice to conclude his message. "But God promises that if you believe you will receive the gift of life … and all He asks is that you trust Him and take Him at His word. Jesus died for each one of you, as if you were the only one in need of this gift, as if you were the only sinner on earth."

Pastor Sterling paused again and looked over the congregation. Then, standing to his full height, he loudly proclaimed, "Today is the day!" Jeremy was startled by his pastor's voice—the man never shouted. "So is there anyone here who wants to receive the gift of God's eternal salvation? If so, I am going to ask you to do something very difficult and come forward. Now, coming forward will not save you, but it will serve as a sign that you are serious about letting God settle your soul's need. I am going to pray now and ask that all of you bow your heads and close your eyes."

Jeremy rose to his feet while the pastor was still speaking. Leaving the safety of his pew, he stepped into the aisle and walked forward, not glancing back once at his father, mother, or grandmother. He had heard all of the things that his pastor had said before, but today he finally understood them. Young as he was, he knew exactly what he was doing that morning.

As he walked toward his pastor, he stared up into the eyes that had been so piercing just a few minutes before. Again, they were filling with tears. But this time, Jeremy knew they were not tears of painful sorrow, but tears of joy for a soul coming home.

"Welcome to the family, Jeremy," Pastor Sterling said softly. He put an arm around Jeremy's shoulders and turned him around to face the congregation. All eyes were now looking to the front. Some of the parishioners were praising God, while others, who knew Jeremy well, were wondering why this sweet young boy—who was obviously a Christian already—would feel compelled to go forward.

"People, meet Jeremy Martel, your newest brother in Christ," Pastor Sterling said. He turned and looked at Jeremy's parents. "We'll be having a baptism tonight at the evening service, and I want Jeremy to take part. I trust that's okay with you, Roger and Virginia?" Jeremy's parents could only nod in approval. "All right then, let's all stand and sing 'Victory in Jesus.'"

Chapter 4

That's What Friends Are For

March 14, 1954, 1:00 PM

Sylvester stepped off his bike and leaned it against the Martel's front porch. He limped up the few stairs to the porch deck and knocked on the front door. After a moment's wait, Mrs. Martel appeared from inside.

"Hello, Sylvester," she said. "If you're looking for Jeremy, he's in the barn." She pointed toward the wide-open doors.

"Thanks," Sylvester said with a polite smile. He quickly turned and hobbled down the stairs. The gravel in the driveway crunched under his feet as he scuffed his way to the barn.

Jeremy recognized the uneven footsteps that indicated his friend was approaching. He did not even look up from what he was doing. "Hey, frog face."

"Hey, pig butt. Sylvester squatted down on the barn floor beside his friend. What are you doing?"

"Playing with Shakey." He was teasing Shakey with a sock tied to a string at the end of a stick. As he dangled it in front of him, Shakey would grab it with his teeth, puppy-growl and then try to rip the sock free by whipping his head back and forth. The boys laughed at the ferociousness of the small pup's growl.

"Can I hold the stick?"

"Sure." Jeremy handed the toy to his friend.

"It's kind of like fishing," Sylvester said after a moment. "But for a dog."

"Yeah. I never thought of it that way."

Sylvester paused. "So … you're getting baptized tonight."

"Yup. You coming?" Both had their eyes glued on the show in front of them.

"I think so. At least Mom is, and she'll probably make us go with her. Dad said maybe, since it's you and all, but he's not much into the church thing."

"*Make* you go? Gee, thanks. Hope I don't put you out too much."

"You won't be putting me out at all. They always serve some good snacks afterward. Besides, I heard Pastor Sterling say he was going to hold you under a little longer to make you pay for all those sins you've committed."

"Yeah, well, here's one more to add to the list." Jeremy reached over, grabbed a fistful of hay from a nearby bail, and threw it into Sylvester's face. Sylvester dropped the stick, grabbed his own handful from off the floor, and returned the favor. The battle was engaged, with hay now flying all over the barn, mixed with belly laughs.

"Hey, hold up a second," Jeremy said after a minute had passed. "Where's Shakey?" Sylvester answered by slinging a fistful of hay that caught him square in the mouth. "Time out! Time out!" Jeremy yelled, spitting out hay and dirt.

Sylvester looked around the barn. "Hey, there he goes, out the door!"

Jeremy ran out of the barn and chased the pup into the yard. Shakey was still holding his sock prize in his mouth, with the stick dragging behind. Jeremy stomped on the stick, jerking Shakey to an abrupt halt. The pup spun, but he never let go of the sock. Sylvester eventually caught up with the two.

Grandma stood on the front porch. She had a pan of chocolate fudge in one hand and a spatula in the other. "You two rascals want to sample some of the fudge I've made for after tonight's baptism?" she asked.

"Yeah!" the boys said in tandem. Jeremy reached down and picked up Shakey. He wrestled the saliva-soaked sock from his mouth, removed the string, and stuffed it into his back pocket. He would need that sock tomorrow for school.

Sylvester slid into one of the straight-backed chairs while Jeremy sat down with his back against the railing and put Shakey in his lap. Grandma handed each of the boys a generous portion of fudge, and then went inside.

Jeremy took a bite, and then bent over to let Shakey lick the crumbs from his lips. "Hey, Sylvester," he said, "how'd you do on the spelling test Friday?"

"Got a 100. How about you?"

Jeremy looked at the front door before answering. "Sixty," he said in a whisper.

"Sixty!" Sylvester shouted. "You got a *sixty*?!"

"Will you hush up that mouth of yours? You heard me. Don't need to announce it to the universe. I can't help it if the Good Lord didn't think it fitting for everyone to have a brain like yours. Well, you may be good with the book learning, but I sure can run like ..." Jeremy stopped mid-sentence as he realized the impact of his words. "I'm ... sorry, Sylvester, I didn't ..."

"Hey, it's okay. It's not like it's a secret or anything. But tell me this: if the Good Lord is so good, how come He made me look like a one-sided metronome when I do run? I can't even ride my bike without the raised pedal my dad made."

"I don't know. But you sure are smart—a lot smarter than me. Maybe it's His way of evening things out. I mean, you can't run so good, but you get all As without even trying. I can run just fine, but I ain't never got an A—or even a B, come to think of it—and I try pretty darn hard."

Jeremy absentmindedly held his last bite of fudge too close to Shakey's mouth, and the pup took advantage. "Hey! That wasn't for you, you little thief."

"Yeah, well," Sylvester said, continuing the conversation, "if that's true, how come God made Willy Garand so he can run even faster than you and be as smart as me? He don't like to show it, but he's smart, and he pushes me around like I was a rag doll."

Jeremy gave a thoughtful pause. "Geez, Sylvester, I don't know. He just did, that's all. Pa says sometimes He lets us in on His purposes, and sometimes He don't. But someday somebody's gonna come up to Willy and—*pow*!" Jeremy punched his right fist into his left palm.

"Oh, like that helps," Sylvester laughed. He licked the last fragments of fudge from his fingers. "Well, Jeremy, I gotta go." He slid out of the chair and hobbled down the steps to his bike. "See you tonight … sinner!"

Jeremy waved at his friend without looking. Then he lowered his face again, allowing Shakey to have a last lick.

Chapter 5

Sin's Reward

March 14, 1954, 6:00 PM

At Pastor Sterling's request, the Martels arrived at church about forty minutes before the service began. The pastor had made the request so he and the deacons could have a few minutes with Jeremy. They wanted to ask him some questions about his decision that morning, go over the meaning of baptism, and tell him what he was about to do.

The church leaders ushered Jeremy into the pastor's office while his parents and grandmother waited outside. Jeremy sat stiffly in a chair in front of the deacons, nervously fidgeting his hands and occasionally rubbing his stomach as he braved out the intimidation he felt. The pastor and deacons quoted some Scripture, and then they began to ask Jeremy questions about his understanding of baptism.

"Jeremy, Satan does not like the decision you have made today one bit," Pastor Sterling said. He leaned forward, folded his hands, and rested his forearms on his knees. "He will try to sift you like wheat to test you and tempt you. He wants to make you run from God and regret this decision to follow Jesus into the waters of baptism. Submit to God, son. Resist the devil, and he will flee from you. Do you understand?"

Jeremy nodded slowly, still rubbing his belly. He felt more nervous than before.

Deacon Stanley gave Jeremy a gracious smile that put him a bit more at ease. "Jeremy, I know all this has to be overwhelming, but we just want to make sure you are prepared for this step. Do you have any questions that you would like to ask us?"

Jeremy thought for a moment, and then slowly shook his head. It was all the response he could muster at the moment. He was fine with the baptism part—he had seen those done before, and he knew how to hold his breath underwater. He just wanted out of this room.

"Okay, then," Pastor Sterling said. "I have one last question to ask before we let you change into your baptismal robe. A pure heart is important, son. Is there any sin you have committed that you need to confess before you are baptized?"

Jeremy looked at the ceiling and thought about the pastor's question. "No," he said slowly, "I don't think so … unless it's the sin of gallantry."

The pastor looked at the deacons, and the deacons looked at each other. They all had puzzled expressions on their faces. "The sin of gallantry?" said Deacon Stanley. "What do you mean, Jeremy? I don't think I know that one."

"Well," Jeremy began, "today at lunch, Pa let me have seconds on everything—you know, because he was proud of me for going forward this morning and all. He said that took a lot of courage. So I had extra steak and mashed potatoes with gravy and beans, and applesauce, and two helpings of Grandma's peach cobbler. Does that count as sin?" He rubbed his belly again.

The pastor let out a loud laugh that startled the other men in the room.

"Jeremy, I think you mean the sin of *gluttony*," said Pastor Sterling, "and, yes, that counts as sin." He leaned forward, patted Jeremy's knee and continued on in a conspiratorial whisper. "But just between you and me, I would have trouble resisting a second helping of your grandmother's peach cobbler too."

With that, the group closed the meeting in prayer, and Jeremy was dismissed to get ready for the big event. A few minutes later, he was sitting in the front pew of the sanctuary, dressed in a white robe with nothing underneath but a bathing suit. Pastor Sterling was in place behind the pulpit, which had been pushed to one side of the platform to give a clear view of the baptismal tank. The congregation was led in a few hymns as Addy blasted out the notes on the organ.

Pastor Sterling gave a short message on the meaning of baptism and then invited Jeremy to come up front. Together they walked over to the baptismal tank and went down the few steps that led into the water. The water came up to Jeremy's waist, and he rubbed his stomach again. No one except his father paid much attention to what Jeremy was doing or to the screwed-up expression on his face.

"What's wrong with Jeremy?" Roger asked, leaning over and whispering into Virginia's ear. "He doesn't look too good."

"It's just nerves," Virginia whispered back. She patted her husband's knee.

"My dear friends," the pastor continued, "it is with great joy that we gather here tonight." He placed an arm on Jeremy's shoulder. "I have had the pleasure of watching this child grow from birth into the fine young man he has become. There is no doubt in my mind that God has some special plans in store for him as he grows and matures in the faith."

Jeremy made the mistake of looking to the far left side of the sanctuary where Sylvester was seated. Every time the pastor glanced to the other side of the room, his friend would make weird, twisted faces at him. Jeremy struggled to keep from laughing and looked down at the water, and then up at the ceiling—any place but back at Sylvester. He could already feel a laugh bubbling up inside him.

Pastor Sterling turned to face Jeremy and spoke directly to him. Jeremy looked up into his face. "Jeremiah Elias Martel, do you here, in front of these witnesses, acknowledge your desire to trust in Jesus as your Lord and Savior and to follow Him all the days of your life?"

Jeremy could only nod. He was still struggling to suppress the laugh that sat on the edge of his diaphragm. Pastor Sterling leaned over. "You need to speak up, son," he said.

"Yes!" Jeremy said in a high-pitched squeak. The muscles on his face began to twitch as he pinched his lips tighter together.

"Then I baptize you in the name of the Father, and of the Son, and of the Holy Ghost." He placed his left hand on Jeremy's back and held out his right hand for the boy to grasp. Then he gently lowered Jeremy back, immersing him into the water.

Jeremy made the mistake of shooting one last glance in Sylvester's direction. His friend now had both forefingers up his nostrils and was twisting them vigorously. Jeremy exploded in laughter just as he hit the water, causing the water to come rushing into his opened mouth. Pastor Sterling felt the boy's panicked struggle and quickly reversed his direction, raising the choking and coughing Jeremy to the surface.

As Jeremy came out of the water, the sin of gallantry at last had its fun. The gluttonous meal that Jeremy had eaten at noon now returned for all to see, but it did not come out in the same form as it had gone in. A collective gasp arose from the congregation. Sylvester, unable to keep from sliding to the floor under his pew, laughed so hard he wet his pants.

Jeremy clung to Pastor Sterling's robe and wretched a second time. Immediately Virginia and Roger were out of their seats, racing to the aid of their distressed boy. Grandma sat in the pew, praying, "Lord have mercy. Lord have mercy."

A deacon standing near the baptismal tank wrapped a towel around Jeremy's shoulders. He and Roger helped the boy out of the tank and led him through the doorway into a side room.

Pastor Sterling, who thought he had seen it all, remained composed and professional throughout the ordeal. As the buzz in the sanctuary quieted, he decided it was best to just move on with the service. Standing in the tank, surrounded by vomit, he instructed the congregation to stand and sing in closing, "Shall We Gather at the River."

Immediately from the back a parishioner yelled out, "Seems a bit late for that, Pastor!" The congregation soon joined Sylvester, who had slid to the floor once again in unrestrained laughter.

Chapter 6

Lessons on Bravery

August 21, 1954

Danger. It was so clear and present that the two warriors, both crawling on their bellies, felt as if they could shovel it. It hung like a shroud around them. The sun, long past high noon, was pushing the temperature to a record-breaking 100 degrees for the third day in a row. It beat down on them, sucking the strength from their bodies as they stealthily moved closer to their enemy. They choked on the dust of the dried soil as they slithered in silence. Yet despite the heat and their discomfort, they knew they must remain focused on their objective: to destroy the enemy before he destroyed them.

Fear tried to play havoc with their minds, but these soldiers were no ordinary just-out-of-boot-camp mud-suckers. They were the best of the best, selected by the general himself. "Failure is not an option," he had warned them before the mission began. Those words now burned in their minds, compelling them to keep moving forward, always forward.

The edge of the forest was coming into sight. The warriors knew the enemy lay just beyond. He was not visible yet, but they could smell him. With practiced stealth, the first warrior—a sergeant by rank—drew his bayonet from its sheath and silently clicked it into place. The second warrior, as if by telepathy, drew out his blade and did the same. Just a few more yards and the enemy would be theirs.

Surprise, the sergeant thought with a smile. *That will be the key to the success of this mission. He will never know—until it is too late—what sent him to his grave.* He could see the enemy now, standing boldly with his back to them. He placed a hand on his co-warrior's back and pointed. *Such a cocky attitude,* he thought as he observed the enemy standing in the middle of the clearing. *If only you knew. We've met before, but you won't be so lucky this time. Nothing can save you now. You're mine.*

The two warriors gave each other a knowing glance. All was silent for a moment, and then the sergeant gave the slightest, almost imperceptible, nod. He raised his fingers and silently began the countdown: three … two … one …

"Eeeeeyah!" The blood-curdling cry came from the depths of the sergeant's soul. The two dashed from the forest's edge toward the enemy, bayonets poised to thrust into the soft underbelly of the foe.

But wait, what was that? The call for retreat? *No, it couldn't be,* the sergeant thought. *Not again.* He skidded to a halt in the soft soil of the clearing. The two warriors and foe now stood facing each other. "We'll meet again, Jack," the sergeant spit out in contempt. "But next time, you won't be so lucky." The warriors lowered their bayonet-tipped rifles and began to back away as the signal for retreat sounded again.

"Jeeeremyyy!!! Supper time!"

"Coming, Grandma!" the squat, seven-year-old yelled back through hands cupped to his mouth. Shakey lowered his head and gave a final threatening growl at the scarecrow. The two turned and raced each other back through the wheat fields, Jeremy with wooden-stick rifle in hand, to the old Kansas farmhouse.

Roger Martel was heaving the last bail of hay from the wagon into the barn's second floor as his son ran past. "Beat you, Pa!" Jeremy cried. He was up the porch steps, two at a time, and through the screened door his grandmother was holding open before his father had a chance to accept the challenge. The one thing Jeremy liked more than attacking scarecrows in the wheat fields was Grandma's roast chicken.

"Come, Roger, supper is getting cold," Grandma, with flour-coated apron and cheeks, called from the top step. Roger looked up and waved an acknowledgment. Grandma turned, muttering something to herself about her son and cold meals, and re-entered the house to put the final touches on the feast that waited on the kitchen table.

Roger soon entered the kitchen and went to the sink to wash up. "Well, Jeremy," he said, "are we safe yet from your archenemy?" He picked up the hand towel that lay on the counter and dried his hands.

"We could have been, general, sir … if Grandma had given us just five more minutes. We were *that* close." He held his thumb and forefinger a hair's breadth apart and squinted through the space. "Me and Shakey were fearless, Pa. That old scarecrow …"

"Shakey and I," Virginia corrected.

"Shakey and I was so fearless, that ol' scarecrow never could've stood a chance."

Virginia rolled her eyes at this abuse of the English language. "You and Shakey sure are brave," she said.

"I guess we'll just have to wait another week for General Martel's orders to be carried out," Roger said as he took his place at the head of the table. "Grandma, this looks fantastic. Let's give thanks." They all bowed their heads as Roger gave the blessing.

"Can I have a drumstick?" Jeremy spoke before the "amen" was finished. He grabbed his empty plate in his hands and stretched it toward Roger.

"It's 'May I' and 'Please,' young man." This time it was Grandma sternly correcting her only grandchild.

"Sooory," Jeremy said, rolling his eyeballs to the top of their sockets. "*May I* have a drumstick … *pleeease?*"

"You watch that tone, son," Roger said, joining in the scolding. He picked up the carving knife and sliced off one leg of the chicken, helping himself to the drumstick. "You're not too old for what for. Besides, your mother or grandmother may want one. If so, you had better find a way to raise a three-legged chicken."

Jeremy knew Grandma only ate white meat, so he did not need to worry about her. But Mom … well, she could go either way.

"Sorry, Pa," Jeremy said. "May I have a drumstick, please?" He looked in his mother's direction and saw her give the go-ahead to give the drumstick to him.

"That's better." Roger sliced off some white meat for Grandma and his wife, and cut off the second drumstick for Jeremy. Shakey lay on the floor beside Jeremy's chair, alert and ready for the inevitable "accidental" droppings that would soon come. After helping himself to seconds on everything, Jeremy—not having learned his lesson on gluttony—topped off the meal with homemade apple pie that Grandma had baked just that afternoon.

When supper was finished, Jeremy and his father went on cleanup duty. As the men of the house scraped and washed plates, Virginia went upstairs to put away laundry, and Grandma went out for her nightly rocking on the front porch. She always selected the same rocker—"her rocker"—from the two oversized chairs that Jeremy's grandfather had made. They still referred to the other chair as "his rocker," even though Jeremiah Martel had long since been buried in the family plot behind the farmhouse. Grandpa Martel had made the chairs oversized because he was too rotund to fit into any store-bought chair, thanks mostly to his love of Grandma's cooking. And it was fortunate that he had made them oversized, for Grandma loved her own cooking as well.

The air had a pleasing warmth this August evening, and the night sky was cloudless. Grandma was sitting in her rocker, looking up at the outline of the Big Dipper in the midst of the starry entourage, when she heard the screen door creak open. "I knew you'd be here, Grandma," Jeremy said, interrupting the silence. Shakey slipped out to the front porch before the screen door slammed shut behind them.

Grandma smiled. "Why, child, how did you get those dishes cleaned up so fast?" She tipped her head down, squinted her eyes, and faked a scowl. "You didn't break any, did you, just so you wouldn't have as many to wipe?"

"Oh, Grandma," Jeremy said with childlike disgust. "No, I didn't break any. Pa said he would finish so I could come out here and sit with you. If that's okay."

"Of course it is," Grandma said, patting the arm of "his rocker" next to her. Jeremy was almost swallowed up by the chair as he struggled to get into it. Grandma rocked in silence as she watched her grandson lean forward, then back, then forward, then back as he tried to get the monstrous chair to rock in sync with hers. Her rocker was angled so she could inch her left foot over and place it on the runner at the base of his rocker if he needed some assistance.

"Tell me a story, Grandma," Jeremy said when at last he had settled in the chair. Shakey, now five months old, dashed off the porch after a rabbit.

"Oh, my goodness, I don't think I know any stories."

Jeremy rolled his eyes. "Grandma, you say that every night."

"Do I, now?" Grandma laughed.

"Yup. Tell me about how I became a Martel and how great-grandpa Elias got his leg blowed off and how we—"

"Slow down, child," Grandma said, interrupting the rush of excitement. "Seems I have told you about every one of your ancestors already. No need to tell those old stories again."

"Oh, pleeeease, Grandma." Even though Jeremy had heard the stories before, he loved how Grandma changed the details with each telling.

"Well, okay. But just one."

Jeremy knew she would tell more than just one. He smiled and kept on rocking.

"Well," Grandma began, "way back in 1839—a long, long time before you were even a twinkle in your parents' eyes—your great-grandfather, Elias Martel, was born. It was way up north. Remember where?"

"Yup, North Dakota. He was born to a fur trader, and he—"

"Hey, hold up there, you little horseradish. Who's telling this story anyway?"

Jeremy pinched his forefinger and thumb together and drew them across his mouth.

"Now, Elias was born to a fur trader named Jack something-or-other and an Indian squaw from the Blackfoot tribe up in Canada. Seems they fell in love and shacked up together, but never married.

May God have mercy on their souls. Anyway, Martel legend has it that Jack was a heavy drinker, and that the more he drank, the more ornery he got. He could get mighty ugly with that devil's brew in him, so it's told, and that mean-tempered cuss got himself into many a barroom brawl. Well, one summer he went to Boston way up in … ?" She paused for a moment, leaving the question hanging for Jeremy to answer.

"Umm … Massachusetts?"

"Very good."

Jeremy beamed from the praise.

"By the way, did I ever tell you I came here from Massachusetts? A little town called Clayton. Why, I was just a brand new bride and …"

"Grandma, you were telling me about Jack."

"Ah, yes, I do go off on tangents, don't I? Well, Jack had a good winter and spring catching and skinning beaver and the like. So with his squaw and two-year-old son, Elias, he went to Boston to find a buyer. He made quite a bit of money for those days, or so I heard. Well, he spent most of the money on drink, and he got a little too drunk and a little too mean. While he was in the bar, an argument broke out between him and some others who were all liquored up. Seems the locals weren't too keen on white men shacking up with squaws and having half-breed sons. Well, Jack drew his skinning knife and stabbed two of the offenders just as the sheriff entered. That ol' sheriff drew his gun and ordered Jack to drop his knife. When Jack turned to throw it at him, that sheriff put a bullet in Jack's knife-throwing hand.

"Jack dropped his knife, but he was so liquored up he had no good sense to quit. So with his good hand, he went for his own gun, which was tucked into his belt. That earned him a hole in that hand as well. Now both of his hands were shot up pretty good, but that didn't stop that crazy Jack. With a screeching howl, he ran at that ol' sheriff, and he was about to knock him over like a bowling pin when the sheriff put a bullet in one of Jack's knees. Jack just kept hopping on the one good leg until he finally fell flat on his face, spitting his teeth all over the place. He landed right at the feet of the sheriff, and, still yelling and cursing, tried to kick him with his good leg. That's when the sheriff decided he'd had enough and put a bullet into Jack's heart."

“That weren’t very smart-brave of Crazy Jack, was it Grandma?” said Jeremy. “That was dumb-brave.”

“Well, I guess that’s one way to describe it.” Grandma laughed.

“When I attack Scarecrow Jack, I’m always smart-brave. That’s what Pa says. He says someday I’ll be a real hero ’cuz I’m so brave.”

“I’m sure you will be.” Grandma patted Jeremy’s hand, her eyes radiating with pride. “Anyway,” she continued, “the next day when Jack hadn’t come home, his squaw went looking for him and found out about the reason for his death. She dropped little Elias on the doorstep of the nearest church and hightailed it out of town. She was never again seen in those parts.” Grandma paused and sighed.

Jeremy waited. He had seen her drift off like this before, and he always wondered where her thoughts were taking her. When the silence continued, he said, “Then what, Grandma?”

“Hmm? Oh, yes.” Grandma sat up in her chair. “Well, Elias was placed in an orphanage. One year later, a young storeowner and his wife adopted him. Jonas and Catherine Martel were their names. They desperately wanted children, but after several years of trying, Catherine had been told by the doctors that she would never be able to bear a child. Adoption seemed like the only solution. So Elias No-name became Elias Martel, your great-grandfather. And that’s how you became a Martel, young man. Oh, and by the way, the doctors were wrong about Catherine. Turns out she was a baby-making machine. After the couple adopted Elias, they had five sons and three daughters.”

The screen door squeaked open. Grandma and Jeremy both looked over to see Roger standing on the porch, holding the door open. They knew what his next words would be: “Bedtime, son.”

“Aw, but it’s Friday night, Pa.”

“And your point is?”

“I’m nearly seven-and-a-half now. I should get to stay up later on Friday nights.” He turned to look at Grandma for support. “Isn’t that right, Grandma?”

“Well, you must obey your father,” she said, giving a quick scowl at her son.

“Just one more story, Pa?” pleaded Jeremy. “*Pleeeease?*”

"Hmm, just one more," Roger said, holding up his forefinger for emphasis. He walked over and sat on the porch railing. Like Jeremy, he was unable to resist hearing his mother's stories—stories he had heard as a child when he was Jeremy's age.

The screen door opened one more time as Virginia, now finished with her final chores of the day, joined the family. "Did I miss much?" she said, sitting heavily in one of the remaining rockers. She rested her head on the back of the chair and folded her hands over her ample belly.

"Grandma was just about to tell us another story about … who, Grandma?" Jeremy's eyes widened in anticipation of the next incredible story his grandmother would tell.

"Hmm, let's see now." Grandma placed her index finger on her chin. "Did I ever tell you about how your great-grandfather Elias lost his leg in the Civil War?" Jeremy lied and shook his head no. Grandma had forgotten it was one of his favorite requests.

"Well, Jonas had made the general store into a successful business, but it was never his first love—farming was. So sometime around 1850, Jonas and Catherine and all their children … how many was that now, Jeremy?"

"Ahh," Jeremy hesitated a moment as he counted on his fingers. "Nine?"

"Right again. So Jonas and Catherine sold the store for a decent profit, and with all nine children, they headed to the farmlands in Kansas. This was right when homesteads were being opened up for settlement. Land was for the taking, and Jonas, being the savvy businessman he was, used the profits from the sale of the store to build up this farm to a quite sizable and profitable operation.

"Then, just a few years later, in 1861, the Civil War broke out. Elias—who would have been about twenty-two, if I did my math correctly—left home, over the protests of his mother, I might add, and joined the Union army. He did some fighting in Missouri, but it wasn't until the Battle of Vicksburg, in Mississippi, two years later, that he got sent home one-legged. Seems General Grant ordered part of his army to assault a redoubt—"

"What's a redoubt, Grandma?" Jeremy asked.

"Well, that's a pile of dirt and logs the Confederate soldiers used for defense. You know, to hide behind. Anyway, your great-grandfather Elias was one of the soldiers assigned to attack the Confederates behind this redoubt. When the order to attack came, he ran yelling and screaming right at those Confederates, loading his flintlock and firing as he went. Cannon ball was a-rollin' and a-burstin' all around, musket balls were whizzing by his head, and good men were falling left and right.

"Elias just kept on a-running, never minding the dead and dying. He got real close to the enemy soldiers hiding behind those logs and dirt, he did. Then he felt a sting in his leg. A musket ball had nipped him. Elias paid no never mind to it, but he figured he'd better start doing some sidestepping. So your great-granddaddy began a-ziggin' and a-zaggin'. First he'd zig left just as a musket ball was about to put a hole in his right ear, and then he'd zag right as another was about to put a hole in his left ear. He said after a while he could hear them musket balls a-comin'.

"While your great-grandfather was doing all this ziggin' and zaggin', he kept on loading his flintlock and firing. Well, just about the time he reached the redoubt, he felt a pain in his leg like someone was trying to saw it off. When he looked down, he saw he had no leg. Seems a cannon ball had taken it clean off just below the knee."

Jeremy screwed up his face as if he were feeling the pain himself.

"He said he should have zigged when he zagged. But that didn't stop him yet. As he lay there on the ground, he loaded and fired three, maybe four more times, before the pain got to him and he passed out. Next thing he knew, he was lying on a hospital bed with some pretty nurse attending to his shot-off leg."

"That nurse became great-grandma Nelly," Jeremy piped in. "Ain't that right, Grandma?"

"Well, land sakes, child, how'd you know that?" said Grandma. "Have I told you this story before?"

Jeremy looked over at his dad, who had a barn-door-wide grin on his face. "Pa, is this a true story?" he asked.

"If your grandmother says it's true, then it's true," said Roger. "At least, most of it." He gave Virginia a knowing wink.

"You know what else, Jeremy?" Grandma said, ignoring her son's last comment. "One day I was sitting here on this porch, and Elias came out and sat beside me. He slapped that wooden leg and said, 'God is good, Martha.' He went on to say that losing the leg was the best thing that had ever happened to him. When I asked how that could be, he told me that if he hadn't lost it, he would have never met Nelly."

"Goes to prove what I've said all along," Roger said. "The end of all things—whether their purposes are revealed or hidden—is good for those who love God."

"Amen to that," Grandma added.

Jeremy, concerned that story time was about to turn into sermon time, quickly spoke up. "Great-grandpa wasn't afraid of nothing, was he, Grandma? He was a real hero."

"That he was, child. That he was."

"I'm gonna be a hero some day, 'cuz I ain't afraid of nothin' either." A picture of a skewered scarecrow popped into his mind.

"Well," Grandma laughed, "I do declare that the Good Lord might just make you one yet."

Roger shifted and stood to his feet. "That was at least one more story, young man," he said. "Time for bed."

"Aw, Pa!"

"Aw, Pa nothing. Now climb aboard." Roger squatted to his son's level, with his backside facing the front of the chair. Jeremy sighed and climbed aboard his father's broad shoulders. Roger bent slightly so Jeremy's head would not hit the porch roof and then trotted along the porch, down the steps, and onto the graveled driveway. Suddenly, all 220 of his pounds transformed into a human bronco as he ran and jumped and spun. Jeremy laughed and held on tightly to his father's thick mane of hair. Shakey nearly got stepped on as he ran around in circles and barked.

"Oh, Roger, be careful," Virginia pleaded weakly, knowing her husband would pay no attention to her whatsoever. Grandma just chuckled in her chair.

After ten minutes had passed, Jeremy waved good night to his audience, and the two headed into the house. Roger, with Shakey still at his heels, followed the ritual path past the fireplace mantel before turning upstairs. He slowed to give Jeremy time to reach out and touch each of the pictures that had been lovingly placed there.

Jeremy first brushed the fading black-and-white picture of great-grandpa Elias. He was standing so his wooden leg showed prominently, and he held a flintlock across his chest. "Good night, great-grandpa," Jeremy said. Next was a picture of Grandma and Grandpa Martel standing in front of an old Model-T Ford. The last picture was of his mother and father standing at the foot of the porch stairs back in 1942. Virginia's arms were around her husband's waist, and her head was resting against his chest. Roger was dressed in his Marine parade dress blues. He and Virginia had been married for only two months when Japan attacked Pearl Harbor, and Roger was just about to leave for the Philippines on active duty.

The ride continued up the stairs. "Watch your head, son," Roger warned. Jeremy, quite practiced in this maneuver, had already leaned forward at the waist to keep from hitting the ceiling. Finally, they reached Jeremy's bedroom, where he was less than graciously dumped onto the soft mattress. No sooner had this occurred than his father began to tickle him mercilessly.

"I … can't … breathe!" Jeremy gasped, his sides splitting from laughing. Shakey jumped up onto the bed and joined the fray, giving Jeremy's face some slobbering licks.

Roger stopped the tickling and sat on the edge of the bed to allow his son to catch his breath. "Well, it's time to get ready for bed," he said. With that, Jeremy got up, brushed his teeth, put on his pajamas, and climbed into bed.

"Aren't we forgetting something?" Roger asked.

"Oh, yeah." Jeremy climbed back out of bed, and father and son knelt together. "Dear God, thank You for this day and for all the fun I had. Thank You for Mommy and Daddy, and for Grandma and Shakey. And thank You for our home and food. And God, thank You for my new brother … or sister, I guess, if that's what You want. Aaaamen!"

"With an 'amen' like that, you'd make a great preacher someday," Roger said.

Jeremy climbed back into bed and under the covers. "Nah, I want to be a ventinarian, or a Marine like you."

Roger tucked the covers on one side of the bed, and then went around and tucked the sheet and blanket in so tightly that the mattress looked like a canoe. He bent over, kissed his son's forehead, tousled his hair, and began to leave.

"Pa?" Jeremy said.

"Yes, son?" Roger stopped in the doorway, his right hand on the light switch.

"How much longer before I get to meet my new brother?"

"Or sister?"

"Or sister." He was still a bit disgusted by that possibility.

"It will all happen in God's gracious timing, but I suspect it won't be long. Maybe another month. Now you get to sleep. We need to be up early. Chores and all. Good night." With that, Roger flicked the switch and slowly closed the door. From the hallway, he could just make out a pair of seven-year-old fingers resting on top of the covers and wiggling a wave good night.

Jeremy rolled onto his right side and dangled his left arm over the edge of the bed. He lay still, except for the fingertip stroking of Shakey's head, who had now moved into his nightly position. Jeremy's eyes were feeling heavy as he watched the hallway light seeping under the base of the door. "One, two, three … he counted. The light almost always went off at twelve. It was then that he allowed the heaviness of his eyes to overtake him.

Chapter 7

Too Young

August 21, 1954

Roger made a side trip through the kitchen and then rejoined his wife and mother on the front porch.

"Roger Martel," Virginia scolded when she saw what was in his hands. "That piece of pie is large enough to choke a mule."

"Want a bite?" Roger said, holding out a fork full of pie.

"Of course I do, and more than one." She rubbed her belly. "I need to keep this little one happy too."

"God is so good," Grandma said. "As I sit here each night, I've often reflected on just how blessed we are."

"Amen to that," Roger said, his mouth stuffed with pie. Virginia reached over, grabbed his fork, and helped herself to a bite.

"And now, blessing upon blessing, I am close to meeting my second grandchild," said Grandma. "Have you two decided on names yet?"

"Well," Virginia replied, "we thought if it's a boy we would name him Benjamin, after my father. If it's a girl, we thought she would be called Martha, after you, Grandma."

Grandma pulled a handkerchief from an apron pocket and dabbed her eyes. "Blessing upon blessing."

"We thought you would find that acceptable," Roger said, smiling. "Now, my dear wife, since you ate my last bite of pie, I need to get myself another one from the kitchen and pour …" He stopped short when he saw a sudden wince crease Virginia's face. She pressed both hands to her belly and gave out a soft moan.

"What's wrong?" Roger said, placing the empty plate on the porch railing and kneeling beside her. "Are you okay?"

"Yes, dear, I'm fine," Virginia replied. "Just a twinge of pain."

"Did the baby kick?"

"No, just a little twinge. I'm fine. Really."

"Well, then, I think I'll make that trip to the kitchen." Roger stood, picked up his plate, and took a few steps toward the door. "Grandma, can I get you—"

"Ooooow!" Virginia groaned, grasping the arms of the chair.

Roger rushed back and stood over his wife. "That was no twinge. I think we need to call Doc Preston and ask him to come over."

"No, it's okay," Virginia stubbornly protested. "It happens every now and then."

By this time, Grandma had struggled out of her chair and was standing in front of her daughter-in-law. "Virginia, I think you better listen to your husband," she said sternly. "Roger, you make the phone call while I help her up to your bedroom. Come, dear." She took Virginia's hand and helped her up.

"Oh, all right," Virginia said, "but I think you're all making too much of a …" She crumpled over in pain. Grandma reached out to try to catch her, but she was not strong enough to hold her, and Virginia crashed to the floor. Roger, who had just reached the front door, dropped the plate and glass, letting them shatter, and rushed back to his wife. "Grandma, you go make the call," he ordered as he knelt by his wife. "I'll get Virginia to our room." He placed his arms under his wife, picked her up, and carried her to their bedroom. There he gently lay her down on the bed and sat beside her, holding her hand.

Virginia looked up. Seeing the concern in her husband's eyes, she tried to reassure him. "Looks like Grandma might be introduced to her new grandchild a bit sooner than planned," she said. She tried to laugh, but another sharp pain raced across her abdomen.

"I'll be right back," Roger said. He left the room and raced down the stairs to where Grandma was just hanging up the phone. "Well, is Doc coming?" he blurted in a demanding tone.

"I talked to his wife," said Grandma, her voice calm and reassuring. "I explained the situation. She said Doc is out on another call, but she is going to try to reach him and let him know to come here as soon as possible. He will call from where he is and let us know when he's on the way. Now I want you to stay here by the phone and wait for the call. I'll stay with Virginia. Everything will be fine." With those words, she turned and walked up the stairs.

Roger did not like having to wait, but he was reassured by the calm finality in his mother's voice. He paced the hallway.

Jeremy sat up in bed. He had been awakened by something that sounded like a scream—a nightmarish scream. He tried to remember if he had been having a bad dream, but he couldn't remember dreaming at all. His nightmares always left him in a puddle of sweat, but on this night his skin was dry.

There was the scream again—coming from beyond his room. Jeremy's head jerked toward the closed door. The light from the hallway was on and filtering into his room from underneath the door. Shakey sat up from where he had been lying at the foot of the bed and whimpered in the dark.

Voices. He could hear people talking, but he couldn't make out what was being said. He looked toward the window. The shades were up, and it was pitch black outside. It wasn't yet time to get up for chores.

What is going on? he said to himself. He swung his legs over the edge of the bed and slid his bare feet to the floor. Shakey immediately jumped down from the bed and stood beside him. Slowly, the two walked toward the bedroom door.

Jeremy approached the door and reached out his hand to turn the knob. Another scream. He jumped and jerked his hand back, as if the doorknob had been electrified. Slowly, he backed up until he bumped into his bed, and then sank to the floor. Shakey moved to his side.

Jeremy pulled him close, hugging his friend as if he were a stuffed animal.

More voices. This time they were louder. Somebody was shouting. He still couldn't make out all the words, but what he did hear frightened him.

"Get the water … clean rags …"

"Quickly!"

"It's a breech … you go over there …"

"No, I can't turn …"

Breech? Jeremy remembered watching his dad try to deliver a calf from their cow, Bessy. She had been ready to birth the calf, but couldn't do it. He could still hear the frightful moaning sounds she made. Pa had said the calf was in the breech position and that he would have to reach almost up to his shoulder inside Bessy to try to turn the calf around. Jeremy remembered the fluid and blood that covered his dad and the painful bellowing Bessy made as the calf was being pulled out. Roger did all he could, but the calf was stillborn. Bessy died a few hours later.

Another scream caused Jeremy to jump again. His face wrenched, and a wetness was now gathering on his forehead that had not been there moments before.

"Don't push!" he heard a man yell through the walls.

More screaming.

Jeremy blocked his ears with both hands, but even that did not shut out the terrible sounds. His body trembled and tears flowed freely down his face. He was desperate for his Pa to rush in, pick him up, hold him, and tell him that everything would be all right. He wanted it all to be just a terrible dream.

Everything went silent. Jeremy waited, listening. Several minutes passed before he dared to release his hands from his ears. When he did, he heard footsteps that stopped just outside his door.

Slowly, the door opened. Jeremy could see the silhouette of Grandma standing against the backlight of the hallway light. She walked across the room and sat heavily on his bed. "Jeremy," she said softly, her voice quivering, "sit up here with me. I have something I have to tell you." She patted the mattress beside her.

Jeremy trembled and rubbed his pajama sleeve across his face. He had never heard this tone in his grandmother's voice before, and it frightened him. He knew he did not want to hear what she had come to say.

Grandma put her arms around her grandchild and pulled him close. "You've been crying." She gently wiped away the lingering tears.

"The screams, Grandma. I was so afraid. I thought I was having a nightmare." Grandma sighed deeply. "Jeremy, do you remember the words your father taught you—the words my father taught me? 'The end of all things, their purposes revealed or hidden …'"

"'Are good for those who love God.' I remember, Grandma." Jeremy sniffed and rubbed his sleeve across his face again, and then looked up into his grandmother's weary, strained face. "Grandma," he whispered, "is Mommy okay?"

Another set of footsteps could be heard coming down the hall. Roger now stood in the doorway. He walked over to his mother and son and knelt before them. He looked into his son's eyes and, for a moment, held his child's face in his trembling hands. Then he fell forward into his mother's lap and wept.

Jeremy had never seen his father cry. The unexplained fear returned.

Grandma Martel put an arm around Jeremy and laid a hand on the back of her son's trembling shoulders. She was now holding the only family she had left in Kansas.

Four days passed. Two caskets—one large, one small—now sat beside the two freshly dug graves in the family plot behind the farmhouse. The funeral service at the church had been well attended, but this gathering was for the family only, with the exception of Pastor Sterling and the two deacons who had volunteered to lay the caskets in the ground and cover them.

"Dust to dust," the pastor concluded. "Blessed be the name of the Lord, into whose loving arms we commit the eternal souls of these two children of God. Amen."

Roger and Grandma whispered an amen and thanked the pastor for his words. Hugs were shared, hands of sympathy were shaken, and Jeremy was patted on the shoulder. Shakey sat silently beside him. The two deacons patiently stood by to begin their unpleasant task.

After the service had ended, Roger, Grandma, Jeremy, and Pastor Sterling walked back toward the farmhouse. "Pastor," Grandma said, "would you like to come in for some coffee and pie?" The look she saw on her son's face made her immediately regret making the invitation.

Pastor Sterling caught the look on Roger's face as well. "Oh, thank you so much, Martha," he said, "but perhaps some other time, if you don't mind."

"Well, you know the door is always open for you."

As soon as Pastor Sterling left, Roger removed his coat and tie and laid them over the porch railing. Without a word of explanation, he left Grandma and Jeremy standing at the bottom of the porch stairs and walked over to the tractor parked beside the barn. He climbed into the driver's seat and started the engine.

"Pa!" Jeremy yelled after him. "Where are you going?" Roger put the machine into gear and drove away toward the fields, ignoring his son's pleas.

Jeremy looked into his grandma's face. "Where's Pa going?" he asked anxiously.

Grandma put an arm around her grandson's shoulders. "Your father needs some time alone," she said. "Now, let's go into the house and I'll cut you a slice of lemon meringue pie, your favorite."

"No!" Jeremy cried out. "I don't want pie! I want to be with Pa!" He broke away from Grandma and began to run after the tractor, with Shakey keeping pace.

"Jeremy, come back!" Grandma cried. But the call was futile.

"Pa! Pa!" Jeremy yelled as he ran.

Roger heard the cries and braked the tractor. As he turned, he saw his son stumble and fall, stretching out his arms in an attempt to break the fall. Jeremy's palms and knees dug into the jagged marble-sized gravel, and for a moment he lay still. Then, ignoring the pain of his torn flesh, he struggled to his feet and began to run again.

Roger leapt from the machine and ran back to his son. He lifted him in his arms and squeezed tightly. Jeremy wrapped his arms around his pa's neck and squeezed back.

Roger carried the boy back to the tractor and lifted him into the bench seat. Together, in silence, they rode through the wheat fields until they came to a small, spring-fed pond near the edge of the farm. Roger reached down, and shut off the engine. For a while he and Jeremy sat together without saying a word. Shakey, who had followed behind, moved to the pond to lap up the water.

Several minutes passed before Jeremy broke the silence. "Pa, are you okay?" he asked, looking up into his father's face.

Roger swallowed hard. "See that willow tree on the other side of the pond?" He paused a moment, rubbed his face with both hands, and gripped the steering wheel. "That's where ..." He stopped again, his voice choking with emotion. "That's where I asked your mother to marry me."

Jeremy turned and looked at the tree. This was not the first time he had seen it. In fact, he had climbed it many times when coming here to hunt for frogs. But it was the first time he had heard this story.

Roger smiled at the memory. "She said no at first—said she was too young. But she told me not to give up."

"Too young?" Jeremy asked.

"That's right," Roger said, still staring straight ahead at the tree. "She was seventeen, and I was eighteen. We dated two more years before I asked her again. That time she said yes." Roger paused, picturing the scene in his mind. "I love you so much."

"I love you, too, Pa," Jeremy said, thinking these last words were meant for him.

"Hmm? What?" Roger turned to look at his son.

"I said I love you too."

Roger said nothing, but slowly reached down to start the engine. He drove back to the farmhouse and parked the tractor near the barn. "You had better go into the house and have Grandma take a look at those cuts," he said, helping Jeremy down.

"Okay, Pa. Are you coming in too?"

"No, son. But you go on now, and do as I've said."

Jeremy headed up to the house. When he reached the porch, he turned for a moment to watch his father walk away toward the hill behind the old farmhouse.

Jeremy slowly opened the door and entered the house. He could hear Grandma in the kitchen and smell the aroma of her baking. It was her way of keeping her mind occupied and dealing with her heartache. Jeremy walked into the room and held up both palms for her to see. "I fell," he said.

"So I see." She pulled one of the chairs away from the table and motioned for him to sit. "You take those pants off and sit right here while I get my first aid kit."

Take my pants off? Jeremy thought. *Why?* Looking down, he saw a tear on his right knee. He was surprised that he felt no pain, until he dropped his pants and began to pull away the cloth from the dried wound.

Grandma returned, placed the kit on the table, ran a pan of warm water at the sink, and grabbed a clean hand towel. With everything now in place, she sat in a second chair and faced Jeremy. Dipping the towel into the warm water, she gently touched the wounded knee, wiping away the dirt and dried blood.

"Why, you didn't even make a whimper when I did that," Grandma praised.

"It didn't even hurt, Grandma." Jeremy lied.

"Well, you are a brave boy."

"Told you I was."

"Yes, you did, but what I have to do next may hurt a bit."

Jeremy's eyes widened. It had been a while since Grandma had worked on any of his wounds, and he had forgotten about the sting of the iodine. "Grandma, it's not that bad," he said with great concern in his voice. "We don't need to—"

"Oh, yes, we do need to," Grandma insisted. "It may get infected, and that would mean a trip to the doctor's office. Now hold still as I poor some of this onto the cut." Grandma held Jeremy's leg between her knees to keep him from pulling away. "When this is over, I will let you have one of my homemade molasses cookies, right out of the oven. How does that sound?"

Jeremy had no time to respond. Grandma tipped the bottle, and the liquid poured out and began to seep into the wound. Jeremy's eyes dilated and he involuntarily sucked in air. The stinging brought tears to his eyes, and his lips quivered. "That hurting feeling is a good sign," Grandma said, trying to comfort him. "It means it's working, pulling out those germs." She sat back for a moment and looked at the face of her grandson, his tears on the verge of falling. "There now. It's not stinging quite so much now, is it?"

Jeremy shook his head slowly. "No," was all he was able to sniffle out.

Grandma found the largest bandage in the first aid kit and pressed it over the wound. "There, all done with that."

"Can I have a cookie now?"

"Almost. But first we need to take care of those scraped palms." She looked closely at his hands. "Looks like there might still be some gravel stuck in there." She picked up a pair of tweezers in the kit and began probing the open wound.

"Ow! Ow!" Jeremy protested loudly through gritted teeth.

"There, I think I got them all. Now, just a bit more iodine." Jeremy held his breath. Tears again welled up in his eyes. "There, all done," Grandma said as she pressed the last bandage into place. "For being so brave, I think you deserve at least two of my molasses cookies. Your father will be so proud of you."

Jeremy did not argue with her, even though he did not feel so brave at the moment. The stinging was almost gone.

Grandma packed up the first aid kit and served the cookies with a glass of milk. She helped herself to a few cookies as well and then sat across the table from her grandson. They enjoyed the treat in silence for a few minutes, until Jeremy came to the last bite of his cookie.

"Grandma?"

"Yes, Jeremy."

"Are Mommy and my sister in heaven?"

"Yes, Jeremy, I believe they are." She had expected to have this conversation, but not this soon. "The Good Lord promises those who love Him will be with Him. Your mother truly loved Him. And God has declared in the Good Book how He loves the little children."

Jeremy ate the last bite of his cookie. "Grandma, is God really good?"

Grandma was taken aback by the question. This was one she had not expected. "Yes, He is," she said in a gentle voice. "I know it's hard to see right now. You are going through a difficult time, as we all are. But you must remember that God is in control."

Jeremy looked straight into his grandmother's eyes. "If He is in control," he said, the anger rising in his voice, "then why did He let my mommy and sister die?"

Grandma shook her head. "I don't know, Jeremy, I truly don't. None of us can understand all His ways and why things like this happen. But He just asks us to trust Him, even in the hard times."

Jeremy slid from his chair and, without saying another word, went to his room and closed the door. Grandma watched him slowly walk away. She did not know what else to say and, of course, she had her own questions. The depth of sorrow that overwhelmed her was almost unbearable. She had suffered other losses—her father-in-law, Elias; her husband; and two miscarriages of her own—but this seemed more devastating.

"Dear Lord," she prayed, folding her hands into her lap. "Help the child to understand Your purposes. For I …" She could not continue. Her own grief overwhelmed her, and she buried her face in her hands.

CHAPTER 8

MORE QUESTIONS

FEBRUARY 23, 1955

Jeremy raced past Grandma, shoved open the front door, and jumped all four steps from the porch to the driveway. Shakey kept pace behind him.

"Hold on just one minute, you little jack rabbit," Grandma scolded as she stood in the doorway.

Jeremy stopped short and turned to face her. "But Grandma, I'll be late for the bus," he said, spreading his arms wide in a pleading gesture.

"That's not my problem," Grandma said, squinting down at him. "You get yourself right back in here and take your lunch and coat. It's going to rain before you get home from school, and I'll not have you coming down with pneumonia because you can't get ready in time."

"Oh, Grandma," Jeremy complained, but he had already started back up the stairs. Shakey, having been through this routine many times, sat where he was and waited, panting with his tongue hanging from the side of his mouth. Grandma helped Jeremy put on his coat and then handed him his bagged lunch.

"Bye, Pa!" he yelled out as he jumped off the porch, again bypassing the stairs. Roger had just stepped out from the barn holding a newlysharpened axe. He waved to his son and Shakey as they raced for the end of the driveway.

"He's getting tall and strong," Grandma said to Roger when he had stepped onto the porch.

"That he is, Mother that he is." He leaned the axe against the porch railing, squeezed past her into the doorway, and entered the house.

"Reminds me of you at that age," Grandma said, opening the door to follow her son inside. "Why, do you know what he did just the other day?" With that, the reminiscing began.

Jeremy could already see the bus approaching by the time he was halfway down the driveway, but he figured he still had a minute. He stepped out into the field, found a stick, picked it up and tossed it as far along the driveway as he could. Shakey, anticipating this daily game, was already in full stride when Jeremy released it. After retrieving the stick, Shakey dropped it at Jeremy's feet and waited for round two, his tail wagging like he was fanning a fire. "Stay!" Jeremy commanded, and then walked ten feet ahead of Shakey before again throwing the stick. Shakey did not move until Jeremy commanded, "Go!" Then they both raced for it.

Even with the head start, Jeremy had never won this race—until today. "I win!" he yelled in victory as he held the stick high over his head. When he turned to tease Shakey with the prize, he saw that his friend had stopped and was staring straight ahead past Jeremy, his head lowered.

Jeremy looked behind him, but saw nothing. "What's the matter, boy?" he said, walking back to Shakey. "Can't take being the loser?"

Shakey continued staring. He bared his teeth and began making a low, guttural growl. It was unlike anything Jeremy had heard or seen from his dog before.

"What's the matter, boy?" Jeremy said, squatting beside his friend. "See a rabbit?" He scratched Shakey's head, but the dog continued to bare his teeth and growl.

Jeremy turned and again looked down the road. This time, a coyote, about half the size of Shakey, was limping into the open from a drainage ditch across the road. Jeremy froze. The coyote stopped where he was, lowered his head, and began to move toward the driveway. Shakey let out a fierce growl and darted from Jeremy's grasp.

"Shakey, no!" Jeremy screamed. "Come back!"

Shakey, flashing his teeth, darted down the driveway and leaped at the coyote. At the last second the coyote sidestepped the attack and sank his fangs deep into Shakey's hindquarters. The flesh ripped away, and the dog yelped in pain. Shakey twisted and turned in an attempt to grab hold of some vulnerable point, but the coyote attacked him with a vengeance.

The German Shepherd was no match for the vicious animal. Within seconds, the coyote had bitten him in several places, and Jeremy could see blood appearing on the fur of his protector. Then, with one swift turn, the coyote grabbed Shakey by the neck and began shaking him mercilessly. Jeremy could only stand frozen in place, as if he were chained to the driveway, unaware of the wet stain growing down his pant leg. Shakey shook free and tried to grab the coyote's neck, but he again found himself in vice-like jaws.

Jeremy was finally able to find his voice. "Pa! Pa!" he screamed.

Roger stepped out of the house when he heard Jeremy yell, but it wasn't until he walked down the porch steps that he saw the battle. Instinctively, he ran back up the stairs, grabbed the axe and raced toward his son. Within moments he had reached Jeremy, who was sobbing and helpless with fear, and rushed past to face the attacker. He raised the axe and lowered it with a crushing blow to the head of the coyote, splitting the animal's skull open. Shakey dropped to the ground and lay still. He was bleeding profusely from several wounds and barely breathing.

The bus driver had stopped the bus a short distance away. After watching the events unfold, he had jumped from the bus to look for some weapon to use to fight off the coyote—a rock or a stick—but had found none. As he approached the scene, he saw the axe was still imbedded in the skull of the animal.

Roger knelt beside Jeremy, holding the boy's arms tightly. "Are you all right, son? Did you get bitten? Are you hurt?" Roger's voice was panicked, and the questions came in a flurry. He was terrified at the thought that it could have been his boy lying in the roadway instead of

Shakey. Jeremy, trembling and unable to stop crying, could only say, "Shakey? Shakey?"

Grandma quickly arrived and gasped when she saw the motionless body of the coyote. Shakey was now trying to stand to his feet, but he repeatedly collapsed in the middle of the road. "Let me have the boy," she commanded, taking him from Roger's arms. "Go get the truck! We have to take Shakey to the vet."

Roger shook his head sadly. "I don't think it will do much—"

"Get the truck and do it!" Grandma snapped back. "We will let the Good Lord decide the outcome."

"I'm … going … too," Jeremy said between sobs.

"We will all go, Jeremy," said Grandma.

The bus driver was still standing nearby. "Anything I can do, Martha?" he called out.

"No, Henry. You go on. Jeremy won't be going to school today."

Roger brought the truck to the end of the driveway, got out, and lowered the tailgate. He walked over to Shakey, reached down, and, as gently as possible, scooped up the dog and placed him in the bed of the truck. He returned to the carcass of the coyote, yanked out the axe from its skull, and tossed the dead animal into the back of the truck as well.

"Jeremy, get in the back with Shakey," Grandma instructed. "Keep him steady. I'll ride up front with your father."

Jeremy thought the ride would last forever. Finally, Roger pulled into the veterinarian's parking lot, where Grandma immediately jumped out and went to the office. Roger stepped out as well and walked to the back of the truck to retrieve the badly mauled dog. Jeremy raced ahead to hold the door open as Roger picked up Shakey and brought him into the building.

Inside, Dr. Pillsbury was already waiting. He took over, directing Grandma and Jeremy to have a seat while he and Roger took the animal into a back room. Grandma grabbed Jeremy's shoulders to keep him from following as they watched the white-coated doctor and his father disappear down a long corridor.

The wait was unbearable. At one point, Jeremy looked up into the face of his grandmother and saw that her eyes were closed and her lips were moving. He knew exactly what she was doing, but he had no inclination to follow her example. He was confused, frightened, and angry.

Finally, Jeremy's father and the doctor, his white coat now stained red, reentered the waiting room. Jeremy sprang to his feet and ran to them. "Can I see Shakey?" he asked in an anxious voice.

The doctor knelt beside Jeremy and placed a gentle hand on the boy's shoulder. "Jeremy, Shakey was a very brave dog. I've seen the coyote that attacked him, and, well, Shakey was just no match for him. I'm afraid ..." He paused and looked up at Grandma and Roger before continuing. "I'm afraid there is not much I can do for him."

Jeremy felt as if he had been struck. He stood in a trancelike state, his eyes staring forward without blinking. The trembling began to return as the doctor's words sank in.

Dr. Pillsbury stood and looked at Grandma. "I'm sorry," he said in a pained voice. "There has just been too much damage. I have talked it over with Roger, and we agree that it is in the best interest of the animal to put him down."

The doctor's words shook Jeremy out of his trance. "Put him down?" he cried, his words laced with tears. "No! Pa, please, *no*!" He darted for the back room, but Roger grabbed him and held him tightly. "Let me go!" Jeremy screamed. "I want to see Shakey!"

"Jeremy," Roger said in a gentle tone, "it's the best thing. We need to—"

"*No!* You can't! Let ... me ... go!" Jeremy punched and kicked to free himself from his father's grasp.

"Doctor," Grandma said quietly. "Is there any chance Shakey can be saved?" Jeremy stopped struggling and looked at his grandmother, and then at the doctor. The doctor paused for a moment, and an unbearable eternity passed.

"Well ... Martha," he said slowly, "I really don't think it would be in the best interest—"

"That's not what I asked you, doctor. I asked if there was any chance that Shakey could be saved. Yes or no?"

"Mrs. Martel, you do not understand," Dr. Pillsbury argued. "The amount of damage is severe. Shakey has lost a great deal of blood. One of his ears is torn off, he has multiple bites in the neck and hind quarters, and one leg is so destroyed that—"

"Doctor, I did not ask you for a description of the animal's injuries. I asked if Shakey could be saved."

Dr. Pillsbury sighed deeply. "Possibly, with a lot of luck. But the expense will be—"

"There will be no luck, doctor, but there will be a good deal of prayer. As far as the expense is concerned, I will take care of that."

Roger looked at his mother with incredulity. He knew how little money she had. "Mother," he said, "you don't have—"

"Hush, Roger. Now, doctor, you just get yourself back in there and use the skills the Good Lord has entrusted you with."

Dr. Pillsbury looked at Roger, who shrugged. The doctor slowly nodded and left.

Four long hours passed. Jeremy sat on the edge of his chair, his every muscle tensed, and stared at the doors. Roger picked up a magazine, but put it down after realizing he had read the same paragraph three times. Finally, the doors swung open and the doctor walked toward them. Each of the Martels studied his face for some hint of the verdict.

"I've done all I can," said Dr. Pillsbury. "Now we just wait and see."

"Can I see him?" Jeremy asked as he slid down from his chair.

"No, Jeremy, not today. Perhaps tomorrow."

"But—"

"Then we will be back tomorrow," Grandma said, interrupting her grandson. "Thank you, doctor." She stood and directed her family to follow her out of the office with a simple, commanding, "Come!"

Back at the farm, Roger stopped the truck in front of the porch to let out his passengers. "Jeremy," he said to his son, "why don't you come and help me in the barn for a while? It will help take your mind off things."

Jeremy ignored his father's suggestion. "I don't want to take my mind off things," he said in a whisper. He walked into the house, up to his room, and closed the door. The late afternoon sun was still high in the sky. He pulled the shades down to block out the sunlight, lay on his bed, and folded his hands behind his head. It was not the first time he noticed the wetness of his pants, but he told himself that he did not care.

Jeremy heard Grandma's labored footsteps on the stairs. He listened for the pause, which usually came at about the eighth step. There it was—a ten-second wait—and then Grandma made the rest of the climb. At the top of the stairs, she usually turned left to head for her own bedroom. Tonight, he heard the footsteps approaching his room. He considered pretending to be asleep when the knock came.

"Jeremy, may I come in?"

At first he said nothing, but then thought better of it. This was Grandma, after all.

"Sure."

The door opened. Grandma stepped in and closed the door behind her. She reached to turn on the lights, but then decided to leave the room dark. "May I talk with you?"

"I guess," said Jeremy, rolling to his right side to face her.

Grandma walked over to the bed and sat heavily on the edge. "I just wanted to see how you were doing. That was quite a scare you went through."

Jeremy sat up. "Grandma, I ain't never been so scared." His eyes went wide as he recalled the terror of the attack. "The coyote came from out of nowhere. I couldn't move. That coyote showed his teeth and growled, and I thought for sure he was gonna come for me. He would've, too, if it hadn't been for Shakey. He ran right at that coyote. I yelled and yelled for him to come back, but he wouldn't."

Grandma sat quietly and nodded, allowing her grandson to shed off some of the fear that was still in his mind.

"I was so scared, Grandma, but Shakey wasn't. He was so brave, and I couldn't help him. Grandma, I ..." He paused and looked away, ashamed of his next confession.

"You what, child?"

"I ... I wet my pants." The tears began to fall. Grandma reached out and pulled her grandson to herself, and Jeremy let himself be swallowed up by her arms. Several minutes passed before he pushed away and wiped his runny nose on his sleeve.

"I wasn't brave, but Shakey was, and Pa. You should have seen Pa, Grandma. He ran right at that coyote and stuck that axe into his head." He stopped and looked up. "Will I ever be brave?"

"Of course you will. Your father is a grown man and has fought in a war. You talk to him. He'll tell you of many times he was so scared he could hardly think straight."

"Pa?"

"Umhmm. And do you think your great-grandfather Elias Martel wasn't afraid when he was attacking them rebs? I think he probably did more than wet his pants." Jeremy giggled at the thought.

"Tell you what," Grandma continued, "I'll go draw you a bath, and we'll get you all cleaned up and in fresh clothes. Then you come to the kitchen and help me clean up the mess I made making chocolate pudding." Jeremy knew this meant he could lick the beaters that would be sure to have extra pudding not yet scraped off.

"Okay," Jeremy said, wiping his eyes and nose again. A faint smile creased his lips. "Grandma?"

"Yes?"

"When will I be growed up?"

"Why, child, I think you've already done a heap of growing up today."

Roger worked well into the evening, and it was after dark when he came in from the barn. Jeremy and Grandma sat on the porch, silently rocking away beside each other.

"Seems you work later and later every night, Roger," Grandma said. "You're going to work yourself to death."

"Can't be helped." Roger leaned against the porch railing and wiped sweat from his forehead with a handkerchief. "Every day something different breaks. Just when I think I've got everything in good working order, what I fixed last month breaks again. I can't afford to buy new tools and equipment, with the way crops have been the last two years."

"We'll get by just fine. You know what the Good Book says: 'Cast all your anxiety on Him, because He cares for you.'"

"Know it well, Grandma. Know it well." He walked over to his son and squatted. "Jeremy, climb aboard. Time for bed."

"Pa, I think I'm too growed up for that anymore. I'll just walk upstairs."

Roger stood and looked at his mother with a puzzled expression. "Okay, son, if that's what you want," he said, not wanting to let his disappointment show. "Go ahead. I'll be up in a few minutes to tuck you in."

Jeremy left and slowly walked up the stairs to his room.

"What's going on?" Roger said to his mother. "He never refused one of my horseback rides before."

"I'm afraid your son *is* growing up."

"Hmm. When did that happen?"

Grandma smiled. Roger shook his head and followed after Jeremy.

"Want to talk about today?" Roger asked when the typical bedtime routines had been completed.

"Nah. I'm really tired. I just want to go to sleep."

"Okay. Let's say our prayers, and I'll tuck you in."

"Pa," Jeremy asked, looking up at his father. "Were you ever afraid?"

Roger hesitated, taken aback by the question.

"Grandma said that when you were in the war, you were afraid sometimes. Is that true?"

"Oh, my, yes. When someone is shooting bullets at you, you'd be a fool not to be afraid."

"Did you ever … wet your pants?"

Roger again hesitated. "Some of the bravest men I knew did that in battle," he said, not wanting to add to his son's embarrassment. "Now, why don't we say our prayers?"

"Pa, why did God let Shakey get so hurt? Shakey's my best friend. I love him. Why did He let it happen?" Fresh tears rose up in his eyes, and his chin began to quiver.

"I don't know, son." He reached over and stroked Jeremy's hair. "But what I do know is that the Good Lord gave you a brave friend to protect you in just such a time as this. I dread to think of what might have happened if Shakey hadn't been with you. I never told you this, but when you picked Shakey out of that litter, I wanted to tell you I didn't think he was the best choice, him being the runt and all. But now I thank God for bringing you two together. Now, it's time to say your prayers and get to sleep."

"I can say them by myself, Pa."

"I guess you can. You're growing up, and I'm very proud of you. But are you too grown up for a good night kiss?" Jeremy smiled and shook his head. Roger leaned over and kissed his son's forehead. "Good night, son."

"Good night, Pa." Jeremy got up and knelt down at the side of his bed. But after Roger turned off the lights and closed the door, he stood again. "Sorry, God," he said aloud, "but I don't like You very much tonight."

Jeremy was not going to school the next day, but his father still made him get up early to do the chores. He did not really mind so much, because he couldn't sleep anyway, and it helped the time go by faster. The vet's office didn't open until 8:00.

A few hours later, Grandma drove Jeremy into town. The drive seemed twice as long as usual that day, but they finally pulled into the veterinarian's parking lot. Jeremy barely let Grandma park the truck before he jumped out and rushed into the office.

"Hi, Jeremy," the friendly receptionist said in greeting.

"Hello," Jeremy replied. "I came to see Shakey."

"Well, let me get Dr. Pillsbury."

Grandma soon entered the office. "Judy's gone to get Doctor P," Jeremy informed her.

The door behind the counter swung open, and the doctor and Judy emerged. "Hello, Martha," Dr. Pillsbury said with a smile. "And Jeremy, how are you doing?"

The impatience on Jeremy's face revealed he had no time for small talk. "I'm here to see Shakey."

"Well, then, come right around here." He beckoned Jeremy to come to the back room and then led him and Grandma down a corridor lined with cages. All kinds of animals in various stages of healing were housed there, and a nauseating medicinal odor hung in the air. At the end of the corridor, the doctor opened a cage door. Jeremy peered in. Shakey was wrapped in bandages, but when he saw Jeremy, his tail began thumping against the side of the cage.

"Shakey!" Jeremy cried out, climbing into the cage to be with his best friend. The doctor let him go and then pulled Grandma aside. "Martha," he said in a soft voice, "it's a miracle, but Shakey is going to survive."

"God is good, doctor."

"Yes, well, there are a few things you need to know. First, full recovery will take a few weeks. Shakey took quite a beating. As I said yesterday, there are multiple bite wounds, his left ear was bitten off, and he had a number of internal injuries. I have been able to deal with all of these issues."

"But there is something you're not saying, doctor."

Dr. Pillsbury turned his attention to the boy and the dog in the cage. Shakey was licking the skin off Jeremy's face as he giggled and wallowed with joy in the saliva. The doctor turned back to face Grandma. "Martha, I had to amputate Shakey's rear leg."

Grandma straightened, narrowed her eyes and pressed her lips tightly together as the doctor's words registered in her mind. She looked over at Jeremy. How would the boy take the news?

"I have some other responsibilities, Martha," the doctor continued. "Do you mind if I leave you with Jeremy?"

"No, that will be fine. And, doctor, I know you did all you could. Thank you."

Dr. Pillsbury nodded and walked away. Grandma walked over to the cage and knelt to speak to her grandson. "It's time for us to go, Jeremy. Shakey's got a lot of healing to do, and he needs rest now."

"Grandma?" Jeremy said as he wiggled out of the cage. "Where is Shakey's back leg? I can't see it."

Grandma sighed deeply. She walked over to a bench along the back wall and sat. There was no easy way to deal with this. "Come here, Jeremy. Sit beside me." She patted the bench to her left, and Jeremy reluctantly obeyed. He didn't like the look in Grandma's eyes. It was a sadness he had seen before, but not in a long time.

"Child," Grandma said, "God used Shakey to save your life. But that leg was so badly damaged that Dr. Pillsbury had to amputate it. Do you understand?"

She expected tears or protests of anger, but none of that came. Instead, Jeremy silently stood and walked back to the open door of the cage. He reached his left hand in and allowed Shakey to once again lick it.

Grandma stood, walked over to her grandson, and put her arm around his shoulders. "Shakey needs his rest."

Jeremy slowly pulled his hand away and closed the cage door. The two began to walk away, but then Jeremy stopped and looked back. "Grandma," he said without looking at her, "Shakey is a good dog. But I don't think God is so good." With that, he continued toward the car.

Grandma followed behind silently. She realized that she was going to have to attack the throne of God ceaselessly and tirelessly in prayer for her only grandchild.

CHAPTER 9

THE RACE

AUGUST 16, 1959

"Pastor, that was one fine sermon. Got right to the heart of the problem."

"Thank you, Eugene," Pastor Sterling said as he shook hands with one of his newest parishioners.

"Yes, sir, my wife really needed to hear that one."

One by one, the parishioners lined up in a traditional exit line to greet and clap their pastor on the back as he stood on the landing. Stern-faced parents in the line held on tightly to their children and clucked their tongues as they watched unsupervised children race past the pastor. No one was holding on to Jeremy, but he was kept in check by being sandwiched in-between Grandma and his father.

Jeremy looked up and saw his friend Sylvester standing near the front of the line with his parents and siblings. "Watch me fly!" he yelled. Before his father could grab hold of him, he leaped from the top step. The flight lasted a full half-second, until gravity rudely introduced Sylvester to the driveway five steps below.

All the well-wishers collectively gasped when the boy landed. His feet hit first as planned, but then he stumbled forward onto both knees. He rolled onto his back, grimacing, and pulled both knees tightly to his chest. As he held them close with both hands, he announced through gritting teeth, “Don’t … hurt … a … bit.”

A small crowd of concerned parishioners gathered around the injured boy. Mr. and Mrs. Pearson pushed through the crowd toward their son. “Oh, Sylvester,” Mrs. Pearson said, squatting to look more closely at the torn knees of her son’s pants. “These were new just this week.”

Mr. Pearson stood over his son with his hands on his hips. “Almost made it this time, son,” he said. “Got to work on that landing, though.”

Some of the newer parishioners were shocked at this seeming lack of concern for the child. Others who knew the Pearsons well just laughed and walked away, shaking their heads. Ira Pearson reached down, took hold of his son’s outstretched hand, and yanked him to his feet. “Those scraped knees sting a bit, don’t they son? Well, don’t worry. We’ll fix ’em up good when we get home.” A quirky grin grew on his face.

Sylvester’s eyes popped wide at the thought of having iodine poured all over his open wounds. “Don’t hurt a bit, Dad, I promise,” he said. “I’ll be okay.”

“Can’t take any chances now, can we?” said his father. “Need to clean them out to keep them from getting infected. Now, come along. You ride in the cab of the truck with your mother and me, and the rest of you boys help your sisters into the bed.”

Sylvester glanced over his shoulder as he slowly made his way to the truck. Jeremy was hopping on one foot and holding the knee of his other leg with both hands, mocking his injured-and-yet-to-be-in-greater-agony friend. Sylvester looked quickly at his parents, and then at the others in the parking lot. No one was watching. With one quick flick of his wrist, he made an obscene gesture with his middle finger.

Jeremy stopped hopping and stood frozen, his mouth hanging open in shock. He had never seen Sylvester use that gesture. Sylvester smiled demonically and climbed into the truck after his mother. Ira Pearson started the engine and the truck backed out of the parking lot. “Hey, hog breath!” Sylvester shouted as he leaned out the window. “Close your mouth. You’re drawing flies. And, hey, why don’t you come over to my house this afternoon and I’ll teach you more sign language.”

Mrs. Pearson grabbed her son by the scruff of his neck and pulled him back in.

"I'll check with Pa and give you a call," Jeremy shouted back, now over the shock. "And enjoy that iodine, dummy!"

Jeremy back-pedaled to bring his single-speed Schwinn bicycle to a skidding halt. Gravel and dust kicked up in front of the wheels of the bike. Sylvester was sitting on the fence at the end of his driveway, watching thunderclouds form in the distance.

"Hey, mouse butt," he said.

"Hey, pigeon turd. How's them knees?"

"Don't feel a thing. Real men can take pain, unlike some wimpy yellow-haireds I know in these parts." He jumped off the fence. The wince did not go unnoticed by Jeremy.

"Yeah, right. Well, ready to ride? Let's go, Shakey. Sylvester, you can eat my dust."

Jeremy and Shakey started down the road before Sylvester could straddle his bike. "Wait for me, you bowl of pig slop!" he yelled as he mounted his well-used two-wheeler, a hand-me-down from his older brothers, and raced after them. It was a challenge for Sylvester to catch up, but Jeremy always held back a bit for his friend—and for Shakey. They headed toward Half Mile Hill, a two-lane highway that rose to several hundred feet by the crest of a mountain in those parts.

The two boys had an easy time getting to the hill, but by halfway up the sweat was stinging their eyes. Both boys gripped the handles of their bikes and stood up on the pedals to get enough force to press down and overcome gravity. Neither wanted to stop to wipe his brow until the other did, which meant that both boys kept struggling up. The last ten yards for both were all grunts. Finally, Jeremy and Shakey crested the hill. Sylvester remained a few yards behind, breathing heavily. For him, death would have been welcome.

"Come on, Sylvester," Jeremy encouraged his friend. "You can make it this time." Shakey barked his encouragement as well.

With one last push, Sylvester crested the hill. He stopped the bike and leaned it slightly so that one foot could lean on a pedal while the other rested on the road. He lowered his head and breathed heavily through his open mouth.

"You gonna be okay?" Jeremy asked with genuine concern.

Sylvester nodded, still catching his breath. "Piece … of … cake." He did not mention the stinging sensation coming from both knees as the salty sweat soaked through the bandages.

Jeremy looked at the view while he waited for Sylvester to catch his breath. The boys had been able to see quite a distance from the low flatlands, but up here they could see for miles. Jeremy glanced at Sylvester's tires. "How many times you gonna patch those antiques before you break down and buy new ones?"

"Hey, I'm saving up," Sylvester replied. "But with the allowance my dad gives me—"

Jeremy pointed down the highway. "Semi coming."

Sylvester looked in the direction Jeremy pointed. "Looks like it will be here in about two minutes. Shall we?"

"Yes, we shall."

The boys turned their bikes around so they faced the same direction the truck was traveling, but in the opposite lane, and watched over their right shoulders as it approached. As the semi began its ascent up the hill, the driver downshifted. The truck's gears ground loudly, and the engine began groaning to reach the crest. "Stay," Jeremy commanded Shakey. The truck was traveling at about fifteen miles per hour as it came to the top of the hill. The bikers sat in the ready position and pumped their right arms up and down in the universal sign for the trucker to blast his horn as he passed. He was more than obliging.

With that, the bikers pushed off, and the race was on. They quickly passed the truck, reaching speeds up to thirty miles per hour. Pedaling became useless—all they could do was coast. The trucker upshifted and quickly began gaining speed. As he passed the boys, he blasted his horn again and waved out from his rolled-down window.

"Wowee! Wasn't that something!" Sylvester shouted as the two braked to a halt at the base of the hill.

"My sentiments exactly," Jeremy replied.

"Again?"

"You sure you're up for it?"

Sylvester swung his bike around and headed back up the hill. "You can eat my dust this time, lizard breath."

Halfway back up the hill, Sylvester got off his bike and pushed it along. Jeremy stopped and waited for him to catch up, and then got off and walked his bike as well. Shakey obediently remained at the top and wagged his tail.

"You ready for the science test tomorrow?" Jeremy asked as they walked.

"Of course," Sylvester replied. "Who doesn't understand the way the digestive system works? Why? Ain't you prepared?"

"Yeah, sure, I understand it. I just can't remember if the large intestine is longer or shorter than the small intestine."

"You've got to be kidding me. It's so simple even my brain-dead sisters could get that one right. It's just a matter of—" Sylvester abruptly stopped and looked off to the southeast. "There's a storm coming. It's moving fast."

"You afraid of a little rain?"

"Of course not, but this ain't gonna be a little rain." Sylvester pointed off in the distance. "Look at that sky. You ever seen a sky that color before?"

"It's kind of greenish. What do you make of it?"

"Whoa! Did you see that lightning bolt? Incredible! Oh, man, and another!"

"Sylvester, I think we better get home. That storm is moving fast, and it's coming straight for us." Jeremy turned his bike around and mounted it. "Shakey, come on!" he yelled, his voice filled with growing urgency. "Sylvester, we need to leave now!"

"Wait, you gutless wonder," Sylvester said without looking at his friend. "Just wait."

The three stood near the top of the crest, watching and waiting. A funnel dipped down out of the cloud. For a moment it hung in midair, and then retreated back up into the sky.

"Tornado!" Sylvester cried. "It's a tornado! Ain't that something!"

"Sylvester, come on. I ain't waitin' no longer."

"Then go. As for me, I …" Sylvester stopped mid-sentence. The funnel appeared again, but this time it stretched down like a dragon's tail until it touched the earth below. It slashed into a field a few miles away and crisscrossed, whipping left and right.

Sylvester stood, hypnotized by the sight. Jeremy's heart was racing, but he remained motionless as well. The funnel moved across the open fields of the Dougherty's farm, about three miles distant, tearing up all the crops. One lone tree stood behind the farmhouse. The dragon tail made a hungry dash for it and tore it out by its roots. Shakey began barking, which quickly brought both boys back to reality.

"Sylvester, come on!" said Jeremy.

Sylvester mounted his bike and paused to take one last look at the tornado. His eyes grew wide as he watched it strike the Dougherty's farmhouse. At first, it only tore the shingles off the roof, but then it sucked up the whole house, piece by piece.

Jeremy stopped pleading and took off, with Shakey following close behind. He looked over his shoulder and saw Sylvester had begun to ride. Shakey quickly fell behind, with Sylvester passing him before they were halfway down the hill.

Jeremy looked back again and, seeing Shakey trailing far behind, hit his brakes to allow the dog to catch up. Sylvester flew past him. Once Shakey was near enough, Jeremy pedaled hard and closed the gap between himself and his friend. In just a few yards they would be at the Pearson's driveway.

Jeremy heard a faint pop and saw the front wheel of Sylvester's bike turn left while the rear flipped upward and over. Sylvester flew over the handlebars and landed hard on the tarred pavement. He slid for a few feet before rolling to a stop in the drainage ditch that ran along the edge of the road.

It took only seconds for Jeremy to get to where his friend lay. He let his bike fall to the ground and rushed to Sylvester's side. Shakey was only seconds behind. Sylvester's eyes were open and staring wildly, but he was not moving or making any sound. Blood poured from his nose and split upper lip. The left side of his face was scraped to the bone, and his right leg twisted unnaturally.

"Sylvester!" Jeremy shouted in panic as he knelt beside him. "Can you hear me? Sylvester?" When he received no response from his friend, he stood and, cupping his hands to his mouth, yelled in the direction of the farmhouse, "Help! Help!"

There was no response.

Jeremy ran his fingers through his hair. "Sylvester, if you can hear me, I'll be right back. I need to get help." He stood and hurried to his bike. As he uprighted it and climbed on to ride to the Pearson's house, he heard what sounded like the roar of a freight train coming from behind. Jeremy turned and froze at the sight. The tornado tail was racing down Half Mile Hill, sucking up fence posts and wire as it travelled. Debris was now spewing around Jeremy—leaves, limbs, boards, and shingles.

Panicked, Jeremy looked at his friend, then down the road to the driveway entrance, and then back at the dragon tail. He wanted to get on his bike and pedal as fast as he could to the safety of the storm cellar at the Pearson house. But with one last look, he dropped his bike, and ran to his friend.

Adrenaline rushed through Jeremy's veins as he grabbed Sylvester by the wrists. With every muscle straining, he dragged the limp body toward the culvert, a ten-foot-long cylindrical tube that channeled water under the entrance to the Pearson's driveway. "Sylvester," he gasped, "you've … got … to … help … me." Shakey grabbed hold of Sylvester's shirt and yanked and pulled.

Jeremy looked behind him toward the culvert. *Thirty more feet,* he thought. He looked up to see the dragon tail whipping back and forth on the near side of the road. It was gaining on them. A gust of wind lashed his body with gravel pellets, throwing him to the ground. He regained his feet and, blocking the onslaught to his face with one hand, latched onto one of Sylvester's wrists. "*Come on, Sylvester,push!*" he yelled.

Ira Pearson was finishing the tune-up on his tractor when he heard the sound of the tornado approaching. In the distance, he could see the funnel cloud tearing down Half Mile Hill. Dropping his tools, he ran to the farmhouse and burst through the front door. His boys were sitting in the living room, listening to a Kansas City baseball game on the radio. "Get into the storm cellar, now!" he yelled. The look on his face was all the boys needed to immediately comply. As they passed him, Ira grabbed the arm of his oldest boy. "Where are your sisters?"

"At the Dougherty's house," his son replied hurriedly.

"What about Sylvester?"

"I don't know. Out someplace with Jeremy, I think."

"And your mother?"

"In the barn."

"Okay, go!" He shoved his son in the direction of the front door and followed close behind.

The Pearson's cellar was no more than a large hole dug into the ground on the other side of the driveway. It was covered by a set of bulkhead doors and reinforced with strong timbers. The boys reached the cellar, lifted up the doors, and climbed down the ladder-style stairs. Meanwhile, Ira ran to the barn and grabbed his wife by the arm, causing her to drop the eggs she had gathered in her apron. "Come quickly!" he gasped. She needed no more explanation.

Ira followed his wife and began to climb down into the safety of the cellar. Just then, he heard what sounded like a boy shouting. He stopped and looked up toward the end of the driveway. There, he could just see the top of Jeremy's head. He seemed to be struggling to pull something into the ditch.

Ira looked in the direction of the funnel. "Lock the doors!" he yelled to his wife over the roar of the wind. "I'll be back in a minute!" Before Mrs. Pearson could protest, he closed the doors over his family and ran toward Jeremy.

Jeremy slipped onto his back again. His strength was seeping away, his breath was coming in gulps, and his leg muscles burned. *Ten feet to go*, he said to himself.

When he glanced down the highway, his eyes widened. The funnel was only 100 yards away. He began to slide as he felt the force of the tornado begin to pull him into itself. Marble-sized hailstones now pelted his body, stinging him like BB pellets. He struggled to his feet and was about to take hold of Sylvester by the wrists again when a hand grabbed him and spun him around.

"Get into that culvert!" Mr. Pearson screamed above the roar of the tornado. Ira picked up his son and led Jeremy to the side of the road, the sucking winds and hail making it increasingly difficult for them to keep their footing. At last, the two reached the pipe, where Ira ordered Jeremy to pull in Sylvester as he pushed. Sylvester groaned in agony as they pulled his twisted leg.

When Ira felt that his son was in far enough, he leaned down, looked inside and yelled to Jeremy, *"Hold onto Sylvester! There's not enough room in there for me! I'm going back to the shelter!"* And he left.

After he had gone, Shakey limped up and looked into the pipe. Jeremy called to him, frantically motioning with one hand for him to come. The dog crouched and crawled into the culvert over the top of Sylvester.

Jeremy clung to Shakey and Sylvester and looked out the opening of the culvert. He could only see the bottom of the funnel as it ripped up the fencing. It seemed to be heading directly for them. As he watched, both of the bikes they had left outside began to slide and then bounce along the tarred road. In an instant, as if invisible hands had reached down and plucked them up, they disappeared. Jeremy closed his eyes and blocked his ears as the freight train rumbled overhead.

An eternity seemed to pass before Jeremy felt he could open his eyes and unblock his ears. The sound of the freight train was more distant now. He lay still, unable to move, paralyzed by fear. The sound of groaning brought him back to his senses.

"Sylvester?" he whispered. "You okay? Sylvester?" There was no response from his friend other than more groans.

"Jeremy! Jeremy!" a voice cried out. Jeremy immediately recognized it as belonging to his father. The grip of fear that had held him slowly began to break.

"In here, Pa!" he yelled. He began to crawl out, with Shakey following. When he reached the opening, he stood and called again, "Here I am, Pa!"

Roger saw his son and ran to him. He fell on his knees, pulled him to himself and crushed him in his arms. "Oh, my son! My son!" He held Jeremy at arms' length and looked him up and down. "You all right, son? Are you hurt?"

"I'm okay, Pa. But Sylvester …" He pointed into the culvert. "He's hurt real bad." Roger let go of Jeremy, leaned forward, and saw the boy lying motionless on his back.

"Jeremy, run to the Pearson's house and tell them to call an ambulance. I'll stay here and—"

"My boy!" a voice cried out. "Jeremy, where's my Sylvester?" They had not heard Mrs. Pearson and her other sons approach. She stepped into the trench and grasped Jeremy by the shoulders with a panicked vice-like grip.

"He's in there," Jeremy said, pointing toward the culvert.

Mrs. Pearson released her grip, bent low, and peered in. She gasped and turned to Roger. "Help him! You've got to help him!" she shouted as she grasped him by the shirt.

"Calm down, Thelma, he'll be all right." He turned to Bert, the oldest Pearson boy. "Bert, you need to go back to your house and call an ambulance. We'll stay here with Sylvester." Bert obeyed and ran for the house, which had been spared by the tornado.

Roger's calm, controlled voice helped Thelma regain her composure. "Jeremy," she said, looking down the driveway, "where is Mr. Pearson? He came here to help you."

Jeremy hesitated and looked at his father, and then at Mrs. Pearson. "He went back to your cellar," he said slowly.

"No. No. He didn't. He came here to help you." She moved closer to Jeremy and placed her hands on his shoulders again. "Jeremy, where is my husband?" She began to shake him. "Where is my husband?"

"I … I … Pa?" Jeremy looked at his father, panic on his face.

Roger took hold of Thelma's hands and pried them off his son. "Thelma, Sylvester needs you!" he said, holding her tightly by her wrists. "Do you understand? Sylvester needs you to be calm!"

Mrs. Pearson struggled against his powerful grip, but then her resistance wavered and her arms went limp. "Yes, you are right," she said, her eyes beginning to glaze over. In a whispered voice spoken to no one, she said, "Felicia? April?"

"Mom," said Henry, the second oldest son, from the edge of the trench. "Felicia and April rode their bikes to the Dougherty's. Remember? They were going to play with Maria."

Jeremy's eyes widened and his mouth opened to speak, but nothing came out.

"Jeremy, what is it?" said Mrs. Pearson. "What do you know? Tell me!"

Jeremy struggled to give his answer. "The Dougherty's farmhouse … we saw it … it was …" He stopped.

"It was what, child? What?" She again reached out to grab him, but Roger restrained her a second time and pulled her tightly to himself.

The tension of the last several minutes caught up with Jeremy and he began to cry. The tears caused Mrs. Pearson's panic to rise, and she struggled violently against Roger's grip.

"The Dougherty's farm …" Jeremy stammered, "it … it was destroyed."

Mrs. Pearson fell silent. The blood drained from her face, and her legs buckled under. Roger grabbed her as she began to fall. In a trance-like state, she stared down the highway as Jeremy explained through tears what he and Sylvester had seen.

Roger carefully released his grip. Slowly, Mrs. Pearson stood and turned in the direction of the Dougherty's. "God, what have You done with my babies?" she whispered, and then began to run toward the Dougherty farm.

A siren was heard off in the distance.

Roger turned to the Pearson boys who were standing together on the lip of the trench. They had a look of confusion mixed with panic on their faces. "Boys, your mother is going to need you. Go to her. We'll wait here with Sylvester until that ambulance arrives." Quickly, the boys darted after their mother. Roger and Jeremy moved to comfort Sylvester, who was beginning to regain consciousness.

The ambulance soon arrived and took Sylvester away. Roger put his hand on Jeremy's shoulder. "Time to go home, son," he said. As the two headed back to the farm, Jeremy wondered why his father had walked to the Pearson's rather than driven there.

From a distance, Jeremy could see their farmhouse. It was still standing. From this viewpoint, it appeared as if not a shingle had been touched, or a tile blown off, or a window even shattered.

Grandma was pacing impatiently on the porch, waiting for her family to return. When she saw Jeremy, she hurried down the four stairs and buried him in outstretched arms. As she held him tightly, Jeremy glanced toward the barn—or what used to be the barn. It looked as if a giant knife had sliced it down the middle, scooped up one end, and left the other end intact.

Jeremy freed himself from Grandma's clutch and walked over to what formerly had been his favorite playground. It was here, in the barn, where he had trained Shakey to shake hands, roll over, sit, and beg for a morsel. It was here that he and Sylvester would jump from the loft onto a haystack, or hold hay-throwing wars. It was here where he used to chase baby chicks, laughing at the cluck-clucking of the mother hens.

Jeremy's mouth dropped open as he witnessed the devastation around him. Then his gaze caught something that completely took him by surprise. Just on the other side of where the barn used to be, he saw a twisted piece of metal that resembled his father's truck. It stood upended, motor end in the air, much like a horse raised up on its hindquarters. A large beam had been driven through the undercarriage, giving it the look of some strange piece of art. Jeremy suddenly understood why his pa had walked down the highway to find him.

A hand slipped gently around his shoulders. "Pa, what about all the animals?" he asked as he looked at the carnage.

"All gone, son," his father replied. "All gone."

Jeremy looked up into his father's face and opened his mouth as if to say something, but no words came. The two stood motionless for a while, silently staring at the scene. Finally, Roger said, "Jeremy, do you know what a 'conviction' is?"

"I'm not sure, Pa."

"It's a strong belief—a belief you live your life by. Sometimes it's a belief you are willing to die for, if necessary. Well, I've struggled with my convictions, especially since …" Roger paused and sighed deeply. "Since we lost your mother and the baby."

Jeremy did not know what to say. Pa had not talked about his mother and the baby they had lost in a long time. *Why now, Pa?* he thought. *I don't want to hear this.*

"One thing I do know," Roger continued, "is that the end of all things …"

Jeremy pushed his father's arm from around his shoulders and backed away.

Roger looked down at him. "Son, I …"

"No, Pa, no. I don't want to hear about God. I don't want to hear it!" He blocked his ears and ran past Grandma, up the porch stairs and into the house.

Roger stood, unmoving. He had not expected this reaction. Recovering from the shock, he began to follow after Jeremy.

"Leave the boy be," Grandma said from where she stood in the driveway.

"But he needs …"

"The only thing that boy needs right now is to be left alone."

"But, Mother, I need to explain to him—"

"The boy needs time, Roger. He's so young, so vulnerable. He's lost so much, and he is not able to see beyond that right now. The last thing he needs is a sermon. Come, sit with me on the porch. Let's talk about what we need to do to get this farm working again."

Roger paused on the porch landing and mulled over his mother's words. He nodded slowly, accepting her counsel, and sat beside her.

Jeremy sat on the edge of the bed and grabbed his baseball glove off the bedpost. An angry fist began punching webbing, each punch harder than the one before. "I hate You, God! I hate You!" he said, the words spilling over his lips through clenched teeth. He threw the glove like a missile against the door, as if it were God Himself standing there. "You took away my mom and sister!"

Unrestrained tears began to fall, betraying the fullness of his rage. "You took away Shakey's leg! And now You killed Sylvester's pa and two sisters, and You almost killed Sylvester! You took away my bike and … and … I hate You." He slid to the floor, curled his legs up to his chest, and hugged them to himself. Anger washed through him—a bitter anger—and it felt good.

After a few minutes he heard scratching at the door, and then whimpering. He stood to his feet and walked over to let Shakey in. He knelt and hugged his best friend, who began to lick his face. "It's you and me, Shakey," he said. "From now on, it's just you and me. We don't need nobody else."

Roger entered the house just after sunset. He had been out in the barn, surveying all the damage so he could plan the rebuilding. When he walked into the living room, he saw Grandma sitting in front of the radio, quietly listening to the news.

"Anything about the—"

"Shhh," she said, waving him off as she leaned a bit closer to hear. Roger quietly settled into his overstuffed chair.

"Governor Docking has said he will do his best to secure funds to help with the costs of rebuilding," the announcer was saying. "As far as casualties, there were seven individuals, two critical, admitted to Groveland County Community Hospital. There is only one reported death. That in itself is a miracle, considering the severity of this tornado. In other news, the governor—"

"Turn it off, Roger," said Grandma, her voice heavy with sadness. "I've heard enough."

Roger turned off the radio and returned to his chair. The two sat in silence for a while, and then Grandma turned on the table lamp next to her and opened her Bible. "Psalm 23," she said. "The Lord is my shepherd; I shall not want—"

Roger listened as his mother read her favorite passage of Scripture aloud. When she was finished, she closed the book and said, "Earlier, while you were out surveying storm damage, Bert Pearson came by with the news that Felicia and April, along with the Dougherty family, were all found safely in the Dougherty's storm cellar. Tonight, we pray for the Pearsons, thanking God for protecting Felicia and April. Tomorrow, we put feet to our prayers."

Chapter 10

A Moment of Truth

August 17, 1959

"George, is that the best you can do?" Roger asked in frustration as he tightly gripped the arms of his chair. An oversized, reddish-brown mahogany desk sat between him and George Evans, the loan officer of Groveland's Savings and Loan bank. George was a kindly-faced man and sympathetic to Roger's pleas, but he was unmoving in his decision.

"I'm truly sorry, Roger," he said, making a teepee with his fingers and leaning back in his leather chair as if to emphasize the finality of his decision. He looked at Roger over the top of his half-eye glasses. "Many folk in this community are in the same boat as yourself, and—"

"But, George, I won't be able to get the barn rebuilt with this amount. My homeowner's insurance doesn't cover 'acts of God.'" He spewed these last words out with disgust. "Not only that, but the automobile insurance company has totaled my truck, and the check they will send me won't even meet replacement costs. I need a few more thousand." He leaned forward on the edge of his chair, his elbows stabbing the desk as he spread his arms in a gesture of desperation.

"I'm sorry," said George, "but my hands are tied. Bank policy only allows loans up to that amount under these circumstances." He pointed at the contract lying on the desk in front of Roger.

"Just what does that mean, 'under these circumstances?'" Roger's anger was rising.

"Mr. Martel," George said, leaning forward for emphasis. He rested his own arms on the desk and folded his hands. "You have several outstanding loans already."

The change from "Roger" to the more formal "Mr. Martel" did not go unnoticed. Roger, enraged, glared into the eyes of the banker. "I've always paid back my loans, George."

George pointed again at the contract. "Unless you have more collateral to back up the loan, that's the best we can do."

Roger, feeling frustrated and defeated, sat back and rubbed his face with his hands. Emptied of arguments, he grabbed the pen that was lying on the desk and signed the loan agreement. He threw the pen down onto the desk and stood to leave.

"I'm sorry," George said to Roger's back, "but my hands are tied."

Roger left the ornately-decorated office in angry silence.

"Thanks, Mom, but not tonight," Roger said in a dejected tone. He stared down at the floor. Grandma set the late-night snack of milk and pie on the porch railing, and then sat beside her son in her rocker.

"You're worried, Roger," she said. "Why?"

"I know what the Bible says, Mom." He had lived with his mother too long not to know where that question was coming from. "But sometimes … sometimes I get so confused with what God is doing, and I just don't have the answers. Today I got angry with George, but to tell you the truth, I'm not sure if he was the one I was really angry at."

Grandma paused, and then said, "Do you remember the story of Job? After he lost everything—his wealth, family, health, reputation—he was confused too. And he questioned God about it all. Remember how God answered Job when he asked why?"

Roger sighed, rested his head against the back of the rocker, and closed his eyes. *No, Mother, and I really don't care,* he thought. But he said, "No, Mother. What?"

"He basically said, 'Job, I'm not going to tell you why. But here's a question for you: do you trust Me?' Job had to think about that, but finally he said, 'Yes, Lord, I trust You.' And that was the end of the matter. Roger, do you trust Him?"

Roger sat in silence. He had been running from this question ever since Virginia and his child had died five years before. Now, with the debt piling up, he was just going through the motions at home and at church on Sundays. He had not shed a tear since he had lost his wife, choosing instead to deal with his pain by busying himself in the needs of the farm. It was his way of dealing with the festering anger he felt toward God—an anger he had denied. Even now, he remembered the sermon he was about to preach to his son the day before about convictions. In truth, he was questioning his own. His soul was doing battle with long-held truths that had been ingrained into him since childhood.

Roger knew his mother's question would have to be answered. "It all seems so pointless," he whispered as he looked toward the heavens. Emotion welled up within his soul, and he buried his face in his hands. Tears surged up from deep within, and his shoulders trembled uncontrollably.

"Oh, God, how I miss her," he confessed through heaving sobs. Grandma looked at her son as silent tears began flowing down her own cheeks. She reached over from her chair, placed a hand gently on his arm, and waited.

Several minutes went by before Roger pulled a handkerchief from his back pocket and wiped his eyes. "I'm sorry, Mother. I …"

"Shh, it's okay," she said. "It was long overdue."

It took a few minutes for Roger to regain some control. "Yes, Mother," he finally said, answering her previous question. His throat constricted, and he coughed. "Yes, I do trust Him. I don't understand any of this, but I will trust Him." Roger said the last words with finality and a new sense of conviction. Long-standing beliefs that he had held for years and never challenged suddenly moved from his mind to his heart. "The end of all things, their purposes revealed or hidden, is good for those who love God," he quoted to himself as the conviction fell upon him that his God was sovereign and in control. He now understood deep in his soul that no matter how bad things seemed, or how tried and tested he was, God would use the trial for His own glory.

Roger glanced at his mother through the tears and gave a smile that she thought had long since been lost. The battle was over. "We're going to be okay, Mother," he said, wiping his eyes again. Strangely, he began to laugh.

"Land sakes, what are you laughing about?" Grandma asked as she dabbed her own eyes.

"I don't know why," Roger said through the laughter, "but I was just remembering that day when we were having a picnic by the pond. I think I was five or six. Dad tried to jump from a limb of the willow tree into the water."

"Oh, my, that was so long ago. And remember what he did then?" Grandma picked up the story, and together they remembered and laughed.

It was late, but Jeremy was not yet asleep. The window that overlooked the front yard from his bedroom had been raised a few inches, and he could hear laughter coming from below. Quietly, he got out of his bed and went over to the window, with Shakey following close behind. The laughter seemed to be coming from the porch.

Jeremy and Shakey moved into the hallway and then down the stairs. Quietly, the two crept to the open door that led onto the porch and listened through the screen door. More laughter erupted, followed by some quiet words, and then more laughter. Jeremy looked down at Shakey with a puzzled expression on his face. Shakey cocked his head slightly to the left and looked up with what Jeremy thought was the same puzzled look. He had not heard his pa laugh like this for a long time—a very long time.

"God is good!" Roger said.

"Amen and amen," Grandma seconded.

The words rekindled Jeremy's anger. *How can they say that?* he said to himself. *How can they believe that after all that's happened? So what if Felicia and April were found safe in the Dougherty's storm cellar. It don't change a thing. God killed their dad. He took Shakey's leg. He killed my mom and sister.*

Jeremy and Shakey slowly crept away and went back to his room, where he closed the door and window to block out the sounds of laughter. He lay on his bed, folded his arms behind his head, and stared at the ceiling he could not see. *It was me who saved Sylvester's life,* he thought, rewriting his own history. *Me! God had nothing to do with it. And I won't have anything to do with Him again.*

With that, the decision was made.

Chapter 11

Pumping Iron

August 18, 1959

Jeremy flung his books on the kitchen table, ran upstairs, changed his clothes in record time, and charged back out the door before Grandma could ask how his day at school had been. "Land sakes, to have that energy again," she said aloud, shaking her head, and then returned to peeling potatoes.

Jeremy ran to the undamaged part of the barn and began searching the area. He quickly found some of the items he was seeking: sections of old pipe, used barn boards, two milking buckets, some bricks, and a few two-by-fours stored in the corner that his father had leftover from repair projects. He gathered the materials together and hauled them back toward the house, where he laid them in a pile next to the bulkhead doors leading to the cellar. He swung the double doors open, and then he began picking up what he thought he could manage.

At first Jeremy overestimated his strength and dropped some of the piping, but then he adjusted and shifted the weight. Slowly, he began making his way down the cement stairs into the cellar, where, using his elbow, he flicked the light switch on at the bottom of the stairs. He carried the goods to the far wall and dumped them onto the hardened dirt floor. After one last trip to the barn for a saw, a hammer and a can of used nails, the sawing and hammering began.

Roger had just finished some fence mending down the road and was driving the tractor into the driveway when he heard the noise. Approaching the house, he noticed the bulkhead doors leading to the cellar were swung open. Curious, he walked over to them. *What on earth is that racket?* he said to himself.

Roger walked down the stairs and stood motionless at the bottom. There he saw Jeremy on his hands and knees, hammering a nail that wouldn't cooperate into an L-shaped piece of metal. He gave an involuntary cough, which startled Jeremy and caused his son to look up in his direction. Jeremy's face grew concerned as he just now realized that he had never asked if he could use the wood or the nails or the tools. "Ah, is it okay if I use these things, Pa?" he asked sheepishly.

"A little late to be asking that, don't you think?" his father replied. Roger turned his head and coughed again.

"Yeah, I … forgot. Sorry."

"I see. Well, since you're already using my tools and supplies, do you mind if I give you a suggestion?"

"A suggestion? On what?"

"On how to hammer a nail without bending it."

"Oh, sure."

Roger walked over to Jeremy and pointed down at the two-by-four he was holding. "You're hammering into a knot," he said. "Move the nail a little to the left."

Jeremy followed his father's advice, and the next nail went in with ease. He looked up at his pa with a grin. It was all Roger needed for thanks.

"What are you building, anyway?" he asked.

"A bench," Jeremy replied matter-of-factly.

"A bench, huh. For what?"

"A weightlifting bench. You know, so I can do bench presses and stuff like that."

"Ah, I see. Well … would you like some help?"

"You mean with building this bench?"

"Yes, and with some exercises. I know a thing or two about weightlifting."

"Yeah, sure."

For the next couple of hours, father and son worked side by side. At one point, Jeremy misjudged a hammer stroke and landed the blow squarely on his left thumb. He had never known such pain, his tears being held momentarily back only by the shock. The thumb soon began to swell and turn black and blue under the nail. Roger took the hand in his for a closer look. "Son," he said, "the bad news is you may lose that thumbnail." Jeremy's eyes betrayed the fear that welled up within him. "But the good news is that you can now consider yourself a true carpenter."

Jeremy sniffled back a few remaining tears and smiled through clenched teeth. "Really?"

"Really."

When the last nail had been hammered into place, Roger said, "Now, how about we try out this masterpiece?" He placed one of the six-foot-long pipes across the supports at the head of the bench and instructed Jeremy to lie down on the bench, his head directly under the bar that was about eighteen inches above.

"Pa, put some weights on it," Jeremy said. "I can lift more than that."

"I know you can," Roger said, "but remember that how much you can lift is not as important as how you lift. If you don't use proper technique, you will really hurt yourself. Besides, you're only twelve, and you've got a lot of growing left in you. Now, place one hand on the bar here and the other here." Roger led Jeremy through the proper method for doing bench presses. When he was satisfied that his son was taking his advice seriously, he hung the milk buckets by their handles over the bar, with one on each end, and put some of the old bricks in the buckets for added weight.

"You two ever going to come up here for supper?" the voice of Grandma called down the stairs. "It's after 6:00, and that boy has got homework to do."

"Be up in a moment," Roger called back. "We got so wrapped up in what we were doing that we lost all track of time."

"Well, hurry up," Grandma said. Though she sounded annoyed, in her wisdom she had actually left them alone for as long as she thought she could.

Once Roger and Jeremy had cleaned up the cellar and returned the tools to the barn, they went into the house, washed up, and sat at the table. Grandma was just placing the last hot dish in the center, and she quickly took her own seat. Roger said grace, and the serving began.

"Land sakes, what was all that grunting and groaning about down there?" Grandma asked as the plates were passed around.

Roger reached over and tousled Jeremy's hair. "Grandma," he said, "here sits the next Charles Atlas."

Grandma raised her eyes to the ceiling. "Dear Lord, what have I done to deserve this … again?"

"Deserve what again, Grandma?" Jeremy innocently asked. "And who's Charles Atlas?" He extended his plate to his pa and nodded at the bowl of mashed potatoes.

"Potatoes, Grandma?" Roger said with a smile on his face, hoping to quickly change the subject.

Grandma held her plate out, but the sidetrack didn't work. "Jeremy, your father got it into his head when he was sixteen that he was going to be the strongest man in the world."

Jeremy looked at his father. "I already thought you were, Pa."

Roger smiled.

"Well, your father found an ad in a Superman comic book for a muscle-building course by a man named Charles Atlas," Grandma continued. "If I remember correctly, this Atlas fellow claimed he went from being a ninety-seven pound weakling to being the world's most perfectly developed man. My, my, such nonsense." She reached for the gravy bowl and ladled a large helping onto her potatoes.

"Pass the meatloaf, would you, son?" Roger said. "And, Grandma, I wasn't a ninety-seven pound weakling when I was sixteen. I weighed ninety-eight pounds, at least." Roger looked at Jeremy and winked.

"Anyway, your father saved up his allowance and sent away for the course," Grandma said, undeterred by her son's remark. "You stayed with it for … oh, let me think now, a whole three weeks was it?"

"Must have been more than that, Mother. Just look at this body. Fit as a fiddle." He slapped his abdomen. "Hard as a rock."

"That it may be, but it wasn't from that Atlas fellow." She turned to look at Jeremy, pointed the gravy spoon at Roger, and continued the lecture. "That's from good hard work here on this farm, Jeremy, just like your great-grandpa Elias and grandpa Jeremiah. Now, they were two strong-backed men, let me tell you. If it wasn't for the accident, why, I do believe your great-grandpa would still be alive today. *They* never needed any Charles Atlas muscle-building course. They just did it the old-fashioned way, through hard work."

"Funny you should mention my Superman comics, Mother," said Roger. "I had forgotten all about them. I think I still have them stored up in the old chest in the attic." He pushed his chair away from the table. "Let me get them for you, son."

"You put that chair right back where it was and finish this meal while it's still hot," Grandma said. "You can wait until after the meal before you go dragging out them old things."

No question who's in charge at this dinner table, Jeremy thought.

"Yes, ma'am," Roger snapped back as if Grandma were a drill sergeant.

"Don't you sass me, Roger Martel," she said, shaking the gravy ladle at him. Specks of gravy hit him in the face, but she offered no apology. "You're not so big that I couldn't take you' 'cross my knee and give you a good whoopin'."

Roger picked up his napkin to hide the smirk the image created in his mind. Jeremy began to laugh. He loved these spats between his father and grandmother. Roger shrugged at Jeremy, giving the sign of defeat, and Jeremy shrugged back. Smirks were plastered across both faces now.

"Now, Pa?" Jeremy asked once dinner was over and the kitchen was cleaned up.

"Now what, son?" Roger answered innocently.

"Pa!" Jeremy said with an exaggerated and disgusted look on his face.

"Race you," Roger challenged. He began to run up the stairs two at a time.

"No fair!" Jeremy complained as he ran behind. "You had a head start!"

When the two reached the second floor, Roger opened a door that revealed steps that led up to the attic. At the top of the stairs, Roger paused and held on to the door frame. He pulled a handkerchief from his back pocket, held it to his mouth, and coughed several times.

"You okay, Pa?" Jeremy asked from behind.

"Yes, I'm fine. Just a little short of breath from running up those stairs. Guess that fence mending today has caught up with me."

After a short rest, Roger walked to the center of the attic and pulled down on a string. An overhead bulb switched on, illuminating the attic. There, in the far corner, sat a chest. Roger walked over to it, knelt beside it, flipped the latch up, and raised the cover. A strong odor of mothballs emanated from it. Jeremy strained to look over his father's shoulder to see what the chest contained.

Roger pushed aside the old clothes and scrapbooks at the top of the chest and withdrew two brown paper bags, each tied with twine. "It's been years since I've looked at these," he said, sitting with his back against the chest. He set one of the bags down on the floor beside him and began untying the twine on the other. He slid his hand into the bag, removed several old comic books, and began reading the titles out loud: "Dick Tracy," "The Shadow," "Popeye." He began to leaf through the pages.

Jeremy sat quietly, waiting for his father to return from wherever he had gone in his mind. *That's enough of this*, he thought. "Hey, Pa, you gonna read all them tonight?"

Roger looked up. "Hmm? Oh, I forgot why we came here. Let's see. Ah, yes, here's the one I was looking for. Superman, the greatest superhero there ever was." He handed the comic book to Jeremy. "Flip it over to the back side." When Jeremy did, he saw a photograph of a man with a muscular physique. He whistled through his teeth.

"That's him, Mr. Charles Atlas," said Roger.

Jeremy began to read the captions to himself—captions that promised the miraculous transformation of any body into one that was just as physically sculptured and perfectly proportioned. Beside the photo was a cartoon. The first frame depicted a scrawny kid on the beach with his girlfriend. In the next few frames, a bully approached, kicked sand into the scrawny kid's face, and stole his girlfriend. The last frame depicted the scrawny kid, some time later and now muscle bound, punching the bully in the face.

"According to Mr. Atlas, that's not just a cartoon," Roger said. "It really happened to him." Roger let Jeremy read and reread the ad, and then began to untie the second brown bag.

"Pa, this says there is a 'Total Health and Fitness Program.' Can I send away for it?"

Roger had already removed a notebook from the second bag. "Here, take a look at this," he said. Jeremy exchanged the comic book for the notebook and read the title aloud: "Total Health and Fitness Program." He flipped through the pages, awestruck by the before-and-after photos of men who had followed the Atlas program.

"Wow! Look at this guy," Jeremy exclaimed, thoroughly impressed by the biceps he saw. He raised his own right arm in a copycat position to the one in the photo and squeezed his biceps with his left hand. Shaking his head, he squeezed harder until his right arm shook. No improvement.

"It takes a lot of time and hard work to build muscles like that," said Roger. "Years, as a matter of fact."

Jeremy made no response, but Roger could see by his expression that he had been bitten with the dream of someday being able to lift a house. "Would you like to hang on to that notebook for a while?" he asked. "If you combine some of those exercises with your weightlifting, you'll have a winning combination."

Jeremy nodded slowly, never taking his eyes off the photographs.

"When you're done with it, though, I would like it back. Deal?"

"Deal."

Jeremy entered the living room, carrying the notebook his father had loaned to him. An all-day sucker he had started on earlier was wedged in his cheek. Grandma was sitting in an overstuffed chair, knitting as she listed to the radio. "The earthquake yesterday at Yellowstone in southwestern Montana registered 7.3 on the Richter scale. Early reports state that the number of fatalities caused by the huge landslide is at twenty-eight. For more on this story, we're going live to our correspondent on the scene—"

Jeremy pulled the sucker from his mouth with a pop he had perfected. "What are you listening to, Grandma?"

"Oh, Jeremy! You startled me. Goodness sakes alive, child, you could choke a horse on that thing."

"Sorry. What are you listening to?" He jammed the sucker back in.

"I'm just listening to the evening news. Seems there's not much good to report these days."

"Did they say how Roger Maris is doing?"

"Not yet."

"He'll probably get traded to the Yankees," Roger said as he entered the living room with a plate full of apple pie. "All the good ones seem to get traded to the Yankees." He sat on one end of the sofa.

"Nah," said Jeremy, "the A's would never trade Maris."

"You just wait and see, son. Just wait and see."

Grandma struggled up from her chair, went over to the radio, and turned it off. "Can't hear a thing with you two jawing about baseball."

Jeremy sat on the rug in the middle of the floor. Shakey soon came up and squatted beside him. "Look what Pa found," Jeremy said as he held up the notebook.

Grandma rolled her eyes.

"Hey, it's story time, Grandma," Jeremy said.

"Story time?" replied Grandma. "What makes you think it's story time?"

"'Cuz it just is, that's all. Right, Pa?"

"Sounds like the boy has a valid argument," said Roger. He winked at his son as he put a bite of pie into his mouth.

"Well, I guess I'm outnumbered."

"Tell me about how you and Grandpa met and how great-grandpa Elias died. You mentioned something about 'the accident' at supper."

"You mean to tell me I've never told you about how old Elias 'Pegleg' Martel was called home to his reward?" Grandma said in mock surprise. She placed the knitting needles and partially-knit sweater—the first of two for the Pearson twins—in her lap. Jeremy shook his head and grinned at the lie.

"Well," Grandma began, "your grandfather, Jeremiah Martel … did you know you were named after him?"

Jeremy popped the sucker out of his mouth, nodded and pointed his thumb at his chest. "Jeremiah Elias Martel," he said, jutting his chin out in pride.

Grandma smiled at her grandson. "Well, your grandfather and I met in Clayton, Massachusetts. That's where my three sisters and I did a lot of our growing up. He was twenty-seven, and I was twenty-nine. Back in those days, that made me a spinster, doomed never to marry. Anyway, Jeremiah and his father, your great-grandpa Elias, had come there to visit family of their own. Goodness gracious, such a small world. We got introduced at the old Baptist Church in town one Sunday morning. Great-grandpa Elias returned to his farm a short time later, but Jeremiah fell in love with me real fast—especially after he sampled some of my blueberry muffins—and found reasons to stay in Clayton. We were married just two months later, and then we moved out here.

"Elias was eighty-seven, but he could still outwork any of us, wooden leg and all. One day, he was replacing some of the tiles on the barn roof that had come off during a wind storm when he slipped and fell. Fortunately, he fell into a pile of hay that your grandfather had just loaded onto the back of a wagon. Unfortunately, your grandfather had left a pitchfork on top of the hay when I called them in for lunch.

"We were all sitting around the kitchen table waiting for Elias when we heard a knock on the door. *Tap, tap, tap.* The sound was not loud, but it was steady. Your grandfather heard it first, and he told me and your father to hush. Then I heard it too. *Tap, tap, tap.* Jeremiah went to the door, and I followed. Well, there was old Elias out on the porch, holding on to that pitchfork that was sticking right out of his belly. He was using one end of it to knock on the door. We all just stared at him and thought it was some kind of joke. But then Elias said, 'Feelin' a bit poorly, son. Think I'd like to lie down for a spell.'"

"Grandma," Jeremy interrupted, "that ain't how the story goes. Great-grandpa Elias is supposed to have said …"

"Hush, child. This is my story, and I'll tell it any way I please. Now where was I? Oh, yes. So your Grandpa and I stepped aside to let Elias into the house. He stepped right past the two of us, went into the kitchen, and grabbed a piece of fried chicken off the table. As he staggered up the stairs, his peg leg clacked on the wood and the end of that pitchfork slapped out a beat against the walls. He sounded like a regular one-man drum set—*clack, tap, tap, clack, tap, tap*—all the while, gnawing on that chicken leg."

Roger looked over at Jeremy, who was obviously mesmerized by this latest version of the story. He struggled to restrain a laugh.

"We were still in shock at the sight and just followed and watched. When Elias got to the top and started down the hallway, he just collapsed. Needless to say, we rushed to his aid. Your grandfather picked up old Elias, while I tried to keep that pitchfork from moving. We wanted to put him into the wagon and get him quick as we could to the doctor, but Elias demanded, 'Take me to my room, son. And Martha—would you be so kind as to hand me that there chicken leg I dropped?' Well, we got him to his room, chicken leg and all, and then your grandfather went for the doctor. That took a few hours.

"Doc Preston finally arrived. When he saw that pitchfork sticking straight out of Elias, he shook his head. 'Thought I'd seen every kind of wound imaginable, Elias,' he said. 'But this is a new one for me.'

"'Can you take it out, doc?' Elias asked.

"'Do my best for ya,' said Doc, 'but I ain't makin' no promises.' He did his best to remove the pitchfork and then left some pain pills for Elias to take.

"'Nothin' more I can do for you now,' he said.

"Elias nodded. 'Thanks anyway, doc,' he said. 'Guess it's 'bout time I was goin' home anyway.' As healthy as he was, it took Elias three days to die from the wound."

"That ain't how you told it last time, Grandma," said Jeremy, "but I like this story better."

"Now, it's off to bed with you, child," said Grandma. "And remember, it's not them fancy exercises in that notebook that's going to help you build up your muscles. You just follow your great-grandpa's example of hard work, and you'll be strong as an ox when you're a hundred. You hear me?"

"Sure thing, Grandma."

Later that night, after all the lights were out in the house, Jeremy slid out of bed and, in the dark, felt his way to his bureau. He fumbled for the handle to the bottom drawer. Slowly, he opened it and withdrew a flashlight and the notebook. Returning on tiptoes to his bed, he climbed in, sat in the middle of the mattress, and pulled the covers completely over himself and Shakey, making a tent for the two of them. Jeremy turned on the flashlight and opened the notebook to the page titled "Twelve Secret Exercises to Developing the Perfect Body."

"Hey, Shakey," he whispered, "they call these i-so-met-ric exercises," carefully pronouncing each syllable of the new word. "Says here you don't use weights; you just pit muscle against muscle." He read the instructions and studied the photographs of Charles Atlas demonstrating each move. "I gotta try one," he said. He pressed his palms together and held the position for several seconds. "Wow! I can really feel that," he whispered to Shakey as he rubbed his chest.

Just then, he heard his father's footsteps coming up the stairs. He shooed Shakey from under the covers, quickly closed the book, turned off the flashlight, and lay quietly in the dark. He closed his eyes and, not willfully, fell asleep, dreaming again of the man he would someday be.

Grandma gently knocked on the bedroom door. "Jeremy, it's long past time to get up and do your chores," she said. Usually she would hear a sleepy protest, but this time when she looked into his room, she saw an already empty and unmade bed. She walked downstairs and looked around in some of the rooms, and then went out onto the porch. "Roger," she called to her son who was just coming out of the barn with a bucket of fresh milk. "Have you seen Jeremy?"

"Nope, but he'd better get himself out here fast and feed these chickens and pigs," he said.

"I'll tell him when I find him. Meanwhile, you come to a good stopping point. Breakfast is near ready." Grandma went back inside the house. *Where could that boy be?* she thought. Just then, she heard some strange noises coming from the cellar.

Grandma opened the door that led down the stairs. "Jeremy, is that you?"

"Yeah, Grandma."

"What on earth are you doing down there this early in the morning? You've got chores to do and breakfast to eat, and you've got to get ready for school."

"Be right up."

A few minutes later, a sweaty, smelly boy emerged from the cellar and entered the kitchen.

"What have you been doing down there all this time?" asked Grandma.

"Exercising," replied Jeremy.

"Exercising? Didn't I tell you that all the exercise you need is—"

"I know, Grandma, hard work." He went to the sink, smiling to himself, and washed his hands just as his father entered the kitchen with a pail of milk.

Grandma went to the stove and put several pieces of crispy bacon on Jeremy's plate. A bowl full of scrambled eggs was already cooling off on the table. "From the smell of you, you'll need to do more than wash those hands," she said.

"So you found him," Roger said. "Where was he?"

"In the cellar, *exercising*, of all things."

Jeremy smiled at his pa. Roger washed his hands, and Jeremy dried his own on a towel. "So, you're going to take this exercise stuff seriously, are you?" said Roger, flicking water into Jeremy's face. "Hand me that towel." Jeremy threw the towel at his father's face, but he was ready for it. He grabbed it before it hit its target and snapped it at the behind of his retreating son, catching him just enough to cause an "ouch!" and a giggle.

"How many times have I told you no horseplay in my kitchen!" Grandma scolded. "Now sit!"

Roger and Jeremy obediently found their places. Grace was said and the bowls of freshly-made powdered biscuits, eggs, bacon and a jug of fresh-squeezed orange juice was passed around the table.

"If you're going to be serious about this exercising," Roger said, sipping his juice, "maybe after school you and I can sit down and put together a routine. How does that sound?"

"You mean it, Pa?"

Roger gave a nod.

From that moment, the day dragged on far too slowly for Jeremy.

Shakey was waiting faithfully at the end of the driveway when the school bus dropped Jeremy off at the end of the day. Jeremy raced his friend to the house and vaulted onto the porch over the far railing. Grandma was knitting in her rocking chair, but before she could begin her usual inquisition—"How was your day? How much homework do you have? What did Sylvester say today that got him into trouble?"—Jeremy had darted past. "Hi, Grandma; bye, Grandma," was all she heard.

Jeremy ran up the stairs to his bedroom, where he stripped off his school clothes and put on his oldest pair of jeans and T-shirt—what he called his new "exercising clothes." He raced back downstairs, flew out the door, and ran into the wheat fields. Roger was riding the tractor in the fields. "Pa! Pa!" he yelled as he chased after him.

The tractor came to a stop. Roger turned around and saw his son running toward him, excitement oozing from the child. He had not seen his son this excited about anything in a long time. "Climb aboard," he said.

"How long you gonna be, Pa?" Jeremy asked as he pulled himself up. "Can we do it now?"

"Lots of work to do yet, son," Roger said. A wave of disappointment came over Jeremy's face. "But … I'll tell you what. You get your chores done, and your homework—"

"But, Pa—"

"Chores and homework. They come first. Then we'll work on the routine."

Jeremy nodded, jumped from the tractor, and ran back to the barn. He grabbed a nearby bucket and threw slop at the pigs, rifled through the chicken coop for eggs (with only a few getting broken), shoved hay at the milking cows, and swept the porch, all in record time. In minutes he was at the kitchen table, working on his homework.

Grandma was impressed when she entered and saw Jeremy with his books open on the table. "What are you working on?" she asked.

"A report," Jeremy said without looking up.

"A report on what?" She moved closer and looked over his shoulder.

"George Washington." The pencil never stopped moving.

"Oh, I went to school with old George. I can tell you a thing or two about him, I sure can."

"That's nice." The joke went right over Jeremy's head as his concentration didn't miss a beat. Grandma quickly realized she was not going to get anything else from her grandson at the moment. She gave up and went about the business of folding laundry.

Jeremy heard the front door open and close. "Pa, now?" he called out. He closed the books, grabbed his pencil and notebook, and ran into the living room.

"Supper's in an hour," Grandma yelled after him.

Jeremy found his father sitting on the couch. He was leaning back with his eyes closed, his fingers massaging his temples. "Pa, can we work on my exercise routine now?" Jeremy asked. "I've got notepaper and everything."

Roger made no reply.

"Pa, you okay?" Jeremy asked, growing concerned.

"Hmm? Oh, yeah. Just a little tired. I'm fine." Roger sat forward and rubbed his lower back. "Now, what were you asking?"

Jeremy sat down beside his father. "Can we work on my exercise routine now?"

"Oh, sure thing." Jeremy sat down on the couch beside his father, and soon the two were making plans for Jeremy to become the next "World's Most Perfectly Developed Man."

Jeremy didn't need an alarm clock to wake up early the next morning. He quickly dressed in the same grubby clothes he had worn the previous night and, with Shakey close behind, took the stairs to the cellar two at a time. The routine that he and his father had put together was already tacked to a beam. The plan called for several minutes of calisthenics, bending and stretching, isometric exercises, and finally, some weightlifting. Jeremy followed the routine religiously, writing down the number of repetitions and the amount of weight he lifted in each exercise.

An hour later, he ran up the cellar stairs and entered the kitchen. Without saying a word to Grandma, he headed into the bathroom and closed the door behind him. He stripped to the waist, stood in front of the mirror and flexed his biceps, just as he had seen in the photos. As he felt his arm, he was sure a bump was now there that had not been there yesterday. "I knew it! I just knew it!" he said out loud to himself.

Chapter 12

The Appointment

January 11, 1961

The appointment had been for 1:30 in the afternoon, but it was now 2:45. For the past fifteen minutes, Roger had been sitting alone in Dr. LeChaise's waiting room. The front door opened, and a man on crutches limped in and sat on the opposite side of the room. After a few minutes of silence, he asked, "So how long have you been waiting?"

Roger looked at his wristwatch. "About an hour and fifteen minutes."

The stranger shook his head. "Shouldn't there be a law that allows us to bill doctors for our time?"

"Good luck with that. But I do have other things to do than sit here all day. In fact, I think I've had enough of this." Roger tossed the magazine he had been reading onto the pile on the coffee table, stood to his feet, and turned to leave. Just then, Nurse Brady entered the room.

"Mr. Martel, the doctor will see you now," she said with the slight hint of a smile. "Please follow me." She was an attractive middle-aged woman, her blonde hair pinned up tightly under her nurse's cap. She led the way along a short corridor and opened the door at the end, where the doctor was seated behind a neatly-organized desk. A stack of manila file folders lay to one side. Dr. LeChaise held one folder in his hands and was reading over the contents.

"Well, Roger, we don't see you in here too often," the doctor said as he placed Roger's medical file on the desk. He stood, walked around the desk, and reached out to shake hands.

"That's a good thing, right, doc?" Roger said as he shook the hand.

"Why, yes, I suppose it is. But with your medical history, it's people like you who would put doctors like me out of business."

"That's a good thing, right?"

Dr. LeChaise smiled. "Don't like doctors' offices, huh? Why don't you have a seat, Roger?" He pointed to a straight-backed wooden chair placed directly in front of his desk. Once Roger was seated, he went back to his chair and sat, leaning forward, with his forearms resting on the desk. He interlocked his fingers in a professional pose. "So what brings you in here today?"

"Well, doc," Roger began, "it's nothing really. I shouldn't even be wasting your time." Dr. LeChaise said nothing in response, but intently watched the eyes of the man sitting across from him. Roger took a long pause. "In fact, I wouldn't be here at all except for my mother's constant insistence," he continued. "She threatened to go on strike from the kitchen if I didn't come." He released a nervous chuckle. "Can't have that, now, can we?" Another nervous chuckle.

Dr. LeChaise smiled again, but still said nothing. "Look, here's the deal," Roger explained. He twisted in his seat and rested his left arm on the back of the chair. "Lately, I've had some trouble catching my breath—you know, from too much work. It seems I'm not getting any younger."

Dr. LeChaise nodded. "Is that the only symptom?"

"Well, there's this cough. Probably just allergies."

"Do you have a history of allergies? I didn't see anything in your medical file that suggested that."

"No, but they can develop at any time, can't they?"

"Yes. Does any blood come up when you cough?"

"No, no blood."

"How long has this been going on?"

"Oh, a few months, give or take."

Dr. LeChaise took notice when Roger absentmindedly rubbed his lower back. "How long have you been having discomfort in your back?" he asked.

"Oh, this? Not long. Maybe a few weeks. I really don't know. I think I may have strained it doing some lifting."

Dr. LeChaise nodded professionally. "Are you under much stress these days? Everything okay with the family? Any problems with the farm?"

"Hey, who isn't having problems with farming these days. I'm still recovering from that tornado. But our family has been through tough times before. We will be just fine."

Dr. LeChaise stepped from behind his desk and removed the stethoscope that had been draped around his neck. "Okay, Roger, why don't you remove your shirt, and we'll take a look." He checked Roger's lungs and heart with the stethoscope, and then, using a small hand-held light, looked into his eyes, ears, nose and throat. He continued to ask questions as he conducted the exam. "Have you had any weight loss?"

"Maybe a few pounds."

"Have the symptoms gotten worse?"

"Not really."

"Any history of respiratory ailments in your family?"

"No."

The doctor finished and instructed Roger to put his shirt back on. He returned to his desk, picked up a pad of paper and a pen, and sat in his chair. He leaned back a bit as he scribbled some notes.

Roger tried to read the doctor's eyes as he buttoned his shirt, but he was unable to pick up any clues as to what the doctor was thinking. "Well, doc," he finally said, "As I told you, I only came so Mother wouldn't go on strike. She can get to be the most fretting woman when she sets her mind to it." The doctor said nothing but continued writing. Roger shifted uncomfortably in his seat. "So I guess I'll be going, since—"

"Roger, I want you to have some more tests. It's nothing to be concerned about, but with your symptoms I just want to cover all the bases. I'm going to have Nurse Brady schedule you for this Thursday at the hospital."

"Tests? What kind of tests?"

"Well, I want to have some X-rays taken and—"

"X-rays? Of what?"

"Of your chest, lungs and that sort of stuff. I also want to do some blood work. It's just routine, Roger. Just routine."

"Is this really necessary? I mean, you can see that I'm in great shape. I'm even working out occasionally with my son. He seems to think he'll be the next Charles Atlas."

Dr. LeChaise looked up and smiled. "It ain't gonna happen, Roger. My son has already laid claim to that title." The two laughed at this, but all too quickly the doctor returned to his professional seriousness. "I also need to do a more thorough exam," he said, standing to his feet. Roger stood as well and followed the doctor to the door. "See Nurse Brady on your way out. Hand her this paperwork, and she will make the appointment at the hospital for you."

The two shook hands. "Okay, doc," Roger said uneasily as he looked at the papers in his hand. "But I really don't think any of this is necessary." As he left the building, he once more absentmindedly rubbed his lower back.

Chapter 13

The Principal's Office

January 18, 1961

Grandma was ironing one of Roger's work shirts when the telephone rang. She looked at the kitchen wall clock. Eight twenty. "Who would be calling at this time in the morning?" she wondered out loud. She stood the iron upright on the end of the ironing board and reached for the phone. "Hello. Martel residence."

"Mrs. Martel, this is Principal Fallworth." The voice was curt and all business.

Grandma put her hand to her forehead and moaned out loud. "Good Lord, not again?" she said.

"I'm afraid so, Mrs. Martel. And because this is the third offense, there will be a mandatory two-day suspension."

"What was it over this time?" Grandma asked in an exasperated tone.

"Same as last time, I'm afraid. I'm sorry to be so abrupt, Mrs. Martel, but I have a great deal to do here. I will need Jeremy's father to come and pick him up."

"Yes, of course. I am so sorry that this happened again. I don't know what's gotten into the boy."

"Neither do I," said Principal Fallworth. "This is not the Jeremy I've watched growing up at this school. Please have Mr. Martel pick his son up as soon as possible. Good day, Mrs. Martel." The call ended.

Grandma replaced the telephone onto the cradle and wondered how she was going to tell Roger that his son had again gotten into trouble for fighting.

Forty minutes later, Roger was sitting in front of Principal Fallworth, with his son sitting quietly in a chair beside him. He was still fuming, but he had finally gotten his emotions under control. He rubbed his forehead. The headache he had woken up with that morning was not helping matters.

He had been mulling over the best way to handle the situation as he drove to the school. His first reaction to the news of this third offense was to come on like a maniacal lunatic and make threats against the boy. But after a while he thought better of this, and decided he would listen to Jeremy as he tried to explain his behavior.

"Well, son," Roger said, "why don't you explain to Principal Fallworth and myself what this mistake is all about and …"

"There's no mistake, Pa," said Jeremy, grinning an arrogant grin. "I beat the tar out of Willy Garand, and he won't—"

Roger quickly threw his tactic out the window along with the patience he had gathered on the way to the school. "You think this is funny?!" he yelled, startling both Jeremy and Principal Fallworth. Roger jumped out of his chair and stood towering over his son. "You think getting into fights is something that makes me proud of you?" Jeremy's grin disappeared faster than a gnat's blink.

Roger's angry tirade continued. He lit into his son and shook his finger in his face. Jeremy had seen his father get angry before, but never like this. "What ever possessed you to get into a fight with Willy? Is this the example that we have set for you in the Martel family?"

Jeremy's eyes darted to Principal Fallworth, where he thought he saw a glimmer of sympathy. "Don't you look anywhere but here," Roger said menacingly, pointing to his own eyes.

Jeremy was now truly frightened. "Pa, I … I …" he stammered, eyes beginning to water.

Roger turned to the principal. "I'll take him home now, Mrs. Fallworth," he said. He looked back at his son and narrowed his eyes. "And believe me, this will *never* happen again."

The ride back to the farm was made in a deathly silence that Jeremy found unbearable. He wondered what his pa was going to do when they arrived home. The fear of the unknown was the worst kind of fear. The last two times he had gotten into trouble, his father had gently lectured him. But this time, his father had not proved to be the gentle giant he expected.

Roger parked the truck beside the barn and got out. "Come with me!" he commanded, storming into the house. Jeremy followed at a distance.

Grandma was hanging freshly-washed laundry on the clothesline out back when the truck pulled in. She pinned one of Jeremy's T-shirts to the line and went inside. When she entered the living room, she found Jeremy sitting stiff and quiet on the couch, his hands folded in his lap. His eyes were following his father, who was pacing the floor in front of him. Roger plowed both hands through his hair.

"Well?" she inquired.

Roger stopped pacing and pointed at Jeremy. "Well, it seems your grandson got himself into a fight … again … and feels pretty proud of it!"

Grandma sat on the couch beside her grandson. "Jeremy, what do you have to say for yourself?" Her voice was gentle and caring, for both Jeremy and Roger.

Jeremy looked up at his grandmother. "I really thought I did the right thing, Grandma," he said. "You know Sylvester can't protect himself, especially since his leg got injured in the tornado and he has to use that crutch all the time. Willy Garand was picking on him and saying all kinds of foul things, and then he kicked the crutch right out from under Sylvester. I tried to catch him, but he fell too fast."

Grandma glanced up at Roger, who had now stopped pacing. "You should have seen the pain on Sylvester's face when he hit the floor," Jeremy continued. "Then, when Sylvester tried to reach for his crutch, Willy kicked it away and stood there with a grin. Well, I got real mad and told Willy that someone needed to wipe that silly grin off his face. And he said, 'What, a piece of manure like you?' But he didn't say 'manure.' Then he shoved me and started toward Sylvester again. I stepped between them and told Willy to back off. Willy said, 'Make me.' So I did."

Jeremy paused and looked up at his father. "One punch, Pa. That's all it took. He dropped like a sack of rocks." He immediately regretted the comment. His father stood stone still, eyes narrowing, jaw muscles pulsating.

"Jeremy, you know we don't approve of fighting," said Grandma, trying to diffuse the situation. She put a fleshy arm around Jeremy's shoulders.

"But, Grandma, Sylvester's my best friend, and …" He stopped and looked up at his father, who was now standing with both hands on his hips and looking menacingly down at him. "I thought you would want me to protect my best friend, Pa," he quickly said. "I thought that was what you would have done. I'm able to do it now."

"What do you mean, 'you're able' to do it now?" Grandma asked.

"It's because of exercising. I ain't never been able to beat up on no one, but now I can." He turned to his father. "I'm strong, Pa, real strong. At least, compared to all my classmates."

"Is that what this is all about?" Roger exploded. "You proving how strong you are?" He locked eyes with his mother, whose lips were pressed tightly together. He threw up his hands and stormed out of the house.

Grandma sat quietly beside her grandson for a few minutes before speaking. "Jeremy," she said, "your father loves you very much. But he …" She paused, searching for the right words. "He has some things on his mind right now."

"What kind of things?" Jeremy asked in a whispered voice.

"Just *things.* But he loves you, and he'll calm down shortly. For now, you go to your room and think about what you've done."

Jeremy left without saying another word. When he had gone, Grandma sat back heavily against the couch and sighed deeply. "Oh, merciful Lord," she prayed, "Your Word says that if anyone lacks wisdom, all he needs to do is ask and You will provide. Well, I'm asking. And You had better make good on that promise, because I don't know where else to turn."

An hour had passed when Jeremy heard a gentle knock on the door. "Son, may I come in?"

Jeremy had been lying on his bed, throwing a baseball into the air and catching it in his glove. Shakey, who had been resting his head on Jeremy's abdomen, quickly looked up. "I guess," Jeremy responded just loud enough to be heard but kept throwing the ball into the air.

The door opened, and Roger entered. He closed the door behind him, walked over to the bed, and sat on the edge. For a moment he said nothing and gently patted Shakey's head.

"Jeremy," Roger said at last, "I need to ask your forgiveness."

Jeremy stopped tossing the ball. "Forgive you, Pa? I don't understand."

"For my anger. I shouldn't have gotten that angry at you. Will you forgive me?"

Jeremy thought about this. His father had never asked for his forgiveness before. Never had to. "Sure, Pa. I guess."

"Also, I need to talk with you about the exercising. To tell you the truth, I never expected that you would take it as seriously as you have. I helped you with it because I loved spending the time with you. It's good to build your body, but it's even more important to build your mind and soul. Your physical strength is only a tool—a God-given tool—to be used for good, not harm. Do you understand?"

"Yes, but Sylvester can't protect himself, Pa. Someone needed to help him, especially when Willy pushed him down."

"Son, it's important to use your strength to make peace with others, not inflict harm on them. Stand in the gap when necessary, but if at all possible, walk away."

Jeremy thought about this for a moment. "But, Pa, you were a Marine and went to war. You fought."

Roger nodded. "There is a time for fighting, Jeremy. But the Willys of this world need to be loved, not rejected." He stopped petting Shakey's head and stood up. "Now, get yourself changed. We've got work to do."

"Work? What kind of work?"

"You live on a farm, son, and I have every intention of making good use of your strong back for the next two days. Meet me in the barn in ten minutes. The stalls need some cleaning. The shovel will be all greased and ready to go."

Jeremy nodded. *Two days hard labor,* he thought. He quickly resigned himself to his punishment.

CHAPTER 14

THE END OF THE MATTER

JANUARY 21, 1961

Roger shuffled through the magazines that had been neatly arranged on the coffee table in the waiting room. He had just selected a copy of *Post Magazine* when Nurse Brady entered. "The doctor will see you now, Mr. Martel," she said.

Roger dropped the magazine onto the table and followed her into the doctor's office. Dr. LeChaise rose from his desk when he entered the room. "Hello, Roger," he said somberly. "Please have a seat."

Roger sat in the same chair as he had about a week before. The doctor sat behind his desk and leaned forward, his hands folded on the ink blotter that covered the desk. Roger immediately had a sense of *déjà vu*. "I'm going to get right to the point," the doctor said. "I'm afraid the news is not good." He paused and looked into his patient's face for any sign of a reaction. Roger remained stoic.

"Roger … you have a tumor in your lungs." There was still no reaction, not even a blink. "Do you understand what I have just told you?"

"Yes," Roger replied, almost too calmly. "I have a tumor. But they have cures for that sort of thing today, don't they? I mean, this is just a temporary condition, right? You just take a knife and cut it out."

Dr. LeChaise looked down at his hands and studied them for several seconds. He tapped his thumbs together a few times before looking back at his patient. "Remarkable strides are being made in this area, that's true. But I'm afraid these types of tumors—"

"Tumors? You mean I have more than one?" Roger tried to remain calm, but he could not restrain the obvious surprise in his voice.

"Yes, I'm afraid it's true. Here, let me show you." Dr. LeChaise stood and flipped on a switch that lit up a white screen on the wall behind his desk. He pulled an X-ray from a large manila envelope and jammed it under some clips at the top of the screen. He removed a pen from the lapel pocket of his lab coat and used it as a pointer. "You can see the shadows right here and here," he said.

Roger leaned forward. He could easily see the dark masses the doctor was pointing out.

Dr. LeChaise turned off the light and sat again. "If we had found them earlier, we might have been able to operate. But I'm afraid the cancer has metastasized."

"It has what?" Roger asked in a stunned tone.

"The cancer has spread beyond your lungs to other parts of your body. This is why you have been experiencing pain in your back—the cancer has spread to your spine. It has also spread to your brain, which is why you have been getting those frequent headaches. Roger, I've consulted with several other doctors who are experts in the field, and they all agree. I'm truly sorry."

Roger slumped back in his chair, shocked by the news. He spread his hand out in a pleading gesture. "Doctor," he asked, "is there anything that can be done?"

Dr. LeChaise sighed deeply. "Well, we can start you on chemotherapy. It will slow the progress of the cancer, but at this stage ..." He looked down at his hands, and then back at Roger's face. Any further explanation was unnecessary.

Roger sat motionless for a long while. Dr. LeChaise said nothing as he allowed his patient to absorb the news. Finally, Roger said, "Doctor, are you saying it is time for me to get my affairs in order?"

Dr. LeChaise cleared his throat. "Yes, Roger."

"How long, doc?" he said in a whispered calmness. "How long before my son becomes an orphan?"

The doctor hesitated for a moment. "A few months, maybe a year at the most."

Roger opened his mouth as if to say something, and then closed it. He swallowed hard.

"Roger, I am so sorry," said Dr. LeChaise. "If there was anything else that I could have done …"

Roger shifted in his chair and stared down at the floor. "It's okay, doc. You know, my father used to say, 'The end of all things, their purposes revealed or hidden, is good for those who love God.'" He looked up at the doctor. "I'm no fatalist, doc. I don't believe it is God's will for me to have cancer. But He's allowed it, and somehow He will use it. So let's give it the good fight. And who knows? Perhaps He will show me mercy."

Roger stood to leave, still numbed by the news. Dr. LeChaise came from around his desk and shook Roger's hand. "I'll contact you as soon as arrangements can be made at the hospital to begin your treatments," he said. With nothing more to say, Roger walked out of the office into the bright sunlight. He stood at the top of the stairs, closed his eyes, and breathed deeply, wondering how he was going to break the news to his son. "Oh, God," he prayed, "I need Your strength."

The truck was parked only a short walk down the street. He slipped in behind the wheel, inserted the key into the ignition, and started the engine. He placed a hand on the gear shift to back out the truck, but then let it go. As emotion overwhelmed him, he laid his forehead against the steering wheel and wrapped his arms over his head. "Oh, my God," he pleaded, "if it be possible, remove this cancer from me, but if not, I will trust You. But, oh God, how do I tell my son? How?"

The few months that Roger thought he had left turned into more than a year. He fought hard, his body and soul refusing to quit, but finally, on May 5, 1962, the inevitable came. Roger lay dying on his bed, his body eaten away from the inside.

Grandma sat in a chair close by and held her son's hand. Jeremy stood at the foot of the bed, with Shakey sitting beside him. He stroked Shakey's head absentmindedly as he reflected back on the day his father had shared the grievous news. "Son, let's go for a walk," his father had said. He remembered wanting to ask why, but as he looked up into his father's face—a face tight with tension—he knew the unasked question would be answered soon enough. In silence, father and son walked through the newly-plowed fields. They came to the pond and sat under the willow tree.

From that day on, Jeremy watched his father's body, which had always been fit and strong, slowly waste away. He watched his father lose his hair from the chemotherapy. Gradually, as Roger became increasingly unable to do any work on the farm, more and more responsibilities fell onto his fifteen-year-old shoulders.

In his mind, he knew his father was dying, but up to this point it had all seemed like some big, sick joke. Any day now his dad would be sitting at the breakfast table again, or puttering around his tractor, or getting his fields ready for the planting season. But now it was clear the cancer had won. There was no denying that fact. The end of his father's life was near, maybe just hours away. All Jeremy could do was watch his father's labored breathing.

"Grandma," Jeremy spoke in a whispered voice, not taking his eyes from his father. "Is he in pain?"

"No, Jeremy," replied Grandma. "He is not in pain." But she did not really know if this was the truth.

As Jeremy looked at his pa, his mind went back to a time when he was four years old. His grandpa Jeremiah had died suddenly, for no reason other than natural causes, as best the doctor could judge. One morning, he didn't show up for breakfast, and they later found him in the fields. Jeremy's memory was fuzzy, but he could still remember walking up to the open casket, hand-in-hand with his father and mother. He remembered thinking how happy his grandfather looked, with just the hint of a smile on his frozen face.

His grandfather was buried on the hill behind the farmhouse. After the funeral service, he remembered walking back to the house in silence with his father, mother, and grandmother. *Was the sun shining, or was it cloudy?* He struggled to remember and found himself frustrated that he could not recall. But he could remember the silence. Grandma did not say a word all the way back to the house, and when they got there she went straight upstairs into her room and closed the door.

Jeremy remembered the suit—his first suit—that his mother had bought him for that day. It made him feel … what, grown up? Yes, that was what his mother had told him. "My, my, what a grown-up young man you look today." He felt so proud. But by the end of the service, he was dying to get out of it. It itched mercilessly.

Jeremy remembered changing out of that prison suit into play clothes and going outside with his glove and a baseball-sized rubber ball. His father joined him while he was throwing the ball against the side of the barn, and the two played catch for a while. But after one toss to his father, his pa held onto the ball and got real quiet. He looked down at that ball as if it were speaking to him. After a moment, his father walked over to him, put an arm around his shoulder, and led him into the barn.

"Have a seat, son," he said as he pointed to a bail of hay. Jeremy tossed the rubber ball a few inches into the air and caught it. "Jeremy," his father said, "some day you will be looking at my body in a casket. But I want you to know that all you will be looking at is an empty shell. My living soul will be with Jesus."

Now, Jeremy watched from the foot of the bed as his father labored for every breath, eyes closed, lips moving, but saying nothing. Jeremy idolized this man. He smiled to himself as he remembered how his dad would come in from a long day's work on the farm. His mother would warn, "Now, Jeremy, you know how tired your father will be. Don't go pestering him to play just now." But he had no need of pestering, for his dad never failed to lift Jeremy, his only child, the apple of his eye, high above his head, then lower him to his broad shoulders and horse trot around the backyard. He remembered the special tuck-ins that made him feel like he was lying in a canoe. *When did Pa stop doing that?*

A gasp from his father snapped Jeremy back to the present. Roger was laboring for every breath, eyes still closed and lips still silently moving. Grandma stood and walked over to Jeremy, nudging him forward off the end of the bed. Roger had opened his eyes and was beckoning with his bony fingers for Jeremy to come closer. Jeremy moved beside his dad and took hold of the hand that had once seemed so massive. He squeezed gently, but there was no response; just a gentle smile creasing his father's lips.

"Son, I ..." his father rasped, but could say no more for a moment. Grandma poured a cup of water and brought it to him with a straw, but he did not have the strength to lift up his head and sip it. She poured a little of the water onto a small hand towel and gently pressed it to his parched lips. "Thank you," he whispered hoarsely. Grandma bent down, kissed her son's forehead and then stepped back, the tears silently streaking down her cheeks.

Jeremy bent closer to his father's lips to hear him speak. "Son," he began again, "it won't be long ... before I ... go home. Remember what I told you ... about the ... empty shell?" He paused, and Grandma again wetted his parched lips.

"Yes, Pa," Jeremy was barely able to choke out. "I remember."

"Know this, my son, 'The end of all things, their purp—'" A cough interrupted him from completing the thought. Jeremy moved closer to his father's ear and finished the well-taught proverb: "... their purposes revealed or hidden, is good for those who love God." His father smiled, and then closed his eyes. Jeremy heard him exhale one last time, and waited to hear the inhale that never came.

Grandma put her hand on Jeremy's shoulders. He looked up into her face, her lips quivering as the tears streamed down her chiseled cheeks and fell to the floor. He looked back to his father. "Say hi to Mom, Pa," he whispered. "I love you both." Then he laid his head on his father's chest and wept.

He did not know how long he lay there—seconds, or maybe minutes. Finally, he sat up and wiped his eyes. "Jeremy," he heard Grandma say, "the Good Lord—"

Jeremy snapped his head around, eyes fierce with burning anger, and opened his mouth to speak. However, changing his mind, he said nothing and swiftly ran from the room. Shakey did not move, knowing that even he was not welcome in his master's presence.

Chapter 15

Final Goodbyes

January 13, 1964

"Mrs. Martel, Mr. Evans will see you now." The receptionist was a bit stiff, but polite.

"Thank you," Grandma said. She had been waiting for twenty minutes, and now, with letter in hand, she entered the financial manager's office.

George stepped out from behind his desk and greeted Grandma as if she were a long-lost friend. He knew this meeting was not going to be pleasant. "It is good to see you, Martha," he said, clearing his throat. "I'm sorry to have kept you waiting." He directed her to a chair in front of his mahogany desk, and then retreated back to his comfort zone. He adjusted his wire-framed half-eye glasses that rested on his pointed nose and leaned forward with his hands folded on the desk.

"Don't you give me that 'it's good to see you' nonsense, George," Grandma said, causing George to sit up and blink. "You know why I'm here." She waved the letter in front of his face. "If I remember correctly, the Martels were the first customers this bank had when it opened its doors. We have always met our financial obligations. We have—"

George raised a hand to interrupt. "But Martha, you have missed the last three payments on the most recent loan."

"Yes, but you know that all the farms around here have gone through some difficult times lately. A few good spring and summer rains, and we should be looking at a bumper crop this year."

"Martha, my—"

"George, don't you dare tell me your hands are tied." She slapped the letter down onto the desk. "You know that this farm has been in our family for generations. And now I receive this letter, signed by you, denying our loan request. Without this loan, we will lose the farm. You know that."

"Martha, you may not want to hear it, but the truth is that my hands *are* tied. I do not make the final decision in such matters."

"But you do make recommendations. Tell me, what was your recommendation this time?"

George's face reddened, and he looked down at his hands.

"That's what I figured. And here I thought we were friends, George. I helped your wife deliver two of your children."

George looked up at this woman with sincere respect and admiration. "It has nothing to do with friendship, Martha. Decisions are based on what's good for the …" He stopped abruptly in mid-sentence.

Grandma nodded slowly. "Good for the bank?" she said, finishing his statement. George made no comment. Grandma sat back heavily in her seat and paused for a moment, trying to think of another line of reasoning. But nothing came. She knew she had been defeated.

"Well, then, I guess that's that," she said, standing to her feet. George stood as well. She looked into his eyes, and there she saw genuine remorse. "George," she said, reaching her outstretched hand across the desk, "we are friends. The Good Lord has not allowed this to come about without some purpose that will reap Him glory."

The hand was clasped. "I truly am sorry, Martha."

"I know you are, George. I know you are." With that, Grandma Martel held up her head and walked out of the bank with dignity. She would pray and cry in private.

Grandma put the property up for sale, and it sold quickly to a real estate developer for a very good price. It would be a farm no more, but she had no choice. She had prayed for a quick sale that would allow her to pay off all her debts and give her and Jeremy enough to live on, and her prayers had been answered. Now she would head back to New England as soon as possible. She had moved to Kansas with her new husband more than fifty years ago, but she had always longed to someday return to her place of birth. Now that time had arrived.

On February 26, 1964, the Chevrolet pickup made its last trip down the long gravel driveway. The truck bed was loaded with everything that remained of their worldly possessions after selling off most of what they had owned at auction. Arrangements had been made for them to stay with Estelle, Grandma's younger sister, until they found a place of their own.

They had not gone more than a few hundred yards on the main road when Jeremy asked Grandma to pull over. She nodded, expecting and wanting what was to come. When the truck came to a stop, Jeremy opened the passenger door and stepped out, pulling the hood of his sweatshirt over his head to protect him from the chill winter air. "I'll be just a few minutes," he said.

Jeremy squeezed between two railings of a fence, crossed a field of tall grass, and climbed the small round-topped hill that overlooked the farm. At the top, he came to a small plot of land surrounded by a square fieldstone wall about three feet in height and twenty feet in length. One four-foot section had been left open as an entrance to the grave sites. He walked past several gravestones and read off the names with which he was so familiar: Jonas, Catherine, Jennifer, Elias, Jeremiah. At the back of the enclosure, he knelt before three gravestones. He reached out to the one on the left and finger-traced the lettering engraved on it, which read:

Virginia T. Martel

1922–1954

Gone Home

The stone in the center simply said:

Martha V. Martel

August 1954

He Loves the Little Children

Jeremy turned and finger-traced the stone on the right, which read:

Roger L. Martel

1921–1962

It Is Well with My Soul

Jeremy spoke no words and shed no tears, but just gave a final, silent touch to say goodbye.

A fourth grave marker was located just to the left. This one was not made of stone but of two pieces of wood nailed together to form a cross. Carved into the horizontal piece of the wood by Jeremy's own hands was the name "Shakey," while on the vertical piece the word "Faithful" had been carved. He remembered the vet telling him that Shakey wouldn't live long after his fight with the coyote, but the dog had fooled them all. Only a month before, Jeremy had stepped off the bus to find Shakey lying by the side of the driveway, unmoving except for a tail wagging at his approach. He carried his friend into the house, where Shakey died in his arms. "He just got plumb tired out, but he waited to say goodbye," Grandma had said.

A raindrop kissed the back of Jeremy's hand. He stood and turned to take one last look at the land stretched out before him—one last look at the barn and the old farmhouse. Then he descended the hill and crossed into the meadow, running to the parked truck as icy drops began pelting his face. Grandma restarted the engine as he climbed into the truck, and they drove away.

About a mile down the road, they passed the Pearson farm. Sylvester was sitting in the rain on the fence railing, his crutch leaning against the fence. Grandma slowed the vehicle. "Would you like me to stop?" she asked. Jeremy slowly shook his head. He and Sylvester had already said their goodbyes. As the truck slowly passed, Jeremy looked out the back window and watched his friend fade from sight in the sheets of rain.

Grandma and Jeremy remained silent in their own thoughts, listening only to the conversation between the rain and the steady swish-swish of the wiper blades.

PART TWO

NEW ENGLAND

Chapter 16

First Impressions

February 29, 1964

After three long, joint-stiffening days of driving, the travelers arrived at Grandma's sister Estelle's home in Clayton, Massachusetts, just before sunset on Saturday. They stayed there for two days, and then Grandma found a small one-bedroom apartment close to the center of town. It was ready for immediate occupancy, completely furnished, with heat and hot water included, and the rent was fair. Grandma had only her monthly Social Security check and what was left from the sale of the farm after paying off the debts, but it would be enough if they were frugal. Jeremy would have to sleep on a fold-out couch in the living room, but that was fine with him.

Grandma and Jeremy spent the first few days fixing up the apartment and scouting the town for the best places to shop. She dragged Jeremy around town at every opportunity, giving him a tour down memory lane. She even took him to Hull on the South Shore, where she had spent the first fifteen years of her life before her parents moved to Clayton. Despite these detours, by the end of the third day, they were settled in.

Jeremy borrowed the truck and drove to the high school to enroll. It was now Thursday, and the principal of the school agreed to let him start the following Monday. After leaving the school, he went to several local businesses and applied for part-time jobs. He filled out several applications, but at each place he heard the same story: "Sorry, kid, there's nothing available right now. But we'll keep your application on file." He would try again tomorrow.

The last place Jeremy applied was at a Stop and Shop grocery store. Once he had filled out the application and handed it to the young brunette behind the courtesy counter, he asked if she had a telephone book he might borrow. "I think we can accommodate that request …" she said, pausing to look at the name on the application, "Jeremy." She handed him a large Yellow Pages.

Jeremy ignored the flirtatious smile and flipped through the book until he found the heading for gymnasiums. Back on the farm, he had made dumbbells by hanging cement-filled cans on the ends of twelve-inch long piping, but he had been unable to take those with him when he left the farm. Even if he had, he realized, there would have been no place in the small apartment to set it up. However, he still wanted to keep up his daily exercise routine.

Jeremy found two gyms listed in Clayton: Gold Medal Gymnasium and Red's Gymnasium. He tried Gold Medal first, where it took all of two minutes for him to figure out that he could not afford their application fees, let alone their monthly dues. He needed to help Grandma with the bills and still have some spending money leftover. He wondered if he should even bother with Red's Gym. He had been clueless as to how much money it cost to join a real gym.

Won't hurt to at least look, I suppose, he said to himself. So he drove to the center of town and asked an elderly pedestrian for directions to Market Street, which was the address that had been listed in the Yellow Pages. The pedestrian pointed in the direction Jeremy had been going. "Turn at the next left," he said.

Jeremy followed the directions and drove slowly, checking all of the numbers on the places of business. He had driven for about 100 yards when he spotted the number "89" over the main entrance of a yellow, three-story, wood-framed building that looked to be in need of some serious renovations. A wide set of stairs led up to a pair of ornately-carved doors that had been painted brown. Over the doorframe was a long, rectangular sign with red lettering against a white background. The paint was peeling, but Jeremy could still make out the words: "The Watering Hole Club."

A weather-beaten sign was hanging over an open door on the left corner of the building. Jeremy drove over to it and looked up. *You have got to be kidding*, he said to himself. He pulled the truck over to the curb and looked up. The sign read, "R d's Gym asiu," followed by a "down" arrow. He shook his head and slowly drove away. *That place obviously houses more cockroaches than people,* he said to himself.

He was about to take a left turn and head back to the apartment when he looked in his rearview mirror and saw two men exit the building from the corner doorway he had just left. He braked the truck and turned to look out the rear window. Each man was wearing shorts and muscle shirts and carried a gym bag. "Holy cow!" he said aloud when he saw the width of their shoulders and size of their biceps. He backed up, parked the truck next to the sidewalk, and got out.

He took a deep breath when he reached the corner entrance. The placed looked even more beat up from up close. *I've got to be crazy*, he thought as he entered. Inside, there were two sets of stairs: a shorter flight to the right that led up to a landing at the main entrance, and a second longer set of stairs that led down. He went down as the arrow had directed.

The further Jeremy went into the basement, the more pungent the odor of sweat became. At the bottom of the stairs, he found another door with the words "Red's Gymnasium" painted in red on an opaque glass window. The letters were readable, but worn.

Jeremy hesitated briefly before opening the door. Inside, he found himself looking into a long, narrow rectangular room. Paint was peeling off the walls, overhead pipes ran exposed along the ceiling, and some of the electrical outlets were missing covers. There were no windows, just long rows of fluorescent lights. Many of these flickered, while others had completely burned out. The floor was potholed cement. Yet to his surprise, almost every piece of exercise equipment that lined each side of the room was in use by some Charles-Atlas wannabe.

Jeremy closed the door behind him and took in the smells, noises, and intense energy he found all around him. He listened to the straining and grunting of the men as metal plates were rammed onto bars. Outside the air had been so cold that he could see his own breath, but down here the heat was stifling. Two large fans, one strategically placed at each end of the room, were running at full blast.

"Four … five … six." Two men, dressed in sneakers, shorts, and cut-off gray sweatshirts, were lifting weights near the door-end of the gym. One was doing curls with a barbell, while the other was screaming encouragement. "Seven! Eight! Two more reps!" he yelled, just inches away from the face of the lifter. "Just two more!" Jeremy saw a spray of spit exit the man's mouth and strike the lifter in the face. The lifter was oblivious to the spit and uttered a gut-wrenching groan. With biceps straining and arteries bulging, he lifted the bar to within inches of his chin, and then slowly lowered it back down to his waist.

"Nine! One more!" the screamer yelled. "Come on! Put some muscle behind it!" The veins in the lifter's neck bulged and pulsed, his muscles rippled, and his face reddened as if he had just swallowed some hot peppers. He clenched his teeth together, creating a demonic expression on his face, and strained until he had pulled up the weight. He then lowered the bar until his arms were fully extended, bent his knees slightly, and dropped the barbell with a crash onto the cement floor.

The lifter unbuckled a four-inch-wide weightlifting belt and sat down on the padded weight bench that was nearby. He leaned forward and planted his thick forearms on his knees, his hands dangling loosely at the wrists. His chest heaved as he swallowed huge gulps of air. Sweat flowed from his brow and formed puddles on the rubber mat at his feet.

Jeremy stared at the two well-muscled men and then at the dropped bar on the floor. He began to calculate the weight. *One hundred forty pounds?* he gasped. *That's almost as much as I weigh!* He began to recalculate his math to make sure he had gotten the figure correct when a thunderous voice from behind made him jump.

"Frank!" the voice screamed, "How many times I gotta tell ya to set them weights down! You don't drop 'em!" Jeremy whipped around to see the owner of the voice approach.

Frank looked up apologetically. "Sorry, Big Red," he said. "Won't happen again."

"Better not," Big Red threatened as he shook both fists in their faces. "Or you'll be answering to Sledge and Hammer!" He spun and saw Jeremy standing there. "Something I can do for you, kid?" he said in the same tone as he had been using with the two weightlifters. "You've been standing there gawking like you ain't never seen a gym before."

Jeremy found himself standing face-to-face with the largest specimen of human flesh he had ever seen. Big Red was wearing nothing but gym shorts—there were not even shoes on his feet. His thighs were bigger than Jeremy's waist, and timber-sized arms hung from shoulders piled up with muscle where his neck should have been. Gold chains hung from each of his earlobes. Nothing but scrub-brush eyebrows grew on his acorn-bald head. Jeremy's 180-pound frame was completely swallowed up by the size of this man, obliterating him from sight of anyone standing on the opposite side.

"I said, Is-there-something-I-can-do-for-you," the Goliath said slowly, annunciating each syllable as he moved closer to Jeremy. "I ain't got all day."

"Hey, Big Red, go easy," Frank said. "I think you're scaring the kid."

"Is that right, kid?" Big Red leaned forward, his nose inching its way deeper into Jeremy's space. "Am I … scaring you?"

"I … I …" Jeremy gasped, completely intimidated.

"Yup, you've got him scared all right," said Frank. "Hey, kid, don't go by first impressions. Big Red here is just an oversized teddy bear. Ain't that right, Lester?" Lester, Frank's screaming encourager, nodded in agreement. "Go ahead, Big Red," he said. "Give the kid one of your great big teddy bear hugs."

Big Red gave a tooth-gapped grin, spread his immense arms out wide, and took one step closer to Jeremy. Jeremy's eyes popped as wide as saucers and he retreated two steps, tripping over a loose weight plate that made him fall on his back to a mat. Frank and Lester laughed as Big Red reached down with his baseball-glove-sized hand. He lifted Jeremy to his feet as if he were a tinker toy.

"Don't worry, kid, I'm just playing with ya," he said. "The only one I hug is my wife." He pointed with his right thumb over his shoulder at Frank and Lester. "Pay no mind to these two. They got gravy for brains." He walked over to a large flattop oak desk that sat against a wall across from the room's entrance and pulled out a well-worn wooden chair. The chair creaked under his weight as he sat. He leaned back so that the chair rested only on its rear legs and folded his hands behind his head. For the first time, Jeremy noticed the two tattoos on Big Red's biceps. The one on the left read "Sledge," while the right one read "Hammer."

Big Red cleared his throat. "Now," he said in a gentler tone, "What can I do for you?"

"Where have you been, child?" Grandma scolded from the kitchen when Jeremy entered the apartment. "I was about to call out the National Guard!" In one hand she held a bowl, and with the other she was doing a whirlwind of mixing.

"Grandma," Jeremy said with a hint of exasperation. "I'm *seventeen*. I'm not a child."

"Okay then, *young man*—is that better?—where have you been?"

"I registered for school. They gave me some papers you need to fill out." Jeremy placed these on the kitchen table, and then moved closer to peer over Grandma's shoulder to see what she was mixing.

"Hand me that bag of chocolate bits on the counter, would you please?"

Jeremy did as asked. "Want me to open them for you?"

"If you do, will there be any left for the recipe?"

"Probably not." Jeremy opened the bag, helped himself to a handful of bits, and stuffed them into his mouth. He was about to reach into the bag for a second helping when Grandma's batter-covered mixing spoon came down across his hand. "I start school next Monday," he continued, licking the batter. "And then I went around and put in some applications for work. Nobody's hiring right now, but I'll keep looking."

"It's okay with me if you want to work, but remember that your studies come first."

"Yes, Grandma."

"Don't you roll your eyes at me, child. I can still whoop you if I need to." She exaggeratedly shook the spoon in his face. Jeremy laughed and reached for a paper towel to wipe off the batter. "Now, what else have you been up to?" Grandma asked as she returned to the mixing.

"What makes you think I've been up to anything else?"

Grandma stopped and looked at her grandson. "Do I look feeble-minded? It wouldn't take you all this time just to go to the school and put in a few applications." She leaned closer and placed her nose near Jeremy's shirt. "And what is that smell?"

"Well, to tell you the truth, I did go to one other place." He paused for effect.

"Well, I am not a mind-reader. Get on with it."

"I'm thinking about joining a gym."

"You *what*?" Grandma dropped the mixing spoon into the batter and turned to face him. "Now, just how do you think you are going to keep up with your studies *and* hold down a job *and* go to a gym? Hmm? Not to mention how you're going to afford it, given the fact that you don't even have a job yet. Do you have any idea—"

"Grandma, don't get so riled up," said Jeremy. "I went to take a look at a couple of gyms, that's all. There's this one called Red's Gymnasium down on Market Street. It's not very expensive and, well, I think it would be—"

"*Not very expensive?* It's expensive if you don't have a job. What are you thinking? Not to mention the kinds of … characters … that go to those gymnasiums. Well, I don't like this idea one bit, Jeremiah Elias Martel." She turned back to her bowl and began mixing with a vengeance. "No sir, not one bit."

Jeremy bit his lower lip. He wasn't sure how he was going to break the next piece of news to her. "Uh … Grandma," he stammered. "I've already … signed up and paid the $5 fee for the first month. I've even got my own key to the place so I can go any time, day or night. And the owner, Big Red, even spent some time showing me how to use the equipment. You wouldn't believe the size of this guy. And is he ever pig-butt ugly. Why, he—"

The expression on Grandma's face shut him up fast. She stopped mixing, stood to her full height, and looked out the window over the kitchen sink. For the past several years, especially since Roger's death, she had watched her only grandson turn what she thought would be a passing childhood fancy into an almost fanatical pursuit—a pursuit that often kept him from attending church with her on Sundays. She removed her apron, wiped her hands with it, and dropped it onto the counter. Taking a few steps over to the table in the corner of the kitchen, she sat and, with a pointed finger, indicated for her grandson to do the same. Her gaze seemed to penetrate him.

"Jeremy," she began somberly, "ever since your father was taken home, you have been driven with this obsession to exercise. I'm concerned for you. The idea of you joining a gym is not what bothers me—my concern is that you're replacing your faith in God with a faith in yourself. You're placing faith in your own strength, as if you don't need Him."

Jeremy sat expressionless as he politely listened to his grandmother. *I don't need Him, Grandma,* he thought.

"God loves you desperately, Jeremy. He has allowed you to go through some hard times in your young life and to suffer some great losses."

Here comes the "end of all things" sermon, he thought sarcastically.

"But He has also blessed you with some great blessings."

What's this? A new sermon?

"Do you remember your father's last words to you?"

Ah, here it comes.

"He said ..." Grandma stopped and looked away, choking up with the thought. She covered her mouth with her hand as her chin began to quiver.

Jeremy immediately regretted his mental mocking. It broke his heart to see his grandmother hurting. *Yes, Grandma, I remember what he said,* he thought.

Grandma regained control, lowered her hand, and opened her mouth to continue. Then she stopped herself again and looked into her grandson's blank eyes. She was unable to discern his thoughts.

"Okay, Jeremy," she sighed. "If joining a gym is what you want, then okay. But you will have to find a way to pay for it." She pointed a finger at him. "And you will go with me to church on Sunday."

"I promise, Grandma," Jeremy said with a smile.

Grandma slapped the table with the palms of her hands—a sign of approval as if to seal the agreement—and in silence went back to her baking. She watched Jeremy leave to go into the living room to watch television. "Oh Lord," she said, closing her eyes, "he's so young to have been through so many trials. I don't know why You're sifting him as wheat, but I can only trust You with him, my grandson, Your child. Amen."

Chapter 17

Second Impressions

March 7, 1964

Jeremy woke at 5:00 AM and hastily scribbled a note on a blank sheet of paper.

Grandma, went to the gym. Be back in a couple of hours.

Jeremy

He left the note on the kitchen table and set a coffee cup down on the corner to anchor it. Then, slowly, he tiptoed out of the apartment.

It was still dark, and much colder than he had expected. He toyed with the idea of re-entering the apartment to put on a heavier coat, but as he began the half-mile jog to the gym, he decided his hooded sweatshirt and sweatpants would be sufficient. By the time he reached the gymnasium, beads of sweat had formed on his brow.

Jeremy turned the handle on the door and, to his surprise, found that it was unlocked. He opened the door and was immediately greeted by the clanking of metal and grunting of voices. He thought he would be the first one there at this time of day. The clock on the wall behind the oak desk read 5:04.

"'Bout time you got here, kid." Big Red was sitting on the end of a vinyl-duct-tape-patched weight bench, tightly wrapping a bandage around his left knee. Several other lifters were scattered around, bench-pressing barbells, curling dumbbells, and pumping at stationary bikes.

Jeremy closed the door and walked over to Big Red. "What's that for?" he asked, pointing to the bandage.

"Don't want my knee popping out when I lift that there weight," Big Red answered. He gave a slight pointing of his chin to the disc-loaded barbell resting on the floor in front of him.

Jeremy walked over to the barbell and put both hands around one end. He squatted and tried to lift it, but it would not budge. He looked at the numbers on the individual weights. Six fifty-pound discs were on each end, and he knew the bar weighed another forty-five pounds. He whistled through his teeth.

Big Red placed his hand, less than gently, on Jeremy's right shoulder and pulled him away from the weight. "Watch and learn, kid," he said. Sucking in his gut, he took a well-worn leather weight belt and placed it tightly around his girth. Then he reached down into a bucket on the floor next to the bench and withdrew a large piece of white chalk. This he rubbed over his hands, shoulders and chest, and then onto the bar itself where he would be gripping it.

Without his saying a word, two other well-muscled men positioned themselves on each end of the barbell. *Frank and Lester,* Jeremy thought, remembering the men from two days before. The gym went silent, and all eyes turned toward the hulk. Big Red stood above the weight, closed his eyes as if meditating, and breathed in deeply. He shook his arms and then, with feet spread shoulder-width apart, opened his eyes, squatted and gripped the bar.

Jeremy watched in awe as Big Red rapidly sucked in a few short breaths and blew them out. With one last rapid suck in, he held his breath and inflated his cheeks like balloons. Suddenly, the bar jerked upward as Big Red stood and lifted the bar to his chest in one powerful movement. The breath was exhaled as Big Red rested the weight against his chest for a few seconds and adjusted his position. Then, again sucking in and holding his breath, Big Red threw the weight upward with a jumping motion and, at the same time, ducked under the bar and spread his feet forward and back for balance. With the bar now over his head and his arms fully extended, he stood to full height and held this position for three seconds.

The weight dropped with a crash to the floor as Big Red broke one of his own rules. Applause broke out around the gym. "Not bad for a warm up," Lester said, throwing a towel to Big Red, who had sweat pouring from his brow. Big Red dried his face and slowly loosened his belt. The two men on each side helped prepare the bar for the next lift.

"See, kid," Big Red said, "it's all in the … what the … ?" The giant had looked for his newest trainee, only to see him bent over a barbell with some small weights on it at the other end of the gym. He watched and shook his head in disgust. He had seen this before—some young punk thinking he was bigger and stronger than he really was, trying to show off his stuff.

Jeremy had been able to get the bar to his chest and hold it there for a few seconds. Straining to push the bar up over his head, he made a jumping motion and spread his feet just like Big Red—but not quite like Big Red. His face contorted as he realized that he had failed to check the locking clips on the ends of the bar that held the discs in place. Now, as he swayed unsteadily, the weights on the left began to slide.

Jeremy stepped left to compensate and tried to get himself under the bar again to push upward. But he was now off balance, and his legs were beginning to buckle. He pushed up again, but now the weights went slightly behind him. Jeremy tried once more to compensate, but he was unable to maintain his balance. The weight fell even further behind him, and at the same time a disc began to slide off the end. The bar shifted up, and now the discs on the right began to slip.

Jeremy stumbled backward and tripped over a workout bench. The bar crashed against the wall, punching a hole in the plaster as his head slammed onto a rubber mat. It was only his second time in this gym, but Jeremy was once again flat on his back. As he sat with his feet draped over the bench and rubbed the back of his head, he heard the room break out into a roar of laughter.

Big Red was *not* laughing. He leaned over the workout bench until he was nose-to-nose with Jeremy and said in a low growl, "Follow me. I want to show you something." This time, he did not help Jeremy up.

Jeremy struggled to his feet and followed after Big Red. His face was red from embarrassment as he walked the gauntlet and followed the giant to the front door. Still rubbing his head, he looked down at the floor when he got near Big Red and asked in a sheepish voice, "What did you want to show me?"

Big Red opened the door. "Step into the hall."

Jeremy obeyed, knowing he was about to receive a lecture. *At least Big Red has the decency to do it in private,* he thought. He turned to see the huge man's body filling the doorway. Seething with anger, his eyes narrowing to slits, he said, "What I wanted to show you, kid, was this side of the door. Don't come back until you think you can learn to do things the right way. And in here, kid, that's my way." He slammed the door in Jeremy's face, leaving him on the outside of the gym. It took several seconds for Jeremy's shock and humiliation to wear off and his anger to rise up within him—a self-righteous anger that replaced his good sense.

Jeremy threw open the door and stormed back inside. Big Red was standing over the barbell again, with Frank and Lester at his side. Jeremy stopped several feet in front of the big man and shouted, "You can all go to—" A finger pointed in his direction quickly made him realize that he had better not finish the obscenity. He sensed others in the gym moving in his direction.

"Got to admit it, Big Red," said Frank as he stood next to the barbell with his arms folded. "The kid's gutsy. Stupid, but gutsy."

A sense of fear descended upon Jeremy. He knew that he had just broken another unwritten law and stepped over some invisible line in Red's Gymnasium. He swallowed hard but unflinchingly resolved to hold his ground, his lips pressed defiantly together, as Big Red, within inches now, towered over him.

"You … don't … scare … me," said Jeremy, looking up at the massive bulk that was now directly in front of him. The swallow went down hard, as he had no saliva.

"I don't, huh?" said Big Red, folding his arms across his chest, which made him seem to grow even taller and wider.

Jeremy shook his head slowly in response. Just now he remembered Sledge and Hammer, and he wished he could back up the clock about sixty seconds.

"Well, that's good, kid, 'cuz I'm really just a big friendly teddy bear. Ain't that right, Frank?" He kept his squinting eyes focused on Jeremy.

"Sure are, Big Red," said Frank.

"And, Frank, whose gym is this?"

"Why, it's yours, Big Red."

"And, Frank, who makes up the rules in here?"

"That'd be you again, Big Red." Frank's smile widened.

"And when I throw someone out of my gym, where do they stay, Frank?"

"Out, Big Red." Frank was thoroughly enjoying the massacre. Big Red lowered his arms, placed his hands on his hips, and leaned forward to within inches of Jeremy's face. Jeremy could now feel the hellish heat of Big Red's breath. "Then, can you tell, Frank," Big Red continued, "why this … juvenile … is standing here in front of me?"

"Haven't got a clue, Big Red."

"Well then, kid," said Big Red, finally addressing a question to Jeremy, "can you give Frank a clue?"

Jeremy opened his mouth, but only a short squeak came out.

"Speak up, boy! I can't hear you!"

Jeremy flinched and took a step backward, but otherwise he held his ground. The humiliation was thorough, but now the anger had returned. "I ain't no boy, *boy*."

There was a collective gasp in the gym, and then silence. Even the smile on Frank's face had been wiped clean. He slowly shook his head, pitying the newcomer.

Big Red rose to his full height, walked over to his desk, and withdrew an envelope from the drawer. From this he withdrew five $1 bills, walked back to Jeremy, and slapped the money into his palm. He strode to the door, opened it, and stood aside in silence. Jeremy knew that nothing more would be said. He walked to the door, gave one skewering look at Big Red, and walked out. He expected to hear the door slam shut behind him, but all he heard was the click of the latch as the door gently closed.

Jeremy climbed the stairs two at a time, the angry humiliation coursing through him and almost bringing him to tears. It was colder out than he remembered, and the sun had still not broken upon the morning. He clenched the $5 in his fist, pulled the hood of his sweatshirt over his head, and began to walk away.

"Hey, kid," said a voice behind him.

Jeremy stopped and turned to see Frank jogging toward him. He turned around again and continued walking.

"Hey, hold up a second." Frank caught up to him, but Jeremy tried to walk away. Frank got in front of him and stopped, blocking his path. "Kid, you really stepped over the boundaries, you know that, don't you?"

Jeremy again tried to walk around the intruder, but Frank stepped into his path. "Just listen to me, will ya?"

"Get lost," Jeremy said, but he did not move.

"Look, everybody in this gym has been browbeat by Big Red. But you got to know he does it because he cares about his people."

"*His* people? What's that supposed to mean?"

"His clients, his customers—you know, his *people*. He doesn't think of any of us as just money in the bank. Good grief, man, look at what he charges. Look at the condition of this building. He ain't getting rich from us. I've known Big Red for ten years. I was about your age when I found this dump of a gym. He cares, kid. He really cares. Sometimes he just doesn't show it in … well … in the most genteel of ways."

"Yeah, I noticed," Jeremy said with disgust.

"But you've got to admit, kid—"

"Name's Jeremy, not 'kid.'"

"Well, you've got to admit, Jeremy, that you really did step out of bounds. What were you thinking when you tried to make that lift?"

Jeremy found his anger draining from him as Frank spoke. He looked down at the sidewalk. "I thought I could handle it," he said quietly.

"Let me tell you something, Jeremy," Frank said, looking into his eyes. "The other day after you left the gym, Big Red came up to me and said, 'There's someone who could really go places with the right training.' He doesn't say that about everyone. And trust me, Big Red can give you that training."

"He said that?" asked Jeremy, astonished.

"Yeah."

"But he threw me out."

"Yeah, that he did." Frank rubbed his three-day growth of beard. "But, to tell you the truth, you deserved it. I probably would have done the same thing. But look, maybe I can put in a good word for you. Just give him a chance to cool down, and try it again. If you can swallow some pride, that is." Frank laughed. "I ain't seen Big Red this angry in a dog's age, not since I almost burned down this cockroach hotel."

"You what?"

"Yeah, I used to smoke. One day—oh, it must have been about two weeks after I joined—I was in the gym by myself. As I said, I joined when I was about your age, and I was just as cocky. Well, I pulled out a cigarette and, instead of coming up here to the sidewalk, I lit up in the bathroom. Just then, I heard someone begin to open the door. Did you notice how it squeaks? It's been like that as long as I've been coming here. Anyway, I panicked and threw the butt into a wastebasket. About fifteen minutes later, smoke is pouring from the bathroom. There were three other guys in the gym now, and it took the four of us to put out the fire. That was when Big Red walked in. Trust me, kid—I mean, Jeremy—you got off easy."

Jeremy tried to suppress a smile. "So, what did he do?"

"Well, if you ever do come back, just take a look at the ceiling outside the bathroom entrance. You'll notice a hole in the plaster about the size of my head." Jeremy shook his head and laughed.

"Hey," said Frank, "I got to get back in before I cool down too much. At least think about what I've said, all right?"

"Do you think he'd really give me another chance?" Jeremy asked as Frank turned to go.

Frank shrugged. "He did with me. It's worth trying, believe me. But I wouldn't go back in there today … know what I mean?"

"Yeah, I know."

"Also, there are two more things you need to know. First, if Big Red does give you another chance, no more swearing. Big Red hates swearing. He used to have a mouth on him that would have gotten him thrown out of hell itself, but he got religion a year or so back, and he's been working on cleaning up his act. Seems he's got a niece who's one of them Bible thumpers, and she convinced him of the errors of his ways. Well, now Big Red thinks he knows God personally." Frank turned to leave and began walking down the street.

"Wait!" said Jeremy. "You said two more things."

"What?" said Frank, looking back as he continued to walk.

"You said there were *two* more things I needed to know."

"Oh, yeah. You need to get rid of that piece of lumber."

"What's that supposed to mean?"

"That chip on your shoulder. Actually, it's more like a log. It's an awful lot of baggage to carry."

Jeremy watched as Frank walked away. He wanted to explain that he didn't swear, at least not as a habit. Back in Kansas, Sylvester had tried his best to get him to swear, and once or twice he had tried a word, but every time, he had felt guilty afterward. He looked to the ground and put his hands into the pouch in the front of his sweatshirt. Slowly, he made his way back to the apartment.

CHAPTER 18

GETTING ACQUAINTED

MARCH 9, 1964

It was Monday morning, and the students at Clayton High were meandering into their classes with the usual banter and pushing and shoving, just as they did every morning when the school bell rang. The students in Mr. Shennet's eleventh-grade biology lab had each found a seat of their own choosing, for Mr. Shennet had informed them on Friday that he would be changing the seat assignments for this new lab. The guys in the class sat mostly with other guys, and the girls sat with girls. A few of the guys, however, sat with their girlfriends, while a few others tried to sit with the girls they wished were their girlfriends.

One of these was Benny, the class clown, whose freckled face and baby fat had plagued him since kindergarten, making him look the part. He tried to sit next to Lizzy, a five-foot two-inch pleasingly plump girl with a great personality, but she slid along the bench-style seat just as he was sitting, pushing his butt firmly onto the floor. The class hooted and hollered. Benny stood, gave an exaggerated bow, and slobbered in Daffy Duck style, "Lizzy, my lovely, I yieldeth to thy wishes for noweth, but somedayeth thou shalt knowest what thowest hast rejectedeth."

More hoots filled the classroom, and even Mr. Shennet smiled at the act. He was a six-foot six-inch beanpole of a man who wore bottle-thick glasses and had a beak for a nose. This had earned him the nickname "Beaker," but the students never said this to his face. He had a sense of humor that endeared most of them to him, and they knew he loved his work with a passion, and loved them all as well.

"Okay, you two," Mr. Shennet said, "fight nicely. And the rest of you bobble heads settle down."

The class was slow to get themselves under control until Mr. Shennet lowered his head and gave his famous over-the-rim-of-his-glasses look—the final warning that it was time to get serious. He was not known for giving out many detentions, but they all knew he would if necessary.

"All right, then. As I promised last week, we are going to continue our study of vertebrate anatomy by dissecting frogs and—"

"Yeeew!"

"Ugh!"

"Yuck!"

"Awright!"

"About time!"

"Show me the knife!"

The complaints and enthusiastic comments that Mr. Shennet received every year when he gave this announcement filled the room. It took another over-the-rim glance to get things under control again. "Okay, you cave dwellers," he continued, "there will be no more of that. I will pass out the materials in a moment, but first I am going to make some changes in seating arrangements." The class grumbled but kept the complaints to a minimum.

Benny glanced at Lizzy, who had looked his way, and silently mouthed, "Maybe it will be your lucky day yet!" He flicked his eyebrows up and down and gave an obscene smile. Lizzy rolled her eyes in disgust and turned away with unmistakable rejection.

"Now then, Benny," said Mr. Shennet," I've assigned you to table one, right up front, as near to me as possible."

"Glutton for punishment aren't you, Mr. Shennet?" someone yelled from the back of the room. The class laughed.

"It ain't fair, Mr. Shennet," Benny objected as he begrudgingly moved forward.

"It'll be okay, Benny. You'll survive. And was that you, Dick, with the witty comment? Well, I'm going to seat you right next to Benny. Seems to me you can use some up-close-and-personal attention based on your latest test score."

Dick's jaw dropped and his arms spread wide in a pleading gesture. "You've got to be kidding me, Mr. Shennet! Please tell me this is just a real early April Fools' joke!"

The teacher pointed with his long, thin index finger to where Dick was to sit. Dick knew he had no recourse. "Hey, Dicky, you get to sit next to your girlfriend after all," whispered Bradley, who was sitting next to Dick. Dick stood and slapped him on the back of the head as the chortles began.

"May we continue?" said Mr. Shennet in a very professorial tone. "Larry and Charles, you sit at table two. Robert and Betty, you're at table three. And now—"

"Oh, oh, Mr. Shennet! Mr. Shennet!" a student named Carmen interrupted with more enthusiasm than the situation warranted. Nicknamed "the Torpedo," she was the class flirt, and as she waived her raised hand frantically, her long, blonde, ironing-board-straightened hair bounced about her head.

"Yes, Carmen, what is it?" asked Mr. Shennet.

"Robert's been dismissed. He got sick—really sick, if you know what I mean—and had to go to the nurse earlier. I sure wouldn't want to have her job, having to clean up all that—"

"Thank you, Carmen. I think we get the picture." Carmen's commentary gave several students cause for expressing exaggerated disgust, and Mr. Shennet again had to glare over the rim of his glasses to get them settled down. Just then, the rear entrance door opened, and Mrs. Parker, the high school's assistant principal, entered the room. Most of the students called her "Honey Bun," because of her sour personality and her hair that was always pinned up in a bun.

A new student followed Mrs. Parker into the class. As the pair walked to the front of the room, the students, as if on cue, went deathly silent and faced forward, their hands folded on the lab tables. "Please excuse the interruption, Mr. Shennet," said the assistant principal, "but I have a new student for your homeroom." She turned, unsmilingly, to face the students and stood there in her buttoned-at-the-neck dress with her hands folded in front of her.

"Class, this is Jeremy Martel," she continued. "He just moved to Clayton. I am sure that you will all make him feel right at home." With this brief and to-the-point introduction made, Mrs. Parker turned and left. The students gave a collective sigh, as though it were now safe to breathe.

Mr. Shennet shook Jeremy's hand. "Pleasure to meet you, Jeremy," he said. Jeremy shook hands and semi-smiled politely back, but said nothing. His gaze rested not at the height of the man before him, but at the huge protruding Adam's apple that bobbed when he spoke. "We are about to start a biology lab, Jeremy. I was just giving out seating assignments. Let's see, you might as well sit next to Betty at table three."

Jeremy looked in the direction Mr. Shennet was pointing and saw the most incredible head of long, wavy, flaming red hair that he had ever seen. Betty smiled up at him as he walked to his assigned seat. Her smile mesmerized him, even with the braces that covered her pearl-white teeth. He paused and stared a fraction of a second too long, causing both Lizzy and Carmen to notice. Lizzy looked over to her friend and mouthed, "Cute," and Carmen nodded and mouthed back, "Way cute."

"Hi," Betty said as Jeremy sat down. He nodded in her direction, a sliver of a nervous smile creasing his lips, and then quickly looked away.

Mr. Shennet continued the seating assignments for another thirty seconds, and then said, "Now class, I am going to pass out the materials for this dissection project. Each table will get one scalpel, forceps, a teasing needle, a half dozen pins, and a dissecting pan. I have already gone over how these tools are to be used, so there should be few questions. I will also pass out step-by-step instructions for you to follow, along with diagrams. Any questions so far?"

Silence.

"One more thing … safety. Remember the safety rules we went over on how to use these tools, especially the scalpel. I expect everyone to follow those rules … to the *T*. Is that understood?"

Again the class was silent.

"I said … is that understood?"

"Yes, Mr. Shennet," the class responded in an exaggerated bored chorus.

Mr. Shennet called on a few students to pass out the papers and equipment, and then some buzzing was heard around the room on who would do the slicing-and-dicing. Jeremy's concentration was fully on his fingers, which tapped nervously on the table. Out of the corner of his eye, he could see Betty looking at him.

Once the materials had been distributed, Mr. Shennet passed out frogs that had been stored in formaldehyde. Jeremy stared at the one that had been placed on the tray in front of him and Betty. "Ah, Betty," he said, "do you want to do the cutting?"

"I don't even want to be in the same room with that smelly thing," Betty replied with genuine disgust. She wrinkled her upturned, button-sized nose in response to the odor and pushed the tray toward Jeremy. "That poor frog."

"Oh, it's just a common grass frog," Jeremy said. He looked over at her, but then quickly had to look away again. "It's a pretty amazing little creature, actually. It can breathe through its skin, so it can hibernate for months under mud. This one is a male."

"And just how do you know that?" she asked, tipping her head slightly to the left to allow her hair to flow across her shoulders. Jeremy's good looks had not gone unnoticed by her any more than they had with Lizzy or Carmen.

"Color," Jeremy replied in a slightly higher-pitched voice than normal. "Color," he tried again after clearing his throat. "This frog is small and dark. Females tend to be a bit larger and darker."

"No, I mean, where did you learn that?"

"Oh, I grew up on a farm," Jeremy explained. "We had lots of these in our pond." He poked and prodded the frog, turning it onto its back and pinning its legs into the wax in a spread-eagle position. "I also was at a school that already covered this," he added. He looked in her direction again, smiled a hint of a smile, and then quickly turned back to concentrating on the frog.

Cute dimples, thought Betty. "A farm, huh. Where?" She studied Jeremy's face as he began to slice the frog down the middle with the scalpel.

"Kansas," he said without looking in her direction.

As disgusted as she was with the assignment, Betty found herself looking at the prone frog. "How come you moved here?"

"Hold this, will you?" Jeremy said, handing Betty the teasing needle in an attempt to change the subject. Reluctantly, she took it.

"Now, hold this piece of skin aside with the needle while I cut … right … here."

"Are you having fun?" Betty asked. There was a touch of a how-could-you-do-that-to this-poor-creature tone in her voice.

Jeremy ignored the question and took the teasing needle from her hand. "There," he said, using the needle as a pointer. "Take a look at that."

Betty leaned forward. "What am I looking at?" she asked.

"That's the esophagus."

"All right, class," Mr. Shennet interrupted. "We have only a few minutes left, and we need to clean up now. As soon as you and your partner have put everything away, you may be dismissed. And by the way, I have written your homework assignment on the board. Oh, and Jeremy, please see me before leaving the class. I need to give you your textbook for this course, along with some information about classroom rules and procedures. It won't take but a minute."

The class spilled into the busy hallway, and the students rushed off to stuff books into already overstuffed lockers. Lizzy and Carmen met Betty in the main foyer, as was their daily routine just before lunch. Amy, Lizzy's identical twin sister, joined the group; and the now-completed foursome headed to the cafeteria.

The last person to enter the cafeteria was Jeremy, who had taken several wrong turns in the unfamiliar building before deciding to ask directions. He had brought a bagged lunch and did not need to go through the lunch line, so he scanned the tables looking for a place to sit. Carmen, "the Torpedo," spotted him.

"Yoo-hoo! Jeremy!" she yelled, waving to the unsuspecting new boy on the block. Jeremy looked over in the direction of the voice. Every eye in the cafeteria looked over to see what new target the Torpedo had locked onto. "Come here and sit with us!" she yelled as she waved him over.

"Carmen," Betty scolded in a whispered and shocked voice. She leaned closer to her friend from the opposite side of the table. "What are you doing?"

"Just being friendly, my dear," replied Carmen with a sly smile.

Jeremy, his face now slightly red, walked with bag in hand to the long table where the foursome was seated. The table was overcrowded, but Carmen, who was sitting in the middle, slid-pushed some of the students aside to make room. She ignored their complaints and patted the newly-created space beside her. "Here. Sit here." Her smile was toothy and barn-door wide. Lizzy, Amy, and Betty looked down at their trays, shaking their heads at this display of unadulterated shamelessness.

Jeremy paused for a moment, looking from the empty space beside Carmen to other possible options in the cafeteria. He wasn't sure if he should take her up on her offer or flee. Betty looked up and tried to undo Jeremy's obvious discomfort.

"Thanks for doing the dissecting, Jeremy," she said.

"Oh, no problem," Jeremy replied without fully looking at her. "Tomorrow, I'll show you how males grip females."

Betty's brows furrowed in confusion, as did her three girlfriends and the rest of the students at the table. Everyone collectively stopped chewing and looked quizzically at Jeremy. A wave of red attacked his cheeks and neck as he realized how that had sounded. "I mean … sex," he hurriedly tried to explain. "I mean, the male frogs have these suction cups on their fingers that …"

"It's okay, Jeremy, I think I understand," Betty lied consolingly. A silent and not-so-silent chuckling began from some of those sitting around the table. Jeremy quickly scoured the room for another seat as far away from this table as possible. This was not how he wanted to begin his first day, and he hurriedly walked away.

"Carmen, how could you?" whispered Amy, darting icy stares at her friend.

"What'd I do?" exclaimed Carmen innocently. "Besides, are you telling me that you haven't noticed how gorgeous he is? Those incredible dimples. And from the way his shirt fit, I'll bet he's got one incredible body. He's mine ladies. All mine."

The final bell sounded and Betty, Amy, Lizzy and Carmen gathered together on the landing outside the doorway before going to their separate buses.

"Hey, Lizzy," Benny called out as he walked past. "Going to the dance Friday night?"

"Not if you are."

"Great! Save me a dance?"

"In your dreams!" She turned her back on her rejected classmate.

"Lizzy, give the poor guy a break," Amy said. "Benny's had a crush on you since first grade, for heaven's sake."

Lizzy shrugged. "But he's got the personality of a fried clam." She turned to her girlfriends. "You're all going to the dance, aren't you?"

"Of course," laughed Carmen.

"Wouldn't miss it," said Betty.

Several other students were now exiting the building, with Jeremy among them. Carmen spotted him as he walked past and grabbed his coat sleeve, pull-yanking him into the group. "Hi, Jeremy," she said with an exaggerated smile and flirtation drooling from her voice. She stood almost eyeball to eyeball with him.

Betty rolled her eyes. She found his shyness appealing and refreshing, and she felt sorry for this poor farm boy. Lizzy and Amy looked down at their feet but were not able to hide their grins at Carmen's trademark boldness.

"Oh," stammered Jeremy, "hi, um, ah …"

"Carmen."

"Hi, Carmen." He gave a sheepish grin and found it difficult to maintain eye contact.

"I just wanted you to know there's a dance Friday night in the gym. At 6:30. Maybe I'll see you there?" She brushed strands of her blonde hair aside with her rose-colored manicured nails.

"Ah, well, Carmen … I don't dance very well." Jeremy lied. He didn't want to guess what they would think if he told them he had never before danced in his life.

"That's okay, I'm a good teacher," Carmen said, resting a hand on his shoulder.

"Yeah, well, gotta go. See ya." Jeremy moved away and quickly headed in the direction toward his bus.

"Took off kind of fast, eh, Carmen?" chided Amy.

"Never to fear," said Carmen. "He will be mine, all six feet of that rock-hard hunk. You'll see."

"I don't know about that, Carmen," said Betty quietly. "I don't think he'll be an easy catch."

"All the better," Carmen replied, as if the future were a known certainty. "I love a challenge."

CHAPTER 19

THE DANCE

MARCH 13, 1964

On Friday night, Jeremy found himself with little appetite as he stared down at the plate in front of him.

"Jeremy, you have hardly touched your supper," said Grandma.

"Oh, I'm not that hungry," Jeremy replied.

"Something on your mind?"

"No."

He spoke these words with so little conviction that Grandma knew just the opposite was true. She sat quietly, waiting for him to speak. She knew he would talk when he was ready.

"Well, to tell you the truth, Grandma, other than the first day, things have been going pretty well at school. I seem to be fitting in all right, and I've made a few friends, but ..." He paused as he searched for the next words.

"Go on, Jeremy," Grandma gently encouraged.

"Well, there's a dance at the school tonight. I would really like to go, but, Grandma, I don't know how to dance, and I'd make a fool of myself if I went."

Grandma smiled. "Come with me, young man," she said. She stood and quickly left the table before her grandson could ask any questions. He didn't move. "Come, young man, right now!" she ordered. Reluctantly, he followed.

Grandma went into the living-room-by-day-bedroom-by-night and plugged in the phonograph player. She searched through her record collection and found one of her favorite Tommy Dorsey records from the Big Band era.

"Ah, here it is. Come," she again commanded as the music began to fill the small room. She held out her arms toward her grandson.

"Grandma, I can't dance with you!"

"And just why not? Am I too old for such a young pup?"

"Well, no, but you're my … grandma."

"No more of this nonsense." Grandma stepped forward and took Jeremy by the hand. "Now, this is how to properly hold your partner. Put your right arm around my waist like this." She guided his hand to her waist. "Now, take my right hand with your left."

"Grandma, I feel silly."

"Just do it. Ah, good. That's correct. Now, always remember to remain a proper eight inches away from your partner at all times. The gentleman should take the lead, but for now, I will do the leading." She slid her feet on the carpet, counting "one-two-three, one-two-three" as she pulled Jeremy gently this way and that. "Your grandfather and I would dance like this for hours."

Jeremy heard little of her reminiscing. He was concentrating on watching his feet to make sure they did not step on hers.

By 7:00 PM, the fourth song of the evening had ended and the students were gathering in groups around the gym or at the snack table. Mr. Shennet, one of the chaperones that evening, slowly maneuvered from group to group, doing his best to make sure everything remained orderly. He approached Betty and her friends, who were standing in a group talking to a few boys.

"Hi, Mr. Shennet," Amy said.

"Good evening, Amy," replied Mr. Shennet. "Having a good time?"

"Oh, Mr. Shennet, I'm Lizzy."

"One, two, three, four. No, you are Amy. I can count. Lizzy has five freckles on the bridge of her nose." The group laughed. Very few people could tell Amy and Lizzy apart, unless they knew the trick.

"I trust your in-depth discussion here is centered on a review of the anatomy of a grass frog for next week's test," Mr. Shennet continued.

"Sure thing, Mr. Shennet," said Harry. "We are definitely talking about anatomy." The students grinned and tried to hide their smirks at Harry's wisecrack.

"Well, Harry, I am truly glad to hear that. I will leave you now so that you all may resume your studies." A quick over-the-rim and he left with giggles in his wake and a smile on his face.

The speaker clicked on and the voice of the disc jockey was heard. "By request, the next song will be 'The Twist.' So grab your partner and start twisting." Benny grabbed Lizzy's hand, Harry grabbed Amy's, and the rest of the boys all but dragged the girls onto the dance floor before they had a chance to protest.

"Looks like your target isn't going to show up," Betty teased Carmen.

"Oh yeah?" smiled Carmen. "Look who just walked in. See ya." Betty's gaze followed the Torpedo as she lowered her head and fast-tracked in Jeremy's direction.

"Fire one," Betty quipped to herself just as three boys surrounded her. "The Torpedo has locked onto target. May God have mercy on his soul." She turned and headed to the dance floor with her three escorts.

Jeremy never saw Carmen coming until it was too late. "Let's dance," she ordered, grabbing him by the hand. Jeremy found himself being propelled to the middle of the dance floor. There, Carmen released his hand and began to twist. He stood motionless before her. He had heard of the Twist—not that Grandma had shown him how to dance to *that* song—but the way she gyrated and contorted her body amazed him. He stood stock still as he watched her move in ways that he did not know the human body was capable of moving, her blonde hair spewing out in all directions.

As Carmen rag-doll-flopped to Chubby Checker's voice, the other dancers began to part and form a circle around the pair. "Go, Carmen, go, Carmen," they chanted. Having an audience seemed to fuel her fire, and The Twist took on a whole new meaning. Jeremy slowly backed away and melted into the crowd.

Unsure of what to do next, Jeremy made his way to the snack table, grabbed a few chips, and munched while he studied the crowd. *This is not for me*, he thought, feeling completely out of place. *I never should have come.* He toyed with the idea of going home—he knew that if he didn't make a quiet exit now, he might be trapped again—but he was fascinated by the way in which the crowd cheered on Carmen.

Just then, he saw Betty looking in his direction from the edge of the circle. He gave a slight wave of his hand from hip level. She waved back and gestured for him to come over and join the group.

After a slight hesitation, he wiped his slightly greasy hands on his jeans and moved toward her. By now, Chubby Checker had stopped singing, and Jeremy's near six-foot height was sufficient for him to see the top of a blonde head moving through the crowd in search of someone. He froze, his eyes darting from Carmen to Betty, and back to Carmen.

Betty looked in the direction Jeremy was staring and was now able to see the blonde torpedo approaching. She understood the situation immediately. Moving toward him, she mouthed the words, "I'll protect you," hoping Jeremy could read lips.

"Thanks," he said with genuine relief when she got close enough, "but I think I should be going, and quickly."

"Carmen is one of my best friends, but she can be a handful at times," said Betty. "Don't go. Like I said, I'll protect you."

A slower song now began playing over the loudspeakers. "So," Jeremy began, "do you come to all these …" He stopped abruptly, and Betty saw the expression on his face turn to panic.

"What's the matter?" she said.

"She's headed this way!" Jeremy whispered back.

"Oh, then you had better ask me to dance."

Jeremy wasn't sure whether he should make a run for the exit or risk making a fool of himself on the dance floor. "Okay," he finally said. They moved to the center of the gymnasium, and stiffly and formally he placed his right hand around her waist. He took her right hand in his left just as Grandma had instructed, checking for the correct eight-inch gap. He had never held a girl before, and his knees weakened. "One-two-three, one-two-three," he whispered, not taking his eyes off his feet.

"Why are you counting?"

Jeremy looked up to answer. "Oh, well, I, uh …"

"Ouch!"

"Oh, did I step on your foot? I'm sorry. Maybe this isn't such a good idea." He released his hold on her and dropped his arms. Betty again took his hand in hers, pulled his arm back around her waist, and began to move rhythmically to the music. "It's okay, Jeremy. Relax. You're stiff as … ouch!"

"No, I'd better go." He started to break away from Betty a second time, but she refused to let him go.

"You're new at this dance stuff, aren't you?"

"You figured that out already, did you?"

"Yeah." She looked up into his red face and started to melt. "I'm quick like that. And just how long have you been dancing?"

"About two hours," he admitted sheepishly.

"Wow. A whole two hours."

"Yeah, my grandma gave me a dance lesson this afternoon." He rolled his eyes toward the ceiling. *Why did you have to go and admit that, you idiot?* Little did he know that, for Betty, his confession had only confirmed her attraction to him.

"Well, Jeremy Martel … ouch … you're doing just fine. A few more dances with me tonight and you'll be a pro."

Jeremy kept moving, but he could not believe he had heard her correctly. *She wants to dance with me again?* he thought.

"Um, are you sure your feet are up to it?" he asked.

"Absolutely! These are steel-tipped sneakers."

Jeremy looked down at her shoes. "Really?"

"No, Jeremy. I'm teasing." Betty wondered if all farm boys from Kansas were this naive.

"I knew that." He lied.

Lizzy and Amy stood on the perimeter of the dance floor with Carmen seething beside them. "Well, Carmen," Lizzy said, "looks like Betty has a new dance partner."

"Just look at them," Carmen said in disgust. "If I had known dancing with him might have put me in traction, I never would have chanced it."

Chapter 20

Lost Notes

March 14, 1964

Betty was still in her bathrobe the following morning when she heard the phone ring downstairs. It rang three times before her father picked it up. "Hello, Maguire residence," he said. There was a pause, and then he repeated, "Hello?"

Betty adjusted her hair, which was still in curlers, and listened to what her father was saying. "Yes, Betty is here. Who is this?" Upon hearing her name, she moved to the top of the stairs, where she could more easily hear the conversation. "Wait one minute, Jeremy, while I …"

Betty took the stairs two at a time.

"… see if she's available." Her father stared in wonder as she snatched the phone from his hand. He gave her a knowing smile as she shooed him away with a few quick waves of her hand. She sat on the chair by the telephone stand, held the phone to her chest, and breathed deeply before answering. "Hello? … Oh, hi, Jeremy … Yes, my feet are fine. The doctor says I'll be out of the cast in a few weeks." She chuckled.

There was silence on the other end of the line. *Stupid! Stupid! Stupid! I can't believe I said that.*

Her father gave her a quizzical look from the kitchen, where he was picking through a bowl of fruit which was on the counter near the doorway. "Jeremy," Betty said, "would you hold on for one moment, please?" She held her hand tightly over the speaker of the phone and said in a desperately-annoyed whisper, "Father, will you please stop eavesdropping!" She never referred to him as "father" unless—and this was one of those "unless" moments.

Betty twisted in the chair for more privacy and returned the phone to her ear. "I am very sorry, Jeremy, but sometimes I have to deal with a juvenile in this house … Oh, no, I don't have any siblings. But sometimes I have to put an oversized child in his place." She turned and glared at her father again. He was now standing in the doorway of the kitchen with an apple in hand and a banana grin stretched across his face.

"What? Going jogging? Oh, no," she laughed, remembering her joke. "I guess I won't be doing that after.… Sure, I have all the notes from the biology labs.… Really? How could you lose them? … Two o'clock? Well, possibly. Let me check my calendar. Could you hold on for just a moment? Thanks." Betty held the phone to her chest again, swung the chair around and waved her free hand frantically to get her father's attention. "Is it okay?" she mouthed, her knees bouncing like nervous pogo sticks.

"Is what okay, dear?" he asked with feigned ignorance. He chomped into the apple.

"Dad, can he come over this afternoon at 2:00?" Her eyes narrowed to glaring slits.

For five agonizing seconds, her father stared at the ceiling in deep thought—a stunt, she was sure, to make her suffer—and then gave the nod. She gave him the look she had learned from Mr. Shennet, though she was not sure how effective it was without the glasses, and again turned her back on him. "That seems like it would work out well," she said, holding the phone to her ear. "Okay, then. See you at 2:00. Goodbye."

"So, 'lost his notes,' did he?" Mr. Maguire mockingly teased.

Betty ignored him and dashed up the stairs to her bedroom. She looked into the mirror over her bureau. *I'm a horror show,* she thought.

I don't have time to get ready. He'll be here in just.... She looked at the alarm clock on her night stand. *Four hours.*

By 1:50 PM, Betty was pacing the floor. "For Pete's sake, will you sit down?" her father pleaded from his overstuffed recliner. He was watching the Red Sox battle the Yankees, but was finding himself distracted by her constant flittering around the room. "Or at least go play the piano. That's the fourth time in ten minutes you've straightened those magazines. I'm sure this boy ... what's his name again? George?"

"It's Jeremy ... and you know that, Father!"

"I'm sure Jeremy couldn't care less what the coffee table looks like."

"I don't want him thinking we live in a pig pen," Betty snapped back. "And would you please tuck in that shirt? And turn the television down?" She walked over to the set and adjusted the volume, and then sat gingerly on the edge of the couch.

The knock on the front door was firm. Betty jumped from her seat and checked herself in the hallway mirror one last time for any out-of-place hairs or wrinkles in her sweater. Mr. Maguire lowered the footrest of the recliner, stood up, and headed for the front door, obediently tucking in his shirt on the way. Betty turned, and with an upraised palm and piercing glare warned her father to back off—or else. Mr. Maguire raised both hands in a gesture of surrender and stood a discreet distance behind his daughter.

Betty inhaled deeply and opened the door. "Hi, Jeremy!" she said, her smile horizon-wide. "Come in."

Jeremy stood where he was on the doorstep. He knew his lower jaw had dropped, but there was nothing he could do about it. For a moment he just stood mute, staring at her.

"Is something ... wrong?" Betty asked, breaking the awkward silence.

Jeremy slammed his jaw shut and swallowed hard. "Ah, no, it's just that ... well, are you planning on going out somewhere? If so, I can come back another time."

"What makes you think I'm going out?"

"Well, you look … great … I mean, you seem really dressed up for a Saturday afternoon."

Mr. Maguire raised an eyebrow.

Betty blushed. *The perfect words.* "Thanks," she said, stepping aside. "Come in."

Mr. Maguire crossed his arms and looked Jeremy up and down.

Oh, great, her father hates me already, Jeremy thought. He was trying hard to keep his knees from knocking together too loudly.

"Dad," Betty said, "I'd like you to meet Jeremy Martel. Jeremy, this is my dad."

Mr. Maguire's handshake was firm. "Pleased, I'm sure," he said.

"Pleased to meet you as well, sir." Jeremy tried to smile, though he had an uneasy feeling that he had just received a warning.

Betty invited Jeremy in and led him to the kitchen table, where she had laid out the lab notes and diagrams. "Did you bring a pencil and paper to copy the notes?"

"Oh, no, I … uh … thought maybe we could just study together rather than waste all that time copying. And since it will be about suppertime, maybe we could go out and get a burger and Coke. If that's all right with your folks, I mean." Jeremy quickly added the last part when he saw Mr. Maguire walk into the kitchen with an apparent sudden need to wrap up the trash in the nearly empty wastebasket.

"Oh, I'm sure it would be. Right, Dad?"

"Fine with me," said Mr. Maguire, "but you had better check with your mother. You know how she gets when—"

"When I get what?" The voice came from the deck off the kitchen through an opened sliding-glass door. Mrs. Maguire entered, holding a potted plant in rubber-gloved hands. Jeremy now knew where Betty had gotten her flaming red hair.

Mr. Maguire made a quick switch from his original intended comment. "When you've been preparing such a wonderful meal, my dear." He moved forward to give her a hug.

"Don't you try to hug me you … you … and be careful. I just repotted this plant."

Mr. Maguire looked at Jeremy. "She's always at a loss for words when she's around me." He then feigned agony from a half-hearted slap on his shoulder.

"Mom, Dad, please ..." said Betty, thoroughly embarrassed that this act had taken place in front of Jeremy.

Mrs. Maguire took the hint and for the first time acknowledged the guest. "You must be Jeremy," she said. "I've heard so much about you." She set the plant in the sink, removed her gloves, and held out her hand. Jeremy shook it and looked at Betty, who seemed to be searching for the nearest hole to crawl into. "And, of course, I do not mind at all if you two go out for dinner. We were just going to have grilled cheese sandwiches anyway."

"But what about the—" Mr. Maguire blurted.

Mrs. Maguire shot her husband a look that said, *If you mention that roast I put in the oven ten minutes ago, you'll be wearing it.* He caught the hint. "Now," she continued, "you two need some uninterrupted time to study, so Mr. Maguire and I will retire to the living room and watch some baseball."

Mr. Maguire looked shocked. "But you never watch—"

Another look from Mrs. Maguire made him shut his mouth in a blink. "Come, dear," she said, taking him by the arm and leading him into the living room.

The two had been studying for about an hour when Betty heard Jeremy's stomach growl. "Time to go for that burger?" she asked.

"To tell you the truth, it was time an hour ago. I'm starved."

Betty smiled. "See you later, Mom and Dad!" she yelled to her parents. They were still sitting on the couch in front of the television, leaning against each other and holding hands. "Be back in a while." Betty dragged Jeremy by the shirtsleeve out the door, leaving the science notes scattered on the table. She walked quickly down the walkway in an effort to escape before her dad had a chance to set a curfew.

She groaned when she heard the living room window being raised. "You two be back before dark, you hear?" Mr. Maguire yelled.

"Yes, Dad!" Betty called back without looking up. "Parents," she said to Jeremy. "Sometimes they drive me nuts."

Jeremy had parked Grandma's truck just out front. He approached and put his hand on the passenger side door handle, but Betty suggested, "Let's walk. There's a place just down the street that serves a great hamburger."

The "just down the street" walk turned out to be almost two miles to the center of town. "So tell me about yourself," Betty said as they walked.

"Well, what do you want to know?" Jeremy asked, his hands firmly planted in his pockets. He was trying hard to avoid looking into her face. He couldn't believe that such a popular, beautiful girl—a natural, no-makeup beauty—would go out with a guy like him.

"Oh, how about everything."

"Well, that won't take too long."

"Okay, then, let's do this. I ask you a question, and then you get to ask one. Let's start with something simple. Do you have any brothers or sisters?"

"Nope. And I know you don't."

"Yup. That's one."

Jeremy assumed that "that's one" meant it was the first question. "Okay, now it's my turn to ask you a question. What nicknames have you been called?"

"You're kidding, right? Look at what I've inherited from my mother. 'Carrot Top.' And the next person to call me that better be able to duck—and fast!" She clenched her fist in a mock threat.

"Wow, calm down. I guess I pushed a button there."

"Sorry. It's just that I've heard it all my life and … well, anyway, you get the point. Next question. What do you think of my lifelong friends since grade school, Lizzy, Amy, and Carmen?"

Jeremy smiled at the image of two beach balls with heads that popped into his mind. Betty stopped walking and looked at him. "What are you smiling at?" she said.

"Oh, I was just thinking about how identical Lizzy and Amy are. And they have really nice personalities." *Good recovery.*

"Yes, they do … don't they," Betty said somewhat suspiciously. "What about Carmen?" Betty enjoyed watching Jeremy squirm at the mention of the Torpedo.

"Well, Carmen is … how shall I put this?"

"Unique?" Betty volunteered.

"Yeah, right. Unique."

"Okay," said Betty, "next question."

"But you just asked one," objected Jeremy.

"My game, my rules. So … what are your plans after high school?"

"Whoa, that's a tough one," said Jeremy, a bit taken aback. "I have no idea. Right now I'm just looking for a part-time job to help out me and my grandma."

Betty smiled, and the two continued to small-talk for almost an hour as they slowly made their way to the restaurant. Jeremy's initial jitters had gone, and he found himself growing comfortable in Betty's presence. For the first time in a long while, he found himself talking about things from his past—not in great detail, just the good memories.

The pair arrived at the restaurant, where a gum-chewing, bleached-blonde waitress seated them in a booth near the back. The two had arrived at the peak dinner hour, and it was the only place left in the popular diner. The waitress placed menus in front of them and then left to tend to other customers. Jeremy and Betty studied the menus in silence.

After a few minutes, the waitress returned and placed two glasses of water on the table. "So what's it gonna be?" she asked, snapping a bubble.

Jeremy nodded for Betty to order first. "I'll have the double cheeseburger with onion, the curly fries and a large Coke, no ice," she said. She looked at Jeremy and noticed he had a strange look on his face. The conversation about his looking for a part-time job returned to her mind, and she realized she might have just over-ordered. "On second thought, make it a single burger, no cheese or fries, and a small Coke."

The waitress, making no effort to write the order down, looked at Jeremy and snapped a second bubble between her teeth. "I'll have the double cheeseburger with onion, the curly fries and a large Coke, no ice," he said. "Oh, and she will have the same." The waitress left to place the order.

Betty leaned forward. "That's two," she said into his ear.

Jeremy looked puzzled. "Two what?"

"I'll tell you later."

When the meal was over, the waitress returned and asked the couple if they would be having dessert. Jeremy said no, and she handed him the bill for $4.75. He pulled his wallet from a back pocket, removed $5—his total weekly allowance from Grandma—and handed it to the waitress. "Keep the change," he said.

The waitress looked down at the $5 bill. "Gee, thanks, a whole quarter," she said and walked away.

Jeremy moved to slide out of the booth. "Well," Betty said, "was I right or was I right?"

"About what?"

"About the burger. Wasn't it the best you've ever had?"

"Oh, yeah, it sure was." He lied. *Some day I'll have to introduce you to one of Grandma's onion and green pepper burgers,* he thought. He glanced down at his watch. "Well, I guess we should be heading back. It will be dark in a little more than an hour."

"Not yet. There's still plenty of time."

"But your dad may not take it too kindly if I get you back after dark."

"Oh, don't worry about Dad. I can handle him. Besides, there's someone downtown whom I want you to meet."

"Who?"

"My Uncle Alex. You'll love him. He's the most fun person I have ever known."

Betty led Jeremy down Main Street, pointing out the best and worst places to shop, and then turned left onto Market Street. "Just a short way down here," she said.

"Uh, Betty, does your uncle live on this street?"

She laughed. "Some people would say that."

A few moments later the two had reached the destination. "Well, here we are," she said, opening the door that led to Red's Gym.

Jeremy stood outside. For the second time that evening, he found his jaw had unconsciously dropped open.

"Well, come on," Betty encouraged, holding the door open.

Jeremy slowly followed and breathed a sigh of relief when she turned right and headed up the short flight of stairs to the small hallway at the main entrance. On the far side of the room, another flight of stairs turned left around a corner and went up to the second and third floors. Betty pointed in that direction. "Up those stairs," she explained, "are rooms that my uncle rents for next to nothing to people who are … well, down on their luck, I guess would be the best way to put it. But we're going in here."

Betty pushed open a set of doors that creaked on their hinges. Jeremy stepped inside and was fascinated by what he saw. The room housed an eight-lane bowling alley, with every lane in use. Several tables had been set around the room, and five or six men were sitting at each table. Most of them had lighted or half-chewed cigar stubs sticking out the sides of their mouths, and they were sipping beer from glass bottles. Loud cheering erupted when a bowler threw a strike, and even louder cheering when one threw a gutter ball. Jeremy wondered how he was going to explain to Grandma—or, worse still, to Betty's father—the smell of stale smoke and alcohol that he knew was beginning to cling to every fiber of his clothes and hair.

The two stood for a moment just inside the doors and watched the crowd. Jeremy noticed one table near the entrance, where five occupants sat ignoring the bowlers. "Come on, Charlie," the gravelly-voiced dealer at the table demanded with impatience. "You want any cards or no? We ain't got all night." He was holding a cigar between the thumb and little finger of his right hand, which were the only fingers he had on that hand. He jammed the cigar back into his mouth, and puffs of smoke rapidly spewed out. His full beard was untrimmed, and his hair—or what there was of it—was disheveled. There was something about him that made Jeremy think he was only about fifty, even though he looked to be eighty.

The one called Charlie looked carefully at the hand he had been dealt and appeared unsure of what to do. He laid the five cards face down on the table, scratched his nose with his forefinger, and then picked them up again. Jeremy noticed the man's shirtsleeve on his left arm was pinned up at his elbow.

"Yeah, Charlie," a third player said. He was squat and had a belly that made him look third-trimester pregnant. He leaned his chair back on its rear legs and held his own set of cards close to his chest. "I got to get home to the little woman sometime this weekend."

The group of men let out a howl. "*Little* woman?" the dealer chided. "Why, Brady, that little woman of yours is a head taller than you and 300 pounds if she's an ounce."

Brady seemed to take no offense at the wisecrack. He smiled a wide, cigar-stuffed grin, planted the front legs of his chair back onto the floor, and said, "You gents are just jealous that I, at least, have a woman. Now, can we get back to playin' cards? I'm about to walk away with the biggest pot of the night."

"Charlie, you made up your mind yet?" the dealer said, his impatience growing.

"Now, now, my fine friends," Charlie said out of the left side of his mouth as he chewed on the unlit cigar stub protruding from the right side. "You can't rush perfection." He looked again at the cards he held and resumed his contemplation.

"Perfection?" said Brady. "Charlie, you ain't won a hand all night."

Betty moved a few steps closer to the table. "Hi, guys," she said. She stood behind Charlie, placed her hands gently on his shoulders, and looked down at the cards he held. The card playing stopped as all the men became aware of the intruders.

"Hey, it's Betty," said Charlie with genuine pleasure. "Look, guys, it's Betty." He placed his cards down and affectionately patted the hand that lay on his left shoulder. Soon the entire room had turned its attention in her direction, with men waving and yelling hellos. Betty returned the wave, and most of them settled back into the Saturday night routine.

"Charlie, have you lost some weight?" Betty asked. "You're more handsome than ever."

"Yeah, down to nearly 200," Charlie said as he sucked in his gut.

"Hey, Betty, been a long time," the gravelly voice said from across the table.

"Too long, Pinky. You still dealing from the bottom of the deck?" The men howled, loving the jibe. Pinky smiled and winked.

"Good to see you, Betty," the fourth player said.

"You too, Henry. How's your wife doing?"

"Oh, she's hanging in there."

"Twins this time, isn't it?"

Henry's scarred, whiskered face broke into a proud grin at the question. "That's what the doc says. Due any day now."

"Let's all pray they look like your wife," said Pinky. Laughter erupted.

Betty walked around the table to where Henry was sitting. She put her arms around his neck and gave him a gentle hug and a peck on his unshaven cheek. "Well, Henry, as for me, I'd be really pleased if they all looked like my favorite guy."

"Hey, I thought I was your favorite guy," said the fifth player with an exaggerated pout.

"That was last month, Macky." She reached over and mussed Macky's hair. He blushed, but he seemed to be enjoying the attention.

"Anyway, Henry," said Betty, "you let me know when they come, and I'll be right over to baby-sit the triplets."

"Thanks," said Henry. "I'm going to need all the help I can get."

Betty walked back to Charlie and looked over his shoulder at the hand he held. She leaned forward and whispered, "Go for it, Charlie."

"Really? You think I should go for it?" he asked, surprised at the advice.

"Yup."

The others looked at each other, and then at Betty suspiciously. Charlie, the last to place his bet, asked for one card. When he picked it up and realized he had just made an inside straight, he could hardly contain his excitement. The others immediately folded and threw their cards into the middle of the table. Disgusted comments could be heard muttered under their breath.

"Anytime he looks like that," Pinky said, "I know it's time to fold."

"You've got to learn how to keep your poker face, Charlie," said Betty as she patted his shoulder.

Charlie laid down his cards and revealed the straight. "Read 'em and weep, gentlemen." He leaned forward and raked in the $2.32 pot in the middle of the table. "I hope you can stay the rest of the night, Betty. You're good luck."

"Not tonight, Charlie. I've got to be going in a few minutes. I just stopped by to see Uncle Alex and introduce my friend to him." She turned and waved for Jeremy, who had not moved from the doorway, to join them. "Guys, this is Jeremy." The men at the table nodded in his direction, with a few giving a finger-tip salute to the forehead. Jeremy smiled weakly, nodded back, and moved closer.

"Has anyone seen my uncle?" Betty asked.

"Yeah," said Pinky. "He'll be right out. He just went into the crapper, and—"

Macky slapped Pinky up the back side of his head. "Hey, dummy, can't you see there's a lady present?"

"Oh, sorry, Betty," said Pinky.

"No problem, Pinky. I'll just wait here until …" Suddenly, massive arms gripped Betty around her waist and lifted her up off the floor. "Uncle Alex," she scolded, "put me down. This is embarrassing."

"Well, well, if it ain't my best girl," her uncle said, gently lowering her.

Betty turned and was engulfed in her uncle's hug. She looked at Jeremy. "Uncle Alex," she said, "there is someone I want you to meet. This is Jeremy. Jeremy, this is my uncle Alex."

The smile immediately disappeared from Big Red's face. "Yes, we've met," he said quietly. He narrowed his eyes as he glanced at Jeremy.

"You've met?" asked Betty. "When? Where?"

"It's a long story," Big Red said without looking at his niece. "How you doing, kid?" He extended his glove-sized hand in Jeremy's direction. Jeremy swallowed hard and cautiously took the hand in his. He expected his fingers to be crushed, but was surprised to find it a gentle handshake.

Betty picked up on Jeremy's uneasiness. "Well, since you already know each other, I guess I can get right down as to why I wanted you two to meet. Uncle Alex, Jeremy needs a job, and since you own this building …" Both men gaped at Betty, and then Big Red's face slowly broke into a smile. "Well, I know you've been looking for someone to work around here. Heaven knows you could stand to have this place fixed up a bit. What do you say, Uncle Alex?"

Jeremy looked horrified. "Betty," he objected through gritted teeth, "I can find my own—"

"Okay," said Big Red, "I'm willing if you are, kid. I'll pay a buck an hour and give you free use of the gym."

"Make it a buck twenty-five," Betty negotiated. "Not a penny less." Jeremy's face turned multiple shades of red, but he could find no words to say.

Big Red looked at Betty, tossed his head back and roared a laugh that caused a few bowlers to throw gutter balls. He turned to Jeremy and placed a bone-crushing hand on his shoulder. "Your manager drives a hard bargain, kid."

"Uncle Alex, I'm not his manager," said Betty, "and his name is Jeremy, not kid."

"Okay, okay," said Big Red. This was not the first time his niece had put him in his place. "Sorry, kid." Betty rolled her eyes. "And, yeah, I could use some help. Seems there's a new hole in the wall that needs to be re-plastered. So, Jeremy, a buck twenty-five plus the gym it is. But I expect no less than ten hours a week of solid work. Deal?" He again extended his hand.

Jeremy was in shock. *A buck twenty-five an hour, plus the gym?* he thought. *Can I afford to pass up the offer? But why would this man want me to work for him, especially after …*

Big Red's hand hung in midair. "Well, deal or not?" he said. Jeremy was amazed to find himself shaking the outstretched hand.

"Good. Be here Monday at 3:00, and I'll show you what I need to have done."

"Oh, my gosh!" Betty exclaimed as she looked at the clock hanging over the entranceway. "Look at the time. We need to be going, Uncle Alex, or Dad will shoot us." She hugged the big man and headed for the door while a chorus of goodbyes from the card players rang out. Betty turned and acknowledged the men with one wave and a smile, and then pushed open the doors. Jeremy followed, still in shock over all that had just transpired.

Betty stopped once she had stepped outside and looked at Jeremy. "I really just needed to get away from that cigar smoke," she said, not wanting the evening to end. "Let's take the long way home, and I'll show you a different side of the neighborhood."

"But you said your father would—"

"I told you, I can deal with Dad," she said. "He's really not the ogre he appears to be. Besides, we've got another good hour before dark."

Betty led him on a longer route back to her house. They walked in silence for a while before Betty spoke. "You're awfully quiet, Jeremy. Is anything wrong?"

Jeremy hesitated a moment. "No … well … yes. It's just that I was downright embarrassed back there at your uncle's place. I don't know whether I should thank you or be mad at you. Maybe I should make you do all the dissecting next week in lab when we do the fish." He laughed.

"Oh, Jeremy, I am so sorry. I didn't think you would mind. Please don't be angry with me. I know I can sometimes be a bit pushy, but on the way here you mentioned that you were looking for a part-time job. I knew my uncle needed someone. He's really picky about who works for him, and he wouldn't have hired you just on my say-so, so I wanted the two of you to meet."

"He's picky about who works for him?" Jeremy asked, genuinely amazed.

"Yes, really picky. Whatever happened when you two met earlier must have really impressed him, though I must say you both seemed to have a bit of an attitude toward each other."

Jeremy chuckled. "Yes, I *really* impressed him." He went on to explain the story of his two encounters with her uncle. Betty couldn't stop laughing when Jeremy pantomimed the lift that sent him to the floor and the way that her uncle had tossed him out of the gym. "Anyway," said Jeremy, wrapping up the story, "I really could use the work. So I guess I should thank you for that. Now, since I answered two questions in a row for you on our way here, you've got to answer two for me. First, why is your uncle called 'Big Red'?"

Betty seemed surprised that Jeremy had not put the pieces together. "Jeremy, think about it. What do you think my mother, my uncle—from ... my ... mother's ... side—and I all used to have in common?"

"Oh, I get it."

"Congratulations," she said with a touch of sarcasm. "You should have seen the head of red hair my uncle had when he was younger. He began to lose it in his thirties, and within a few months he was completely bald. It was a shock the first time I saw that monster bald as an eagle. And your second question is ..."

"Yeah, those men back there. Who are they? How do you know them so well?"

"Well, as I said, many of those men are down on their luck, and others are homeless war veterans. Charlie is the oldest. He's just shy of seventy and still tough as nails, but he's the sweetest old man. He lost his arm in World War I at the Battle of Belleau Wood. A machine gun tore it off, and he almost died on the battlefield. Pinky lost his fingers during World War II when he picked up a German grenade that had landed in his foxhole. It exploded just as he was throwing it back. That's how he got his nickname, 'Pinky,' as it's the only finger he has left on that hand. As for the others ... well, some are veterans from the Korean conflict. They're not that old, but they still carry a lot of baggage from those horrors. Others are just having a hard time finding a job. Uncle Alex hires them from time to time, and he puts them up in his building."

"You seem to genuinely like them. And they obviously like you."

"Every now and then I'll bake some cookies and bring them over. It gives me a chance to sit and listen to them reminisce. They are all such sweet men. They're a bit rough around the edges, but God loves them, and I've grown to love them as well."

Jeremy had been watching Betty's face with great interest, but at the mention of God his face fell and he looked at the sidewalk.

"I hope I didn't say anything that offended you," Betty said when she picked up on the change in his demeanor.

"Oh, no, not at all," Jeremy said, almost too quickly. "We're taking a long route back to your house."

Betty noticed the change in the topic, but said nothing. The two walked on, and Jeremy continued to share stories about growing up on the farm in Kansas. He told her about swimming in the pond on the far side of the farm with Sylvester, and about the tornado, and about his great-great-grandfather Jonas and his great-grandfather Elias. Betty noticed that Jeremy seemed to be enjoying his own reminiscing. At first she had thought she would have to pull his teeth to get this shy boy to talk.

"I'm named after my grandfather and great-grandfather, Jeremiah Elias Martel," he said at length. He did not know why he felt it important to share that information.

"You seem proud of your family, Jeremy," said Betty softly, wondering what had happened to his parents. She assumed they had died, given the fact that he lived with his grandmother, but he volunteered no details of the events or the pain he still felt.

Jeremy nodded and looked away. "I guess I've been running off at the mouth. I don't usually talk so much."

"Don't be sorry. I've enjoyed every minute of it. Would you like to know my middle name?"

"Sure."

"It's Virginia. Elizabeth Virginia Maguire. Virginia was my grandmother's name. She died when I was eight."

Jeremy stopped and gave her a strange look. "Why are you looking at me like that?" she asked.

"Virginia was my mother's name," he said quietly.

Betty was tempted to ask about his mother, but thought better of it when Jeremy became silent and seemed to drift away. They walked on for several minutes when their hands bumped together. Jeremy felt a shockwave pass through his body, as if he had accidentally touched an electrified fence wire. He jumped and pulled his hand away.

"I don't bite," Betty said. Uncertain of the message she had just given him, he moved his hand closer and locked his little finger onto hers. She accepted it, which gave him the courage to take her whole hand in his. The sounds of nature were the only conversation they heard for the rest of the short walk back to Betty's house. Each was afraid that words would break the magic of the moment.

Betty let go of Jeremy's hand when they turned onto her street. "Dad," she said, offering a one-word explanation. Jeremy nodded his understanding. He stopped and shoved his hands into his pockets when they reached the walkway that led to Betty's front porch. She turned to face him. He paused before speaking, and then said, "Betty, I have a confession to make."

"Oh?" she said, feeling a little concerned at the tone in his voice. "You're not married, are you?" She giggled at her attempt at humor as she tried to read his face.

"No," he replied as if missing the joke. "I … lied to you."

"What do you mean? When?"

"I didn't really lose my notes. I just wanted to see you, and couldn't think of anything else to say."

Betty was filled with relief. "Feel free to lose your notes any time."

"Okay … well then, I was planning on losing them again next Saturday, and I was wondering if you would like to go to Paragon Park to help me look for them. If I can borrow Grandma's truck again, that is."

Betty's heart raced. "I would love to go. But what's a 'Paragon Park?'"

"It's an amusement park down on the South Shore," he replied. He was a bit surprised she didn't know about it, as he was supposed to be the new kid on the block.

"Oh, now I remember. Carmen has talked about it, but I've never been there, or to any amusement park, really, except for the occasional local carnivals."

"Really?"

"Really. Carmen keeps telling me I need to get a life."

Jeremy chuckled.

"How did you find out about an amusement park on the South Shore? You've only been here two weeks."

"My grandma. She grew up on the South Shore until her family moved to Clayton. She thought Paragon Park was her personal playground. Before I started school here, she showed me all around the area. Paragon Park was on her must-see list. It was part of her drive down memory lane."

"Well, then, starting next Saturday I'll 'get a life' and go there with you."

"You'll love it. My favorite ride is the roller coaster."

"Uh oh. Carmen told me about her first experience on the roller coaster. She threw up when the ride ended and swore she would never go on it again. Maybe I'll just watch you. Anyway, I'll have to check with my parents, but I think you passed the test this afternoon with my dad."

"Test? What test?"

"The handshake test. It's how my dad checks a person's character when he first meets them. Did you notice it was just shy of bone crushing?"

"Yes," Jeremy said as he rubbed his hand.

"Well, you didn't wince. So for the moment, you're in with him. But then there is my mother."

"You think she'll object to your going out with me again?"

"Not if we meet her basic requirement for a second date."

"Which is?"

"My mom told me not to get involved with a guy unless I have three things in common with him."

"So, Elizabeth Virginia Maguire, was that what the 'that's one' and 'that's two' all about?"

"Yes, Jeremiah Elias Martel, it was. We have two things in common. One, we are both only children; and two, we both like double cheeseburgers with onion, curly fries and large Cokes, easy on the ice. All we need is a number three. Got any suggestions?"

"Hmm, let's see." Jeremy rubbed his chin in thought. "When is your birthday?"

"August fifth."

"Well, then, there's number three."

"Don't tell me your birthday is August fifth."

"No, but we both have birthdays."

Betty looked at Jeremy and shook her head. "You're weird."

"Yeah, I've heard that before. So what do you think?"

"It works for me."

CHAPTER 21

THE GREAT DECEPTION

MARCH 21, 1964

The wait for his next date with Betty was agonizing, but finally Saturday arrived. Jeremy arrived at the Maguire home and was welcomed at the door by Betty's mother. She led him into the living room to wait while Betty finished her primping. "So, Jeremy," she said, "how is the job going? Is my brother treating you well?"

"Yes, ma'am," said Jeremy, "though I don't think I worked this hard even back on the farm. I've been scraping and patching and painting, and I haven't even begun to scratch the surface of what that building needs. And the wiring! I do okay with the painting and carpentry, but when it comes to electrical and mechanical things, I'm lost. But that wiring is *long* overdue for an update. I think I could have a lifetime of employment there."

Mrs. Maguire smiled at the comment. "I know what you mean. Alex has never been one to show an aptitude for that kind of work—which, to be honest, surprises me, because our father was a handyman's handyman. But I know he is quite taken with you. I talked with him just yesterday, and he said you're the best worker he's ever had. Trust me, that is no small compliment. For some reason, the help he's hired in the past just hasn't stayed very long. Can you imagine?" There was a twinkle in her eye.

"No, ma'am," Jeremy laughed. "I can't imagine why."

Just then Betty came down the stairs and entered the room. "What have you two been talking about?" she asked. Mrs. Maguire looked at Jeremy and smiled when she saw his eyes widen and noticed the sudden trouble he seemed to have swallowing.

"Jeremy was just telling me about the work he's doing for Uncle Alex," Mrs. Maguire replied. "Isn't that right, Jeremy?" Jeremy could only nod, unable to take his eyes off Betty.

Betty looked at her mother, and then back at Jeremy. "Is anything wrong?" she asked coyishly. She seemed to be enjoying herself immensely.

Jeremy shook his head slowly and squeaked out, "Not a thing." He cleared his throat and tried again when he realized his words hadn't come out quite right. "Not a thing. It's just that you look …" He glanced down at his vintage sneakers covered with paint spots, his clean but less-than-new dungarees, and his pullover T-shirt. "You look incredible," he finally managed to say.

Betty laughed. "Oh, you mean these old things?"

Mrs. Maguire rolled her eyes. "These old things" had just been purchased that morning after Betty had dragged her from store to store looking for the perfect amusement park outfit. But she would keep the secret.

Mrs. Maguire watched the pair leave from the living room window. Although her daughter received a host of invitations from many young men, she was particular about the boys she went out with, and she did not date all that much. When she did accept an offer, the guy would usually sit in his car and honk the horn. If Mr. Maguire was home, he would not even let Betty get off the couch until the date came to the front door so he could shake his hand.

Mrs. Maguire noticed that Jeremy opened the passenger side door of the truck for Betty before going around to let himself in. She nodded her approval as the two drove away.

After a few minutes, Betty realized they were not headed for the highway. "Jeremy, are we taking a detour?" she asked.

"No, but my grandmother insisted I bring you to meet her. Do you mind?" This was only a half truth. Grandma had mentioned a few times that she would like to meet this new friend with whom her grandson was so taken, but Jeremy actually wanted to go home to change his clothes.

A few minutes later, Jeremy opened the door to the apartment and called out, "Grandma?"

"I'm in the kitchen."

"Of course, where else," Jeremy said. He invited Betty inside and closed the door. "The kitchen is my grandma's pride and joy." Betty made a quick survey around the room and noticed there was not a thing out of place or speck of dust on any surface.

"What are you doing back here so soon?" Grandma said from the kitchen. "I thought you had a date with that young lady you keep talking about."

Jeremy had a sudden need to look at the ceiling. "You keep talking about me?" teased Betty, enjoying his discomfort. "And just what do you say?"

"Oh, the usual."

"Which is?"

Just then, Grandma entered the living room, temporarily saving Jeremy from further punishment. "Oh, my," she said, wiping her hands on her apron. "Why, Jeremy, she is more stunning than you described." She walked to Betty with outstretched hand.

Jeremy picked up a magazine and began leafing through it. Betty noticed that it was upside down. "Thank you, Mrs. Martel," she said as she shook hands.

"Oh, everyone calls me Grandma. If you call me Mrs. Martel, I won't know who you're talking to. Now come with me." Grandma took Betty by the hand. "I can use your help in the kitchen while we get acquainted." Betty looked over her shoulder at Jeremy, who only shrugged.

Once in the kitchen, Grandma handed Betty an apron. "Don't want those new clothes getting all floured up now, do we?" she said. She took some bowls out of the cupboard and handed one to Betty.

A half-hour later, Betty and Grandma re-entered the living room. "Really?" Betty exclaimed. "He really did that when he was seven?"

Jeremy, now in slacks, a dress shirt and his best pair of shoes, was sitting on the couch, browsing through an old *Sports Illustrated* magazine he had found at Big Red's. "Did what?" he asked. "Grandma, what have you been telling her?"

"Just women's talk. Now you two go on and have a good time. Maybe later you can stop by and we can enjoy some of that chocolate layer cake."

The first ride inside the entrance to Paragon Park was the Scrambler. "Shall we?" Jeremy said. Not waiting for an answer, he headed toward the ticket booth.

Betty watched the ride spin and twist. She was not sure she wanted to get on it, but she said nothing while Jeremy bought the tickets. The ride started slowly, but within seconds it was up to full speed. Jeremy was in his glory. Centrifugal force caused Betty to be pushed up against him. She held onto the side rail.

Two minutes later, the couple stepped out of the ride. "Well? What did you think?" Jeremy asked.

"I think I'm going to like this park," she said with childlike excitement. "I guess I really did need to get a life. What's next?"

Jeremy took her on the Tilt-a-Whirl, followed by the Caterpillar. Then they stopped at a ring toss game, where he became obsessed with winning her a stuffed animal. After the fourth try, she took him by the arm and pulled him away.

"But I wanted you to have something to take home," he said.

"I already do," she said softly as she looked at him. Her green eyes sparkled, and her face was lit with a radiance that melted Jeremy's heart. "I have my memories of this night."

Jeremy swallowed hard. He opened his mouth to say something in return, but no words came out. Betty took him by the hand. "Let's make some more memories," she said. "Hey, what's this ride?" She was standing too close to the entrance to see the sign above her head.

"Oh, this is the … ah … the Tunnel of Love." He lied. He couldn't believe Betty swallowed it. "Shall we?"

Jeremy paid for the tickets and led Betty to the front seat. When the attendant came by to check that the safety bar was firmly in place, Betty looked at Jeremy, but he would not return the glance. "Jeremy," she said, "are you sure this is the Tunnel of Love?" He said nothing as the ride began to pull away and ascend a steep hill.

"Jeremy?" He reached over and, in silence, took Betty's hands and placed them on the bar in front of her. Then, looking straight ahead, he simply said, "Hold on … really tight."

Betty stared in disbelief. *How could I have so misjudged you?*

Jeremy quickly realized that he had just made the biggest mistake of his life. He turned to apologize for his practical joke, but the roller coaster had reached the apex of the first hill. *Too late now*, he thought. The ride crested the top, and then plunged almost straight down. He heard Betty's scream but still did not dare look in her direction. He couldn't believe anyone could yell that loud for that long. For the first time, he took no pleasure in his favorite ride.

The roller coaster came to an abrupt, jerking stop back at the starting gate. The safety bars were lifted, and the passengers got up to leave. Jeremy sat still, not daring to look at Betty. "Will you forgive me?" he asked.

"Never in this lifetime, you creep!" said Betty.

"I'm sorry," he whispered in a repentant voice. "Well, I guess it's time to take you home." He stood to leave.

"Not so fast!" she said. "You may be a creep, but that was *great!*"

"Seriously?" he said, puzzled.

"Seriously."

"Want to go again?"

"Absolutely!"

The climb. The plunge. The scream. Then again. Betty did not want to get off. After the third time, Jeremy insisted they take a break.

"Can't take it, eh?" Betty mocked. She was feeling a bit rubbery-legged, however, so she welcomed the break.

"Hungry?" asked Jeremy.

"Starved!"

Jeremy ordered two hot dogs at the concession booth and handed one to Betty. He laughed as he watched her load it with the works: onions, relish, mustard, and catsup. They downed the dogs with Cokes and finished off the meal with cotton candy.

"Well, after that meal I think I'm ready for a bit slower ride," said Jeremy.

"What did you have in mind?" asked Betty.

Jeremy pointed to the Ferris wheel just ahead. As they waited in line, Betty again took Jeremy's hand.

"Does this mean you forgive me?" he asked.

"No, you're still a creep," she said. "But tonight, you're the only creep I've got."

The attendant held the seat steady while the two passengers settled in. The ride moved a few feet, and then stopped to let the next riders on. It continued this way until Jeremy and Betty reached the very top. "Oh, Jeremy, the view is wonderful!" said Betty. "You can see the ocean and … oh, look, someone is shooting off fireworks."

Jeremy ignored the fireworks and looked into Betty's face. She was truly beautiful. He put his arm around her shoulders. She kept staring at the view but leaned back and rested her head on his shoulder. The Ferris wheel slowly began to move.

"Jeremy, could we go for a walk along that beach after this ride?"

He looked toward the ocean. "Yes, I'd like that very much."

With sock-stuffed shoes in hand, the two entered the beach. The wet sand felt cool and soft under their bare feet, and the waves crested and crashed onto the shore. The pair played tag with the incoming white froth, talked and laughed, and looked for sand dollars by the light of the full moon. Then, for a long while, they walked in silence hand-in-hand, completely unmindful of anyone else.

"Jeremy?" Betty said at length. There was a serious tone in her voice that caught him off guard.

"Yes, Betty? Is something wrong?"

"Wrong? Oh, no." She stopped walking, let go of his hand and began to play in the sand with her toes. "This has been a perfect night. But …"

"But what?"

She looked into his face and started again. "Jeremy, this has been a wonderful night, and I hope we do it again. But there is something I need to share with you. Something you need to know about me."

"All right. What is it?"

"Jeremy …" she paused briefly, unsure of how to proceed. "You know that I am a Christian, right?"

The question took him by surprise. "Yes … Big Red mentioned it."

She took another long pause. "Jeremy, could I share my faith with you?"

"Sure," he simply said. He really did not want to go this route, but he also did not want to offend the first girl he'd ever dated.

"When I was twelve, I became a Christian. I mean, before that I was a nice girl and all—or at least I thought I was. But I knew something was missing in my life. One night, a girlfriend invited me to sleep over at her house. It was just the two of us. I remember how we talked and laughed and had pillow fights.

"At around 10:00 that night, my friend's parents ordered out for pizza. I was famished by the time it arrived, and I began to help myself. But then my friend—Christy was her name—said, 'Let's say grace.' I was holding a piece of pizza up to my wide-open mouth. We never said grace in my house, and I was a bit embarrassed. I put down the pizza and bowed my head as Christy prayed. I remember being struck by that. Well, later that night—well after midnight—we were in her bedroom, and she was braiding my hair. I asked her why she wanted to say grace. She began to tell me about Jesus and …"

Jeremy listened politely, even though this was all familiar territory for him—territory that he had no intention of treading again. He bent over, picked up a piece of broken clamshell, and played with it while they walked. As Betty spoke, his mind returned to the time when he was six years old and a tearful Pastor Sterling gave an invitation to come forward to accept Christ. He remembered stepping out of the pew, going forward, agreeing to be baptized, and confessing his sin of "gallantry." He smiled at the memory as he tossed the clamshell into an oncoming wave.

"What are you smiling at?" Betty asked.

"Oh, nothing."

Betty continued, but she wondered if anything she was saying was getting through to him. "Well, that night I asked Jesus into my life, to be my Savior and Lord. Jeremy, does any of this make sense?"

He hesitated for a moment. He didn't want to offend Betty, but he didn't want to share his own attitudes toward a God he had once trusted. Betty immediately sensed his discomfort. *Oh, God, was it too soon to share about this with him?*

"Perhaps we can talk about this again sometime," she offered.

"Perhaps," was all Jeremy said. He looked at his watch in the light of the moon. "Uh oh, I don't know if we have enough time to get you home before your dad's curfew." He turned and ran in the direction they had come, shouting, "Race you to the truck!"

Jeremy parked the truck by the curb when he reached Betty's house. He got out, walked around to the passenger side to open her door, and then walked her to the front door. The porch light was on, and the walkway was lined on both sides with tall bushes and trimmed evergreens. Even though it was late, they could see that the living room light was on.

"Looks like my parents are still up," Betty said as they lingered outside the front door.

"Yeah," said Jeremy. "Do you think I will be in trouble for getting you home ten minutes late?"

"Probably," Betty said playfully, "but I'll see what I can do to protect you. Of course, you may not want to shake my dad's hand for a while."

"Just the thought of it hurts," Jeremy said with an exaggerated wince. "So … if I called you during the week to ask you out again, do you think you might say yes?"

Betty hid her surprise. "Well, I'll have to think about that," she teased.

"If you don't, Grandma will be very upset. I can guarantee that she will be saving you a piece of that chocolate cake."

"Well, in that case—"

"Great!" He looked at his watch. "I'd better be going," he said, but made no attempt to leave.

He wants to kiss me good night, Betty thought. *Some day, Jeremy, but not tonight.* Jeremy reached forward with his right hand, took Betty's hand in his and shook it. "Well, good night," he said, and then hurriedly walked back to the truck. She watched as he got into the pickup and drove away.

Betty found herself smiling at the gesture. *Would I have let you kiss me, Jeremy?* she wondered. She entered the house, turned off the porch light, and went into the living room to say good night to her parents. To her surprise, they were not there. *They must not have been waiting up for me after all,* she thought. She turned off the living room light and quietly went upstairs to her bedroom.

"Well, what do you think, dear?" Mrs. Maguire said to her husband. They were standing by the window in the unlit kitchen that overlooked the front walkway.

"The jury is still out, but a good night handshake? He may be all right after all."

Chapter 22

No Time for Fear

January 23, 1965

The weather report had called for a light dusting of snow, but by 9:30 p.m., there was already two inches of the heavy wet stuff on the ground. Cutting gusts of wind whipped across Jeremy and Betty's faces as they left the theater.

Jeremy wiped off the hood and windshield of the truck and jumped inside to start the engine. "I think we had better cancel phase two of our date," he said, breathing into his hands to warm them. There was no argument from Betty.

Jeremy drove slowly in the snow and turned off Route 128 to enter Clayton. "Jeremy," Betty said, "would you mind taking a detour through the center of town? I want to do a quick check on Uncle Alex and the guys."

"I don't know if that's such a good idea," said Jeremy. "We really need to be getting you back. I can barely see fifty feet ahead, and the traction in this snow isn't so good." He leaned forward to wipe off some of the moisture from the front windshield that the old defroster could not handle.

"Please, Jeremy, it will only take five minutes."

"Well, okay, but I'm sure they are all right."

Big Red closed up the club at 9:00 that night, ordering all those who had not rented rooms to go home. The electrical lines that led into the building sagged under the weight of the heavy snow and whipped back and forth with the wind. The remaining half-dozen men sat around a table in the club and finished off their beers, each trying to outdo the other with recycled accounts of war exploits. With one final flicker, the lights went out with a strange buzzing sound.

Big Red had found a couple of flashlights for just such an emergency, which he now set on the table. He turned one on and handed it to a couple of the men nearby. "You guys can put yourselves to bed," he said. "I've got to get home before the boss sends out the bloodhounds." He threw a woolen, checkered scarf around his neck and, with no coat, left the building. Minutes later, the others broke up the meeting and headed to their second- and third-floor rooms.

Just after Big Red left, the limb of an oak tree on the edge of his property broke under the weight of the moisture-laden snow. It fell onto the main electrical wire that led into the building above the sidewalk entryway. No one was out walking the streets to see the sparks when the wire snapped.

Jeremy drove through the center of town. The businesses had closed early and only the streetlights were on to guide anyone foolish enough to be out in this weather. He turned left onto Market Street and immediately slammed on the brakes, causing the truck to slide in the unplowed snow. They bumped hard against the curb.

"What's wrong?" Betty asked. She had been rummaging through her purse for a tissue and had not been looking out the front window.

"Look over there!" he said in a panicked voice.

Betty looked where Jeremy was pointing and instantly froze. He opened his door and stepped out. "Get to the nearest house and have the owner call the fire department!" he yelled. Betty remained motionless, staring ahead at the blaze. He reached back in and shook her arm. "Betty, do it now!"

She snapped out of her shock, opened her door, and ran for the nearest house that had lights on. "Fire!" she yelled, pounding at the door. An eternity seemed to pass before the owner opened the door. "Call the fire department!" she screamed once more, pointing up the street. The man nodded and went back inside. Betty turned and ran back toward the Watering Hole Club.

By the time Jeremy reached the building, the fire had already broken through the roof on the left side. Flames erupted thirty feet into the air, giving the wind-whipped snow an eerie glow. As he approached, the large front doors burst open, and several people stumbled down the main stairs. He grabbed one of the fleeing tenants by the arm and shouted into the man's ear, "Are there any others in the building?" He could just recognize the man in the light of the flames.

"What?" Pinky said. He choked from the smoke he had inhaled.

"Pinky, listen. Are there any others in there?"

Pinky gave a quick look around at those who had fled the building and were now staring up at the inferno. "Yeah, I think so," he said. He coughed again and sank to his knees in the wet snow.

Jeremy let go of Pinky's arm and ran toward the burning building. *Not a good idea, Jeremy. Not a good idea at all.* The words echoed in his mind as he threw open the door and ran inside.

Betty arrived just in time to see him enter. "Jeremy, don't go in there!" she screamed. But it was too late. He had already disappeared into the smoke that was pouring out the open door. She heard sirens in the distance.

"Oh, God!" Betty began to pray, "Oh, God! Oh, God!" A part of the roof to the left collapsed. The sparks and flames flew up, and the old building continued to burn. Then, through the smoke, Jeremy stumbled out of the structure carrying Macky across his shoulders. He lowered Macky slowly to the ground as Betty ran to help him. "Oh, thank God you're safe," she said. Her voice quivered with relief.

"Charlie," Macky coughed out from where he lay.

Betty knelt in the snow beside him. "Macky, what about Charlie?"

The man pointed toward the building and coughed. "In there. Third floor."

"Take care of him," Jeremy ordered. Betty stood and grabbed his arm as he attempted to go back inside. "You can't go in there!" she pleaded in a panic. "The fire department will be here any minute. Let them do their job."

"No time," he said as he quickly pulled away.

Macky lay coughing in the snow. Betty knelt beside him and held his head in her lap. "Oh, God! Oh, God!" she cried.

"Clayton fire department. What is your emergency?" The intercom system at the fire station automatically began broadcasting the conversation.

"There's a fire," the voice at the other end of the line said with forced calmness. "I'm calling to report a fire."

"What is the location, sir?"

"It's the Watering Hole Club on Market Street." The pitch in the caller's voice began to rise.

"Calm down, sir," said the dispatcher. "Engines One and Two are leaving right now."

The main doors of the fire station opened, and Engines One and Two pulled out. Engine Two, with a 500-gallon attack pump, would be the first to arrive on the scene. Fireman Noble, the driver, turned left and headed toward Main Street. Lieutenant Danner, riding in the passenger seat, and Fireman Hanscom, sitting in the rear, had already equipped their fireproof turnout gear and were strapping on their air packs and helmets. Their face masks hung loosely to the side.

"Do you know if anyone is in the building, sir?" the dispatcher asked.

"I don't know," the caller replied. "There could be some renters in there." He moved to the front window and pulled back the curtains. "I can see flames shooting through the roof. It looks like some people are running from the building."

"Okay, thank you, sir." The dispatcher hung up and radioed Engine Two. "Lieutenant Danner, confirming the address is 89 Market Street, the Watering Hole Club."

Noble turned left onto Main Street and headed for the center of town. The dispatcher radioed Danner again. "Our records show a hydrant 100 feet north of that address. There may still be people inside the building."

"We're approaching that block now," said Danner. "I can see the flames."

The dispatcher struck the working fire alarm. Immediately, the ambulance was dispatched along with Engine Three and whatever spare firefighters were available.

Engine Two arrived at the scene, with Engine One and the ambulance only seconds behind. Engine One drove past the scene to get their hoses hooked up to a hydrant further up the street. The emergency medical team jumped out of the ambulance and was immediately directed by onlookers to Macky, who was still lying on the street. They placed an oxygen mask over his mouth and lifted him onto a gurney. With a roar of sirens, he was taken off to the hospital.

Lieutenant Danner quickly surveyed the situation while Hanscom and Noble began laying hose from the attack pump to the burning building. *Looks like this will be a complete loss*, Danner said to himself. He began shouting orders when suddenly Betty grabbed his arm. *"My boyfriend is in there!"* she screamed hysterically into his face. *"You've got to do something!"*

Lieutenant Danner pulled her hands away and held her firmly by the shoulders. "We're doing all we can right now, miss," he said with professional calmness, and then walked away toward his men.

Betty stood alone, staring at the lieutenant's back as he walked away, and then up at the inferno. She was at a complete loss as to what to do. She could no longer feel the biting snow that whipped across her face.

She felt an arm being placed around her shoulders. Looking to her right, she saw Uncle Alex next to her. She burst into tears. Big Red wrapped his arms around her. "He's … in … there," she cried and pointed. "Jeremy is … in there … trying to save Charlie."

Big Red's eyes went wide, but he said nothing. The two stood holding each other, unable to do anything except stare at the disintegrating building. The left side of the building was now completely engulfed, and the fire raced deeper to the right, aided by strong winds.

"There's at least one person in there, maybe more," Lieutenant Danner shouted to his crew. "You're going in." Hanscom and Noble acknowledged the command with a nod. They put on their face masks and turned the knob on the oxygen tanks strapped to their backs. Then, with Hanscom leading the way, they entered the burning building.

The first time Jeremy entered the building—a building he had come to know well—he encountered smoke that stung his eyes, but no flames. Inside, he saw the fire was coming from the left. So he crouched low, covered his mouth with his coat, and took the stairs on the far right. He dropped the coat when he found Macky crawling on his hands and knees on the second floor corridor.

By the second trip, the situation had deteriorated significantly. Jeremy tore off his shirt and used it to cover his mouth, but by the time he reached the second floor, he could see the flames creeping across the ceiling on the left side of the hallway. The heat was intense, and the hallway felt like a broiler oven. He moved low and quick up the stairs to the third floor, where the smoke billowed above him.

When he reached the top landing, he turned left and removed the shirt from his mouth. "Anybody here?" he yelled. Hearing no response, he covered his mouth again, coughing and choking with the amount of smoke he had inhaled. Flames crept toward him along this ceiling as well, and the smoke blinded him.

He crawled along the floor and yelled again. Still no response. He felt along the wall as he moved until he came to the legs of a wooden bench seat, and then to a door he knew led into Charlie's room. He rolled onto his back and kicked at it, and the door quickly gave way. The sound of coughing came from inside. "Charlie, is that you?" Jeremy gasped. His eyes burned as he crawled on his stomach into the room.

He heard one faint cough and moved in that direction until he felt a body. "Charlie!" The body lay motionless. There was no coughing now, or any response. Jeremy found Charlie's one good arm and began dragging him across the floor into the hallway. At the top of the staircase, he looked back and saw the glow of flames through the thick, black smoke. Ahead of him, the heat was rising up the stairwell.

Firefighters Hanscom and Noble moved cautiously into the main entrance, turned right and up the stairwell, and then moved around the corner toward the second floor. A red glow began to surround them as they neared the second floor landing. Even with their protective gear, they could feel the intensity of the heat. "Lieutenant!" Noble called through his radio.

"I hear you, Noble."

"We can't see a thing. The smoke is thick as molasses."

"Can you make any progress at all?"

"We'll try. Turn the water on now."

Within seconds, the end of the nozzle burst with water. The two men advanced behind it, using the spray as a shield. As they moved up several stairs, they saw the water begin to turn to steam as it struck the walls. Each man realized there was no way they were going to reach the second floor landing, let alone the third floor, in time to save anyone.

Just as they had made the decision to retreat, they heard the voice of the lieutenant coming over their radios. "Abort! Abort! Get out of there, *now*!" Suddenly, they heard a sound like breaking timbers. Another part of the roof was caving in. The men dropped the hose and retreated to the exit.

A second and third alarm from the station brought help from neighboring towns. The trucks arrived within minutes and began setting up. The hoses were no longer pointed at the Watering Hole Club, but at the structures nearby that were now in danger of catching fire as well.

Jeremy could not go down the stairwell, and there was no way to go up. He was beginning to feel dizzy, and his breathing labored under the smoke that burned his throat and lungs. As he lay on the third floor landing, fear began to course through him. "Think, man! Think!" he said as his body trembled.

Just then, he remembered the wooden bench against the wall. *There is a window at the top of each landing*, he thought. He let go of Charlie's arm and quickly found one of the legs of the bench. He took as deep a breath as he could and used the shirt to cover his mouth as a filter. Then, with eyes squeezed shut, he stood up, grabbed the bench, and hurled it in the direction of the window. As he dropped back to the floor, he heard the sound of glass shattering. Smoke billowed out of the opening.

Still holding his breath, he felt for Charlie and grabbed the arm of the unconscious man. He stood to his feet again, faltering once before catching his balance, and then lifted the man's dead weight across his shoulders. Slowly, he reached out with his left arm and felt for the window. Some of the shards were still imbedded in the frame, but he had no time to worry about those. He lifted his left leg and then his right until he was able to maneuver into a sitting position on the edge of the windowsill. Shards of glass sliced into his flesh, but he ignored the pain and grasped the frame with his left hand. He thought about the tarred walkway he would land on below should he slip from this third-story perch. *God, help me*, he thought. Even at this moment, he realized how strange that was for him to say.

Unable to hold his breath any longer, he exhaled what little was left and then sucked it in. Most of the smoke was above his head now, but not all. He coughed and choked, involuntarily sucking in, which caused more choking. Pain shot through his body as glass shards cut deeper into his flesh. The stinging wind whipped snow into his face, while heat from the inferno blistered his back. He felt himself start to slip and instinctively released his hold on the side of the window frame, grabbing the window ledge as he slid off. More glass shards knifed into his palm.

Charlie slipped from Jeremy's shoulders and began to fall. With his right hand, he grabbed the man's wrist and held on. His muscles reached their limit, and he felt as if he were being stretched on a rack. He knew he was losing the battle to stay conscious. His left hand slipped from the sill. He felt himself falling.

"Stay here," said Big Red to Betty. "I have an idea." He had been thinking about where Jeremy would be if he were searching for Charlie. Betty, still in shock, made no response as she watched the building burn out of control and collapse before her eyes.

Big Red ran to Engine Two and lifted a ladder from off its hooks on the side of the truck. "You can't take that," Lieutenant Danner shouted over to him.

Big Red ignored the order and quickly walked toward the building, ladder in hand.

"I said you can't take that," Lieutenant Danner shouted again as he tried to block Big Red's path.

"Yeah, Danner, I heard you the first time. Now get out of my way!" He plowed directly ahead, forcing Danner to step aside, and headed for the far side of the building. *If I can just get to the third floor window, I might give Jeremy a chance of escape,* he thought. *God, please help him to have made it to the third floor.*

When he rounded the corner, he saw a bench laying splintered on the snow-covered tarred pathway. There, directly above him, were two bodies dangling from the third-floor window. "Hang on!" he yelled. He threw the ladder down and, in a mad dash, ran toward the building to get under the window. Just then Jeremy's grip let go, and the two limp bodies plummeted to the ground. Big Red placed his massive body in the path of the falling men, took one quick deep breath, and tensed every muscle.

The bodies partly struck his outstretched arms and his chest. Heads cracked. The impact knocked the air out of Big Red, and he fell to the ground. He did not know how long he lay there—seconds, minutes perhaps—as he tried to suck air back into his lungs. Finally his lungs cooperated, and air gushed in. Regaining his senses, he stood, picked up the two bodies, slung one over each shoulder, and carried them toward the ambulance.

"Look!" someone in the crowd shouted. All who heard turned to look in the direction the man was pointing. Several of the onlookers quickly rushed to take the bodies from Big Red as he collapsed to his knees.

Lieutenant Danner saw the movement, and then saw the bodies. He turned to the emergency medical team on the site and ordered the stretchers to be brought. Betty saw what was happening and bolted to them. She pushed her way through the crowd and threw herself on the ground beside Jeremy.

"Jeremy! Jeremy!" she cried, holding his face between her hands. There was no sign of life.

The medical team arrived with the stretchers, along with some oxygen tanks and masks. One of the technicians gently, but forcefully, moved Betty aside. The team placed the masks over the men's mouths, and for the first time Betty saw Jeremy's chest heave, followed by a wracking cough, as he sucked in life. Both Jeremy and Charlie were placed onto the stretchers and quickly carried into the ambulance. Betty followed closely behind. She tried to enter the ambulance, but the technicians wouldn't allow her. She screamed her protests as the doors were shut and the ambulance drove away.

Big Red, who had refused medical treatment, came to her side. "Follow me," he said, rubbing his forehead where skulls had clashed. He led Betty to his vehicle parked down the street, and they followed the ambulance to the hospital.

Betty was still in shock when they arrived at the Boston hospital, but she had the presence of mind to realize that she needed to make some phone calls. She called her parents first and gave them as calm and brief an explanation of what had happened as she could. Then she called Grandma Martel and repeated the information, adding, "My parents are on their way to pick you up and drive you here." She hung up the phone and returned to the waiting room to sit beside her uncle. Alex put his arm around her, holding her tightly. "He's going to be okay, Betty," he said. "Trust me." She nodded, tears wetting the hands she had pressed to her face.

"You know how you're always telling me about how God has a plan for me and all?" Big Red said, trying to raise her spirits. Betty slowly looked up at her uncle and nodded. "Well, I think I figured it out. His plan was for me to be the largest cushion on the planet." Betty did not want to laugh, but she couldn't help herself. "Betty, a piece of advice," he added. "Don't let this guy go. Jeremy is one special guy."

She nodded again and wiped her eyes with both palms. "I have no intention of letting him go."

Two hours passed before Grandma walked into the waiting room, followed by the Maguires. All three rushed to Betty, who was pacing the floor, and smothered her in hugs. The questions quickly flooded out. Big Red, who had been sitting on the couch, stood but did not join in the group hug.

A doctor entered the room and looked at the group. He did a double-take when he saw Big Red. "Ah, which of you is Mrs. Martel?" he asked.

"I am," Grandma replied firmly.

The doctor walked over to her. "I am Dr. Layton. I want to assure you that Jeremy is going to be fine." Grandma immediately reached out and took Betty's arm to steady herself, and then collapsed onto a nearby couch. "Thank You, Jesus!" she whispered, pressing a shaking right hand against her quivering lips.

"He will need to remain hospitalized for a few days," the doctor continued. "He has had quite a bit of smoke inhalation, and he has suffered some first- and second-degree burns on his left arm and back. In addition, there is quite a lump on his forehead." The doctor looked at Big Red, who was again rubbing his own lump. "He possibly has a mild concussion, but nothing to worry about. We also had to remove some pieces of broken glass from his side, and his left arm and hand, which will require a few stitches. There will be a small amount of scarring, but in time he will heal completely."

Grandma looked up from where she sat. "May I see him?" she asked.

"He's resting right now. Perhaps in the morning."

"Doctor," Betty asked as he turned to leave, "what about the second man who was brought in?"

"I did not treat him, but I did consult with the doctor who did. I understand he will be fine as well. He also had quite a bit of smoke inhalation, along with some burns, bruising, and a few cracked ribs. It's amazing that a man of his age could live through all this. He was one lucky man."

"No, doctor," Grandma said, "not lucky. A sovereign God was watching over him. And over Jeremy."

The doctor nodded, turned and left.

"Betty," Mr. Maguire said, "what on earth happened? You said very little on the phone—just enough to make your mother and me sick with worry."

Betty opened her mouth to speak, but immediately burst into tears. The emotion she thought she had under control broke free like a levy.

Two days later, Betty entered Jeremy's hospital room, holding a copy of the Clayton local newspaper in her hands. Without a word, she unfolded it and held up the front page for him to read. The bold-print headline read:

LOCAL BOY HERO

Beneath the headline was a picture of Jeremy being carried to the ambulance on a stretcher. "Well, I'll be darned," he said. "A hero. Guess I'll have no trouble getting dates now."

Betty carefully folded the paper and set it on the foot of his bed. Moving closer, she put her face within inches of his and held his face between her hands. "You listen, and listen good, buster. You look at any other girl and I'll give you another lump on your head. And don't let me ever see your picture like this on the front page of a newspaper again. You got that?"

Jeremy started to say something, but the kiss that followed shut him up quickly.

Chapter 23

The Confession

August 30, 1965

The birthday party for Amy and Lizzy had ended, and Jeremy and Betty were now parked in front of Betty's house. They had spent the last ten minutes in small talk. Finally, Jeremy gripped the steering wheel and drummed it with his forefingers.

"Jeremy, is everything okay?" asked Betty.

"Yeah, fine," he replied without looking at her. "Why?"

"Well, it just seems you're a bit nervous tonight."

Jeremy took a deep breath, turned, and placed his right arm over the back of the seat. He cleared his throat. "Betty, we've been dating for more than a year now—"

"One year, five months and twenty-two days."

Jeremy blinked. "Really?"

"Really."

"Well, there's something I have wanted to tell you for one year, five months and twenty-two days."

Betty looked, hopefully, into Jeremy's serious facial expression. Jeremy slid closer, took her left hand in his, and gazed intensely into her green eyes. "You know I leave for Strickland State college up in New Hampshire tomorrow, and—"

"Do you have my senior picture someplace safe?" Betty teased. "I don't want you to forget me when you see all those gorgeous freshman girls."

"Sure do," Jeremy said as he patted the wallet in his back pocket. "Every time I open my wallet and see I have no money, there you'll be."

"Gee, thanks."

"Now, stop interrupting. This is important. Where was I?"

"You leave for college tomorrow, and—"

"Yes, and, well, I just wanted to tell you that I … that is, before I leave, I wanted you to know that …" He paused and looked away.

I love you, too, Jeremy, she thought.

Jeremy's right hand moved to caress her left cheek, and he again looked into her eyes. "I've never told this to a girl before, but … I want you to know how … fond I am of you." He was pleased with the courage he had shown in admitting his true feelings and slid closer to follow up his confession with a kiss.

Betty quickly leaned back and let go of his hand. She placed her hands against his chest and pushed him away. She looked as if she had been slapped.

"You're … fond of me? You're fond of me? Oh, thank you so very much." Jeremy's eyes opened wide, and he quickly retreated to a much warmer side of the truck. "Jeremiah Elias Martel, you are the biggest jerk I have ever met." With that, she opened the passenger side door, got out, and slammed the door.

Jeremy sat for a moment in the truck, blinking and wondering what had just happened. He started to get out, but then thought better of the idea. "I'll call you tomorrow before I leave," he yelled through the open passenger-side window. She never looked back.

Women. Go figure, he thought as he turned the ignition and drove away.

Mrs. Maguire was sitting with her husband in the living room when Betty opened the door and stormed inside. She put down her novel and looked up. "Did you have a nice time, dear?" she called out.

Slam!

Mr. Maguire put down the sports section of the newspaper and looked at his wife. Betty stormed up the stairs and stomped down the corridor. Her parents stared up at the ceiling and followed the sound of the footsteps with their eyes. They did not hear her bedroom door open, but they did hear it close. *Slam!*

Betty grabbed the pillow off her bed and threw it against the headboard mercilessly. For a while she sat on the edge of the bed, fuming, and then retrieved the weary pillow into her arms. She hugged it to her body as if it were an overstuffed teddy bear. "Fond of me?" she mumbled. "How wonderful for him. He's fond of me."

Mr. Maguire again looked at his wife. "Your turn, honey," he said.

"It's always my turn," she complained.

"Well, this sounds to me like it needs a woman's touch. That's all I'm saying."

"In my next life, I'm having sons." She stood and headed upstairs.

Mr. Maguire watched her go and then went back to the sports page. "Well," he said to himself, "however bad a night she had, it couldn't have been as bad as the one the Red Sox had last night."

Mrs. Maguire approached her daughter's door and knocked quietly. "Betty, may I come in?" she asked.

There was no reply.

She slowly turned the knob, opened the door a crack, and poked her head inside. Betty, still hugging the pillow, was now sitting cross-legged in the middle of the bed. She opened the door wider, folded her arms, and leaned against the doorframe. "Want to talk?" she asked.

A tear trickled down Betty's check and spilled onto the pillow. "Oh, mom, are all boys jerks?"

"Actually … yes. What did Jeremy do this time?"

"He told me he was … *fond* of me. Can you believe that? After a year and a half of dating … and *only* him, mind you … he decides he's fond of me. The big jerk." She squeezed the pillow tighter while another tear trickled down her face.

Mrs. Maguire bit her lower lip to subdue a smile that desperately wanted to be released. "Want to hear a story about your father?" she asked.

Betty looked at her mother, and then slowly nodded.

Mrs. Maguire leaned back and looked down the corridor, as if to see where Mr. Maguire was, and then began in a hushed voice. "Well, your father and I dated for several years. Our very first date was to the movies, and then he took me to the local drugstore for ice-cream sodas. Nothing fancy, mind you, but it was a wonderful evening. I knew then that I wanted to marry him. He was polite, smart, and funny, and … well, he kind of swept me off my feet."

Betty nodded and waited for her mother to continue. "Anyway … he drove me home, and we sat in front of my parents' house. I thought we would talk a bit before he walked me to the front door. But do you know what he did? He pulled out a piece of paper and a pencil and began calculating the cost of the date. Then he subtracted the cost from what he had started out with when the evening began. He actually took out his wallet to see if what he still had matched the difference. I … was … furious! I didn't think I ever wanted to see him again, the insensitive brute."

Betty gave her mom her full attention. "What happened then?" she asked.

"Oh, I eventually forgave him, of course. A week later, he called to ask me out on a second date. But this time, when he drove me home and began to take out his pencil and paper, I pulled out a gift that I had wrapped up for him. He took the package, and I asked him to open it. Inside was a giant pad of paper and a pencil. I still remember the look on his face. He was clueless. Some things never change." Betty and her mother both had to cover their mouths to suppress the giggles. "Well, I informed him that since we were going to be going out steady, he would need a larger notepad. I planned on becoming a very expensive date."

Betty's face brightened. "Do you have any more stories?"

Mrs. Maguire looked down the hallway again, entered the room and closed the door behind her. "Move over, kid," she said. "This will take a while."

Chapter 24

The Letters

September 13, 1965

September 13, 1965
Betty,

Classes have only been in session for a week, but I wanted to let you know that I have not found any gorgeous freshmen yet. A few upper-class girls maybe. Just joking.

Before I forget, I want to give you the telephone number of my dorm here at Strickland State College, just in case you ever need to hear my voice or something. I'm in Doberman Hall. The number is 603-555-2346.

I'll try to keep my promise to write as often as I can, but I have to tell you, the workload is so much more than it was in high school. I'm taking a five-course load, and I have a thousand pages of collateral reading in just my history course alone. Give me a break! I thought the professor was joking at first when he announced the reading, just to see if we were paying attention.

You know what kind of reader I am. I always choose books by weight. If anything seems more than an ounce, I reshelve it.

Now each of my textbooks must weigh a few pounds at least. Anyway, I'll give it my best shot.

I hope you will write to me soon, as I miss you already. A few dozen pages would do. Maybe I could count them as part of my collateral reading. Ha! Ha!

Say hi to Big Red, Charlie, Pinky and the rest for me, will you? I meant to drop by the Watering Hole Club II before I left, but did not get a chance to do so.

That's it for now. I know it's short, but I'm afraid all my letters will be short with my studies and all. Got to go hit those books now. Hope I don't break my wrist.

Miss you,
Jeremy

October 25, 1965
Dear Betty,

I got the care package last week that you and Grandma put together. The cookies were out of this world. Thank you! It's amazing how many friends I had for about twenty minutes when I opened the box and pulled them out. Two dozen chocolate chip cookies didn't last long.

Thanks for the prayers that I would do well on midterms. Maybe you needed to pray harder, though. I just got the results and, oy, not good. Mostly low *C*s, and one *D*. But at least it was a high *D*. Gotta stay positive.

Are you enjoying classes at Essex South Community College? The business courses sounded pretty boring to me, but to each his own. And congratulations on your new bank teller position—you sounded excited about it in your last letter. You always were good with numbers. And you get banker's hours … what a deal. That should make it easy to work during the day and go to school in the evening.

Forgive me for not writing as often to you as you write to me. I always look forward to getting your letters, but writing is not my gift.

Well, that's it for now. I look forward to hearing from you. I miss you *very much.*

Jeremy

January 4, 1966
My Dearest Betty,

Our time together at Christmas was precious. I hated to leave you.

I hope I can keep up with writing to you this second semester. The workload is no easier than the last, and I need to put in more time with my studies. I can't figure out how some of the other guys do it, especially with all of the reading I have to do. What takes my roommate one hour takes me three. I tried going out for basketball, but there was no way I could keep up my studies *and* have practices every day *plus* games on weekends.

Thank you for checking in on Grandma from time to time. She really likes you, and I know she appreciates it. When she drove me back to campus, all she did was talk about you. Every time I see her, she seems to have aged so much more. I worry about her being in that apartment by herself.

Well, I've got to get to dinner before they lock the doors on me.

Love,
Jeremy

May 7, 1966
Dear Sweetheart,

In just two weeks I'll be done for the summer. Can't wait to see you!

I'm exhausted. I still have a few more classes, and after that I have to put in some long hours—maybe some all-nighters—to get ready for finals. If I don't do well on those, I may be placed on academic probation next year. I think my grade point average is about 1.9. Not good.

I don't know, maybe I wasn't cut out for college. I haven't even declared my major yet. Grandma is using so much of her savings to help put me through school. I feel like I am wasting her money.

I talked with her on the phone the other day, and she sounded so tired. I hate that she has to come and pick me up at semester breaks, but she insists on doing it.

Enough about my woes. So glad to hear the job is going well. Congratulations on the latest evaluation. Who knows ... bank teller today, bank president tomorrow!

I can't wait to see you back home. Try to write one more time and remind me how much you miss me. I need to hear it.

All my love,
Jeremy

Chapter 25

The Gifts

July 16, 1966

Jeremy looked around and was pleased to see his grandmother's funeral was so well-attended. The old Baptist Church normally held about seventy-five, but today it was standing room only. It was apparent that Grandma's life had impacted many people in the few short years that she and Jeremy had lived in Clayton.

Five days earlier, Jeremy had returned home late in the evening to find Grandma sitting in her oversized rocker in her bedroom. The second rocker, his grandfather's, was close beside it—two of the few possessions Grandma had refused to leave behind in Kansas—and her left arm was resting on it as if holding the hand of an invisible person. She had her Bible in her lap, and her chin was resting on her chest. At first, Jeremy thought she was praying or that she had fallen asleep, but when he touched her hand to wake her, he knew that she was gone.

Jeremy had often found excuses to not attend Sunday services with Grandma, but he liked this pastor. He appreciated the way he talked about Grandma's practical faith—the way she knitted blankets for the elderly in nursing homes, sent letters of encouragement to those going through tough times, and gave bear hugs. The congregation laughed tearfully at the last comment. Nobody could give a bear hug like

Grandma, and many present had first-hand knowledge of that fact. The ushers were hard-pressed to find enough tissues to go around.

Jeremy and Betty hung back at the grave site as the other mourners left to return to the church for a reception of sandwiches and punch. Many of them patted him on the shoulder as they passed and expressed their condolences.

"She was a wonderful woman, Jeremy."

"She's done with the weariness of this life, son."

"Your grandmother is in a better place."

After everyone had left, Jeremy stood in silence beside the casket. Betty moved closer to him and quietly took his hand. "Do you know what she used to say to me all the time?" he asked her, his eyes still fixed on the casket. "She said, 'Jeremy, let your life be one long, loving response to God for His first loving you so much.' She lived by that conviction."

He let go of Betty's hand, pulled a handkerchief from his back pocket, and wiped his eyes. It took him several moments to regain his composure so he could continue. "She never complained. Not once. She saw her grandfather die a lingering and painful death, and her husband suddenly drop dead in the fields. She saw my mother die and endured the loss of her second grandchild. She watched as her son, my pa, wasted away from cancer. We lost the farm that had been in our family for generations. But she never complained. Not once." He paused for a moment, and then turned to look at her. "Is this how God loves us so much? By taking away everything that is important to us? Everything we love?"

Betty wasn't sure if he was asking the question to her or to himself—or, perhaps, to God. But she continued to remain silent, her heart breaking for this man she loved so deeply. They had talked many times about God, and Betty knew from the few things Jeremy had shared about his past that he was hurt and angry with Him. But she remained confident that God would somehow make him see.

She looked down at the casket in front of them. Betty had often visited this woman she had come to love and also call "Grandma." The two would talk together while they baked in the kitchen, and from what Grandma told her, she had come to learn quite a bit about Jeremy.

She knew that he had trusted in Jesus and been baptized when he was almost seven, and even about his confessed sin of "gallantry." She knew details about his great-grandfather Elias, his grandfather Jeremiah, and his mother and father. She knew about Sylvester and the tornado, Shakey and the coyote attack, and many other things that Jeremy had never shared with her personally.

"Thank you," Jeremy said at length.

"For what?" Betty asked, her mind snapping back to the present.

"For being here. For listening and not preaching at me."

Betty smiled and put her head on his shoulder. Then, hand in hand, they walked back to where the limousine driver waited to take them to the church.

The reception ended, and the deaconesses began cleaning up the church. "Jeremy, let's go for a ride to our place," Betty suggested. "There's something I want to give you."

"What is it?"

"You'll see."

They drove in Grandma's pickup truck—a truck that now belonged to him—in silence for about a mile until they reached the outskirts of town. When they came to a dirt parking lot, Jeremy pulled off the road. Just beyond the lot was a path that led into several acres of town-owned forest.

Jeremy turned off the engine and looked at Betty. "Well, here we are," he said. "What's the surprise?"

"Jeremiah Elias Martel, this is not *our* place. Now come!" She opened her side door and exited with her pocketbook in hand.

"I think you spent too much time with Grandma," he said, but he obediently followed.

The two walked along the path for a few hundred yards until it opened up onto a small pond covered by lily pads. Red-winged blackbirds darted in and out of unseen nests that they had built among the reeds on the shore. A symphony arose from croaking, courting frogs. A great blue heron, surprised at the sudden appearance of the couple, took flight from where it had been feeding near the shore and glided to a safer location on the opposite shore.

At the end of the path sat a large boulder that nature had carved into a rough-hewn bench of sorts. Jeremy and Betty were pleased to find that "their place" was vacant. In fact, this was "the place" of dozens of other lovers, as evidenced by the number of hearts with initials and arrows carved into the neighboring trees. One tree had a heart with "JEM fonds EVM" inscribed on it.

The two sat down on the rough bench. "Well, what's the surprise?" Jeremy asked again. He turned to Betty and looked into her eyes. She smiled, opened her pocketbook, and withdrew two small packages. Each had been wrapped in colorful paper and tied with a ribbon.

"Here, open this one first," she said.

Jeremy was genuinely surprised as he took the gift. "What's this for? I mean, it's not my birthday or anything."

Betty said nothing, but waited quietly as he untied the ribbon and undid the wrapping paper, revealing a thin rectangular box. He removed the cover and withdrew a black leather wallet from inside. The initials "JEM" were engraved in gold lettering on the front.

Betty watched as Jeremy's eyes lit up. "Like it?" she asked.

"I love it! But why?"

"Just because I wanted to give it to you. Besides, it's not like you don't need one."

Jeremy pulled his old wallet from his back pocket and laughed. "Well, it's not *that* bad," he said, peeling away some of the duct tape that held it together. He transferred his driver's license and the few dollars he had into the new wallet, and then slowly removed the pictures from their plastic casings. He held each one for a moment before sliding it into its new home. "There's my mom and pa," he said. "He used to give me the greatest horseback rides at bedtime. Oh, and here's me and Shakey by an old scarecrow. That was before Shakey lost his leg. And here is Grandma ..." He suddenly choked up as the memories of Grandma rushed back into his mind. Betty gently placed her left hand on his.

After a moment, Jeremy pulled out Betty's high school picture. She was posing with a broad smile, proudly showing off her braces. She reached over and slowly took the picture from him as she handed him a second wrapped gift. "Open this, and then I'll give you back my picture."

"I don't know what this is all about, but I sure am enjoying it." As he unwrapped the package, he was more than surprised to find that it contained a pocket Bible. "Well … uh … thanks."

"Don't thank me, thank Grandma."

"What do you mean?"

"About a week ago, just two days before … before she went home, I was visiting and she told me how she wanted to buy you a Bible. She asked if I would go with her to pick one out. Of course I said yes, and we shopped around until we found this. Look, she even had your name engraved in gold letters on the front cover: 'Jeremiah Elias Martel.' Jeremy, she was so proud of you. When I would bake with her in the kitchen, she would always start in on 'Jeremy this' and 'Jeremy that.' She told me more about you than you may realize."

Jeremy didn't know what to say. He sat there quietly and held the Bible.

"Look inside," Betty said.

He opened the front cover and immediately recognized his grandmother's handwriting. He read the words out loud:

> The true measure of a man is not in the possibles he accomplishes that last a lifetime, but in the impossibles he allows God to accomplish through him that last for eternity. With forever love, Grandma.

Below those words, she had written:

> "The end of all things, their purposes revealed or hidden, is good for those who love God."

"Those were the last words my pa said to me," Jeremy said, his voice choked with emotion.

Betty took the Bible from his hands, opened it to the middle, placed her picture there and handed it back. "Every time you take out this Bible, I want you to think of me. And I want you to think of me *a lot*." With no more words, she slid her left arm through his right and rested her head against his shoulder. Together, they sat without speaking, listening only to nature's symphony.

The rest of the summer passed quickly. Jeremy spent many hours with Betty, and many hours in Red's Gym. Studying came hard for him, but he loved physical work. The harder he worked under Big Red's tutelage, the more satisfied he felt.

He worked two jobs that summer. During the week, he worked full-time as a gopher for a construction company, and on weekends he worked as a stock clerk in a local grocery store. At the end of the summer, his boss at the construction company told him that if he wanted to continue to work for him and learn the business, he would train him personally. "You've got what it takes to succeed," he said. "You have a strong back and know how to follow orders." Jeremy politely refused his boss's offer, feeling he owed it to Grandma to try and finish college.

Jeremy realized that his grandmother must have sensed her days on this earth were numbered. In her wisdom, she had placed money into a savings account under his name that he could access without having to go through probate court, which would have taken at least a year. The cost of the funeral had used up some of the money, but there was enough left to pay for one more semester at college. The truck, which had been registered under both his and Grandma's name, would have to go once he returned to school—there was just no way he could afford the gas and upkeep on the old Chevy. He would sell it for the best offer, probably a few hundred dollars, and put the money into the account.

Jeremy and Betty spent their time together taking long walks on the beach, sometimes in nonstop conversation, and sometimes in silence. They took fishing trips along the banks of the pond at "their place" and went on picnics, with Betty using Grandma's recipes for fried chicken and peach cobbler. They had little money to spend, but neither complained. All they wanted was to be together.

CHAPTER 26

THE HINT

SEPTEMBER 1, 1966

The summer was over all too soon, and Jeremy returned to Strickland State College at the beginning of September. He was struggling with his studies more than ever, but he was determined to press on. Finally, in late October, the inevitable occurred.

October 26, 1966
Love of my life,

This letter will be real brief. Earlier today, I was called into the Dean of Academics' office. I am now officially on academic probation based on my recent midterm grades. I've been given the rest of this semester to bring up my grade point average to 2.0, or I'm history. No pressure there.

The dean strongly—and I mean strongly—encouraged me to take part in a tutorial program they have on campus. Some of the seniors do the tutoring for a few bucks an hour. I guess it will help, but I just don't know how I can afford it.

Anyway, I miss you, and your cooking. Care packages are always welcome. After the first one you sent, I learned how to hide them. I miss you terribly!

All my love,
Jeremy

By winter, Jeremy had settled some things in his mind and wanted to start sharing more of these thoughts and feelings with Betty. As he wrote a special letter to this woman he loved, he hoped that it would be received favorably by a loving heart that would hear and understand his decisions.

February 6, 1967
My Dearest Betty,

On many occasions, I have shared with you how I am struggling at school. As I sit here today in the campus library, I think I have figured out the reason. My days and nights are filled with thoughts of you. When I am not with you, my heart aches to be in your presence. Have I ever told you how desperately I love you?

Having said that, I want to come to your house and ask you something. It's not something I can ask over the phone or in a letter—I need to ask it in person. The problem is that I still have five weeks to go before the semester break, and I will be very busy between now and then as I try to get my grade point average up. So far, I've been able to raise it to a 2.0, but I think that will only be temporary.

I also have some sizable debts to pay before the semester ends. So on Friday I will be starting a job in town as a night security guard in a factory. The hours are from 10:00 PM to 6:00 AM, Wednesday through Sunday. It's an easy two-mile hike to get there from campus. I know it's a lot of hours, but I will be able to get some studying done between rounds. And maybe some cat naps. I have dropped one course from my load to see if that helps.

Between the academics, the need to work, and the need to sleep, I will try to write you as often as I can. I am trying my best to get my act together here so I can leave at the end of the semester without debt—and of my own free will. I have just about made the decision not to return next fall. I'm not giving up completely on college yet, but I don't think I was ready for it.

One more thing. I spoke with the powers that be, and they wouldn't allow me to take the night job and still live on campus. School policy with curfews and all that. So this weekend I will be moving to a small room in a private home within easy walking distance of the campus. It will be affordable, as I won't have to pay for room and board at the college.

I will be sharing the cost with Carter Southerbee, who, you might remember, is my current roommate. We seem to get along well, even though we have only known each other for a short time. When we talked it over, he liked the idea—he says there are too many rules on campus for him. He has a car, so we can do our laundry and grocery shopping in town as needed. The owners of the house have given us kitchen privileges. We think we can make it work, though it will be tight.

The owners of the house said I can make a few calls from there if they are kept short. The address is 28 Fairview Street, Strickland, New Hampshire. The telephone number is 603-555-9884.

Please be patient with me. I will be at your house on Saturday afternoon, March 18, if that's okay with you. Let me know soon. I so love you and miss you.

Jeremy

Jeremy placed the letter into an envelope, addressed it, and walked across campus to the student union building to mail it. He was giddy with excitement as he thought about the question he was going to ask Betty. He had calculated the earnings he would make at the factory and determined that he would have enough to pay off his college debts by the end of the semester—and have enough to purchase the diamond ring he had seen in the window of Woodman's jewelry store downtown. He might even have some cash leftover for a small nest egg that he and Betty could use to pay for a couple months' rent on an apartment. The honeymoon would have to wait.

Jeremy dropped the letter into the mail slot and headed back to his dorm room, now highly motivated to work on pulling up his disastrously-low grade point average.

CHAPTER 27

A COMEDY OF ERRORS

FEBRUARY 10, 1967

Jeremy didn't remember to check his mailbox again until late Friday evening. When he did, he found that the letter he had mailed on Monday had been returned for insufficient postage. "How could I have been so stupid!" he moaned, slapping his forehead in disbelief. In his excitement, he had forgotten the stamp.

Back at the dorm, Carter was sitting at his desk, deeply engrossed in some textbook. He waved his hand to acknowledge his roomie's presence when Jeremy entered, and then continued on with his studies. Jeremy quietly rummaged through his own desk drawer and found an envelope and stamp. He addressed the new envelope and made sure to place the stamp on it this time. Instead of removing the letter from the old envelope, he simply folded it and placed it into the new one.

On his way back to the student union building to mail the letter, he suddenly realized that it was Friday night, and that the mail from campus would not be going out until Monday morning. He desperately wanted it to go out on Saturday, and for a moment he thought about mailing it from the post office in town. However, that was on the opposite end of town from the factory, and he had less than an hour to get to work. He briefly considered holding on to it until morning and mailing it on the way home from work, but he did not want to carry it with him all night, and he knew there was a better-than-fair chance that he would have to work overtime. The first-shift guard had complained the previous morning of coming down with a cold, and he said he would probably not be in for a couple of days. Jeremy decided he couldn't risk it, especially since the post office closed at noon on Saturdays.

He walked back to the dorm and re-entered his room. "Hey, Carter, sorry to interrupt," he said. "Can I ask you to do me a favor?"

Carter swiveled in his chair and faced Jeremy. "Sure, buddy," he said. "What's the emergency?"

"Are you going into town this evening?"

"As a matter of fact, I'm going in about," he pushed up his shirt-sleeve and looked at his watch, "ten minutes. Wanda and I are going to see *Born Free*. Need a lift?"

"Thanks, but no. What I need is for you to mail this letter at the post office for me so that it goes out tomorrow. I have to shower and shave before I leave for work, and I don't have the time to mail it."

"No problem, my friend. It would be my pleasure."

Jeremy handed the letter to Carter, who slipped it into his shirt pocket. "Thanks, Carter," he said. "You will never know how important it is."

"Matters of the heart would be my guess," Carter mused, tapping his pen to his lips as if in deep philosophical thought.

Jeremy smiled. "Think you're pretty smart, don't you?"

"Well, I do have a 4.0 average," Carter said with a shrug.

"Mind sharing some of that with me?"

"Would if I could, my friend." Carter swiveled around to study for a few more minutes before leaving for his date.

Jeremy went into the bathroom to get ready for work.

Four weeks later, Jeremy was returning home in the early hours of the morning after a long night at work. He met Carter at the door, who was leaving for an early-morning jog. The look on his roommate's face told him that something was wrong.

"Hey, roomie, what's the matter?" Jeremy asked.

Carter bit his lower lip. "I need to apologize for something, Jeremy," he said quietly.

"Okay …"

"Remember that letter you asked me to mail for you a couple weeks ago?"

A knot began to form in Jeremy's stomach. "Yes, what about it?"

"Well, when I went to my car to pick up Wanda, I put the letter in the glove compartment." He walked over to his desk and picked up a white envelope. "I totally forgot about it, and just last night I found it. I'm so sorry." He handed the letter to Jeremy, who stood dumbstruck as he looked down at the envelope in his hand.

"Carter, I told you that this was important. How could you forget?" Jeremy's voice was soft and controlled, but he was finding it difficult to suppress his anger.

"I know, I know, I really messed up. I'm sorry." He reached out his hand. "Here, give the letter back to me. I'll drop it off at the post office after breakfast."

"Uh, no … that's okay, I'll take care of it." He dared not look Carter in the eyes or say anything else for fear of losing his temper.

"Okay, I understand. Really, I can't tell you how sorry I am." He patted Jeremy on the shoulder and slipped past him out the door.

Jeremy walked over to the window and watched Carter jog away. The anger suddenly flooded through him, and he punched the sheetrock wall, blasting a hole through it like a shotgun. The pain in his hand snapped him back to his senses, and he immediately regretted his act. *Not sure how I'm going to explain that to Carter—or the landlords,* he thought.

He walked over to the bed, sat on the edge and looked at the letter again, not sure of what to do next. After considering the problem for some time, he finally decided to simply write Betty a short explanation and re-mail the letter at the post office. It might mean missing his first period class, but that was a chance he was willing to take.

March 16, 1967
My Dearest Betty,

You would not believe the trouble I have had in getting this letter mailed to you. First, I forgot to put a stamp on it, and a week later I found it in my mailbox stamped "insufficient postage." Then I asked my roommate to mail it for me before heading to work. That was four weeks ago. Today, he told me that he had forgotten to mail it and just now handed it back to me. I hope you have not made plans for Saturday afternoon, as I really need to see you. I hope to be at your house by 3:00.

Jeremy

He stuffed the note and the first two envelopes into another envelope and put two stamps on it just as a precaution. He wrote out Betty's address and was about to write his return address, but then hesitated. New ideas began to play in his head. *It's really too late to mail it,* he thought. *It will never get to Betty in time. Maybe I should call her. No, better yet, I think I'll surprise her. Yeah, I'll take a sick day and surprise her.*

The more Jeremy thought about the idea, the more it began to appeal to him. He set the letter down and picked up a little black box that sat on his desk. As he opened it, he smiled to himself. "I hope I got the ring size right," he said aloud.

At around 7:00 that night, the phone rang at the Maguire house. Mrs. Maguire answered and said a few friendly words to the caller at the other end before yelling upstairs to her daughter. "Betty! It's for you!"

"Coming!" Betty called back. A few moments later, she picked up the phone that her mother had laid on the telephone stand. "Hello?" she said.

"Betty, it's me," said the voice.

"Hi, Carmen. What's up?"

"I wanted to ask you something—and don't say no right away, okay?"

"Maybe. What's the mystery?"

"Are we best friends?"

"Is that your mystery question? Of course we are."

"Then you know I would never do anything to hurt you. Right?"

Betty paused a moment before responding. "Carmen, what are you getting at?"

"Betty, how long has it been since you've heard from Jeremy?"

"Let me think. About four or five weeks, I guess. Why?"

"Isn't that kind of a long time? I mean, does he ever go that long without writing to you?"

"It is a little longer than usual, I guess, though we do have about a two-to-one writing ratio. But he has got a lot on his mind with his studies and all. And besides, he's a guy. Why are you asking?"

"Well, as you know, I have a friend who has a sister who goes to Strickland State College."

"Actually, I didn't know that."

"Oh … well … anyway, this friend's sister told her—who told me—about a guy there she dated. And believe me, she shared some juicy details that would make Lucifer blush. I told her that I knew a guy who went to Strickland."

"Carmen, stop the cloak-and-dagger stuff and get to the point." Betty was beginning to lose her patience and not liking where this conversation was headed.

"Okay. Are you sitting down?"

"Carmen!"

"Betty, I hate to be the bearer of bad news, but when I told her the name of the guy I knew … well, I couldn't believe it, but it was the same name as the guy her sister dated."

"Carmen, you're crazy. Jeremy's not dating anyone else."

"I know this is a shock. But how many Jeremy Martels can there be at Strickland? She says he's dating anything in a skirt."

"I'm hanging up now, Carmen. You can …"

"Betty, I know this hurts, but you needed to know. You said yourself that you haven't heard from Jeremy in five weeks, and that he never goes that long without writing."

Betty thought about this for a moment. "He must have a good reason."

"Betty, facts are facts. Now … there is another reason I called."

"Carmen, I'm not sure I can handle any more of your news. And I don't believe Jeremy is seeing anyone else. We've had our bumps along the way, but he's not that kind of guy."

"Well, if you ask me, from my experience, all guys are 'that kind of guy.' Now, I want to ask you to think about something. I have a cousin in town who is visiting for the next few weeks. His name is Robert, and he is twenty-seven and very good-looking. He's a really great guy. Anyway, we were looking at my high school yearbook yesterday and he saw your picture. I told him you were my best friend, and he asked if you still lived in the area—and, if so, if he could he meet you. I thought—"

"Stop right there. Don't go any further with this idea. I trust Jeremy, and I will not be going out with your cousin."

"Betty, just hear me out. Think about it. You remember Fred? Well, he and I are going on a date to a Celtics game this Saturday night, and Fred has an extra pair of tickets. Some pool he won at work. I thought you might like to join us. We could do a double date."

"Carmen, I meant what I said." She loved Jeremy, and she resented Carmen for laying these seeds of suspicion.

"I know, Betty, I know. Well, just think about it."

"No, I won't!" She slammed the phone down to put an end to the nonsense. She could feel her face growing hot from the anger that was welling up inside her. *How dare she accuse Jeremy of such deceit. He would never … don't even think about such things, Betty. Ooooh, that Carmen makes me so mad sometimes I could scream.*

"Mom!" she yelled. "I'm going for a jog."

"Okay, dear."

Three hours later, Betty found herself sitting by the telephone, not believing what she was about to do. She opened the card index of telephone numbers that sat by the phone and found the one Jeremy had given to her in his first letter nearly two years ago. As she dialed, she was struck by the fact that this was the first time she had ever used the number to call him at school.

The phone rang twice before someone picked up. "Doberman Hall, what's your pleasure?" said the male student at the other end.

"May I speak with Jeremy Martel, please?"

"Hold just one." Without bothering to place his hand over the mouthpiece of the receiver, the student yelled out, "Hey, any of you mutton heads seen Martell?"

"Yeah," came a more distant voice over the phone. "He went to Goose Neck Lake with Candice. And you know what that means!" A few hoots and hollers arose from some of the other students.

The first student came back on the line. "Sorry, he's not here right now. Can I take a …"

Click.

Betty sat in shock, trying to mentally absorb what she had just heard. She wanted to cry, but she refused to let the tears spill. Confusion overwhelmed her, followed by hurt, and then anger, and then a sense of betrayal. She breathed in deeply, picked up the phone again and dialed a number.

"Carmen? What time on Saturday?"

Chapter 28

Best-laid Plans

March 18, 1967

It took Jeremy longer than he expected to hitchhike from Strickland to Clayton, and he didn't arrive in town until after 6:30 PM on Saturday night. He counted his blessings that the mid-March weather was unusually mild. A hooded sweatshirt was all that he needed for now, but he had a backup coat jammed into his backpack just in case.

His last ride dropped him off at the outskirts of Clayton, and he had to walk the last two miles to Betty's house. The sun had already set, and the porch light was on as he walked up to the door. He rang the doorbell. There was no answer.

Jeremy tried the bell again, but there was still no answer. He checked the garage on the other side of the house and found that Mr. and Mrs. Maguire's car was missing, but that Betty's lemon-colored VW bug was there. *I should have called,* he thought. *Surprise might not have been the best option. Maybe they just went out for a family dinner.*

With that thought, Jeremy went back to the front of the house, slipped the backpack from off his shoulder, and sat on the steps. He unzipped the backpack and took out a copy of Dante's *Inferno*. It was required reading for his classical literature course, and he hated it with a passion. *Might as well make the most of the time,* he thought.

Several hours passed. A chill began to permeate his clothing, so he took his coat out of his backpack and put it on over the sweatshirt. Exhausted, he pulled the hood of the sweatshirt over his head, tucked his hands into the pockets of his coat, and laid his head back against the porch door. He picked up the book again, but sleep soon overtook him, even under these uncomfortable conditions.

A sudden breeze woke him up. He looked at his watch and was surprised to find that it was now 10:50. *Maybe they all went out to a movie after dinner,* he thought. He stood and began to run in place to warm himself, and followed this by doing a few jumping jacks and other calisthenics.

After twenty minutes had passed, he sat and pulled out the letter he planned to give to Betty to explain his last five weeks of no communication. He chuckled to himself, thinking about the comedy of errors that had occurred. He was certain Betty would see the humor in it as well.

He set the letter on the step beside him and removed a little black box from the backpack. He opened the box and gazed down at the diamond that he was about to give to the love of his life. Just then, he heard a car pull up out front.

The tall bushes blocked his vision from where he sat, but he could hear the car door open and close, followed by a second door. The vehicle's motor continued to run. The sound of hurried footsteps started up the brick walkway, followed by a second set of footsteps close behind.

"Betty!" a man's voice called out. "May I see you again?"

"No, Robert," Betty replied. "I had a very nice time, but this was a mistake. I never should have agreed to go out with you."

"But what did I …" Robert stopped mid-sentence and looked past Betty. "Who is that?" he said, pointing with his chin. Jeremy had moved from where he had been sitting and was now visible in the porch light.

Betty turned. "Jeremy?" She gasped.

Jeremy stared at her, but said nothing. Several seconds passed in awkward silence. Suddenly, he remembered that he was still holding the small black box in his left hand, and he snapped it shut and slipped it into his left pocket. He swallowed hard and turned to pick up his backpack, brushing the envelope still laying on the edge of the steps into the dirt below. He slowly walked toward Betty.

"I'm sorry. I should have called." He brushed past her and started down the brick walkway.

"Jeremy, I …"

He turned and stared into her face. "It's okay, Betty. Really. It's okay. You know, the end of all things … yadda, yadda." There was a tone of bitter sarcasm in his voice. He raised his hand, turned, and walked away.

"Jeremy, wait," she said, following after him. "We need to talk." He ignored the pleading voice and quickened his pace. "Fine!" she said. "Then just leave!"

Without saying another word to her date, Betty turned and ran onto the porch. She fumbled for her house key in her purse and entered the house. Tears of frustration flooded down her cheeks as she ran up the stairs and into her room. She fell onto her bed, her shoulders shaking from the sobs, and buried her face in a pillow.

"Oh, God, what have I done? I don't understand what just happened! Oh, God, what have I done?" She cried for a few more minutes, and then suddenly stopped herself. *No, it's not my fault,* she thought. She rolled onto her back. *Jeremy, you betrayed me! You … betrayed … me!* Her mind wrestled with her disbelief until exhaustion finally overcame her.

Betty stayed in bed until noon the next day. Her parents were away until Monday evening visiting friends on Cape Cod, so there was no one to nag her to get up. It was just as well, because she did not want anyone to counsel her or try to comfort her or even come within a football field of her. She just wanted to wallow in her grief, her self-pity, her anger, and her sense of betrayal. *I didn't do anything wrong,* she kept telling herself. *He was cheating on me. He deserved it.*

She spent the rest of the day in a mental court, with her as the plaintiff and Jeremiah Elias Martel as the defendant. She brought the courtroom into the kitchen, where she tried to eat a bowl of cereal, but she threw it out after two bites. Arguments flooded her mind, justifying her actions. The jury needed only minutes to come back from its deliberations: "We, the jury, find the snake guilty as charged."

Betty broke down in tears again and raced back to her bed, depression cloaking her like a shroud.

The following Monday, Jeremy entered the admissions office at Strickland State College at 9 AM. He had already been to town to close out his small savings account.

"What can I do for you?" the secretary asked with a polite smile.

"I am going to withdraw from school," Jeremy replied in a barely audible voice. "What do I need to do?"

"I'm sorry," the secretary said, not sure she had heard the question correctly. "Would you repeat that?"

Jeremy looked her straight in the eyes, and this time the tone of his voice caused several others to stare in his direction. "I said, I'm going to withdraw from school. Just tell me what hoops I have to jump through to get out of here. I want the process started immediately."

The secretary was quite taken aback, first by his tone of voice, and then with the idea that he would withdraw halfway through the semester. "Are you sure you want to do this? Perhaps you would like to talk with a counselor first."

"No!" Jeremy said with bitter anger.

"Okay, then." The secretary's smile disappeared, and she reached into a drawer and pulled out a slew of official-looking papers. "You need to fill out these forms. You will have to go to several departments around the campus and to the library to get signatures stating that you have no outstanding debts or books overdue." She handed the papers to Jeremy and expressed her regret that he would be leaving.

"Thanks," he said curtly as he took the papers. He stood and left the office to head to each of the required places. Three hours later, he returned with the paperwork properly completed and turned it in.

"Anything else?" he asked impatiently.

The secretary quickly looked over the paperwork. "No, that should do it," she replied. "I truly wish ..." She stopped voicing her regrets when she saw that she was now speaking to Jeremy's back, as he was heading for the door.

Back at his room off-campus, he called the factory and announced to whoever answered that he would not be in to work again, and he gave no further explanation. It was just past noon, and now he was not only a college dropout, but an unemployed college dropout. He took out his suitcase from under his bed and quickly began to pack his belongings, leaving all of his textbooks on the shelf over his desk. Then he placed $300 on Carter's desk and wrote a brief note of explanation.

> Carter,
>
> I've withdrawn from school. This money should cover my part of the rent for the rest of the semester, and get the hole in the wall fixed. Take care, buddy.
>
> Jeremy

By 2:25 PM, he found himself standing in front of a building in downtown Strickland for the second time that day. He was about to do what he had only dreamed of doing since childhood. He entered the building and was immediately greeted with the friendly smile of the recruiting officer.

"Hello," the man said. "Can I help you?"

"Yes. I want to join the Marines."

"Well, you have certainly come to the right place. Have a seat, and let's talk."

"Hello, we're home," Mrs. Maguire announced that evening when she and her husband entered the front door. The only light in the house seemed to be coming from the porch light, which, unknown to her, had been on since Saturday evening. She flicked on the hallway light, set her handbag down on the telephone stand, and looked around.

"She must be out with her friends," Mr. Maguire concluded from the silence. He set down the two suitcases he was holding to the left of the door.

"No, I'm right here," came a faint voice from the living room.

Mr. and Mrs. Maguire quietly entered the living room. There, sitting curled up on the couch in the dark, was their disheveled, red-eyed, bathrobed daughter. She held a container of ice cream in one hand, and the other hand now held a spoon between her lips. Mrs. Maguire moved closer to the couch. "Oh, sweetheart, are you ill?"

Betty shook her head once and dipped the spoon back into the container.

"Then what's the matter?" Mr. Maguire asked. "You look like you just lost your best friend." The look she shot him made him instantly realize that he had struck a nerve.

"Dear," Mrs. Maguire said to her husband without taking her eyes off her daughter, "go out to the car and bring in the packages." It was not so much a request as a command, and it was readily obeyed. "Now," said Mrs. Maguire to Betty when he had left, "Do you mind if I sit down?"

Another shake of the head. Betty desperately wanted comforting now.

"Do you feel like talking?"

"Oh, mom …" said Betty, falling into her mother's arms. She quickly began unleashing the burdens of her soul.

Meanwhile, Mr. Maguire had retrieved Monday's mail and was now struggling to carry all of the packages into the house. He climbed up the few stairs to the porch and tried to open the door by pushing down on the latch with his right elbow. A package slipped from his hands and he reflexively grabbed for it, dropping the mail and another package in the process. The second package tumbled down after the first and landed in the dirt alongside the dropped mail.

Mr. Maguire placed the items still in his arms on the porch, and then went back to retrieve the items that he had dropped. Once he had everything in the same place, he opened the door and started placing the packages next to the luggage in the hallway. He dropped the mail on the telephone stand and then grabbed the first piece of luggage and lugged it upstairs. He had no desire to be part of the heavy discussion that was taking place in the living room, so once he had brought the luggage upstairs into the bedroom, he retreated to the basement and puttered around.

Mrs. Maguire listened patiently for twenty minutes while her daughter explained the story. Finally, she said, "Betty, is there any way you might have misunderstood? This just doesn't sound like Jeremy."

Betty was irritated that her mother could even consider she might be in the wrong. "How many Jeremy Martels can there be at Strickland?" she said, quoting Carmen's words. With that, she got up and headed for the bathroom off the kitchen, taking the ice cream along with her. Fifteen minutes later, she returned to the living room, where her mother was still waiting. "I'm sorry, Mom," she said. "I had no right to bark at you." She sat again beside her comforter.

"It's okay, dear," said Mrs. Maguire. "You're hurting, and I understand that. But I truly think you owe it to yourself—and to Jeremy—to call him and talk this out."

Betty sighed. "I guess." But she did not move.

"You really need to do it now."

Betty struggled in silence for a few moments with what she knew she had to do. Finally, she stood, went to the phone, and dialed the number that she had used last Thursday.

The same student picked up on the third ring. "Doberman Hall."

"Jeremy Martel, please," said Betty in a quavering voice.

"Sure, he's just down the hall. Once again, the student did not bother to cover the mouthpiece. Hey, Martell! It's for you!"

"Yeah? Who is it?" came a distant voice.

The student put his mouth back up to the phone. "He wants to know who it is."

"Tell him it's Betty," she said in almost a whisper.

"Some chick named Betty!"

Seconds later, another voice came on the line. "Hey, babe, what's cookin'?"

Betty was startled and didn't know how to respond. The voice did not belong to Jeremy—and he never referred to her as "babe."

"Hello? Betty? You there?"

"Uh, yes," said Betty, recovering her composure. "I'm calling for Jeremy Martel."

"You got him, sweetheart, alive and ready for action. Now what kind of action are you looking for?"

"I think … there has been a misunderstanding. You're Jeremy Martel?"

"Last time I looked in the mirror. Look, I haven't got all night, babe. What do you want?"

Betty's anger began to take over. "Uh, tell me. Did you go out with a girl named Candice last Thursday night?"

"Oh, you heard about that, huh? You some friend of hers? Maybe you want to get in on some of the action as well?"

"No, I certainly do not want to 'get in on the action.'" Betty was irate now. "And this is not the Jeremy Martel I've known for four years."

"Oh, wait a minute. You don't want this Jeremy Martell. You want the other one in …" he put the phone down and yelled down the hall. "Hey, any of you cockroach brains know what dorm the other Martel is in?"

"Yeah," came a reply. "He's in the sophomore dorm."

"Well, Betty, darlin', I think we have our mystery solved. This is the freshman dorm. You want the sophomore Jeremy Martel, with one *l*. I'm the freshman Jeremy Martell with two *ll*s. We've had a few mail mix-ups over this." He chuckled to himself.

Betty suddenly needed to sit as the realization of this horrible mistake began to overwhelm her and a wave of guilt enshrouded her. Softly, in a controlled tone, she asked, "Could you give me the sophomore dorm number, please?"

"Sure, same as here, just change the 6 to a 5."

"Thank you."

"Hey, Betty," the freshman Jeremy Martell said, "you sound like a nice girl. If things don't work out between you and the other Jeremy Martel just give me a—"

Click.

For a long moment, Betty sat staring at the telephone. She looked up when she noticed that her mother was standing in the doorway. "There *are* two Jeremy Martels at Strickland," she said.

Mrs. Maguire's heart broke for her child.

Betty picked up the phone and dialed the new number.

"Hello, Brighton Hall," said a voice.

"May I speak with Jeremy Martel, please? Tell him it's Betty." Her voice was barely audible. She had no idea how she was going to explain herself to him.

"Jeremy? He ain't here."

"Can you tell me when he will be back?"

"No, I mean he *ain't here*. He moved off campus weeks ago."

"What?!"

"Yeah. You said this is Betty, the redhead? I'm surprised you didn't know that. You're all he ever talked about." Betty lowered the phone to her lap and placed her free hand over her face.

"Hello? Betty, are you there?" The distant voice was barely audible. Mrs. Maguire tapped Betty on the shoulder and pointed to the phone.

"I'm sorry," Betty said, picking up the receiver. "Can you tell me where he moved?"

"Someplace not far from campus. But I don't have the address or anything. Sorry."

"Thank you." Not knowing what else to say, she hung up.

Without another word, she went upstairs to her room, closed the door, and began pacing. *Okay, Betty, you fouled up royally,* she thought. *You listened to your best friend, and she was wrong. I owe Jeremy an apology. But he's got some apologizing to do. It's not all my fault.* Fresh anger was overtaking her feelings of guilt. *He doesn't write to me for weeks, and then he moves off campus and doesn't tell me a thing about it. And to top it off, he doesn't tell me anything about a second Jeremy. What's with that? As if it's some minor detail he knew nothing about. Jeremy the slime-ball even said they had some mail mix-ups. Well, Jeremy Martel with one* l, *you owe me an explanation.*

With that settled, she picked up a magazine from her nightstand, flopped onto her bed, and flipped through the unread pages.

Downstairs in the living room, Mrs. Maguire put her face into her hands and prayed. "Oh, Lord, help us. My little girl's heart is broken, and I know it breaks Your heart too. Show me what to do."

Mr. Maguire came up from the basement, picked up the mail from the hallway stand, and entered the living room. "Anything I can do?" he asked as he sat beside his wife. She shared the story while he absentmindedly leafed through the mail. He set aside a few pieces of junk mail and some obvious bills, and then came to an envelope addressed to Betty, but with no return address. "Hon, look at this," he said, handing her the envelope. "I wonder how this letter got through the post office without them canceling the stamps."

Mrs. Maguire took the envelope from her husband's hand and immediately went upstairs. Betty was not in her room, but she heard the sound of water running in the bathroom. She walked to the door and knocked gently.

"Betty, you have some mail," she said to her daughter through the closed door.

"Just put it on my bureau, Mom. I'm not in the mood."

"I'm not completely sure, but I think it's from Jeremy."

After a few seconds, Betty unlocked the door and opened it. Mrs. Maguire handed the letter to her daughter, who proceeded to throw it into the bathroom wastebasket and head back to her room.

Mrs. Maguire opened her mouth to speak, but no words came out. Dumbfounded, she retrieved the envelope from the wastebasket and stood there for a moment, considering the implications of reading someone else's mail. Finally, she sat down on the toilet seat and opened the envelope. Inside was a single, loose page and a second envelope. She read the single page, and then placed all of the contents back in the envelope. She headed to Betty's room and knocked on the door. "Betty, I think you need to read this. May I come in?"

There was no response.

"Betty, you really need to read this."

The door opened a crack, and Betty stuck her hand through. Mrs. Maguire handed her the now opened envelope.

"Forgive me, dear, but I read the—"

The door closed.

"Lord, do Your thing," Mrs. Maguire prayed as she turned to leave.

Betty sat on the edge of her bed for several minutes, staring down at the single page she held in her hands. With a deep, quivering sigh, she set the page on the bed beside her and opened the second envelope. Her hands shook as she read, and then reread, the contents of the letter within.

"Oh, Jeremy," she groaned as she pressed the love letter to her chest. "Oh, my Jeremy." Suddenly, she sprang to her feet and hurried downstairs, where she found her mother sitting in the living room. She sat beside her on the couch and handed her the letter. "Mom, would you read this?"

Mrs. Maguire read the letter, handed it back to Betty, and looked at her watch. "It's not too late. Call him, dear."

Betty rushed to the phone and dialed the number that Jeremy had given in the letter. "Hello, Fairchild residence," a voice answered.

Betty struggled to get control over her emotions.

"Hello?"

"Hello, I'm sorry to bother you," said Betty. "Is a Jeremy Martel there?"

"Whom shall I say is calling?"

"Tell him it's Betty, please."

"Oh, Betty, I'm Dorothy Fairchild. Jeremy has talked of you so often. I can't believe anyone could have such beautiful red hair! Let me see if he's in his room."

Betty pondered Mrs. Fairchild's words. *How would she know? Wait, my picture. Jeremy showed her my picture. Oh, my Jeremy.*

Another voice came on the line. "Hello, Betty?"

"Yes, who is this?"

"My name is Carter. I was Jeremy's roommate."

"Was?" Betty said with a gasp. "What do you mean 'was'?"

"Yeah, it happened kind of fast, but Jeremy withdrew from school today. I just got in about five minutes ago and found a note from him. There was no explanation of any kind. I knew he was having trouble in school, but I didn't think it was this bad."

A feeling of numbness came over Betty, and she did not know what to say. She let the phone sink into her lap.

"Hello? Betty, are you still there?"

Her mother entered the hallway and, seeing the look on her daughter's face, walked over and picked up the phone.

"Hello, I'm Mrs. Maguire, Betty's mother," she said. "Who is this please?"

"I'm Carter, Jeremy's roommate."

"Carter, would you put Jeremy on the line, please?"

"I'm sorry, ma'am, but as I was just telling Betty, he withdrew from college today. He's gone."

"*Gone?* Gone where?"

"I don't know, ma'am. He just packed up and left. Didn't even take some of his personal stuff. He did leave me some money for the rest of the semester's rent, along with a note saying he withdrew, but not much more than that."

"Thank you, Carter. Would you do me a favor?"

"Sure."

"If Jeremy comes back, would you please ask him to call the Maguire home? It's an emergency. He has the number."

"I will do that, ma'am."

"Thank you." Mrs. Maguire hung up the phone and looked down at Betty. "He *will* call, dear," she said, trying to be reassuring. "Don't worry. He will call."

The shock that had paralyzed Betty was wearing off. "Oh, Mother," she whispered, "I love him so much. He was going to ask me to marry him, wasn't he?" Mrs. Maguire pulled her daughter to herself and embraced her in silence. For several minutes, the only sound that could be heard was Betty's quaking sobs.

CHAPTER 29

A FINAL LETTER

APRIL 6, 1967

April 3, 1967
Dear Betty,

I have had a lot of time these past two weeks to think about what happened the last time I saw you. I now know that I should have called before making the trip down. I left that night feeling hurt, angry, and confused. I thought you loved me as much as I loved you. But I now realize that we had not made any commitments to each other. You had the right to go out with anyone you wanted to date.

I have left college, which should come as no surprise to you. In two days, I leave for basic training for the Marines. To tell you the truth, I don't really know if this is something that I wanted to do, or if it was a knee-jerk reaction in my moment of anger. I am no longer angry, but what is done is done. I have already been sworn in.

This will be my last letter to you. Our country is at war, and I do not know what my part in the conflict will be. But I intend to give myself fully and completely to my new responsibilities.

Perhaps our paths will cross again someday. If not, I want you to know that you were the best part of my life. I will always remember you.

Goodbye, my love.
Jeremy

Betty gently touched Jeremy's name. A final tear fell onto the page like melting wax on the letter she held in her lap.

PART THREE

VIETNAM

Chapter 30

Boot Camp

April 6, 1967

The bus pulled into Casual Company, the first stop at the Parris Island training grounds, at precisely midnight. From the moment the forty-three recruits had been herded onto the bus, they had ridden in absolute silence—not by choice, but by command.

Each man had used the time to ponder the decision he had made. Some viewed it as an adventure, like going off to summer camp for the first time. Others were now second-guessing their decision, wondering if they had just made the biggest mistake of their lives. A few men, close to tears, stared out the windows into the total darkness. Most had heard stories about Parris Island, and many had seen movies about it, but few believed it would actually be *that* bad. After all, that was just a Hollywood depiction.

The door of the bus opened, and suddenly all hell broke loose. With no preamble or warning, two military police stormed the bus and began waging an assault on its passengers. "Pack up your bags and get out, now, you maggots!" one of the MPs ordered. "Out! Out! Out! You aren't worthy to be on this bus, you pieces of turd! What's the matter with you, boy? Trip over your elbow? Slime!"

The recruits—mostly teenagers—were shaken out of their complacency and found themselves running at the commands. The MPs were masters at filling their charges with terror, and they shouted out orders faster than they could possibly be obeyed. The recruits were stunned, and within seconds it dawned on each man that he was no longer a human soul. Feelings? Forget it. Self-worth? Forget that too. Their weariness was instantly dissolved, and their dreams of home abruptly dashed.

The shocked recruits stumbled over each other and staggered off the bus. "Line up here on these footprints, you worthless excuses for pus!" the MPs ordered. Each recruit, in no particular order, found a set of footprints and stood on it with bags in hand. "Drop those bags and stand at attention! Eyes forward!" The recruits dropped their bags—all the worldly possessions they had been allowed to bring—stood ramrod straight, and focused their eyes on whatever was in front of them.

The next voice the recruits heard was loud, but the man did not shout at them. As they watched his six-foot three-inch body move with practiced exactness up and down the line, they had no doubt that he was the one in charge. "I am your drill instructor, Sergeant Holliway," he said, keeping his hands folded behind his back. "For the next ten weeks I will be your mother, your father, your brother, your sister … your god. You will not eat, you will not talk, you will not pass gas unless I tell you to do so. Am I making myself clear?" A few recruits timidly answered yes. "I said, *Am I making myself clear?*"

"Yes, sir!" the chorus rang out.

"It is not, 'Yes, sir.' It is, 'Sir, yes, sir.'"

"Sir, yes, sir!" the recruits snapped in unison.

The unfortunate recruit at the front of the line had turned his head and was watching the drill instructor as he addressed the men. Too late, he snapped his head back and looked straight ahead. The drill instructor moved in his direction.

Sergeant Holliway stopped directly in front of the man and put his nose almost into his right eye. In a slow, measured voice that none of the other forty-two recruits could miss, he said, "Don't you ever look at me when you have been told, 'eyes front.'" The recruit had never experienced a threat level of this magnitude.

"I … I … am … s … s … sorry … sir," he stammered.

"S … s … sorry?" Sergeant Holliway mimicked. "You're *s … s … sorry?"* He turned and faced the men down the line. "The only thing that's sorry around here is this piece of afterbirth standing in front of me." The recruit, not knowing what to do with the spittle that had just landed on his face, stood motionless, his eyes like saucers. He suddenly had the need to urinate. Sergeant Holliway straightened to full height and yelled to all the recruits, *"And don't you ever answer me back* unless *I ask you a question!"* He bent over again and looked into the face of the frightened recruit. "Now, did I ask you a question?"

"Uh … no, sir."

"Are you deaf, maggot? I just asked if I had asked you a question."

The recruit blinked his eyes. "Uh … yes, sir. I mean, no, sir. I mean … I'm confused, sir."

To the recruit's relief, the man to his left suddenly gave out a nervous giggle. The drill sergeant's head snapped in that direction, and his whole body followed. He stuck his nose directly in the man's face. "You find something funny?" he said. The second recruit opened his mouth to speak, but nothing came out but a squeak.

"Nothing to say now, boy? Close that mouth. You're letting out more pollution than we have room for. Where are you from?"

"South Dakota, sir."

"It's, 'Sir, *the recruit is from South Dakota, sir.'* Now, where are you from?"

"Sir, the *recruit is from South Dakota, sir."*

Sergeant Holliway nodded and moved to his left, where he looked Jeremy up and down, and then straight into his eyes. "And what's your name, recruit?"

"Sir, the recruit's name is Jeremy Martel, sir," he said with a snap to his voice. *There, that wasn't so hard to learn. I think I've got this figured out.*

The drill sergeant turned to the MPs who were standing nearby. "Well, looky here, gentlemen. I think we got ourselves a college boy. A real quick study." He turned back to Jeremy. "You a … college boy, boy? No, you're not a college boy, are you? You're a flunky. What college you flunk outta, boy?"

Jeremy was stunned. *How did you figure that out so fast?*

The flickered-eye response confirmed Sergeant Holliway's suspicion. "Well, what college, boy?"

"Ah, Stickland Strate, sir. I mean Strickland Sta …"

"Shut up, flunky. It's, 'sir, the recruit flunked out of life, sir.' Running away from life, boy? Looking for someone to take care of you now, boy? Need someone to wipe your nose and empty your diaper, boy? Or maybe your girl dumped you. Is that it, boy? Did your girl dump you?"

Jeremy had no idea what had just happened, but he was suddenly missing Grandma real bad.

Without waiting for an answer, the drill sergeant moved on. The next recruit was wearing a tight T-shirt that revealed his sculpted, muscular body. He stood eyeball-to-eyeball with Sergeant Holliway and did not seem the least bit intimidated. "And why did you join the Marines, puke?"

The recruit looked straight ahead and gave a slight smirk. "Sir," he said, "the recruit was tired of people telling him what to do, sir."

Sergeant Holliway took one step back, folded his arms across his chest, and looked at the two MPs with a satisfied expression. The MPs looked at each other and mirrored that same expression. The recruits went bug-eyed, each man realizing that something had just gone seriously wrong with the universe. "Corporal," the drill sergeant said to one of the MPs, "would you be so kind as to bring me 'the helmet?'"

Without a word, the corporal left. "So, you don't like being told what to do, eh, recruit?" Sergeant Holliway's voice was soft, gentle and almost father-like. "Well, I guess you came to the right place, son. After all, we don't call this the Parris Island Country Club for nothin'."

The corporal returned with "the helmet" and handed it to the drill sergeant. As he paced up and down the line, he announced in a low growl, "There's one thing you're gonna learn and learn right now. From the moment you stepped into that bus, you became a team. You became one. Individuality does not exist on Parris Island. When one of you screw-ups screws up, the whole team screws up." He planted himself in front of the still-smirking recruit, drawing himself so close to the man's face that he had no choice but to lean backward. "And one of you just screwed up! Put this helmet on, you sorry excuse for vomit."

The recruit looked at the object in the drill sergeant's hand. "But that's a bucket," he said.

Sergeant Holliway's teeth gnashed and his face contorted into a nightmarish double of Lucifer himself. *"It's 'Sir, the recruit observes that it is a bucket, sir'"* he yelled, the spit flying from his mouth. He thrust the bucket into the recruit's hands, which now had started to tremble. The drill sergeant narrowed his eyes and clenched his teeth. With jaw muscles pulsating, he said, "Put ... it ... on."

The recruit slowly looked left, and then right. All of the other men's eyes were facing squarely front, their backs stiffly straight and arms tucked tightly at their sides. All he could hear were crickets in the distance and the sound of Sergeant Holliway breathing through his nose, like a bull ready to charge. The recruit placed the bucket over his head.

"Take two steps forward and do an about face," the drill sergeant ordered. The recruit obeyed. "This recruit will now lead you in a series of calisthenics," Sergeant Holliway shouted to the men. "Recruit, start jogging in place." When the man hesitated an instant, the drill sergeant slapped the bucket. "Now!" The bucket started bouncing, and all the recruits joined in. The MPs quickly re-entered the nightmare, swearing in a staccato fashion without, it seemed to Jeremy, ever repeating a swear.

After forty-five minutes of jogging and doing jumping jacks and deep-knee bends, the drill sergeant called the recruits to attention. "Recruit, take that bucket off." The man removed the bucket and was ordered back into line. "One more time, recruit. Why did you join the Marines?"

Sweat leaked into the recruit's eyes. His throat had gone dry, and he choked on his own saliva as he tried to swallow. Humiliated, he broke down into tears.

"Corporal, Private," Sergeant Holliway said, directing his orders to the MPs, "take these recruits to their barracks and bunk them down." With that, he strutted off, hands once again clasped behind his back. *A good and satisfying day's work,* he thought to himself. *Very good indeed.*

Not a word was spoken as the men were marched to their sleeping quarters. When each man had identified his bunk, stripped to his underwear and laid down, it was lights out. No further sound was heard except for the silent weeping of the utterly humiliated recruit who, for the first and last time, had been the leader.

Morning came all too quickly. Routine became the order of the men's days—days that began with them being awakened at 5:30 AM, and sometimes at 3:00 AM, by thunderous noises as the MPs hurled metal trash barrels around the barracks. The rest of their day was spent being torn down, shredded, and skewered. Nothing the recruits did was right, even when it was right.

The first few weeks were agony for the men. But as the "team" drilled together, crawled in the mud together, slept together, and ate together, they increasingly began to respond as one. Some of the men could not handle the disciplined life of the corps and were discharged, but the remaining thirty-four slowly transformed into a well-oiled machine. Before long, they were responding as a unit to every command with instant obedience and precision. Gradually, they came to realize that this was how it had to be if they were to serve their country with honor—and survive on the front lines.

Eight weeks into basic training, Jeremy found himself lying in his bunk after lights out and reminiscing as to how he had gotten there. His heart ached for Betty, and he longed to see her again. But he had to confess to himself, he loved the Marines. He sighed and fell into a deep, satisfying sleep.

Chapter 31

A Thorn in the Flesh

June 16, 1970

Sergeant Major Martel stood on the lip of the mound of dirt that he had known as home for the past three months. He and the other 476 Marines had been charged with defending "Firebase Trumpet," a small piece of real estate located near the Cambodian border. Jeremy wasn't sure, any more, why this was their responsibility. Two years ago, he would have agreed that the United States could win this war. However, now, as he neared the end of his third tour of duty, it seemed that nobody wanted victory in Vietnam, especially the politicians. It was a thought that he dared share with no one.

Jeremy placed his hands on his hips and looked westward. The sun was about two hours from setting. *Should be a gorgeous sunset, the way those clouds are lining up on that horizon,* he thought. He refocused his attention on the tree line located a thousand yards from the base of the hill across an open field. That line represented the edge of hell, and at dawn, he knew, hell would release its fury. Until now the attacks had only been slight skirmishes, the enemy willing to sacrifice many of its troops to test the strength and weaknesses of their defenses.

Sergeant Major Martel reviewed in his mind what still had to be done to prepare this section of the perimeter, but he could think of nothing. A smile creased his face. He found no humor in the situation, but he was struck by the irony of thinking a glorious sunset was about to reveal itself over the hell that was about to break out in front of him.

Jeremy turned to make one final inspection around the portion of the perimeter for which he was responsible. The click of a camera shutter caught his attention. He looked down to see Palowski, a photojournalist, lying on his back in the dirt to his left side. "Great shot, Sarge," he said. "Now if you could just move a bit to your left, I could get more of the flag over there into the frame."

Jeremy walked away instead. Palowski was a thorn in his flesh, but there was nothing he could do about it. If it were up to him, no civilian—regardless of how much the politicians wanted photos of this war to use for their public relations back home—would be allowed on this firebase. Or, for that matter, anywhere in Vietnam ... if it were up to him. But orders were orders. Palowski was an intrusion, but Central Command had given him full access to the men. He was allowed to photograph them and interview them, as long as he did not "interfere" with the Marines' ability to accomplish their duties. Of course, Jeremy's definition of "interference" and his colonel's were worlds apart.

As Jeremy walked away, he reflected on his first meeting with Palowski. Four days of nonstop rain had abated enough for the mail helicopters to land. Palowski had arrived on one of those helicopters, and after stowing his gear in his assigned sleeping quarters, he began his craft.

Palowski first approached the sergeant major's tent—Jeremy's sanctuary—and, without asking permission, parted the curtain over the doorway and entered. Jeremy had been sitting behind his "table"—an empty crate with a piece of plywood across the top—where he had been writing letters to the mothers of fallen soldiers, attempting to explain why their son or daughter would be coming home in a casket. He leapt from behind the table when Palowski began taking pictures and asking questions, reaching him in two steps. He grabbed the photojournalist by the shirt collar and lifted his small frame off the ground. In one quick motion he had thrown him back out the opening, ripping the curtain hanging from the bar in the process.

Palowski landed on his back in the mud. Sergeant Major Martel followed him outside and, in no uncertain terms, made it clear that he would not allow this kind of intrusion. The photojournalist, obnoxious to the core, looked up with his camera still in hand and said, "Smile!" *Click.*

Jeremy rushed toward Palowski, who had made no move to get up, and again grabbed him by the collar. "Sergeant Major! Back off!" said a sharp voice. The command came from Lieutenant Moorland, and it was to be obeyed.

"Lieutenant, sir," said Jeremy, "if this piece of—"

"I said back off, Sergeant Major! Palowski, I suggest you get yourself and your camera as far away from here as possible. Now!"

Palowski slowly stood, smiled a toothy smile at Jeremy, and said, "Got some great shots, Sarge." He walked away with a victory laugh.

Lieutenant Moorland approached and stood nose to nose with Jeremy. "Sergeant Major Martel, you will not—I repeat, you will not—lay hands on Palowski again. Do you understand?"

Jeremy quickly realized that if he spewed out the ticker-tape parade of language that was rolling around his tongue, he would immediately be demoted to buck private. With a smart, crisp salute reeking his disdain, he said, "Sir, yes, sir! May I be dismissed … sir?"

The lieutenant returned the salute, missing none of the tone in Jeremy's voice. "Dismissed."

Jeremy turned and re-entered his tent. The lieutenant followed. "Sergeant Major," he said in a more controlled voice, "We're all under stress these days. I know how you feel about journalists, but you have to let up on them. Each one that's come to this base has complained that he was more intimidated by you than by any other Marine—or by the Viet Cong, for that matter. Palowski has a reputation for being a thorn in the butt, but you have to deal with it. Colonel's orders—public relations and all that. And of all the people who ought to know about orders, you should."

Jeremy paused for a moment. "You're right, Lieutenant," he admitted. "It won't happen again."

Jeremy smiled. This memory could have occurred a lifetime ago, and it was hard for him to believe that it had happened just two days before. He shook his head and walked away from Palowski as the photojournalist continued to snap pictures of him.

Sergeant Martel continued his inspection, pausing at various locations along the perimeter to give a word of encouragement to the men, or make sure the trenches were dug deep enough, or ensure the sandbags were piled high enough, or confirm that the weapons were clean enough. "A little deeper on that trench, Marine," he would say, or, "Pile on a few more sandbags, Private." Jeremy knew that none of these things really needed to be done, but he wanted to give his men something to do to keep their minds off tomorrow's dawn and the inevitable losses that would follow.

CHAPTER 32

THE CONFRONTATION

JUNE 16, 1970

The sun slowly worked its way toward the horizon as Jeremy continued his inspection along the perimeter. "Hey, Sarge, big day tomorrow, huh?" a voice called up from one of the trenches as he passed by. There was a nervous twinge in the man's voice.

"It's gonna be like any other day around here, Private," Jeremy replied. "Long and hot, or long and wet. Better get some rest."

"Hey, Sarge, wanna see a picture of my girl?" The private held up a picture for him to admire. "Ain't she a beauty?"

Jeremy could not make out any of the woman's features from where he was standing, but he said, "She sure is, Private. How'd a butt-ugly sucker like you get hooked up with someone like her?" The man smiled and returned the picture to his front pocket.

Jeremy walked a few feet down the line. "Hey, Private," he called out to a Marine who had just opened a C-ration of hash. "What's for supper tonight?"

"Steak, Sarge. Thick, juicy and smothered in mushrooms. Why, it's so rare a good veterinarian could save it."

"Nothing but the best for the Marines," Sergeant Martel laughed. He continued to move along the trenches and speak to each Marine under his command. He knew their names and rank, but did not want to know about their personal lives—whether they had girlfriends, or if they were married, or if they had kids. He felt such information only made it more complicated for him when he had to lead them into battle—battles in which many would be severely wounded, and others would not survive at all. Command was difficult enough, and he did not need the extra burden.

"Sarge?" the voice of Private Noonan called out from below. He was hunkered down in a three-foot-deep trench, cradling his M-16 rifle.

"What is it, Private?"

"Ain't that gonna be a great sunset?"

"Sure is, Private." Jeremy began to walk away. Private Noonan paused a moment, and then said, "My first child is supposed to be born in four days."

Jeremy stopped in his tracks, and a wince appeared across his face. *I don't need this tonight, kid. Not tonight.* He turned back to face the soldier. "That's great, Private. When this is all over, you and your son will watch many sunsets just like this one." He turned and took a step forward.

"You really think it'll be a boy, Sarge?" Private Noonan called after him.

Jeremy looked back and gazed into the shadowy face of the frightened soldier. "Of course it will be, Private. What else would be the firstborn of a Marine?" Private Noonan lay back in the trench, a grin on his face.

Jeremy cut short his rounds and headed back to his tent. It had now been more than twenty hours since he had slept—and that had been only for a few hours at best. He needed some time to himself. *Just an hour's rest*, he told himself, *and then I'll return to the trenches and join the men until dawn.*

As he pulled the flap back to enter his tent, a voice called out to him. "Sergeant Major Martel, may I have a word with you?" Jeremy turned and saw Captain Mike Harrington, the firebase's chaplain, beckoning to him from his own tent. "It will just take a moment."

No, you may not have a word with me, Jeremy thought, but he let the flap of his tent drop. The captain's voice made it sound as if he was making a request, but Jeremy knew an order was an order. He walked over to the chaplain's tent, entered, stood at attention, and saluted. Captain Harrington returned the salute.

Jeremy removed his helmet and tucked it under his left arm. "Yes, sir, you wanted to speak with me, sir?"

"Yes, Sergeant Major," said the chaplain. "Have a seat." He pointed to a straight-backed wooden chair positioned in front of his own "desk"—a piece of plywood placed across a couple of carpenter's horses. Jeremy reluctantly obeyed and waited while the chaplain picked up a file that had been lying on his desk and browsed through it.

"Uh, Captain, may I ask why you called me in here?" Jeremy asked. "I have some things to do before I get back to my men."

"Yes, Sergeant Major Martel, I know you have many things to do to prepare for what is coming tomorrow. But I have been looking over your file: two unit citations, three purple hearts, a Bronze Star, a Silver Star, a Distinguished Service Medal. Very impressive." Jeremy sat motionless. It took every ounce of his restraint to keep from getting up and walking out.

"Tell me, Sergeant Major," the captain continued, reviewing another document in the file, "why three tours?"

"Sir?"

"You could have gone home after one tour of duty. Why three?"

"Sir, what does this have to do with—"

"Just humor me, Sergeant."

Jeremy paused. "Yes, sir. It's simple, sir. This is what I do."

"What does that mean, exactly?" The chaplain leaned forward, folded his hands in front of him, rested his arms on the desk and looked intensely into Jeremy's eyes.

"Sir, the Marines. This is my life. I am very good at what I do." He paused and shifted uncomfortably in his chair.

"Go on, Sergeant."

Jeremy leaned forward, a look of intensity on his face. "Sir, I know how to make sure as many of my men get home as is humanly possible—and not in body bags or with any missing body parts. I can get them through this mess and back to their families and sweethearts. I just want to get them out of this hellhole in one piece."

Captain Harrington sat back and nodded. He rested his elbows on the arms of his chair, folded his hands and tapped his lips with his forefingers. "And what about you, Sergeant?"

"What do you mean, sir?"

The chaplain again leaned forward and looked into Jeremy's eyes. "It's time for you to come home, son."

Jeremy blinked and shifted in his chair. "I still don't know what you're getting at, Captain."

"I think you do. Three tours. Multiple battles. Shot up. And yet here you are, like a mother hen protecting her chicks. I have watched you, Sergeant. You spit nails when you must, bring these men to the breaking point, and work them and drill them until they are ready to drop. You want me to tell you why, Sergeant?" The chaplain did not wait for Jeremy to respond. "It's because you love these men—*your* men—whom God has placed under your care. I can see it in you. They are not just 'Marines' to you. They are living souls, and you love them."

Jeremy's face contorted with the heated anger he suddenly felt. His eyes narrowed to slits and his jaw muscles pulsated, but he said nothing.

"The way you love these men is the way God loves you," the chaplain said in a gentler tone. "You would die before leaving one of your men in the field. And that's just how God has loved you. You had an encounter with God at some time in the past—I can see it in you. I don't know what happened to make you so bitter toward Him, but I can tell you that your main battle is not with the enemy beyond that tree line." The chaplain pointed westward. "Your battle is with God, and it's time you surrendered. He has allowed you to be sifted like wheat and tested beyond what most could endure. Yet even though His purposes may have been hidden from you, He has kept you in His hands. Do you really think you could have survived all the things you've gone through if that were not true? It's time to come home, son. It's time to come home."

Jeremy clenched his teeth and angrily stood to his feet. "This is my home, Captain. May I be dismissed, sir?"

"Just one more thing." The chaplain reached for a book that rested near the edge of the desk, picked it up and handed it to Jeremy. "Here, Sergeant Major, take my Bible and read Luke, chapter fifteen, starting with verse eleven. You may find it—"

"No thank you, Captain," Jeremy said as he put on his helmet. "I have my own Bible. Now, may I be dismissed?" The chaplain nodded. Jeremy smartly saluted, and then turned and left before the salute could be returned.

Jeremy entered his own tent and angrily threw his helmet onto the gray, blanket-covered cot. He sat on the floor, rested his back against the foot of the cot, and doubled up his knees. He held out his right arm, but immediately clenched his fist when he saw that he was shaking. He wanted to chalk it up to the anger he was feeling toward the chaplain, but the truth was that this was not the first time he had experienced these symptoms.

God, I'm not afraid to die. It would almost be merciful. The thought surprised him. The problem was not fear, but his nerves—nerves made raw by the blood, suffering, and death of war. *Oh, God, so much death.* He had sworn to so many men that he would not let anything happen to them, but in the end, he had been powerless to do anything to prevent the inevitable from happening.

He realized that for the first time in a long time—just how long, he could not remember—he had breathed the name of God.

He unbuttoned his lapel pocket and removed a leather-bound, weathered, and battle-worn pocket Bible. He flipped open to the middle and took out the picture of the redhead with braces whom he had once dated and planned to marry. He shook his head as he remembered back to those days. That was another life—a safer, joy-filled life—when he was with her. He closed the Bible and placed the picture on top of it, allowing himself a few moments to dwell on what might have been.

After several minutes, he turned the picture over and looked at the 1,057 dots he had imprinted on the back. Each dot represented one day he had been in the Marines and one day he had looked at Betty's picture, thought about her, and yearned for what would never be. He withdrew the stub of a pencil from the same lapel pocket and inscribed another dot.

Jeremy placed the picture on the mattress of his cot, and then opened the front cover of the Bible. His eyes fell on his grandma's inscriptions:

> The true measure of a man is not in the possibles he accomplishes that last a lifetime, but in the impossibles he allows God to accomplish through him that last for eternity. With forever-love, Grandma.
>
> "The end of all things, their purposes revealed or hidden, is good for those who love God."

He had once believed those words. How long ago had that been? Did it even matter?

Jeremy reached around, picked up the picture he had laid on the bed and, with one more longing look, replaced it in the pages. He began to place the Bible back into his lapel pocket, but something he could not explain suddenly stirred within him. He took out the little book again and held it in his trembling hands. Slowly, he turned to the passage the chaplain had suggested and began to read: "A certain man had two sons."

Jeremy instantly recognized the familiar parable of the prodigal son. He thought about the number of times as a child that he had heard Sunday school lessons and sermons centered on just this one passage. He continued to read, and as he did, the words seemed to leap off the page at him:

> The younger of them said to his father, Father, give me the portion of goods that falleth to me ... the younger son gathered all together, and took his journey into a far country, and there wasted his substance with riotous living.... And when he came to himself, he said, How many hired servants of my father's have bread enough and to spare, and I perish with hunger! ... I will arise and go to my father and will say unto him, Father, I have sinned against heaven, and before thee, and am no more worthy to be called thy son.

A peace settled over Jeremy as he read the words. Strangely, it was like reading a letter from an old friend.

> But when he was yet a great way off, his father saw him, and had compassion, and ran, and fell on his neck, and kissed him.... This my son was dead, and is alive again; he was lost, and is found.

"It's time to come home, My son," a voice said.

"What?" Jeremy said, looking up. He expected to see the chaplain standing in the doorway, but no one was there. He understood. A single tear slipped from his eye, and then another. His shoulders began to shake with sobs of emotion as the years of rebelliousness, anger, and bitterness he had held inside began to be released. The Bible fell from his hands, and through his tears, he cried out to God to forgive him for the years of running from Him and rejecting Him.

Just then, he felt the arms of his Father surround him in love. "Oh, my God, my God," were the only words he could find to say. In the back of his mind, he could hear a still, small voice whisper, "My son, My son!" He wept in agony over the lost years, and for joy at the burdens that had been lifted. He still did not understand all the reasons for the sorrows he had endured, but it no longer seemed to matter.

Jeremy did not know how long he remained there, weeping from sorrow, and praying, and rejoicing in his heart, but the last thought that came to his mind before he drifted off to sleep was, *Welcome home, My son.*

CHAPTER 33

PEACE

JUNE 16, 1970, 10:00 PM

"Hey, Sarge," said Private Jimmy Noonan from outside the tent flap. Cautiously, he pushed aside the curtain and poked his nose through the entrance. "May I have permission to enter?"

Jeremy was startled awake. *Beat it, Private, this is my sanctuary*, was the first thought that entered his head. But he said, "Sure, Private, for just a moment." He rubbed his face, vigorously wiping away any tearful remains. It wouldn't do to have some private thinking his sergeant had been crying.

Jeremy remained seated on the floor and looked up at the tall, lanky Marine that now stood before him. "What's on your mind, son?" he asked, expecting the Marine to spill his guts about his fears of the dawn. He smiled to himself. *Son?* This Marine couldn't have been more than three years younger than himself. *Have I gotten that old?*

Private Noonan stepped closer, reached down and picked up the picture of Betty which had fallen from Jeremy's Bible. "This your girl, Sarge?" he asked. "She's a beauty." He turned it over to the other side. "What's with all the dots?"

Jeremy reached up and took the picture from Private Noonan's hand. He found the Bible that had slid to the floor, slipped the picture into the center, and placed it back into his lapel pocket. "You wanted something, Private?" he asked with obvious impatience. He again rubbed his face.

"Well, I've written this here letter to my wife, and I was wondering if, when tomorrow is over, if I'm not able to ..." He left the sentence hanging and held the letter out for his sergeant to take.

Jeremy marveled at the timing of God. He stood to his feet, ignoring the letter in Private Noonan's hand. "You have some concerns about tomorrow, Marine?" he asked.

Private Noonan dropped his arm. "Well, I guess. I mean, I ain't afraid of dying or anything. It's just that ... well, I don't know how my wife and baby will get along without me."

Jeremy thought for a moment. "Private, may I share something with you? Something very personal?"

"Of course ... Sarge." He was not used to his sergeant asking for his permission, and he was suddenly feeling a bit awkward.

"Sit down, Private." Private Noonan obeyed and sat on the cot. Jeremy sat beside him and removed the Bible from his lapel pocket. He opened the Scriptures and slowly began to share his faith for the first time since he was a child.

A half hour later, the two Marines walked out of the tent and returned to the trenches. Private Noonan, with a peace in his soul that he did not know was possible, soon found sleep. Meanwhile, Jeremy sat on the edge with his rifle across his lap, looking toward hell as he waited for the dawn.

Chapter 34

Dawn

June 17, 1970

Sleep evaded Jeremy, and the night passed slowly. He spent the night alternating his gaze between the tree line and the cloudless, star-studded, moonlit sky that slowly disappeared behind a thick shroud of milky-gray clouds. A blackness he had never before experienced seemed to descend and blend all creation together into one unknowable mass.

Jeremy held his hand out in front of his face, just as he had done as a child after his father tucked him in and turned off the lights in his bedroom. Back then, he had eventually been able to make out the image of his hand as his eyes got used to the ambient light coming through the window. But this darkness was something different—the blackest darkness he could ever recall. *Hell is over there,* he thought. *It wants to come here and destroy us.*

Dawn approached, but Jeremy's uneasiness only grew. *You would think I'd be used to this after three tours of duty.* He raised his binoculars and looked through them. He knew it was a wasted effort, but it made him feel better, as if he was doing something productive besides waiting. That was the worst part of battle—the waiting—because it gave a man time to think and allow his imagination to run wild. There was no time for thinking in the heat of hand-to-hand combat, when instinct and training took over.

Although it was still too dark to make out any movement, a faint *whomp, whomp* sound caught his attention. He realized what he was hearing. *Mortars.* He jumped to his feet and raised his hand to his mouth. "Incoming! Incoming!" he yelled, and then dove into the trench.

Many of the other Marines had heard the same faint sound coming from the tree line and were now hunkered down in their trenches, wishing they had dug a few feet deeper. Others, completely exhausted, were still fast asleep. They would soon be awakened by the sound of the shells bursting.

The first few shells landed harmlessly behind the trenches, exploding in the latrine and in the empty tents. Jeremy knew these first shots were for measuring the distance and for effect. The enemy would soon close in on its target.

Jeremy picked up his rifle and began to walk along the line. As the fires broke out, he appeared as a silhouette in front of them. Mortars from the firebase engaged as more shells from the tree line exploded among them.

Flares suddenly burst open the darkness of the field. Jeremy looked up and saw that black-clad figures had already left the safety of the trees and were swarming toward them like an army of ants. The mortars from the base's guns were adjusted, and soon shells began landing among the "ants."

Jeremy's men peered over the edges of the trenches, straining to see the advancing enemy. "Steady, men," he said. "They're just testing your nerves. Keep your heads down. I'll let you know when you can look at the scenery." More flares descended, illuminating the field. A withering sheet of steel from M-60 machine guns began to cut the enemy to pieces. But they kept coming.

Two mortar shells from the tree line landed to the left and right of the observation tower. Jeremy quickly realized the enemy was targeting it, and that the next shell would be a direct hit. He jumped out of the trench and began running toward the tower. "Get out! Get out!" he yelled. The two Marines who were there wasted no time in obeying, but as they started to climb down, a shell burst on the roof. The bodies of the men flew horizontally before falling to the ground. Jeremy knew they were dead, but he had no time to mourn.

He ran back to his men and walked up and down the line, even as more shells began to fall from the sky. Ammunition exploded, turning Firebase Trumpet into an inferno. A fireball, once a jeep, rose into the air and fell back to earth twisted and mangled. Bodies of men caught in the open were torn apart by shrapnel.

"Steady, men." Jeremy's voice was calm and controlled. "Any minute now, you will—I repeat, you *will*—let them know the full fury of the United States Marines. Steady, men." The Marines turned and watched as their sergeant major walked along the edge of the trench, giving encouragement and last bits of advice as he passed from soldier to soldier. "Take aim. Don't rush your shots. Make every bullet count."

A faint light began to appear on the horizon. The dawn had come.

"Hey, Sarge," said a voice.

"What, Marine?" Jeremy replied.

"Ain't you afraid?"

"No time to think about that, soldier."

"Where's God when you want Him?" another man yelled, a tinge of fear in his voice.

"Why, can't you see Him, Marine?" Jeremy replied. "He's right here, carrying me."

Movement caught his attention as he walked down the line. In the faint light, he saw Palowski kneeling in the open a few yards left of a sand-bagged machine gun emplacement that was set on the flank of his command. A camera was in his hands, and he was snapping pictures of the gunners as fast as he could. A mortar shell exploded about twenty yards to the right of the machine gunners, but Palowski only glanced momentarily in that direction before resuming his picture-taking.

"Palowski! Get out of there!" Jeremy yelled. The journalist either did not hear him or chose to ignore the warning. Jeremy began to run.

A second shell burst a few yards closer. Palowski flinched, but he ignored this blast as well. Jeremy knew where the next shell would land. Already the two Marines stationed at the machine gun were hunkered down behind the relative safety of the sandbags. Palowski remained exposed, oblivious to the danger.

As the Marines sunk down, Palowski stood to get into a better position to film them. Jeremy hit him on his blind side like a linebacker blitzing a quarterback. The two fell over the sandbags and landed on top of the two Marines already in the pit. At that moment, the third shell burst just a few feet to the left of where Palowski had been standing.

Palowski gasped and wheezed as he tried to regain the breath that had been knocked out of him. Jeremy struggled to his feet and climbed out of the pit. The two gunners unceremoniously shoved Palowski out and, with ears still ringing, returned to spraying lead into the enemy.

"What the? Why'd you do that?" Palowski screamed, struggling to regain some ability to breathe. "You just cost … me a Pulitzer … prize-winning … picture!"

Jeremy knelt, grabbed Palowski by the shirt collar, and pulled him close to his face. "That's the first and last time I'm going to save your miserable life, Palowski," he said, spitting out his anger through gritted teeth.

"Thanks for nothing," the photojournalist shot back. "I can take care of myself."

"Is that right? Tell me, Palowski, are you left- or right-handed?"

Palowski looked puzzled. "What does that have to do with you costing me my Pulitzer?"

"Answer me, Palowski. Are you a lefty or a righty?"

"A lefty."

"Well, not any more." With that, Jeremy released his grip, stood up and walked away, ignoring the gash in his right calf.

Palowski stood and rocked a bit, quickly realizing that he was shaken up more than he realized. He bent over to pick up his camera lying next to the machine gun emplacement, and noticed some blood on his left shirt cuff. He pulled his sleeve up a few inches and stared at a hand that was now missing all of its fingers and half of its palm. "Hmm, I wonder how that …" He dropped and fainted into a heap. Twenty minutes later, he awoke to find his left hand throbbing and covered in bandages.

The mortar shells from the tree line were now falling all over Firebase Trumpet. Jeremy turned his gaze back to the front lines and found the Viet Cong were about halfway across the open field. "Hold your fire, men," he ordered as he continued to walk the edges of the trench. "Wait for my command."

Seconds that seemed like an eternity passed. "Where the devil is our artillery support, Sarge?" one Marine yelled. It was a question that every grunt in the line was silently asking himself. Jeremy was wondering the same thing. "Any minute now, Marines. Steady. Now! Fire! Fire! Fire!"

The Marines opened fire just as the firebase cut loose with every weapon at its disposal. The bodies of the enemy soldiers began piling up in the open field at an unbelievable rate, their flesh torn apart by machine gun bursts, rifle-propelled grenades, mortar shells, and cannons. Yet they kept advancing.

Some of the Viet Cong stopped to aim their rifles at any exposed heads of the Marines they found, while others shot from the hip on the run, and still others lobbed grenades into the trenches. "Medic!" the Marines shouted across the plateau as their comrades fell. The medics responded as fast as they could, but in a short time they were overwhelmed with their task.

By now, a few of the Viet Cong were drawing close to the 200-foot embankment covered with land mines and rows of barbed wire that they would have to climb. As they charged, the barb wire entangled them and slowed their progress, but it did not stop them. A few of the fighters threw themselves on top of the wire to form bridges their comrades could use to cross. In short order, the bodies of the Viet Cong soldiers began to pile up in front of the Marines, creating an obstacle for the enemy. But still they kept coming.

"Sergeant Major!" a voice called out. An out-of-breath runner from another sector jumped into Jeremy's trench.

Jeremy squatted down next to the man. "What is it, corporal?"

"Lieutenant Moorland's down, Sarge. Shot in the leg. I think it's broken. Also, our radio is out of commission. He sent me to tell you the enemy is about to break through. We can't hold. He wants you to send whatever help you can."

Jeremy stood and gave a quick analysis of his defenses. He turned back to the runner. "Get back to the lieutenant and tell him I'll bring what I can."

Jeremy turned to a man close by and yelled over the thunder, "Corporal Yastremski! You're in charge here now." Then he ran along the line, yelling, "Every fourth man follow me!" Forty-three men left their positions and followed their sergeant major to a second line of defense.

"Gather round, Marines," he shouted. The Marines obeyed. "Men, the southwest sector is about to be overrun. We're going to make sure that does not happen. Fix bayonets." In one movement, the bayonets were fixed. "Now, follow me!"

Jeremy turned and sprinted toward the enemy. As they approached the endangered sector, they saw the enemy had already pushed into the American defenses. Marines were engaged in hand-to-hand combat, and the bodies on both sides were falling. *"Show 'em how it's* done, *boys!"* Jeremy yelled. As one unit they charged, screaming and yelling, into the battle.

The enemy was stunned by the sudden appearance of the Marines and the violence of their onslaught. Bayonets found their mark and pierced the hearts, lungs, guts, and throats of the Viet Cong. Jaws were shattered by butts of rifles wielded like battering rams.

Private Noonan took down two enemy soldiers before he was run through the belly with a bayonet. The attacker violently yanked the bayonet free and was about to run it through Noonan a second time when Jeremy put his own bayonet through the man's throat. Jeremy yanked it out and let the dead Viet Cong crumble to the ground.

Noonan dropped his rifle, held his hands over his stomach, and collapsed into a sitting position. Jeremy knelt beside him and gently helped him lay back. "You're going to be just fine, Private." He lied. "It's just a flesh wound."

Jeremy stood to his feet. "Medic!" he yelled. He could do no more. The battle raged around him, and he had to move on to support the rest of his troops. *Better one Marine out of action than two,* he thought.

A medic came seconds after Jeremy left. He tore open Noonan's shirt and did a quick analysis of the wound. "Stay still," the medic said as he ripped open a sulfa packet and dumped the contents into the wound. He applied a field dressing and turned to leave. There was no time to do more.

Private Noonan reached up and grabbed the medic's vest. "Am … I … gonna … make it, doc?"

"Sure you are, Private." The medic also lied. "Hold your hands over the dressing and press." Then he was gone. Noonan lay motionless, closed his eyes and began praying for his yet-to-be-born son. "Oh, God," he said aloud through gritted teeth in short, painful breaths. "Take … care of my … boy.… Just take … care of him."

Private Noonan did not see the three Viet Cong charging toward him with their bayonets pointed at his chest. Just as they reached him, a rifle blast sounded, removing the first enemy's head from his shoulders. The soldier fell dead on top of Private Noonan, who screamed in pain. The other two fighters stopped and looked in the direction from which the rifle blast had come.

Jeremy had already pulled the trigger of his M-16 again, but this time it jammed. The second attacker rushed him and thrust his bayonet at his throat. Jeremy parried with his own bayonet and deflected the enemy's strike, but the knife sliced through the skin and bone of his left cheek. Immediately, Jeremy smashed the butt of his rifle into the groin of the Viet Cong, and then slashed his bayonet in a downward movement. The knife cut across the enemy soldier's throat, almost severing his head from his torso.

The third attacker made the same mistake. Again, Jeremy parried the thrusting blade, and this time brought the butt of his rifle into the jaw of the enemy. The stunned Viet Cong staggered backward, blood spraying from his nose and mouth. Jeremy turned his rifle and thrust the bayonet into his heart.

Jeremy turned to see if any more enemy solders were close by. He nodded in satisfaction. The battle was well under control, and the enemy was retreating from the sector. A groan from the ground caught his attention. Holding his rifle in his right hand, he leaned over and pulled the dead Viet Cong off the wounded Private Noonan. He knelt and looked at the wound. Blood seeped through the dressing.

"I'm gonna die, Sarge," Noonan said, wincing as he spoke. "Would you … do me a favor?"

"What is it?" asked Jeremy.

"When this is all … over, would you look in on my wife and son and … tell them how much I love them? That my last thoughts were … of them?"

"I won't need to, Private. You're going to do that yourself."

Noonan had no more to say. He lay still, looking into the eyes of the man who had led him to a source of peace he had never before known. The sounds of thunder roared overhead. The American artillery support had finally arrived. A rolling barrage moved across the open field, shredding the Viet Cong reserves that had been sent in to join the attack. Within minutes, those still standing began to fall back to the tree line. Others on the hill tried to retreat, but they were shot in the back as they ran.

"I have more to do now, Private," said Jeremy. "But I'll be back and check in on you." He stood to his feet. Just then, someone shouted, "Sniper!" A wounded Viet Cong, thought to be dead, had risen to his knees and was holding a rifle in his hand. He aimed it randomly and pulled the trigger just as a round from a submachine gun perforated his body.

The bullet caught Sergeant Major Martel in the forehead, just below the hairline. Private Noonan looked up to see Jeremy's head snap back. It remained in that position for what seemed like an eternity, and then Jeremy crashed to the ground. Noonan lay still, not comprehending what had just happened. "Sarge? Sarge!" Ignoring his own pain, he tried to crawl to his fallen leader. "Medic!" he cried.

The medic arrived a short time later, knelt beside Jeremy, and made one quick check for any vital signs. He shook his head and began to walk away.

"No, don't leave! Do something!" Noonan pleaded.

"There is nothing I can do for him," the medic replied. He picked up his bag and quickly walked away.

It was now two hours after dawn, and the battle was finally over. It had been a decisive victory for the American forces, but one that had come at a heavy price. More than 800 Viet Cong were dead, and many more were wounded. Fifty-seven Marines entered eternity that day, and another 102 had been wounded. A continual stream of MedEvac choppers arrived and departed the base throughout the day.

Private Noonan was one of the first to be evacuated, but not before he saw the body of Sergeant Major Martel placed into a bag and laid alongside the other fallen Marines. Another man, holding his camera in his right hand, stood over the body as the medics zipped it closed. The man put the camera down and, using his one good hand, tried to help the Marines lift the body into the chopper. Then he stepped back, gave a civilian salute to the man who had saved his life, and picked up his camera.

"Hey, Palowski," Noonan choked out as the photojournalist walked away. "You gonna write something about Sarge?"

Palowski turned toward the voice. "Yeah, Private," he said.

"What are you gonna say?"

Palowski watched as the helicopter with Jeremy's body rose into the air. "I don't know yet, Private. Why?"

"They don't come any finer, Palowski. Just make sure you say that."

"I'm beginning to see that, Private." He nodded and walked away.

Three weeks later, Mrs. Maguire held a copy of the *Clayton Daily News* in her lap. A fresh wetness appeared on her cheeks as she looked at the picture of the Marine on the front cover. The caption read, "Fallen Hero—One of Our Bravest, One of Our Own." Her eyes moved down to again read the beginning of the article written by Palowski.

> There is a time to live, and a time to die. For Sergeant Major Jeremy Martel, it was his time to die. His time was too soon, as is true of all those who have fallen, or will yet fall, in this war. But he did not die in vain, for before he was struck down by a sniper's bullet, he made sure that as many of his comrades as possible would remain

> behind and continue to see life—to see loved ones, to see sons and daughters again. We have nothing to fear in this country if this is the kind of man who is leading our fighting men. Many—myself included—owe our lives to him.

Mrs. Maguire heard Betty's car out in the driveway. *Oh, Lord, how will I break this to her?* she thought. The porch door opened, and then the front door to the house. Betty entered and hung her sweater in the front hallway closet. "Mom! Dad! I'm home."

"In here, dear," her mother replied.

Betty entered the living room and saw her mother sitting on the couch, dabbing her eyes with a tissue. "What's wrong, Mom? Did something happen to Dad?"

Mrs. Maguire shook her head and patted the seat beside her, motioning for Betty to sit. Betty held her breath and slowly sat beside her mother. "There's some bad news," Mrs. Maguire said, gaining control of her emotions. "It's about Jeremy."

"What about Jeremy?" Betty asked quietly. Her mother handed her the newspaper. She recognized Jeremy's picture immediately, and then she read the caption. For a moment she sat in disbelief, unable to cry, or to speak, or to do anything but stare at the newspaper.

"This must be a mistake," she finally choked out. "They must have mixed up the photo with the wrong caption. Oh, Momma, tell me it's a mistake!" The tears rolled from her eyes, and she fell sobbing into her mother's arms.

PART FOUR

HOME

Chapter 35

New Beginnings

September 13, 1974

It had been several months since Roy Napier had been to Boston's Dudley Square Financial Savings and Loan to meet with Robert Raymond, the loan manager. Most of the bank employees knew Roy by sight, and some knew him by name.

He approached the receptionist's desk. "Mr. Napier, good to see you," she said. Gloria's smile—though Roy understood it was just professional courtesy—was in itself reason enough for him to bank there. He understood the bank's rationale for having such a beautiful woman be the first thing that any customer—new or existing—saw when they entered. He had applied the same philosophy to his own businesses.

"Mr. Raymond will be with you in just a few minutes," said Gloria. "May I get you a cup of coffee while you wait?" She asked the question, but made no attempt to follow through on the offer. She knew what the response would be.

"Thanks, but no thanks, Gloria," he said. "Never touch the stuff." *You are one good-looking woman,* Roy thought. *If it weren't for that ring on your left finger ...*

Doreen, the head teller, walked past on her way back from a break. "Hello, Mr. Napier," she said. "It's been a while."

"Hello, Doreen." Roy left Gloria and followed the head teller to her counter. There was something about Doreen that had always fascinated him. Maybe it was her genuineness and her unpretentious manner, or maybe it was because she reminded him of his mother. It certainly wasn't her looks—she was rather grandmotherly, overly made-up, and on this day displaying a too-tight permanent. But he genuinely liked her, which was not something he could say even about his closest associates.

"You are looking as radiant as ever. When are you going to leave that no-good husband of yours and run away with me?"

"I'm off at 5:00. How about then?" The two chuckled. This flirting had been going on between them for years. Roy knew that she adored her truck-driving man.

"Tell me something," Roy said, leaning forward so he could lower his voice. "I thought I knew all the tellers at this bank. Who is that?" He pointed with his dimpled chin toward a girl with flaming red hair a few windows down.

"Oh, that's Betty Maguire," Doreen whispered back. "You are not the first to inquire about her, I might add. She transferred from another branch and has been here for a couple of months. She's going to take my spot when I retire next month. Really knows her stuff, and she's the sweetest thing." She paused a moment to look in Betty's direction. "She's also not married … and for the life of me, I can't figure that one out."

"Mr. Napier," a voice said, startling Roy out of his concentration on Betty. Gloria had approached quietly from behind. "Mr. Raymond will see you now." Roy took one more look in Betty's direction, and then followed Gloria to Mr. Raymond's office.

Roy finished his business twenty minutes later and headed for the exit. On an impulse, he turned and looked back over his shoulder where Betty was working. *Give it a shot, Roy,* he told himself. *Nothing to lose.* He walked to her window and stood behind the only other customer in line.

"Mr. Napier, I can help you over here," Doreen said a bit too loudly. He shot her a look. "Oh, I'm sorry," she quickly said, "I just remembered I have to check on something." She looked at Roy and left with the hint of a knowing smile.

The customer ahead of Roy finished his business and walked away. "Yes, how may I help you, sir?" Betty said with a practiced and yet genuinely sincere greeting.

Roy froze. *That smile. She's even more gorgeous up close.*

"May I help you?" Betty inquired politely again.

Roy realized he had no purpose for being in line other than to meet her. He reached his hand over the counter and said with a sheepish grin, "Hi, my name is Roy." *I don't believe this. What was I thinking?*

Betty gave no response, but her smile slowly faded. She stared at the offered hand. "Uh, Roy Napier." *Come on, Roy, where's that bold confidence you always exude? Where's the take-charge guy? The winner?*

Seeing his discomfort, Betty reached over, shook his hand, and said with a full smile again, "Nice to meet you, Mr. Roy Napier. I'm Betty. Now, how may I help you?"

Doreen said "not married." No diamond, either. He released her hand, fumbled for his wallet, withdrew a $100 bill and placed it on the counter. "Would you be able to break this for me?" *Of course she can break it. This is a bank, dummy.*

Betty picked up the bill. "I believe that is possible. What denominations would you like?"

"Ah … twenties?"

"That sounds like a question, Mr. Napier. Are you certain you want twenties?"

I'm an idiot, and she knows it. But that smile is so infectious. "Yes, I'm sure … I think. Yes, definitely twenties." *You take out million dollar loans and can't hold an intelligent conversation with this girl? Roy, baby, you really have to get out more.*

Betty counted out five twenties and placed the bills on the counter one at a time, recounting each out loud for Mr. Napier.

"Thank you," said Roy.

"You're very welcome. Will there be anything else?"

"No, I think that's all I needed." Roy did not move. He could not take his eyes off this vision standing in front him.

"Are you sure?" asked Betty.

"Uh, yes." Roy blinked and turned to leave, but then turned back again. *Here goes nothing.* "Betty, would you go out with me?"

"No, Mr. Napier!" The surprise and shock in her voice caught the attention of Clarice, the teller at the window to her left.

"Well, then, okay. That settles that, doesn't it?" Roy again turned to leave, but once more turned back. "May I ask why? Do you have a boyfriend or something?"

Betty's original look of surprise returned to her face, and immediately Roy sensed that he had just crossed the line. She leaned forward slightly so she could speak to him in a hushed voice. "No, Mr. Napier." Her voice dripped with ice, and her eyes narrowed. "There is no … boyfriend, as if it is any of your business. It's because I've only known you for two minutes, and what I've seen so far does not impress me."

"Oh," was all Roy could say. No one had ever been quite that direct with him. This time when he turned to leave, he kept on going.

"Betty, did I hear you right?" Clarice asked. There was a look of astonishment on her face. "He's tall, dark, and gorgeous … and rich … and available. And you turned him down?"

Betty shrugged. "He's not my type."

"Not your type? Betty, that's Roy Napier, the owner of King's Rooke Restaurant."

Betty wanted to tell Clarice to mind her own business, but instead she just shrugged again and said, "Never heard of it. And, like I said, he's not my type."

"Well, he sure is my type. Next time, send him over to my window."

"Clarice, shame on you. You're married with children."

"Sure, go ahead and throw that in my face." The tension was broken, and the two laughed at the absurdity of the moment.

Roy climbed into his car and grasped the steering wheel with a white-knuckled grip. He wanted to find a cement block to bang his head against. *Idiot! Idiot! Idiot!* He sat for a moment and struggled to regain his composure. *But I will win you, Betty Maguire,* he determined. *I will win you.*

Chapter 36

Lessons Learned

September 14, 1974

The King's Rooke Restaurant was as busy that Saturday night as Roy had ever seen it. Customers without reservations lined the front entrance, willing to wait an hour or more to be seated. Roy leaned against a railing on the balcony level and surveyed the tables below, and then looked out of the large glass panels to watch the ships heading into port in Boston Harbor. The restaurant had been the love of his life, but now all his thoughts returned to Betty.

He had started the business only three years ago out of a desire to have a more challenging career—to succeed where so many others had failed. Since then, he had been overwhelmed with its success, receiving a five-star rating every time a gourmet magazine did a review. He smiled and, not for the first time, wished that his father could have been there to see it.

Not that he loved his father—far from it. Roy L. Napier was actually a "Jr.," but he never signed his name that way. His feelings for his father bordered on hatred mixed with sadness for what would never be. *Five-star rating, Dad,* he thought. As the sun slowly set and the waiters balanced their trays and tended their tables on the floor below, he thought back to his earliest memories as a child.

Six-year-old Roy handed his second-quarter report card to his mother as soon as he got home from school. She removed it from the large manila envelope, scanned the grades, and beamed with delight. "All A's! I am so proud of my first-grader!" she exclaimed as she bent to hug him. "Your father will be so pleased when he gets home from work. This deserves a celebration. Why don't you take two cookies from the jar and have them with a glass of milk."

This truly was a treat, as Roy's mother seldom allowed him to eat such a snack between meals. Roy didn't hesitate. "Your father will be so pleased," his mother repeated as he reached for the jar. "Let's leave this great report card right here on the kitchen table for him to see when he gets home."

Roy was not so sure about how pleased his father would be. During his first quarter, he had received one B-plus, and his father had thrown a tantrum that he didn't get all A's. "Do you think you could try a little harder, boy?" he had shouted as he waved the report card around in the air. His mother later explained that his father was not really upset with him; he had been drinking at his nightly post-work trip to the local bar, and it was the alcohol that had caused him to become angry.

Two hours later, Roy's father drove into the driveway. His mother stopped preparing the supper meal when he entered and turned to greet her husband. "Did you have a good day at work, Sweetheart?" she asked.

"Yeah, sure," he said indifferently. He sat and began to browse through mail that had been sitting on the kitchen table. "Supper almost ready?" he snapped.

"In about ten minutes. While you wait, why don't you take a look at Junior's report card? We have such a smart little boy." Roy's father picked up the report card and frowned. "Where is he?" he asked with irritation. "In his bedroom playing, I'll bet."

Roy's father stormed up the stairs to his son's bedroom, where he found Roy playing with a stuffed animal collection. The child looked up from where he sat on the floor. "You should be outside running around," his father said gruffly, "not playing with girlie toys. Now, about this report card. You happy with this, boy?"

Roy nodded, remembering his mother's pride.

"Well, I'm not! This is how losers are made, being satisfied with mediocrity."

The smile disappeared. "But Mamma said—"

"Mamma? You listen to your father, boy. No excuse for an A-minus. Let me tell you something. There's no room for slackers under my roof. You better have that A-minus wiped off the next report card. Understand? And what is this note scribbled by the teacher about your social skills? You not getting along with classmates?"

Roy nodded, his eyes watering with tears yet to be spilled. He desperately wanted to please his father.

"Are those tears, boy? You gonna cry like a baby? Loser. Here, wipe your nose with this." His father walked over to him and pressed the report card into his face.

Roy walked down to the floor and, with his typical charm, checked in with the customers seated at the tables. He received glowing reports on the food, the service, the atmosphere and everything else. *Loser, Dad?* he thought. *Not today.*

"Thirty-seven to nothing," he overheard a staff member report to a customer dressed in a military uniform. Roy gave his employee a quizzical look. "The score in the game between Air Force and Idaho," the man said. "Air Force is killing them." Roy smiled and patted him on the back. As he returned to his balcony railing, his mind returned to a game he had once played back in high school.

"Thirty-seven to nothing," the local play-by-play announcer reported to anyone who may still be tuned in. "This is the worst shellacking the Cougars have ever received, and it looks like they're going to end the season with an 0-9 record. This football game was over in the first quarter."

"No," his colleague beside him corrected, "this game was over before the Cougars took the field. They were eliminated from the playoffs long ago. Do you see any Cougar out there who seems to care about this meaningless game?"

"Apparently their coach does. The way he's pacing the sidelines, he better be careful not to gouge a trench to China. Oh! Look at that kick! Coach Garrety just kicked the water bucket further than the last punt."

"Time out! Time out!" Coach Garrety called with ten minutes left in the game. "Second string, get your helmets on and get out there. Maybe you guys can do something to turn around this disgrace. At least you can't be any more of a disaster than this first string of incompetents."

Roy ran out onto the field for the second time that season. He stopped in the middle and scoured the stands. There, high up in the bleachers, he spotted his dad. He waved and hoped his dad would wave back, but all he received was a disgusted shake of the head followed by a tip of a beer can. "My son, the second-stringer," he remembered his father saying. *Why does he even bother to come at all?*

The drive home was torturous, not because of anything his father said, but because his father said nothing. Every now and then, Roy glanced in his father's direction, watching this former football hero fuming in silence over his disappointment of a son. He tried to press his body further down into the seat. His father hit the brakes and pulled to the side of the road, skidding in the loose sand. He shoved the stick shift into neutral.

"Somebody grease your hands, boy?" his father spit out, causing Roy to cower into the passenger side door. "Any good reason you couldn't hold that ball? Good grief, son, two fumbles! Two! Do you know how embarrassing that was? And all those people yelling things like, 'Try something different, kid, use your hands.'" He rubbed his hands through his thick head of graying hair in frustration. Roy knew the next line by heart. "When I played ball, I never scored less than one touchdown in a game. Usually three. Do you know why?"

He paused, but Roy said nothing. "Well, do you?"

"No, Dad," Roy said, looking down at his hands in his lap.

"Because even when I wasn't practicing, I was practicing."

Roy screwed up his face in confusion. "That doesn't make sense, Dad."

"In my head," he said, tapping his right temple. "When I wasn't practicing on the field, I was practicing the plays … in … my … head." The saliva-coated words sprayed out as he thumped each word on his son's forehead. Roy tried to move away, but couldn't escape the reach, or the force, of his father's long arm.

"But … ow … Dad, the score was thirty-seven-to-nothing. None of it was my fault; not really. All the guys—"

Another thump. "Don't you ever tell me you weren't part of this screw-up! Where was the team spirit? The pride? You better change that attitude of yours, boy, or you'll never be anything but the loser you are." The look of pain on Roy's face stopped his father short. It wasn't the first time Roy had heard these words, and they always cut deep. His father gripped the steering wheel with both hands, took in a deep breath, and let it out slowly.

"Son, I know I come on pretty strong sometimes," he said. "But it's for your own good. I want you to be a winner. In this dog-eat-dog world, there are winners, and there are losers. It has nothing to do with who plays the game. It's only who wins that matters, which is why you must do anything they want you to do in order to win. They want you to run, you run. They want you to walk, you walk. They want you to laugh, you laugh. They want you to cry, you cry. They want you to be one of them goody-two-shoes Christians, you be a goody-two-shoes. They want you to be a fat-bellied Buddha lover, you be one. *Whatever* it takes to win. Got that?"

Roy didn't have a clue as to who "they" were, but he knew enough to nod and keep his mouth shut. His father seemed content that Roy had gotten the point, and he shifted back into first gear and drove off. They drove the rest of the way home in silence.

When they reached the driveway, Roy's father opened the door and started to get out. "Dad?" Roy said. His father sat back down and looked over at his son.

"What?" he said impatiently.

"How … do you know when you win?" He raised his hands to guard a blow, unsure of whether the question would earn him another thump on the head.

"That's the first intelligent question I've heard from you in a long time," his father said, looking pleased. "You'll figure it out." He belly-laughed all the way into the house.

I certainly did figure it out, Dad, Roy thought. After high school he had been accepted into Harvard, and then worked for Matthews & Matthews law firm in Cambridge, Massachusetts. He went on to receive his Masters in Business Administration, also from Harvard. The law firm was a good job that paid the bills, and it might have even resulted in a partnership in the future. But that had been the problem—it was just a job. The experience was priceless, but it gave Roy no real satisfaction.

Roy had always enjoyed eating in restaurants, and he began to take note of what it was about certain places that brought him back—and what it was that made him want to head to the exit before the meal was even served. Service was always at the top of the list. A waitress with an attitude could spoil the most expensive gourmet meal, while an overly well-done hamburger at a truck-stop diner could be saved if it was delivered with a smile and a joke. All of this captured his attention.

Roy got his first chance to purchase a small establishment during the late 1960s. The owner of a restaurant on the North Shore of Boston was up to his ears in debt, and the bank was threatening foreclosure. Roy was aching to take on the challenge. So at the age of twenty-nine, he bit the bullet and entered the realm of entrepreneurship. The grand opening of Roy & Friends Restaurant took place in April of 1967. Sure, it wasn't the most creative name ever, but he was confident that people didn't visit restaurants based on their names. Besides, to him, the name seemed personable and friendly.

As much as Roy hated his father, he took seriously his advice on how to be a winner. "Be all things to all people," his father had told him, and Roy was willing to play the game. He became Mr. Personality and learned how to use his good looks, disarming smile, and practiced charm to manipulate people. Roy could flirt and sweet-talk himself out of any situation with a sincere, "Yes, ma'am, I agree with everything you've said," or, "No, sir, it was entirely my fault, and it will never happen again." He used people as a means to an end, and once the prize—whatever that might be—was won, he moved on and set his sights on the next goal. His work was like a drug to him. He considered more than five hours of sleep a night to be wasted time.

Within two years, the profits of Roy & Friends Restaurant went through the roof, and Roy opened up a second restaurant—"Roy & Friends II"—and got even less sleep at night. But the idea of owning a high-class establishment obsessed him. He wanted a place that would draw movie stars, sports heroes, mayors, governors, senators, and maybe even a president of the United States.

His chance came in 1972, when a factory in a suburb of Boston burned to the ground. The cause was determined to be arson, and the owner was charged with the crime. Boston's Dudley Square Financial Savings and Loan had been in the process of foreclosing on the factory when the fire was set, and Roy negotiated with the bank to become the new owner of the property. He built the restaurant from scratch, overseeing each detail personally. The King's Rooke Restaurant would be his legacy, the love of his life, his crowning glory.

Roy smiled as he reflected on this thought. "Well, my beauty," he said, "today, I'm afraid you might have become my second love." He only wished he didn't have to wait another day to visit Betty at the bank again.

Chapter 37

Audacity Personified

September 16, 1974

Roy was carrying a white business-sized envelope in his hand when he entered the bank on Monday morning. He stood in Betty's line and waited for the three customers ahead of him to be served. Betty groaned softly when she saw him standing there, looking at her with a slight smile and nod of the head. Clarice looked at her and cleared her throat just loud enough to get Betty's attention, and then slid a small piece of notepaper over to her. "If you don't want him, send him to my line," the note read.

Betty read the paper and then looked up at Clarice. "You're married, remember?" she mouthed. Clarice shrugged and got back to helping her own customers.

The last customer ahead of Roy finished making her deposit and left the bank. Betty sighed. "Hello, Mr. Napier. How may I help you today?"

Hmm, tone a bit icy. Smile forced. Not very professional. Can't blame her, though. At least she remembered my name. That's promising. Roy walked up to the window. "Betty, first of all, my behavior last Friday was rude," he said. "I was totally out of line. Will you accept my apology?" *Straight and to the point. I think I sounded sincere.*

Betty paused, a bit taken aback. "Well, yes ... yes I will, Mr. Napier."

"Thank you." *Phase one: success.* "Second, I have some papers here for you." He placed the envelope on the counter and slid it across to her side. It was labeled, "Miss Betty Maguire: For Your Eyes Only."

"What kind of papers?" Betty said in a businesslike tone.

"Well, last Friday, you said that you would not go out with me because you did not know me." *Actually, that's not quite what she said, but maybe she doesn't remember.* "I respect that. So ... in the envelope I've placed letters of reference from three people who do know me. I would like you to read them. I will return tomorrow at five minutes to 3:00, just before the bank closes." With that, Roy turned and walked away, giving Betty no chance at a rebuttal.

Betty stood mouth agape and watched him leave. "Do you believe the gall of that man, Clarice?" she said after a moment. She dropped the envelope unceremoniously into the wastebasket.

"I think it's romantic," said Clarice. She looked over to the wastebasket. "Well, if you're not going to read those letters, I will." She reached down, retrieved the envelope, set it on the counter between them, and began reading. Betty tried to ignore her as she helped more customers, but before long her curiosity got the best of her.

"Oh, all right!" she said, slipping the envelope into her purse.

That night, in the privacy of her apartment, Betty pulled out the envelope that was still in her pocketbook. *Might as well get this over with,* she thought. She sat in her overstuffed recliner, broke the seal, removed the papers, and began to read.

Dear Miss Maguire,

Thank you for accepting my apology earlier today. If you had not, I never would have given you this envelope. Enclosed you will find character references from three people who know me best. These will give you some insight as to who I am. Once again, I thank you for taking the time to read them.

Sincerely,
Roy Napier

Betty set the cover letter aside, shook her head in disbelief, and began reading the first letter.

Dear Miss Betty,

On behalf of my son, Roy, I would like to say that he is truly a fine and gentle man....

Betty put the letter down. *His mother? He asked his mother to write a character reference for him? Un-be-lieve-able!* She picked up the letter and continued reading.

Roy works hard at being honorable and always does his duty. He is obedient and helpful to others at all times. He does his best to keep himself strong, mentally awake, and morally straight. I know he can sometimes come across as being a bit pushy ...

A bit pushy! He's the king of pushy!

... which he gets from his father's side of the family. But when you get to know him, you will come to find that he is really quite lovable.

Sincerely, Mrs. Napier
P.S. Roy is nothing if he's not punctual.

Just a bit prejudiced are we, Mom? I've got to send this to Dear Abby.

Betty set down the first letter and began to read the second. "Hey, wait a minute!" she said aloud. She set down the letter and picked up the third, and then looked back at the cover letter. *Well, I'll be darned! They are all written with the same pen, and they're all in the same handwriting. Does this guy think I'm a fool?*

She tossed the letters into the wastebasket and went to bed. Her last thought before she fell asleep was, *No, Mr. Napier, I will not be going out with you, except in your dreams! What a creep!*

The next afternoon, Roy entered the bank as promised and went directly to Betty's window. Betty had been watching the clock. *Five minutes to 3:00. Yes, very punctual.* There were no customers in front of her window, but she looked down and pretended to be distracted by some paperwork. Roy waited for her to finish and look up. After a while, he began clearing his throat to get her attention.

"Oh, Mr. Napier," said Betty, looking up in mock surprise. "How may I help you?" She gave an exaggerated smile that was even more forced than the one she had given the day before.

"Hello, Betty. Did you read the references?" Roy politely inquired.

"Yes, I did. They were … unique."

"Oh, in what way?"

"Well, for one thing, most people do not write their *own* references."

"So … you noticed that."

"Did you think I wouldn't?"

"Not really. But I only wrote what those people would have said if I'd had time to ask them." His grin was contagious.

Betty frowned, and then began to crack a smile. She did not want to give him the satisfaction of knowing that something he said had amused her—but it just happened. Roy noticed, and his grin widened.

"Betty, I would very much like to request your presence this coming Friday night, if you will allow me the honor," he said. He immediately regretted the way the words had come out. *Too formal. She's going to think you're a class-A jerk. No, she already thinks that.* "That is, if you're not already booked, of course."

"Um, Mr. Napier, I …"

"Look, I know it's not much notice. But if you're free, I would really like to go out with you. So here's the deal. I won't come to your place to pick you up. We can meet anywhere you like and go to any place of your choosing. You can even drive if you like. What do you say?"

"I don't know what to say, Mr. Napier," Betty replied. *That was not the response I rehearsed. Just say no, dummy!*

"Say yes." Roy's voice had a slight touch of pleading.

"*Any* place of my choosing?"

"Any place."

"Okay, Mr. Napier, I—"

"Please, no more Mr. Napier. It's Roy."

"Okay, Roy. I would like to go to Paragon Park."

The request took Roy by surprise. "What's a 'Paragon Park?'" he asked.

"It's an amusement park down near the South Shore, in Hull."

"I've never been to an amusement park before. But, hey, a deal's a deal." *It sounds boring, but ...*

"Fine. Meet me here in the bank's parking lot at ... well, you tell me."

"How about 5:00?"

"Five it is."

Roy turned and walked out with an ear-to-ear grin. *Roy Napier, winner of round one!*

"Never been to an amusement park?" Clarice quipped. "That man has got to get a life."

Betty went back to her paperwork and tried not to smile, but she was not entirely successful.

Chapter 38

The Competition

September 20, 1974

It was a few minutes past 5:00 when Betty drove into the parking lot. Roy was leaning against the trunk of his black Corvette convertible. The top was down, and he was glancing impatiently at his watch. He looked up when he saw her, smiled, and waved.

Betty parked her six-year-old lime-green Volkswagen Beetle beside his Corvette and got out. Roy opened the passenger door of his car and gestured with a sweeping, exaggerated motion of his left arm for her to get in. Betty, in turn, went around to the passenger side door of her Beetle and gestured with her finger for him to get in. "This is where you'll be riding tonight," she said.

Roy shrugged. "Give me one minute," he said. He re-entered his Corvette, put the key in the ignition and turned a switch. Betty heard a noise, and the canopy slowly began to go up. She watched as Roy walked back around the trunk-end of the vehicle, paused, pulled out his handkerchief, and polished a spot on the trunk where he had been leaning.

Betty started the car once her date was seated beside her and then began to pull out of the parking lot. She was amused when she noticed Roy squirming. "A bit of a tight fit?" she asked.

"Just a tad. They certainly didn't build this for a six-foot-two frame."

"There's a handle on the front of the seat near the floor. Pull up on it, and you can adjust the seat to stretch out some more."

Roy found the handle and pulled it up. The seat slid rapidly backward. "Whoa!" he exclaimed.

Betty laughed out loud. "It needs a gentle touch."

"Yeah, tell me about it. But that seemed to do the trick. Plenty of leg room now. So how far is it to this Paragon Park?"

"About an hour." She clicked her blinker and turned left onto the main road.

"An hour! Oy!"

"Roy, you need to learn to suffer in silence."

"No, not in silence. I want you to tell me all about yourself."

"That's not going to happen. Instead, I thought we would play a little game."

"A game? What kind of game?"

"A simple one. It's a way for you and me to see how observant we are, even though we've only known each other for a short time. I'm not going to tell you about me. You are. And then I'm going to tell you about you. For example, I know that you were a Boy Scout."

Roy's eyes widened. "I'm impressed. I never told you that."

"Yes, you did. Not in so many words, but your 'mother'"—she emphasized this title by making a quote sign with her fingers—"said you were honest, dutiful, obedient, and helpful, and that you kept yourself physically strong, mentally awake, and morally straight. Isn't that the Boy Scout pledge?"

"Well, who would know better than my mother? But, look, about those letters, I—"

"Don't be embarrassed. I actually thought it was kind of cute. Your turn."

"Okay. Let's see … well, you're a lady who's not impressed with material things."

"Are you referring to my little love bug?"

"Your what?"

"My love bug. You never saw the Disney movie *The Love Bug*? It came out a couple of years ago."

"Uh, no.... Actually, I was referring to the fact that you didn't want to ride in my Corvette. It's a classic, you know."

"No, I didn't know."

"Well, it is. Most of the women I've dated loved to go for a spin in it. But not you. That impressed me."

"And just how many women might that be?"

"Well, truth be told, not that many. I ... don't get out socially that much."

"Oh, really!" Betty exclaimed in mock surprise.

"Yes, my business keeps me busy," Roy explained, hoping this conversation would lead to him talking about his successful business.

"Okay, I'll let you off the hook. My turn."

The hour-long drive to the amusement park went by quickly, and soon they were pulling into the main parking lot. As the two walked to the entrance, Roy looked up in wonder at the lights and the rides before him. "Where do we start?" he said.

"The roller coaster. I love the roller coaster!"

Roy noticed that a change had come over Betty. Up to this point, she had seemed a bit distant and reserved, but now, as she led him to the ride, he marveled at her childlike exuberance. He found it adorable.

"I have a confession to make," Roy said when they reached the ticket stand. "I've never been on a roller coaster."

"Then you're in for a real treat. Follow me." Roy paid for the tickets, and then Betty led him to the front seat. The safety bar clicked into place, and the roller coaster slowly made its way to the top of the first hill.

"This isn't so bad," Roy said. He nonchalantly placed his left arm across the back of the seat and rested his right hand in his lap. Betty smiled as the coaster neared the top of the crest. The car paused for a moment, as if hanging over the top of the ledge, and then began the slide down. She looked over at Roy. His eyes were now dilated, and he was grasping the safety bar with both hands. Betty screamed in pure delight, her long, red hair trailing behind.

Seconds later, Betty said, "You can let go now, Roy. The ride is over."

Roy attempted to stand, but he found his legs to be a bit rubbery. He had to hold on to the railing for a moment when he stepped onto the platform.

"Are you okay?" Betty asked.

"Give me a minute. I just need to get my land legs back."

"Want to go again?"

Roy stared wide-eyed at her. "You have got to be kidding!"

"Oh, you poor baby," Betty said in a mock-motherly voice. "Here, let me help you down the stairs." Roy was irritated and wanted to protest, but then he realized she had taken hold of his arm.

"Thanks," he said, swallowing his pride to make the moment last. "So where now?"

"I think the hobby horses would be about your speed." Betty smiled up at him. "But next it's the Tilt-a-Whirl." This was followed by a ride on the Caterpillar and the Scrambler, and then the two went to the snack area to get a hot dog and a Coke. Roy put one thin layer of catsup on his dog, while Betty got the works.

They found an empty picnic table and sat on opposite sides. "This is the only way to eat a hot dog," she informed him, biting into one end. The fixings dripped down into her lap from the other end. "The mustard stains are just part of the price one must pay," she quickly added.

Roy washed down his last bite. He looked into Betty's eyes and noticed that she had a distant look. *I wonder what she is thinking right now,* he asked himself. Betty shook her head as if waking from a dream and took her last bite. "Just one more ride now," she said. "It's the way I always ended my trips here. Come on."

The attendant at the Ferris wheel helped the pair get into their seats and locked the safety bar into place. The ride moved a few feet, and then stopped to let on the next few passengers. When Betty and Roy had reached at the top, the wheel stopped again. Roy was struck by the majestic view of the park, and the glitter of the lights. In the distance, he could just see the waves of the ocean cresting and crashing onto the beach in the light of the full moon. He turned to Betty to comment on the view, but then saw that same distant look in her eyes. It was as if she were far away, in another time. *Where are you, Betty?* he thought.

"Sometimes … in the past … I've seen fireworks from here," she said at length. She seemed to be disappointed by the memory. Before Roy could ask any questions, the wheel began to turn again and pick up speed as the actual ride began.

"Hey, Betty," Roy said when the ride ended, "why don't we go for a walk along the beach?"

"Oh, no, Roy. Not tonight. I … I'm tired. Let's go home."

The two walked back to Betty's car in silence. She unlocked his side door, and then let herself in on the driver's side. She put the key in the ignition and started the car, but Roy reached over and turned the key to off.

"Why did you do that?" Betty asked.

"Betty, where were you just now on the Ferris wheel?"

"I don't know what you mean."

"Several times when I looked at you tonight, you seemed to have a far-away look. You've been here many times, haven't you?"

"Oh, yes," she confessed. "Not for several years, though. This was always one of my favorite places to come. I had many precious memories here."

"You mean from when you were a child, with your parents?"

"No, my parents weren't amusement-park type of folk."

"Then you came here with friends?"

"Several times each summer during high school. Why all the questions?"

"These friends—were any of them boyfriends?"

Betty stiffened and looked away. She again put her hand on the key to start the engine, but Roy placed his hand over hers.

"Please, Betty. I need to know."

Betty pulled her hand from his, leaned back against the seat and looked out the window. "Why do you need to know, Roy?"

"Betty, I'm a businessman. Success or failure in my line of work depends on the degree to which I know the strengths and weaknesses of my competition—why one succeeds while another fails. Then I try not to make the same mistakes that led to failure, and I try to do the things that resulted in success. So … I need to know who my competition is. Who is causing you to drift into a time gone by?"

Betty turned from the window and looked directly into Roy's eyes. "There is no competition," she said softly. "It was a long time ago."

"He was very special." Roy meant this as a statement, not a question. Betty nodded slowly, her eyes beginning to glisten.

"What was his name?" Roy asked quietly.

Betty hesitated before speaking. "Jeremy."

"When was the last time you saw him?"

Betty again looked out her window. "Seven years ago."

"Betty, I only met you a few days ago, and I already know what a wonderful woman you are. This Jeremy must have been a fool to break up with you." Betty had no response and Roy said no more. For a few seconds, he allowed the silence to linger.

"He wasn't the fool. I was," Betty said, her voice just a whisper.

"I'm sorry, Betty, I had no right to pry. Thank you for talking to me and sharing this. But it's obvious to me now what my competition is."

"No, Roy," Betty snapped back more harshly than she intended. "There is no competition. Jeremy is dead. He died in Vietnam four years ago." She reached for the key and started the engine.

Roy sat back and stared at Betty. There was much more to this story, but it would have to wait. He slowly put his left hand on her shoulder. "I am so sorry, Betty. But what I meant was that I now know my competition is your memories of Jeremy. I will never ask you to give up those memories, but I hope we will be able to build our own."

Betty shifted into first gear without another word and drove away. The hour-long drive back to the bank was spent in awkward silence. When Betty finally pulled into the parking lot, she left the engine on and waited for Roy to leave. He opened his door, but paused.

"Betty, may I see you again?" he asked. He no longer had any confidence that he would get the desired answer, or if he had any chance left with her at all.

"Yes, you may," she said with a smile.

Roy closed the door and went to his Corvette, his heart leaping. Betty backed out, and then rolled down her window. "But next time, we go in that classic," she said. As she drove away, she looked into her rearview mirror and laughed. There, by the light from the streetlights, she saw Roy doing some kind of dance that she was certain had just now been invented.

Chapter 39

The Prize

September 10, 1975

Roy paced the floor of the King's Rooke Restaurant as he waited for Betty to arrive. He stopped to check his watch, and then began pacing again. The two had been dating for almost a year, and Betty had yet to arrive on time for one of their dates. *I told her 6:30,* he thought. *Eight minutes late.* He knew that she finished work by 4:00 PM, which would have given her plenty of time to do all that primping women seemed to need to do. *Must be some kind of test,* he mused. *She's trying to teach me a lesson, I suppose. One of these days, I'll break her of this habit.*

Roy had been driving his employees crazy with his nervous pacing and his constant checks with the kitchen to see if the special creation he had ordered was being properly prepared. He was also annoying the service staff in the main dining room with his continual checks on whether his favorite table in the far corner was being set up just right, with candles lit, rose petals on the tablecloth, and cloth napkins folded just so.

Marvin, the *maitre 'd,* also had his instructions. As soon as Betty arrived, he was to escort her directly to the table. At 6:40 PM, he saw her coming through the doors. "Ah, good evening, Miss Betty," he said with genuine pleasure at seeing her. Betty took his arm and allowed herself to be escorted to the table. "Always a pleasure to see you," Marvin said. "And, my, you are looking stunning tonight."

"Why, thank you, Marvin," Betty replied. "And how are those granddaughters doing?"

"Growing like weeds." He took delight at how Betty always inquired about his grandchildren.

"And how is Roy handling my being ten minutes late?"

Marvin raised his eyes heavenward. "Thanks be to God that you finally got here. He's wearing a hole into the carpet."

Betty giggled. "Some day I might just show up on time, but for now I think he needs to learn patience, don't you?" Marvin stifled a chuckle.

Roy thought his heart would burst when he saw Betty approach. He hurried down the stairs and rushed over to the table he had instructed to be so lovingly prepared. "Thank you, Marvin," he said, wringing his hands. "I'll take over from here."

"Very good, sir," replied Marvin. He gave a slight bow, winked toward Betty, and left.

Roy took her hands in his and looked at her. She was dressed in a black lace blouse with a white pearl necklace and earrings to match and white pants with matching heels. Her silken, red hair flowed over her shoulders. "Betty, you are breathtaking. And that outfit—it's perfect."

Roy, dear, thought Betty, *if I told you all this was purchased at a Salvation Army secondhand outlet for less than $40, you'd probably go ballistic.*

Roy seated Betty at the table and then sat on the opposite side facing her. Right on cue, a waiter approached with a dozen long-stemmed roses and silently presented them to her.

"Oh, Roy, they are absolutely beautiful!" Betty exclaimed. She cradled them in her arms and breathed in the fragrance.

"They're imported," said Roy, beaming with delight. Everything was going perfectly so far.

"They are lovely, but I wish you wouldn't be so extravagant."

"Okay, my dear, never again. But do accept them just this once." He took the bouquet and placed it into a vase that had already been set on the table, and then signaled the head waiter to begin serving the appetizer.

For the next hour, the conversation was light, and the meal exquisite. The waiters were almost too attentive. Betty noticed a few of them were nervously stiff.

Finally, the moment of truth arrived. Roy's eyes were so focused on Betty that he did not even notice several of the staff peering in their direction, anticipating what they all knew was about to happen. Some of the staff wondered—though never out loud—what on earth such a stunning and gracious lady as Betty saw in the likes of Roy Napier.

"Betty," Roy began, and then paused to catch his breath.

"Yes, Roy, what is it? You haven't seemed quite yourself tonight."

"Yes … well, there is a good explanation." He reached across the table and grasped Betty's hands. "Betty, we have been seeing each other for a year now, and you know I have declared my love for you many times." He stopped to clear his throat, and then released her hands to take a sip of water. Then, sliding out of his chair and dropping to one knee before her, he asked, "Betty, will you marry me?"

Betty was stunned by the proposal. She knew it might come someday, but it had never entered her mind that it would be tonight. She watched as Roy reached into the side pocket of his suit coat and withdrew a small black box. He held it up to her, and then opened it. Betty was speechless.

Roy removed the one-carat diamond from the box and took Betty's left hand. She was too stunned to resist. "Will you accept this ring as a token of my undying love?" he said, placing the ring onto her finger.

"Oh, Roy, it's beautiful! But I … oh, Roy, is one year enough time to be sure?"

"For me, it has been an eternity waiting for this moment. I have loved you from the time you first rejected me, and I want to spend the rest of my life showing you how much. Will you let me?"

Betty gave no reply.

A bead of sweat began to form on Roy's forehead. His face went expressionless as he waited for her answer. The silence was deafening.

"Yes, Roy, I will marry you," she said at last. She helped him slip the ring fully onto her finger.

"You said yes," he whispered. "You said yes!" He stood and raised his hands into the air like a boxer who had just won the heavyweight title fight. "She said yes!" he cried out to the audience in the restaurant.

The entire room—which had been breathlessly watching the drama unfold from the moment Roy had fallen to his knee—arose to its feet in unison and applauded. Glasses of wine were raised in celebration with shouts of congratulations. The staff breathed a collective sigh of relief. The thought of what life would be like at the King's Rooke Restaurant had Betty rejected him was cause enough for several employees to consider submitting applications elsewhere.

Roy turned back to Betty. He took her hands in his and pulled her up to himself, his lips meeting hers in a passionate kiss. "Come," he said. He took her by the hand and led her toward the exit. "Let's go for a walk. We have plans to make."

Getting to the front door was like walking a gauntlet. Well-wishers patted the couple on the back, shook their hands, and expressed their humorous advice. "Learn how to say, 'Yes, dear,' Roy," one bystander said. "Make sure you get that pre-nup signed, buddy," said another.

The newly-engaged couple waded through the crowd. Roy wallowed in the attention, while Betty, though overwhelmed, graciously accepted it. Nothing was going to dampen their joy on this day.

Outside, the couple made their way to a gazebo at the back of the restaurant. "Good, nobody is using it," Roy said. He again took his fiancée into his arms, and they kissed deeply.

Betty gazed at the engagement ring as he held her in his arms. "It truly is beautiful … and so big. I can't wait to show it off at the reunion next week."

"The … reunion?"

Betty shook her head. "Roy, please tell me you didn't forget. I told you about it a month ago, and you even wrote it down in your pocket calendar. I'm meeting some friends from Clayton on Thursday. We've rented a room at the Greystone Hotel, and then on Friday evening we are going to my ten-year high school reunion at the Cedarvale Country Club. I asked if you would meet me there for the banquet. I even bought a ticket for you."

Roy slapped his forehead with the palm of his hand. "How forgetful of me. Will you forgive me?"

"Yes, of course, but you will meet me at the country club at 6:00 on Friday night, won't you? I want to show you off."

"Honey, I truly would like to go. But next Friday I have some important business meetings, and I don't know if I can fit this in."

"*Fit* this *in?* Roy, I asked you a month ago."

Roy saw the frustration and hurt on Betty's face and knew that his perfect evening was quickly slipping away. He reached for her hand, but she pulled away. "I'm sorry, sweetheart. Really I am. I'll tell you what. I'll be there. I will end the meetings early and be there."

"Do you promise?"

"I promise. Scout's honor."

Chapter 40

The Good Samaritan

September 13, 1975

The 1964 Ford pickup rolled northeast along a lonely stretch of Texas highway. The driver knew his truck was in need of some serious body work—a brake job, tires with tread, a muffler without holes, and an exhaust pipe that was not held in place by a coat hanger. The slide-on camper did not do much for gas mileage either. *Oh well, not to worry,* he comforted himself. *When the money gets low and the repairs start screaming to be tended to, the Good Lord will provide.*

Usually, that meant the Good Lord would provide him with a short-term job. In the past few months alone, he had worked as a dishwasher in a restaurant, a gopher on a construction site, and a picker and combine operator on a farm. No, he wasn't worried about money. Right now, he just needed the freedom of the open air.

The road had few curves, and he could see for miles ahead. He watched as the heat rose in waves from the black tar in front of him. Even though he was stripped down to the waist, wearing only cutoff jeans and leather sandals, the heat was still oppressive. "One hundred-five degrees with no rain in sight," the weather reporter announced every ten minutes. *Sure could use some rain,* he thought. *Might help get some of these bug carcasses off the windshield.* Just then, a kamikaze beetle crashed into the windshield with a thwack. "Well, little fella, I guess you won't have the guts to do that again." He chuckled at his own stale joke.

He rested his arm on the open window frame. The sun, now just low enough to require swinging the visor around, was working on his driver's tan. He listened to the country western music blowing through the speakers, using his fingers like drumsticks to tap out the beat on the steering wheel. Every now and then, he used the drumsticks to scratch the itch caused by his two weeks of beard growth.

An object appeared in the distance that caught his attention. As it came into view, he saw that a vehicle had pulled off into the breakdown lane just off the road. An elderly man was sitting on the outside edge of the driver's seat with the door open, his feet resting on the hot tar. The left rear tire was clearly flat.

He drove past the man and pulled over, and then backed up to within a few feet of the breakdown. The car was a Hudson sedan, maybe twenty years old by his estimate, but well-maintained. "Need any help?" the Good Samaritan asked as he got out of his truck.

He was struck by the contrast in the way he and the elderly man were dressed. The old man was wearing a pair of gray, cuffed pants held up by red suspenders; a long-sleeved white shirt rolled up to the elbows, with sweat stains in the armpits; a red bow tie; and dust-covered, black leather shoes. A gray suit coat lay across the back of the passenger's seat.

The old man wiped his brow with a large, red handkerchief. "Why, as a matter of fact, I could, young man," he said. He grunted as he struggled to stand with the use of a cane. "Seems I got me a flat tire. There was a day I would have changed it myself, but I'm afraid those days are long past." He chuckled and then coughed into the handkerchief.

The Good Samaritan gestured at his truck with his right thumb. "Changing tires is something I'm a pro at doing. Let me have a go at it." He walked back to his truck, opened a side compartment on the camper, and took out a lug wrench and jack. He returned to the elderly man and said, "If I can borrow your keys, I'll get your spare out of the trunk."

"Would you mind getting them?" the old man asked. "They're in the ignition." The Samaritan did as he was asked. "Oh, and would you hand me my glasses?" the elderly man added. "They're on the dash. Can't see a dang thing without them."

The old man leaned against the automobile while the Good Samaritan set about changing his tire. He breathed on the glasses and meticulously went about the business of cleaning them with the red handkerchief. Slipping them on his face, he was finally able to study the tire changer. He was immediately struck by the rippling muscles in the man's back and shoulders, and then by the bulging biceps as the man applied pressure to the lug nut wrench. He squinted slightly and could make out several scars on the man's back, and a longer one on his right calf. As the tire changer turned to jack up the car, the older man also noticed a prominent scar running diagonally down his left cheek.

"Say, how long have you been sitting here in this heat waiting for help?" the Good Samaritan asked. By now he had jacked up the car and was in the process of loosening the lug nuts.

"Oh, let's see," the elderly man said. He reached for a chain attached to a belt loop and pulled out an antique gold stopwatch. He pushed a small button, and the cover popped open. "It's about 4:00 now. Got the flat around 11:00 this morning."

"That's five hours in this heat!" the Good Samaritan exclaimed. Without another word, he went back to his camper. After about two minutes, he returned with a tall plastic cup filled with water and three ice cubes. "Here, take this," he said, handing it to the man.

"Thank you," the old man said. He took the cup and drank the icy liquid in one continuous swallow. When he had finished, he looked at the now-empty cup and said, "I've always found it interesting how the flavor of water is enhanced on a day like today. It actually becomes sweet. May I trouble you for another cupful?"

The Samaritan fulfilled the old man's wish and then returned to the task of removing the damaged tire. The old man sipped the second cup a bit more slowly, as if to allow the pleasure to linger a bit longer this time. Sweat rolled down the Samaritan's forehead and into his eyes. He wiped them frequently, leaving grease marks behind.

In twenty minutes, the job was done. The Good Samaritan put the flat tire in the trunk of the Hudson and closed it. He returned the tools to his truck, retrieved an old rag he found in the toolbox, and walked back to the old man. "Well, that should hold you until you get to the next town and a garage," he said, wiping his hands with the rag. "You really need to get that flat fixed."

"Yes, thank you, I will do that," said the old man.

"By the way … during those five hours, there must have been other cars that passed by while you were waiting. Did no one stop?"

"A few drove by, but no one stopped until you."

"Not a good commentary on neighborliness, I guess."

"I suppose. Now, here, let me pay you for your kindness." The old man reached into his pocket and held out a $5 bill.

"Oh, no," said the Samaritan, taken aback by the offer. "I didn't do this for pay."

"I understand that, but I am truly grateful, and I want to thank you in this way."

"I'll tell you what. This Sunday, you go to some church and put that money in the offering plate. It will be much more needed there."

The old man glanced at the stranger's truck and smiled. "If that's what you want," he said.

"It is," said the Good Samaritan. He walked toward his truck and gave a wave of his hand as a goodbye.

"Goodbye to you, and Semper Fi."

The Samaritan stopped and turned around. "Why did you say that?"

The old man pointed with his cane at the well-worn sticker on the rear window of the camper. "Oh," the Samaritan said. "I forgot I placed that sticker there. I put it on there a couple of years ago."

"I'm a former Marine myself," the old man explained. "World War I."

The Samaritan paused for a moment. "Parris Island?"

"Yup."

"Hmm, tell me, do you like beans and hot dogs?"

"I haven't had beans and dogs in … well, in a dog's age." He chuckled heartily at the bad joke.

"It would be my pleasure to cook up some in exchange for some of your stories." The strong bond of brotherhood which Marines shared had stirred the Samaritan's soul with compassion for this elderly stranger now sitting alone by the dusty road.

The old man agreed and, with the Samaritan's help, climbed the stairs into the camper. An hour and a half later, the door opened and the two former Marines, now well fed but far from storied-out, emerged from the camper. The Good Samaritan helped the old man down and waited for him to get into his vehicle before driving away himself. It was only a short time before the road curved and the Samaritan could no longer see the Hudson in his rearview mirror.

The old man started his vehicle and slowly pulled away. "Thanks for the kindness, young fella," he said out loud to himself. "But as far as putting this five dollars in an offering plate … that'll happen the day I can shinny up a thirty-foot icicle."

Chapter 41

Ghost

September 18, 1975, 2:00 PM

The parking lot at the Hartford Stop & Shop grocery store was nearly full, and the Good Samaritan had to park several rows away from the front entrance. He welcomed the exercise, as he had been driving longer than he should have without a break and his muscles were cramping. He grabbed a cart on the way in.

He negotiated the cart around the store until he came upon a man who was blocking the way to the snack aisle. "Say, fella, would you mind moving a bit to your left so I can get by?" the Samaritan politely asked.

"Oh, sorry. Give me a moment here and I'll …" The stranger's jaw suddenly dropped open, and he stared wide-eyed at the Samaritan.

The Samaritan looked behind him to see what had caught the stranger's gaze. When he saw that no one was close by, he looked back at the man. "Is something wrong?" he asked. "If you don't mind my saying so, you look like you've seen a ghost."

"I…. I'm not sure. Maybe I have. You're … Sergeant Major!"

Now it was the Samaritan's turn not to blink. He stared at the stranger more closely. "You look a bit familiar. Do I know you?"

"If you're my sergeant major, you do," the stranger said in an excited voice. "Vietnam, 1970. Were you there?"

"Yes," the Samaritan said slowly, his mind racing to remember, "I was. Who are you?"

"But … that's impossible. You're dead, man. I saw you get bagged and tagged."

Jeremy raised his hand and pointed his finger at the man. "Yes, I know you. You were with the Marines on Firebase Trumpet. You're Private, uh—"

The stranger left his cart in the aisle, rushed over to Jeremy, and bear-hugged him. Jeremy looked around to see if anyone was watching. "Private Noonan, Sarge. Jimmy Noonan," the man choked out. "You saved my life." Tears filled his eyes.

"Noonan," Jeremy said. He wrapped his arms around the private, and the two stood there hugging, oblivious to the stares from the other customers. "I do remember. You got a bayonet in the gut. I thought you were dead too."

The men released from the embrace but still gripped each other by the arms. "You told me I would be fine … that it was just a flesh wound."

"I lied." Jeremy grinned.

"We gotta talk. Come on, let's check out. There's a restaurant next door. My treat."

"Well, I can't refuse a free meal."

The hostess led the two men to a table at the far end of the restaurant and gave them their menus. Noonan put his aside without looking at any of the food. "Sarge, you gotta tell me. How are you alive?"

"I'm not saying anything until you show me a picture of your son," Jeremy replied.

Noonan pulled his wallet from his back pocket and flipped it open to a packet of pictures. "You were a prophet, Sarge," he said, holding up a picture of a woman with a newborn baby. "That's my wife, Jeannie, holding my son, Elijah. Ain't he something?" He flipped to the next photograph and beamed with pride. "He's five now. This picture was taken when he was in kindergarten. And we've got two more on the way."

"Two more?"

"Yep. Twins, due in three months. Jeannie is a blimp." He leaned forward and lowered his voice. "That's not to be repeated, of course. She's very sensitive about her figure and all."

Jeremy shook his head slowly. "God is good."

"Ain't that the truth. Now, get to it. How is it that you're sitting here talking to me instead of fertilizing some cemetery?"

"I never knew you had such a way with words, Private. Anyway, here's the story, as best I can give it. The last thing I remember about the battle that day is standing up after I had checked on you. The sniper shot me right in the forehead, and I went down, and you and everyone thought I was dead. I was bagged, tagged and shipped to the body depot at Long Binh Medical Center."

"No kidding? That's where they sent me."

"You gonna interrupt my story, Private?"

"Sir, no sir, Sergeant Major, sir," Noonan said with a quick salute and a wide grin.

"And don't call me 'sir,' Private!" Jeremy commanded. Neither man noticed that a few of the other customers had stopped eating and were leaning in their direction.

"Now, where was I? Oh, yeah. Anyway, it seems that as I was being removed from the MedEvac chopper, the fellows handling my bag got a bit careless and dropped me. When I hit the tarmac, they heard a groan. I hear they were rather stunned, to say the least. They unzipped the bag, checked me for a pulse, and were shocked to find one. They put me on a stretcher, laid it across the back of a jeep, and drove to the MASH unit, where I was stabilized. It seems the bullet entered at such an angle that it followed the curve of my skull and exited out the back of my head. It missed my brain.

Noonan let out a low whistle.

"I spent a week in that facility," Jeremy continued, "and then they flew me to the States. It took about three months of physical therapy for me to get back to normal. Or close to it. I had planned on making the Marines my career, but the powers that be would have nothing to do with that. So … I was discharged, and here I am."

Noonan shook his head in disbelief. "Un … be … lieveable!"

"Strange things happen in war, Jimmy. I heard a story of a Marine in World War I who threw himself onto a live grenade and survived. Heard that from the old Marine himself, just a week ago."

The reminiscing went on for two hours. Jimmy looked down at his watch. "Oh, man. I'm in trouble with the wife now. We're going to her high school reunion tomorrow, and we were supposed to leave for the motel … well … an hour ago." He called the waitress over and asked to borrow her pen, and then took one of the paper napkins from off the table. "Here's my address and telephone number," he said. "We'll be gone until Saturday afternoon. Any chance you can come by? You've got to meet Jeannie. I can't tell you how many times I've told her the story of how you saved my life."

Jeremy took the napkin, folded it, and placed it into his wallet. "I would love to, Jimmy, but I'm heading up to Canada. I won't be back in this area until … well … I don't know when. But I promise that when I'm back this way, you'll find me on your doorstep. I want to meet that boy of yours, and those twins."

"Okay, then," Jimmy said. They stood to leave. "But I'm going to hold you to that promise. When you do come, I'm going to throw the biggest barbecue with the thickest steaks you've ever seen."

"I'll bring the steak sauce, Private."

They walked to the parking lot and, with a bear hug, parted ways.

Jeremy shook his head at the chance meeting as he walked to his truck. "The end of all things, Lord," he said out loud. "I know You've got a purpose in all this. Maybe someday You'll share it with me?" He got into the truck, put the key into the ignition, and heard the familiar click-click sound as he tried to start the engine. "Not again!" he groaned.

He reached under the dashboard, pulled the hood release, and then grabbed a hammer from the toolbox he kept on the floor. He slowly got out of the truck and raised the hood. *Whack!* He pounded the starter one time with the hammer and slammed the hood shut. He re-entered the truck and turned the key. The engine started this time, and Jeremy was quickly on his way.

CHAPTER 42

A Reunion

September 19, 1975, 5:30 PM

Four-freckled Amy and five-freckled Lizzy, the married and unemployed ones in the foursome, arrived together and checked in at the Greystone Hotel in Clayton. Betty was the last to arrive. *Late again,* she thought. She went to the front desk, learned the room number and, in great anticipation, hurried to the elevator. She put down her one small suitcase and pushed the "up" button, mentally encouraging it to move faster. *I should have taken the stairs,* she said to herself just as the elevator doors parted.

She took the elevator to the second floor, turned left, and quickly found room 243. She had no key—the front desk only gave out two per room—so she knocked on the door. Almost instantly, it burst open.

"Betty!" Carmen exclaimed, wrapping her arms around her friend. Amy and Lizzy rushed to join in and make it a group hug.

"Hold … the … phone!" said Lizzy, giving her signature expression since high school. "Hey, Amy, Carmen. Look at that rock on Betty's finger!"

"What, you mean this old trinket?" Betty said with mock nonchalance as she flashed it before their eyes.

"What did you land?" asked Lizzy.

"When did this happen?" asked Amy.

"Does he have any brothers?" asked Carmen.

For the next half hour, Betty was the center of attention. She told the story, giving every last detail from her and Roy's first meeting at the bank to the proposal. She took great delight in seeing her friends' eyes light up in envy of the romance. Then the group began their reminiscing of the days they had spent together back in high school.

Jeremy decided to take a detour on the drive up from Connecticut and visit his grandmother's gravesite. It would be the first time he had been there in years. *Maybe I'll break the bank afterward and treat myself to a room for the night,* he thought. *It would be a nice change from this rolling motel.* After leaving Connecticut, he entered eastern Massachusetts and eventually traveled along the way to the cemetery. The gravesite kindled sweet memories of the precious woman who loved and cared for Jeremy throughout his growing-up years. His heart was stirred with many emotions of the time he had lived in this area.—It seemed so long ago.

After visiting the gravesite, he drove past his high school and then through the center of town to the Watering Hole II. It was now a double-decker structure, and the outside looked clean and modern. He went into the basement and saw the gym was now air-conditioned and had state of the art equipment. He did not find Big Red, but he did meet up with some of his old weightlifting buddies. Once they had gotten over the shock of seeing him alive and had heard his story several times, he pumped a bit of iron, just to show them he still had it. Then he went upstairs and found Pinky, Charlie, and the guys smoking cigars and playing poker. The reunion had the same effect: disbelief and lots of back-slapping.

He said his goodbyes and, against his better judgment, went to the other end of town toward Betty's house. An unsettled feeling crept over him as he drove down her street—a street he and Betty had often walked along, hand in hand, just to be together. He read the name on the mailbox as he drove past: The Bertrands. *Just as well,* he thought. *I had no intention of stopping anyway.* An involuntary sigh escaped from somewhere deep within.

Jeremy drove back to the other side of town and entered the parking lot of the Greystone Hotel. He parked his truck, went in, and walked up to the front desk. His only baggage was an old backpack he had picked up at a yard sale in New Mexico.

"Hello, how may I help you?" the female clerk behind the counter asked politely.

"Do you have any rooms available?" asked Jeremy.

"We are pretty booked up, but I think we still have a few rooms left. Let me check. How many are in your party, sir?"

"Just one." He couldn't believe he was doing this. Motels were expensive, and he seldom rented rooms for the night. The bulk of the money he had saved up during his time in the Marines—including his hazardous duty pay—was long gone. But every now and then, he needed a break from the camper and to sleep on a bed with a real mattress.

"I have one room available on the third floor. Two queen-sized beds. Will that do?"

"Sure. How much?"

"That room is $67 plus tax." The clerk saw the pained look on Jeremy's face and smiled to herself.

"Ouch! Sixty-seven dollars, huh?" It wouldn't break the bank, but he seldom paid more than $25—and usually $15—for the motels he stayed in. He looked around. "Any chance I could just rent that couch over there for one night?"

"I'm afraid not," the clerk said with a smile and a touch of sympathy in her voice.

"Okay," Jeremy said. He was too tired to look elsewhere in town for a room.

"Very good, sir. I just need you to fill out this registration card. How would you like to pay for the room?"

"Cash."

The clerk did some calculating. "That will be $75.35," she said.

"Ooh, boy. Let's see what I've got." Jeremy pulled out his wallet and laid three twenties, a ten and six ones on the counter. As the clerk recounted the money and retrieved his 65 cents in change, he checked to see if he still had enough cash to treat himself to a halfway-decent restaurant meal.

He was surprised to find that he had only $2 in his wallet. *Two bucks? I thought I had an extra $10 in there. Oh, that's right—I put $10 worth of gas in the truck earlier. Well, it looks like it's time to dip into the old checking account.* He kept several hundred dollars in the account—which amounted to his life's savings—for use in emergencies.

"Say," he said to the clerk, "are there any banks in the area that might still be open? I need to cash a check."

The clerk handed him his change. "Yes, just down Route 1, about a quarter mile, there is a savings and loan that stays open until 7:00 PM on Thursdays. I think you will have just enough time to reach it."

It only took a minute for Jeremy to complete the registration card. The clerk handed him a key to room 362, and he left the hotel. He found the bank easily and cashed a check for $100.

The first restaurant he saw looked good enough. He went in, ate his meal, and left around 8:30 PM. *I'm feeling wild tonight,* he thought. *Think I'll take in a movie.* By 11:30 PM he was back at the Greystone. He headed for the elevator, but then turned and walked up to the front desk.

"Yes, sir, what can I do for you?" the night clerk asked.

"I just wanted to let you know that I parked my truck at the far end of the parking lot, and it's awfully dark out there. I don't think any of the lamp lights are working."

"Yes, sir, we are aware of that. It seems some punks came through last night and shot out most of the light bulbs in the lot, probably using BB guns. We reported it, but we can't replace the lights until Monday at the earliest."

"Okay, then. Good night."

"Good night, sir."

Jeremy entered his room, stripped to his underwear, pulled back the sheets on the bed and collapsed into it. He closed his eyes and waited for sleep to surround him. Minutes went by. He was exhausted, but the longer he lay in bed, the more wide awake he became. "I don't believe this," he said. He turned on the television, and then read one of the many magazines the hotel had provided. Nothing worked.

"Darn!" he said. He got out of bed and dressed in a pullover T-shirt, a pair of shorts and his running shoes. He left the room, went down to the lobby, and exited the front doors. When he had these bouts of insomnia—and they happened frequently—jogging was the only remedy that seemed to work.

"Is anybody getting tired?" Amy asked. The clock on the table read 1:35 AM.

"Not me," said Betty.

"Not me, either," said Lizzy.

"Not *I*," Carmen corrected.

"Ooh, always the English teacher," said Lizzy. Carmen threw a pillow in her direction that missed her head, but Betty's return strike connected. The pillow caught Carmen square in the face, and the brawl was on.

"I give up!" said Betty after receiving a few direct hits.

"Not me!" said Amy.

"Not me, either!" said Lizzy. The foursome had been laughing and horsing around like this since they had arrived.

"Say," said Amy when the brawl had died down, "I'm in the mood to paint my toes."

"You have got to be kidding," said Carmen. "It's past 1:30."

"So what? None of us are tired. And besides, who's watching the clock?"

"Carmen is, apparently," said Lizzy.

"Now, where did I leave my pocketbook?" said Amy to herself. "Ah, there it is." She opened it but did not find the cosmetic case she was certain she had brought with her. She never went anywhere without it.

"Did you use it in the bathroom earlier?" Lizzy asked, trying to be helpful.

"No, I'm sure I … oh, I remember now. I left it in the glove compartment of my car. Be right back."

"You're not going to the parking lot alone at this time of night," said Lizzy. "I'm going with you."

"Okay, Mother Lizzy, if you insist. Hey, Betty and Carmen—no juicy gossip 'til we get back. And if we're not back in ten minutes, send out the Marines."

The beer bottle landed with a crash into the vacant lot next to the hotel. The three men in the Chevy convertible erupted in drunken laughter, and then one of the men threw another bottle. "Hey … it's good to be free, eh fellows?" he said to his friends. All three had worked at the same plant, and all three had been fired the day before. It wasn't their fault, though—they had just misunderstood the company's no-drug policy.

"Hey, Twomby," the first man continued, "whadya think about the way old man Stryker lit into Bobby when he caught him lighting up?"

"Twern't fair, Arny," said Twomby. "No sir, twern't fair at all. He's the boss … and he had his own bathroom to go to. It was like he was just snoopin' around lookin' for things to bust a gut over. That's all I gotta say about it. You agree, Bobby?"

"Course I do," said Bobby. "Stryker never did like me nohow. But it sure was funny when he heard you two on the johns, puffing away and laughing your fool heads off."

"Well, if you ask me," replied Twomby, "I think we oughta go in there tomorrow and kick his—"

"Hey, guys," said Arny. "Shut up a minute."

"Who you telling to shut up, Arny?" said Twomby. "You shut up."

"No, I mean it," said Arny. "Look what's comin'." Bobby and Twomby looked in the direction where Arny was pointing.

"Whoa!" said Twomby. "Can't make out the faces, but I like what I see from the neck down."

"Look a bit plump to me," Bobby commented.

"Plump works for me," Arny replied. "How long's it been since you guys had any action, huh?"

"Don't matter," said Twomby. "Gonna get me some tonight." Arny and Bobby covered their mouths to muffle their sniggering.

The three slid over the side door of the convertible. They stayed low to the ground as they moved behind other parked cars and circled behind the twins. From there, they could hear the two women talking.

"How far down this row is your car?" asked Lizzy.

"Almost near the end," replied Amy. "I didn't realize how dark it would be out here. You would think a classy place like the Greystone would have this lot lit up like a Christmas tree. Anyway, here we are." She opened her pocketbook and withdrew her car keys.

The three men jumped out from their hiding places. "Ladies," they said, "may we be of service?"

Amy jumped and dropped her keys. "Ah, no," she said, "but thanks. We were just—"

Twomby grabbed her and put his hand over her mouth. Lizzy tried to scream for help, but Arny quickly grabbed her and covered her mouth as well. The women kicked and struggled, but they could not fight off the men.

"Ladies, relax," said Twomby. "We just want a little … *ow*! This one's no lady. She just kicked me in the shin. But, hey, I do like my women feisty. It's a real turn-on for me, know what I mean?" He grabbed Amy's chin and turned her face toward his. "How about a little kiss now? You know, to say you're sorry."

"Shut up and get them into the car," said Bobby. "I know a real quiet place where we can—"

"Excuse me, gentlemen," a deep voice said from behind.

The three men stopped and turned in the direction of the stranger's voice. "Who the devil are you?" Arny yelled at the intruder.

"I just want to know if there is anything I can do for the young ladies," Jeremy replied in a calm voice. "I know it's a bit dark out here and all, but they appear to be a bit distressed."

"Get lost, Jack," said Arny, "or you'll be the one who's distressed!"

"Now, gentlemen," said Jeremy, "I think there must be a way we can negotiate out of this situation. That's what all civilized men do. So let me make a suggestion—"

"Here's a suggestion, butthead," Arny said, giving Jeremy the finger.

"Good one, Arny," Bobby sniggered, wiping his nose on his shirt sleeve.

"Here," said Arny, turning Lizzy over to Twomby, who was struggling with Amy. "Think you can control the two of them while Bobby and me turn this piece of scum into hamburger?"

"Now, Meeny," said Jeremy, "I must warn you that if you pursue this line of negotiating, I will be forced to deal unkindly with you and Eeny."

Arny looked puzzled. "Who the devil is this Eeny and Meeny you're talking to?"

"Why," said Jeremy, "I figured you guys were part of the famous quartet—Eeny, Meeny, and Miny."

Arny looked at Bobby and chuckled, and then looked back at Jeremy. "That ain't a quartet, you idiot. That's a trio."

"Oh, did I forget to tell you? I'm *Moe*."

Arny's face contorted. He lunged forward, aiming a fist at Jeremy's jaw. Jeremy sidestepped the blow, grabbed Arny's right wrist, and pulled him down with his right hand, using Arny's own momentum to make him fall off balance. Then, in one continuous motion, he placed his left hand on Arny's back and slammed him head-first into the trunk of the car that was behind him. Arny slid to the ground, blood flowing from a broken nose.

Bobby looked shocked. He had been in numerous bar fights with Arny, and his friend never missed landing a blow—even when half-drunk. He leaped at Jeremy with both hands extended, intending to wrap them around his opponent's throat and put him down without mercy.

Jeremy placed a right fist squarely into Bobby's gut. The man's eyes went wide, and he dropped to his knees, gasping for air. Jeremy grabbed him by his belt and shirt collar and threw him like a rag doll into the air. Bobby slammed face-first into the rear window of the same vehicle that Arny had hit and began to slide down, leaving a trail of blood as he went. He landed on top of Arny and vomited onto his head.

Arny shook himself and stood. He wiped the vomit from his eyes and glared at Jeremy. He clenched his fist and made another attempt at landing a blow on Jeremy's jaw. Jeremy again sidestepped the off-balance blow, and then grabbed Arny's arm and twisted him around so they faced one another. He grasped him by the front of his shirt collar and, pulling him close, placed his knee firmly into Arny's groin. Arny gasped for air and dropped to his knees, holding his injured groin. He let out a groan and slowly fell forward into the tar.

Jeremy bent down beside him. "Don't worry, Meeny," he said. "You'll still be able to have kids someday … I think."

He stood and looked over at the third intruder, who was still struggling to hold the two girls. "Well, Miny, what do you think? Shall we call it a day, or do you want this tarred lot to be your bed for the night as well?"

Twomby didn't move.

"I'll tell you what," said Jeremy. "I'll give you to the count of three, and then it's you and me, pal. One …" Twomby immediately released the girls and took off into the night. "Smart move," said Jeremy.

He walked over to the two girls. "Are you ladies all right?" he asked.

"I … I think so," said Amy, leaning against her vehicle for support. "If you hadn't come along, I don't know what might have happened."

"I do," said Lizzy. "We would be dead."

Amy nodded. "How can we ever thank you, Mr. … what is your name?"

"Oh, just call me Sergeant Major Moe." Jeremy smiled.

"Thank you, Sergeant Major Moe," Lizzy said. She was beginning to tremble as the events of the past few minutes began to fully register. "It was certainly a lucky coincidence that you came along when you did."

"Luck had nothing to do with it," said Jeremy. "As my pa used to say, 'The end of all things, their purposes revealed or hidden, is good for those who love God.'" He glanced down at the two men groaning on the tar. "But not so good for those who don't."

"Then thank God you showed up," Amy said. "Lizzy, we had better get back to the hotel."

"What about your cosmetics case?" said Lizzy.

"I think my toes can wait."

"Good night then, ladies," said Jeremy. "I'll stay here and do a little 'clean up.' Will you be all right getting back inside without an escort?"

"Yes, we'll be fine," said Amy. The two girls walked away, glancing over their shoulders every few steps to make sure all was still well. Amy began to run for the door, and Lizzy followed suit.

When they reached the room, Amy banged on the door, having forgotten that she had taken a key with her. Betty quickly opened it. "Where have you two …" she started to say when Amy and Lizzy bolted in past her and collapsed onto the beds. Lizzy began to shake and sob uncontrollably, and Amy quickly followed suit. Carmen and Betty looked at each other, and then together rushed to their friends.

Betty pulled Amy into her arms and held her close while Carmen held Lizzy and gently stroked her hair. Several minutes passed before either Amy or Lizzy could gain some measure of composure. Finally, Carmen asked in a gentle, soothing voice , "Are you able to tell us what happened? Should we call the police?"

"No, there's … no need …" Lizzy said between sobs, "to call … the police." Slowly, the two poured out the story, with each sister picking up where the other left off. Betty and Carmen sat in silence and shook their heads in disbelief.

Jeremy lifted the two men less-than-gently into the convertible and returned to his room. It was now after 2:00 AM and, according to the notice posted on the door, he needed to check out by 10:00 AM. He certainly did not want to get charged for a second night. He picked up the telephone, pressed zero for the main desk, and asked the clerk if he could have a 9:00 AM wake-up call. Without bothering to undress, he fell into bed and quickly was asleep.

The telephone rang at precisely 9:00 AM. Jeremy fumbled to pick up the receiver. "Hello?" he said, stifling a yawn.

"This is the front desk. You requested a 9:00 AM wake-up call."

"Oh, yes, thank you." He clumsily replaced the receiver and slowly got out of bed. He showered and thought a moment about shaving, but then decided that he liked the bearded look. *It gives me a fuller chin*, he thought. Revived from the shower, he dressed quickly and packed the few items he had brought.

His pickup truck was parked at the end of one of the rows close to where the previous night's events had occurred. The drunken men's convertible was long gone, but as Jeremy slowly walked past the spot, he could not help but notice the blood and vomit on the road. *Hope the ladies are okay,* he thought. *Hope Meeny is still holding his groin.*

He unlocked the driver's side door, got in, put the key into the ignition and turned it. Nothing happened. He turned it again. Still nothing. He could not even hear the familiar *click, click* sound that his truck always made before starting. "What the … I don't need this right now, Lord." He pulled the hood latch, grabbed the hammer, got out and opened the hood. *Man, this had better work,* he thought. *Whack!*

He returned to the driver's seat and again turned the key. Nothing. *Good golly, Miss Molly.*

After two more whacks, the engine would still not turn over. Jeremy sat motionless behind the steering wheel, weighing his options. Anger boiled up inside him, severing his clear thinking. He picked up the hammer and once more stepped out of the truck. "I'll show this rust bucket who's boss," he said, raising the hammer above his head. Then, with a sigh of resignation, he lowered it and locked up the truck. He walked back into the hotel and went to the front desk.

"Is anything wrong, sir?" asked the clerk behind the counter.

"Afraid so. Starter trouble."

"Been down that road," came the sympathetic reply.

"Do you know of any garages in the vicinity that might work on trucks?"

"You're in luck. There's a garage just down the street on Route 1 called Smiley's. You can use this phone to call there."

"Thanks. Do you happen to know the number?"

"No, but let me look it up for you." The clerk pulled out a telephone book from under the counter and turned through the pages. "Here it is," he said, keeping his finger on the entry. He dialed the number and handed the phone to Jeremy. A gruff female voice answered on the eighth ring.

"Hello? Yeah, look, I'm in the Greystone Hotel parking lot down the street. I seem to be having starter trouble. Any chance I can get a tow and have it looked at? … A '64 Ford pickup.… A half hour? Sure, that will be fine. I'll meet you out there.... Not until tomorrow? You don't have any slots open until tomorrow to work on it? ... Well, okay, I guess there's not much I can do about that.... My name is Jeremy Martel.... The license plate is 398 AKE ... hey, I just take the plate they give me, but it does fit.... Okay, thanks." He hung up the phone and turned to the clerk.

"Well, it looks like I'm going to be in the area another night," he said. "Any chance that room is still available?"

"Let's see. No, I'm sorry, we are booked up solid. It's Friday night and all. Oh, wait a minute. It seems that room 241 had a cancellation at the last minute. Everything is the same, except for the floor."

"That will have to do, I guess." Jeremy reregistered and paid for the room. "Say, what's the telephone number for this place? I want to give it to the garage so they can reach me if needed."

"It's 555-3856, extension 241." The clerk wrote it down for Jeremy and handed the paper to him.

"Thanks." He went outside to wait for the tow truck, which arrived twenty minutes later. Once he had given the driver his keys and the telephone number of the hotel, he retrieved his bag from the cab and slowly walked away. His stomach was growling, so he walked across the street to a restaurant he had seen from the parking lot. By noon he was back in his room taking a short nap.

The ringing telephone jarred Jeremy awake. "Hello?" he answered, rubbing his eyes. He glanced at the alarm clock on the nightstand. It was now 5:40 PM.

"Is this Mr. Martel?" a terse female voice said.

"Yeah."

"This is Smiley's Garage. Truck's ready."

"But ... I thought you weren't going to be able to work on it until tomorrow." He sat up, realizing he had just wasted another $67, plus tax, for the room.

"We had a car that needed a part the local auto parts store didn't have in stock, but they did have your starter—a rebuilt one. So we were able to take your truck in early. Didn't take long to pop your starter out and put the new one in."

"Great, I guess. So what's the damage?"

"Bottom line: parts and labor, $77 even."

Jeremy rubbed his face with his free hand. *The whole truck isn't worth that much,* he thought. "Okay, then. I'll be right over and pick it up."

"Yeah, well, make it quick. We close at 6:00." *Click.*

Jeremy quickly got dressed and jogged over to the shop. Fifteen minutes later, he was standing before a fiftyish-looking woman who seemed desperately in need of a visit to the hair dresser. She rummaged through a pile of bills in her desk when Jeremy gave her his name. "Martel … Martel. Ah, here it is. That will be $77."

Jeremy began to open his checkbook.

"We don't take checks—cash or credit only, just like the sign says." The woman impatiently tapped the sign on her desk with a pen, and then looked at the clock on the wall. It was now 6:01 PM.

"Well, we have a bit of a problem then," said Jeremy. "I don't have that kind of cash on me, and I also don't have a credit card." The woman started tapping her pen on the desk. "Perhaps if I could speak to the owner …"

The woman tossed the pen onto the grease-stained appointment calendar that covered her desk and walked to the door that led into the work area. "Hey, Smiley!" she yelled over the noise of revving engine. "A customer can't pay and needs to talk with you." She shot Jeremy a look on her way back and again glanced up at the clock on the wall. It was now 6:03 PM.

Lord, help me out here, Jeremy prayed.

A moment later, a short, semi-bald mustached man walked into the office. "Yeah, what's the problem, Marge?" he said, wiping his greasy hands on a greasy rag.

"This here guy can't pay his bill."

"Oh?" Smiley turned to look at the customer.

"Well, that isn't quite true," said Jeremy. He noticed Marge fold her arms, lower her head, and glower at him. She was obviously not used to customers disagreeing with her. "You see, I can pay by check, but

I don't have a credit card or the cash to pay the whole bill. Perhaps if you would trust me to take my truck, I could make a quick trip to the bank and—"

"Banks close at 6:00 … same time as us," Marge interrupted, pointing to the clock. "It's now five past."

Jeremy scratched his head in frustration.

Just then, Smiley noticed the type of vehicle that had been written on the bill. "Hey, you're the owner of that '64 Ford, right?"

"Yes …" said Jeremy.

Smiley reached out with his right hand and gave a wide smile, showing exactly how he had gotten his nickname. "Semper fi," he said.

"Semper fi," Jeremy replied, cautiously shaking the outstretched hand.

Marge rolled her eyes and pushed herself away from her desk. "I'm going home," she said. "You can lock up. And don't be late for supper."

"Yes, dear," Smiley said, slapping her on the rear with the greasy rag as she walked past. He ignored the intimidating look he got as his reward. "Women," he said mostly to himself after the door to the office had closed. "Sometimes I wonder if God would be willing to renegotiate for a rib. Anyway, tell me, were you in 'Nam?"

"Yes," Jeremy said. He didn't really want to get into any war stories right now.

"I was a Navy man myself, but my youngest son insisted that real men only went into the Marines. He was shipped to 'Nam in '73. He was there only three months before he lost a leg. Landmine."

"I am truly sorry to hear that." A pained look came over Jeremy's face as he recalled some of the injuries he had seen while he was on active duty.

"Is that where you got that there scar?"

Jeremy touched a finger to his left cheek and nodded slowly.

"Look, as far as the bill is concerned, write me out a check for parts only—$47—and we'll call it even. If the thing bounces, though, I'll send my wife after ya." He grinned.

Jeremy was taken aback. "Look, I don't need charity. I—"

"Ain't charity. It's my way of saying thank you."

A lump formed in Jeremy's throat. It was the first time anyone had ever said thank you to him for serving in Vietnam. He set the check on the desk and wrote out the amount. "I really appreciate this," he said, handing it to Smiley.

"Hey, are you hungry? We live just across the street. It would be my pleasure to have you join us. What do you say?"

"Ah … well, I—"

"Yeah, I know my Marge comes across like a bull dog, but she sure can cook. And she really is a great woman. After all, she's put up with me for thirty-five years."

Smiley picked up the phone on the desk without waiting for Jeremy's response. "Hey, honey," he said after a short wait, "put an extra plate on the table. We've got company coming for supper." There was a slight pause, and then he hung up and smiled at Jeremy. "She said the extra plate's already on the table. Maybe I won't trade for a rib after all."

Most of the class of '65 had showed up for happy hour at 5:00 PM at the country club. The foursome, not as much interested in that part of the reunion, arrived shortly after 6:00 PM. They entered the large function room and reserved five seats at a table for eight—saving the fifth seat for Roy, who had not yet arrived. Two other classmates joined them at the table, and then the foursome joined in the mingling.

There were hugs, greetings, handshakes, backslapping, introductions of spouses, and stale jokes about guys who still had their hair and those who were complete acorns. There were loud exclamations when some of Betty's friends saw the size of her diamond, which served to draw others to the group. She began to feel self–conscious, and at the first opportunity she twisted the ring around so the diamond was less visible.

About 6:30 PM, Joey "Stubby" Owens, the class president, stood behind the lectern and started fumbling with the microphone attached to the front. Carmen had made the rounds, and she remarked to all within range how nicely Stubby had slimmed down, and that he was still a bachelor. She watched as Joey leaned into the mike and then made a hasty retreat as the ear-piercing feedback made everyone cringe.

"Sorry about that," Joey said after a moment. "What I wanted to say is that the meal is about to be served, so please find your tables." He waited for a few moments while everyone settled into his or her place, and then continued. "Before we begin the meal, we, the reunion committee, felt that it would be appropriate to remember those in our class who have passed away. I have asked Brenda Bennett, our class secretary, to come and read their names, followed by a moment of silence."

Brenda took Joey's place behind the lectern and asked everyone to stand. She held up an index card and solemnly began to read the names, pausing appropriately after each was read: "Barry Chase, Lydia Salome, Victor Blanchette, and Jeremy Martel. Let us now have a moment of silence." Several pairs of eyes looked at Betty's table as the last name was read, but she did not notice because she had closed her eyes.

When the minute of silence had ended, Joey took over and announced, "Let the party begin!" Everyone sat, and the waitresses began to serve tossed salads. The noise of talk and laughter again filled the room as the former classmates enjoyed the meal, shared about degrees they had earned, discussed who was working where (and who was not working), gossiped about those who were not present (and those who were not within earshot), and shared pictures of babies.

Twenty minutes into the meal, Lizzy exclaimed, "Look who just walked in!" All eyes turned toward the entrance to the hall. "It's Donna Demarko! Whoa, is she knocked up or what?"

"Lizzy! Don't be so crude," her sister scolded.

"Well, she is, isn't she?"

"Hey, Donna! Over here!" Betty waved and called out.

"Hi, everyone," Donna said when she had approached the table. She gestured toward the full room. "What a turnout!"

"Sit here at our table," said Carmen. " We have some spare seats."

"Thanks. I guess I do look like I could use a couple, huh?"

Carmen's face turned red. "Oh, no, I didn't mean—"

"It's okay, Carmen. I'm teasing. And since when did you start getting embarrassed by anything I said?" She sat and placed her hands on her belly. "My husband will be along any moment. He dropped me at the front door, and then went to park the car. Less distance for me to have to waddle."

"Well, we still have one seat left for him," Carmen said, and then remembered that the last seat was being saved for Roy. She looked at Betty. "Oh, Betty, I'm sorry. I forgot your fiancé was coming."

"It's okay, Carmen. Apparently so has he." Disappointment dripped from her voice.

"You're engaged, Betty?" asked Donna. "Do you have a ring? Let me see it."

Betty twisted the ring back in place and reluctantly held up her left hand.

"Holy smokes!" Everyone at the table laughed, momentarily breaking the tension. "What did you land?"

"Apparently, a guy who doesn't know how to read a clock. So where are you staying?"

"My husband and I are staying at the Greystone."

"The Greystone? Great!" said Amy. "So are we. What room number? Maybe we can all party-hearty after we leave here."

"Room 244."

"Room 244?" said Betty. "We're in room 243, just across the hall."

Amy glanced over toward the entrance. "Hey, Donna, does that guy standing in the doorway looking lost belong to you?"

"Oh, there you are," said Donna, waving her husband over. He saw her and quickly made his way over to the table. "Everyone, I'd like you to meet my husband, Jimmy. I am now Mrs. Donna Jean Noonan."

Chapter 43

The Revelation

September 19, 1975

At 9:00 PM, the disc jockey cranked up the volume of the music and the dancing began. Betty sat alone at her table, watching her friends—even Amy and Lizzy, the married ones without husbands tonight—out on the dance floor doing the twist.

"I am so sorry, sweetheart," a voice said from behind. Roy put his hands on her shoulders and kissed her cheek.

Betty was startled by his sudden arrival—she had given up on the idea that he would show up at all. "Where have you been?" she exclaimed. "You promised you would be here at 6:00!"

"I know, I know," said Roy. "I am truly sorry." He sat beside her and took her hand. "The meetings were intense. This new business deal that I'm putting together is worth millions." His eyes widened with excitement at the thought, and his voice became more animated. "When I realized the time, I put my lawyer in charge and got here as fast as I could. Will you forgive me?"

"I'll think about it," Betty said dryly. She turned her back to him and pretended to watch the dancing.

"That's my girl," Roy said, patting her arm.

The disc jockey announced that he would be taking a fifteen-minute break, sending those on the crowded dance floor back to their seats or outside for a smoke. Betty, still angry and hurt, put on an award-winning smile and introduced Roy to her friends. They all congratulated the couple and wished them well. "Got any more like you at home?" Carmen asked.

The evening passed quickly, and by midnight, many at the party were saying their goodbyes. The foursome and company remained. "Hey, guys," said Carmen. "Anyone want to look at our yearbook?" She knew this was always a highlight of such an event.

"You brought a yearbook?" asked Lizzy. "I looked for mine, but couldn't find it."

"I was just waiting for the right moment," Carmen said, reaching into her oversized handbag and withdrawing the book. The white cover had begun to yellow and show signs of wear-and-tear. The group pulled their chairs in closer together as Carmen laid the book on the table and began to turn the pages.

The memories flowed with each turn of the page. The friends laughed until they nearly had stomach cramps when they saw the out-of-date hairstyles and pictures of skinny classmates who were so no longer.

"Oh, look, Roy," said Carmen. "There's Betty's picture."

"I think I would have fallen in love with you even then, with the braces," said Roy.

Betty groaned and playfully slapped her fiancé on the arm.

"Uh, oh," Donna moaned.

Jimmy looked with concern at his wife. "What's wrong, honey?"

"Nothing serious. I just need to make a quick trip to the ladies' room. These twins are …" She left the table without finishing the sentence.

Betty had started to stand, but Jimmy put a hand on her shoulder. "It's okay, Betty," he said. "Happens often these days. There's not much room in there for the twins and a full bladder."

Carmen flipped to the next page. "Wait! Go back to the page before," Jimmy said. Carmen did as instructed and was surprised when Jimmy took the book from her hands and held it up to his eyes. "I've seen that picture," he mumbled.

"Which picture?" Carmen asked.

"This one … of Betty. I've seen that before … I think."

"You probably saw it in Donna's yearbook," Amy suggested.

"No, I'm sure that wasn't it. I've never seen her yearbook. Wait, I remember now. It was in Vietnam."

Betty looked shocked. "That's impossible, Jimmy. What would my picture be doing in …" She went quiet.

"Beauty has a way of getting around, dear," said Roy.

"Yeah, I'm sure of it," Jimmy continued, ignoring Roy's attempt at a joke. "My sarge in 'Nam had this picture." He tapped it with his index finger. The silence was acute, and those around the table shared shocked looks among themselves. No one missed the look on Betty's face.

"Go on, Jimmy," Betty gently prompted. The group grew deathly quiet.

"He used it as a bookmark in a small pocket Bible."

Betty stiffened. Roy, who had his arm around his fiancée, felt the change. "Are you okay, Betty?" he asked.

She ignored the question. "Go on, Jimmy," she pressed, her voice reflecting her increasing tension.

"I had arrived in 'Nam a few days earlier, straight from Parris Island. I only saw the picture once. Sarge was a very private man. One night, a short time before sunset, I went to his tent and asked if I could come in. I was really bothered—well, more like scared silly—by what I and the others knew was going to be a tough time the next morning. Sarge was sitting on the floor next to his cot. I could tell he was not pleased with my intrusion, but I had to talk to him and give him a letter I had written to Donna … in case I didn't make it. He let me come in, and I saw this picture lying near him. I picked it up and turned it over to see if there was any note written on the back. There was no signature or anything, but the back was covered with little dots."

"Dots?" asked Betty.

"Yeah, hundreds of dots. I don't have a clue what that was about."

"You're absolutely certain it was this picture?" Roy said, tapping on the yearbook.

"Absolutely. How many redheads look like *that*?" All eyes fell on Betty. Her face was frozen, completely stunned by Jimmy's revelation. What they couldn't see was the fresh torment she was experiencing as the story unfolded.

"Well," continued Jimmy, "I asked Sarge if it was a picture of his wife or his sweetheart. He said nothing—he just reached out and snatched it from my hand and put it into his little Bible. That was it as far as the picture was concerned. Then I began to tell him why I needed to talk with him, and I handed him the letter. He told me I could deliver it myself and didn't take it from me. Then he asked if he could share his faith with me.

"I said sure, though I must admit I was a bit taken back by a sarge who wanted to do such a thing. We sat on his cot, and he opened the Bible and began sharing. I tell you, he was one tough sarge, but that night he seemed … well … different. An excitement seemed to overwhelm him as he talked about Jesus. After we talked, we went back to the trenches, and believe it or not, I slept like a baby. But here's the strangest thing. I just saw—"

"What's wrong, Betty?" Roy asked, interrupting Jimmy's story. He had noticed that Betty was beginning to tremble.

Betty ignored him and, as calmly as she could, asked in a shaking voice, "Jimmy … what was his name … your sergeant?"

Jimmy hesitated a moment. "Betty, I don't know," he said. "Like I said, I had only arrived, and we never called him anything but Sergeant Major, or just Sarge. But you won't believe what happened just yesterday—"

"Sergeant Major?" gasped Amy. She turned to look at Lizzy. "That was what the man who saved our lives last night said we could call him."

"Yeah," said Lizzy, "Sergeant Major Moe. He nicknamed the drunks Eeny, Meeny and Miny, and he called himself Moe."

"You never mentioned that detail," Betty choked out.

"I know," said Amy. "We were so shaken up that we both forgot."

"What are you talking about?" said Roy, his frustration taking over. "You were *attacked*? And who is this 'Sergeant Major Moe'?"

Betty put her hand on Roy's arm. "Jimmy, go on."

"I just remembered something," said Jimmy. "After he shared his faith with me, he turned to the front of the Bible and read a quote that he said had been written there by his grandmother. It was something like, 'The end of all things …'"

"'… their purposes revealed or hidden, is good for those who love God,'" Amy finished in a hushed voice. The blood drained from Betty's face, and she covered her mouth with her hands.

"How did you know that?" Jimmy asked in astonishment.

"Yes, how did you know that?" Betty asked. Her mind was reeling with confusion, and she felt a sense of panic coming over her.

"Sergeant Major Moe quoted it last night just before Liz and I ran back to the hotel," said Amy.

"This doesn't make any sense," said Betty, shaking her head. "Jeremy's grandmother wrote that passage into a Bible she bought for him just before her death. But he was killed. This has to be a mistake." Her hands were shaking as her fingers twisted a cloth napkin.

"Who's Jeremy?" Jimmy asked.

Roy looked into Betty's eyes. His concern was rising as he saw his competition being resurrected. He reached over to take Betty's hand, but to his surprise, she rejected the gesture.

"Jeremy was a boy Betty used to date during and after high school," said Carmen.

"Jimmy, when were you in Vietnam?" Betty asked, her voice constricted with emotion.

"I was there in 1970."

Betty's eyes filled with tears. "Jeremy was killed in Vietnam in 1970."

"Was he a member of this graduating class?"

"Yes."

Jimmy handed the book to Betty. "Show me his picture."

Betty took the book from his hands and turned one page over. She pointed to the name "Jeremy E. Martel" printed beneath a picture. Jimmy fell silent for a moment as he studied the photograph. No one moved.

"That's my sergeant major," he said at length. He showed the picture to his wife, who had just now returned from the ladies' room. "Jeannie, honey, that's the man who saved my life. And Betty, he's not dead. Just yesterday—and you're gonna love this—I was at the—"

"How … do … you … know … this, Jimmy?" Betty said, barely able to choke out the words. Her mind was racing and she was having trouble catching her breath. None of this made any sense.

"I've been trying to tell you all," Jimmy said, smiling at the story he was about to tell. "I saw him yesterday, in Connecticut."

"But that's … not possible," said Betty. Her whispered voice was barely audible. "I read his name in the paper. He was … killed in action."

"Yeah, that's what we all thought. I saw him fall in battle just after he saved my life. He took a bullet to the head."

Betty gasped and again covered her mouth with her hands. Donna gave her husband a tightlipped look, and Jimmy quickly realized that he had just shared too much information. "But trust me," he quickly added, "he's alive and well. Amy, you said you are staying at the Greystone?"

"Yes."

Without further explanation, Jimmy got up from the table and hurried out of the room.

"Where are you going?" Donna asked, but she received no response.

Roy stood and looked into Betty's tear-filled eyes. He put a hand on her shoulder. "I'll be right back," he said. He caught up with Jimmy just as he was asking the attendant at the front desk for the number of the Greystone Hotel. The attendant produced it quickly, and Jimmy asked if he might use the desk phone.

"Sure, since the call is local," the attendant replied with a yawn.

Jimmy dialed the number. "This is the Greystone Hotel," the voice said on the other end of the line. "How may I help you?"

"Would you tell me if you have a Jeremy Martel registered there?"

"Let me check." After a slight pause, the clerk answered, "Yes, we do."

"Would you be able to connect me to his room?"

"But, sir, it's almost one o'clock in the morning."

"Yes, I'm aware of the time, but this is an emergency." Jimmy had no trouble making his voice sound desperate.

"May I inquire as to the nature of this emergency?" the clerk replied, sounding a bit suspicious.

"Yes, I'm his brother. There has been a death in the family . . . his . . . our mother." Jimmy was surprised at how quickly the lie came out of his mouth, but he felt no guilt. If he needed to confess that was fine, but later. God would understand.

"In that case," said the clerk, "give me one moment."

Jimmy heard the telephone ring once, twice, three times. "Come on, man, pick up," he whispered. Roy was breathing down his neck.

"This had better be real important," a yawning voice answered.

"Sergeant Major—AKA, Jeremy Martel?"

There was a pause on the line. "Who is this?"

"Sarge, this is Jimmy. Jimmy Noonan."

"Jimmy? Do you know what time it is? And how the devil did you find me here? I didn't even know I was going to be here tonight."

"Sarge, you ain't gonna believe the story I have to tell you. Can I come over?"

"What? Right now?"

"Yeah, right now."

"Can't this wait 'til morning?"

"Trust me, Sarge, it can't."

"Well, okay. Room 241. But I'm telling you, Private, this had better be good, or you're going to fry."

"Yes, sir, Sarge. Room 2-4-1."

"And don't call me sir!"

Jimmy hung up the phone and raced back to the banquet hall. Roy was right on his heels.

"Betty, come with me," he said when he reached the table.

"No, she's going with me," Roy said firmly. Jimmy slowly backed away and let Roy take over.

Betty had already grabbed her purse. "Where are we going?" she asked.

"I'll explain on the way," Roy replied.

Chapter 44

The Meeting

September 20, 1975, 1:20 AM

Roy and Betty entered the hotel together and headed for the elevator. Betty looked at him as they waited and gently touched his arm. "Roy, my darling," she said, "I must go alone."

Roy looked shocked. "No, please, Betty. I have to come with you. What if—"

"What if what, Roy? I'll be fine. But I must do this alone. Please understand." Her voice was still shaky, and her body trembled.

"No, I *don't* understand," Roy replied bitterly.

"I'll come back," she said as she slipped her small purse into his suit coat pocket. "That's my guarantee."

The bell on the elevator rang and the doors slowly opened. Roy watched as Betty stepped in. "I'll wait right here until you return," he said. Betty tried to smile. The doors closed.

Betty rode the elevator to the second floor, wondering at the irony of having this man she had so dearly loved—and even once had hoped to marry—being only one thin wall away. She thought about what she would say when, in seconds, she would look into his face.

Hi, how ya been?

Hey, where ya been hiding yourself?

How dare you make me suffer like this!

The elevator stopped and the doors parted. Betty's mind quickly snapped back to the reality of what was happening, though she still could not believe it. She stepped into the hallway and hesitated for a moment. The elevator doors closed behind her. She took a deep breath and walked down the corridor to the room.

When she reached the door, she stiffened her posture, clenched her teeth, and locked her lips tightly. It was her way of taking control over the emotions she was feeling and the emotions she knew she was about to feel. She knocked softly on the door.

"Jimmy?" a voice responded from inside. The door opened. "All right, this had better be …" Jeremy stopped, and his jaw dropped open. He and Betty stood there motionless, eyes holding each other like two mute scarecrows.

Memories of times from long ago flooded into her mind. A dance. Lost notes. A roller coaster ride. A walk along a sandy beach under a full moon. Voices inside Betty's head cried for her to run to him, to wrap her arms around him, to tell him how much she loved him. Other voices told her to slap him, kick him, punch him, and scratch his eyes out.

She opened her mouth to speak, but choked on the first word. All of her prepared defenses vanished. Ever so slightly her jaw began to quiver, and then the floodgates burst open. A kaleidoscope of emotions overpowered her, with her growing anger leading the assault.

"You're alive," she whispered. She heard herself speak, and the words became a barrage. She clenched her fists and pounded his chest. And pounded. And pounded. Jeremy remained stunned, mute, immovable, his arms by his sides. "Why?" she yelled, pounding the question into his chest through gnashing teeth. "Why … didn't … you … call … me? Why didn't you … come for me?" Her shoulders heaved, and she buried her face into his chest, weeping uncontrollably.

Jeremy slowly slid his arms around her and gently pulled her closer to himself. Betty made no attempt to resist, her clenched fists unfolding in his embrace. Seeing her, holding her, and touching her was the culmination of the desire that had consumed him. "I'm sorry," he said. "I am so sorry."

Moments went by before Jeremy began to release his embrace and gently push Betty away. He stepped aside. Wiping tears with the palms of her hands, she entered the room. She turned to look at him and gave a weak attempt at a smile. "You … look good," she sniffled out, giving a nervous laugh at the absurdity of the comment.

"I was just thinking the same about you."

Betty lifted her hands to dry her eyes again. Jeremy immediately noticed the ring on her left hand.

He walked over to the nightstand beside his bed, retrieved a box of motel-supplied tissues, and handed it to her. She withdrew a few, wiped her eyes and nose, and placed the box on the bed. Several moments passed in awkward silence.

"Jeremy, we need to talk," she said. She wondered how long it had been since she had last used his name in his presence.

"Yes," he agreed. He sat on the edge of one of the beds, and Betty sat on the other. "How did you know I was here?"

"Did you know it's our tenth-year high school reunion tonight?" she asked as she absentmindedly played with the moist tissue in her hands.

"No, I didn't. Ten years?"

"Jimmy pieced it together."

"But Jimmy didn't go to our high school, did he?"

"No, but his wife did. Do you remember Donna Demarko?"

"Yes, but Jimmy said his wife's name was Jeannie."

"Yes, Donna Jean Demarko, now Donna Jean Noonan."

Jeremy slowly shook his head. "Amazing!"

"Jeremy, do you remember the last words you spoke to me on that Saturday night?"

Remember? He remembered those words as if he had spoken them yesterday, rehearsing them over and over in his mind each day. "Yes, I do." He looked down at his hands, which were folded in his lap. "That was so long ago. Another life."

"Yes, another life. All these years, I thought you were … dead."

Jeremy looked up. "I guess I was as good as dead for a while. But how did you learn of it?"

"It was printed in the local newspaper. Back in 1970." Betty was now looking at her hands and at the twisted tissue she held in her lap. She again dabbed her nose with it.

"I … took a wound that should have been fatal," he said. "I didn't know that it had been misreported." Suddenly, the realization struck him. "Palowski!"

"Who?"

"It's a long story," he said, not wanting to get into all the details at the moment. He returned his attention to his hands, and both sat without talking for several minutes. Jeremy could see that Betty wanted to ask him something. He waited.

"Jeremy," Betty began again, continuing to play with the shredded tissue in her lap, "did you …" She stopped, took a deep breath and looked into his eyes. "Did you ever think of me while you were in Vietnam?" She already knew the answer from Jimmy's earlier account, but she wanted to hear it from him.

Jeremy stood and walked over to the windows. He had opened them earlier to look at the city lights, and he paused a moment when he caught Betty's reflection. Her gaze had followed him. The agony he felt was unbearable.

He went over to the table next to the window. There lay his wallet, a comb, keys, a small leather pouch attached to a leather lanyard, his dog tags, and the small pocket Bible he had carried with him throughout the war. He reached for the frayed and blood-stained book and brought it back to Betty. He again sat on the bed opposite her and held it out for her to take.

"I carried this with me in 'Nam," he said. "Open it."

Cautiously, she took the Bible and held it in both of her hands. Memories of the day she had given him this gift from his grandmother flooded through her mind. The leather-bound cover was stained and split, and it felt as if one careless breath would blow it away like dust from her hands.

"Open to the middle," Jeremy said in a soft voice.

She followed his instructions and found the picture. The corners were bent, and there were creases across it at different angles. She could only imagine what this book and picture had gone through.

"Turn it over."

Again, she did as he instructed. She gave a puzzled look when she saw the dots. "I don't understand."

"There are 1,058 dots there—one dot for every day I was in the Marines and in 'Nam." His voice choked with emotion. "You asked if I ever thought about you. I thought about you every day when I took out your picture and placed a dot on the back."

Tears streamed down Betty's face, but she let them fall. "Why didn't you come find me?" she whispered.

Jeremy looked away. He did not want to answer the question, yet he wanted to tell her everything that was in his heart. "I was afraid."

She stared at him. "Afraid? Afraid of what?"

Jeremy stood and ran his hands through his hair, struggling to find the right words to say. "Betty, war changes people. It changed all of us who went through that hell. It changed *me*." He walked over to the table by the window and leaned against it, placing his palms down on the surface for support. "I did things that no human should have to do." He kept his back to her as he spoke. "The problem is that I did them too well. It was my job." He straightened and began to pace again. He knew that he had said far more than he intended, but he could not help it. "It's been five years, and I still wake up in the middle of the night from the cold sweat of the nightmares."

Betty watched him pace. She wanted to rush to him, to hold him, to caress him, to tell him.... Tell him what? That everything would be all right?

"I'm not able to stay in one place," Jeremy continued. "I get a job, and a few weeks later I have to move on. I live in a beat-up truck and camper. I ..." He stopped and again leaned against the table by the window. He hung his head, and his body shook. "I couldn't bring you into this kind of life."

Silence hung like a fog in the room. Betty said nothing as she sat in the stillness, absentmindedly twisting the ring on her left hand.

Jeremy turned and faced her. "I'm sorry, Betty. You didn't need to hear all that. I think you should go now."

Betty stayed where she was and continued to twist the ring. "You were holding a small black box that last night you came to my house. What was inside?"

Jeremy was stunned. He didn't know she had seen the box. His mind raced to find an answer other than the truth, but it would not come. He walked over to Betty, reached down and took her by the hand. When she stood, he released it and again said, "You need to go."

She started to speak, but Jeremy softly touched her lips—lips he had so often kissed, and desired to kiss even now. He walked over to the door and began to open it.

"Jeremy, I …"

His eyes said there was nothing more to say. Betty moved to the door as if she were in a funeral march. When she was within inches of him, she looked up into his face, perhaps for the last time. "You loved me once," she said. "Do you still love me?"

My heart aches from the love I have for you, Jeremy thought. *If all the sand on all the beaches in the world were words, they would not be enough to describe my love for you.* He took her left hand in his and touched the ring. "What's his name?"

Betty looked down. "Roy," she said after a moment of hesitation, almost with a sense of guilt.

"Did he come to the reunion with you?"

She looked down at Jeremy's hand and nodded.

Jeremy swallowed. "Is he downstairs in the lobby waiting for you?"

Betty nodded again, almost imperceptibly, still gazing down at the ring.

"If it were me waiting, I would be pacing the floor right now, wearing a hole in the carpet." He let go of her hand. "Go to him."

Betty looked again into his eyes and tried to read the words that he was not speaking—the words she wanted him to say. "Jeremy, do you still love me?"

He looked directly into her eyes. "No, Betty," he answered. "It's over. Go to your fiancé. He's waiting. He loves you."

Betty held his look for a moment, and then turned and walked away. She heard the door latch click behind her. She leaned heavily against the wall when she reached the elevator, feeling as if something inside of her had just died.

Jeremy walked back over to the table and picked up the leather pouch. He poured the contents into his right hand and then spilled it into the palm of his left. A small diamond ring rested there—a ring he had worn around his neck since 1967. He gripped it tightly, turned, and fell to his knees at the foot of his bed.

"Oh, my Father," he cried out, covering his face with his hands. "I lost her once. And now this? Why? Why did you allow her to come back into my life for such a short moment? Would it have been too much to …"

He stopped himself short. He knew he had no right to accuse God, but his heart was filled with anger, confusion, and resentment at this cruel trick. "You protected me all those years in war. You brought me back from the dead. Would it have been too much to protect me from this pain? I don't understand You, God. What was the purpose? Help me to understand. Oh, God, help me!"

He stayed on his knees until dawn, pleading for release and for answers, but he received only silence in reply.

The elevator doors opened, and Betty stepped out. Roy stopped pacing. He had no idea in what state she would return to him—or even if she would return at all. Seeing her red-rimmed eyes, he rushed to her and put his arms around her. "Oh, thank God!" he said. "I thought I had lost you." He stroked her hair and kissed the top of her head.

Betty released from his grip and pulled away. He put his hands to her cheeks and kissed her lips. "I love you! I love you! I love you!" he cried. There was no response. Panic gripped his mind as he realized something was not right. "What, Betty? What is it?"

"Roy, I … I need some time by myself."

"Sure, sweetheart, anything." The panic registered in his voice. "But just tell me. Do you love me?"

Betty stood silent for several seconds as she reflected on the fact that she had just asked that same question to another man from another life. She took his hands from her face and lowered them. "Yes, Roy, I love you."

Roy saw the hesitation and heard the lack of conviction in her voice. "Really, sweetheart, do you mean it?"

"Yes, I mean it. But I need some time alone—time to think." She reached into his pocket and removed the purse she had placed there. "Do you understand, Roy?"

"Yeah, sure, babe. I understand." That was a lie. His mind raced to think of why she needed time to think. What had happened in that room?

Betty started to walk away, but he held her hand and refused to let go. "No, Betty, wait. I *don't* understand. What is happening? What do you need to think about?"

"Oh, Roy, just let me go … for now. Please?"

He slowly released her hand. She turned quickly, not wanting to look into his pained face any longer, and began to run to the stairs. She did not want to wait for the elevator to take her to the second floor.

For the second time that night, Roy found himself standing alone in the lobby. "I'll be right here," he said weakly.

CHAPTER 45

A DECISION

SEPTEMBER 20, 1975, 6:00 AM

Betty stood in front of room 243, wondering how she was going to get any time alone. She was sure that her girlfriends by this time would have returned to the room. She had no desire to talk to anyone, but she removed the key from her purse and quietly opened the door a crack. The lights were out, and she could hear snoring.

She entered the dark room, closed the door carefully behind her, and stepped lightly to the far end of the room. The girls had left the curtains open, and there was sufficient light for Betty to see the table and chairs by the windows. She walked over to them, sat at the table, and began to pray in silence.

Dear Father, I know full well that You are good and gracious and loving. You know my heart. Help me to know what to do!

She prayed as the tears flowed down her face until exhaustion overtook her body and mind. Her head slipped gently to the table, and she slept.

Jeremy rose from where he had been praying through the night and began packing the few belongings he had. It was now 6:20 AM, and though he hadn't slept, he needed to be back on the road. He took the stairs to the lobby, where he noticed a disheveled man sleeping on the couch. His suit coat was draped over the back, his shirt collar was unbuttoned, and his tie was askew. *They wouldn't let me rent that couch,* he couldn't help thinking in spite of the horrendous night he had just experienced.

He returned the room key at the front desk and hurried to his truck in the parking lot. He placed the key into the ignition and turned. It started on the first try. Shifting into first gear, he drove away.

Ten minutes later, Betty was startled from her sleep by Amy's snore. The others in the room stirred, but they did not wake up. She was confused by her surroundings when she looked around, but the events of the night before quickly returned to her mind. She now knew what she needed to do.

She rose stiffly from the table and quietly walked to the door. She first went down to the lobby, where she found Roy sleeping on the couch. "Roy," she said softly, gently shaking his arm.

He awoke with a start and looked up at her. "Oh, Betty," he said lazily. The disorientation slowly began to lift, and he leaped to his feet. "Oh, Betty!" He reached out to pull her to himself, but she put her hands in front of her to prevent him from coming any closer.

"Betty, what is it?" he asked. "Do you need more time? Because I certainly—"

Betty took a step forward and put her fingers to his lips. "Oh, sweet Roy. You need to listen."

"I'm listening." His face froze when he saw Betty remove the ring from her left hand. "No!" he gasped, grabbing her hand. "No!" The desk clerk looked up, but quickly went back to his business.

Betty again gently removed his hands from hers. She took his right hand and placed the ring into his palm.

Roy stared down at it. "But … why?"

"Roy, my dear Roy." There was no easy way to do this, but she would try to hurt him as little as possible. "I now know that it would be unfair for me to marry you. Every time I held your hand, I would be holding his. Every time we kissed, I would be kissing him. Every time we made love, I would be making love with him. You must try to understand."

"No, I don't have to understand," he said, spitting out the anger he felt inside. "I love you, don't *you* understand?"

Betty stepped back and blinked in surprise. At this moment she could only look on him with pity, but not with love—at least, not the kind of love he needed. "I know I have deeply hurt you, but—"

"Hurt me? You think all you've done is hurt me? No, Betty, you have deceived me, embarrassed me, and humiliated me. I'll be a laughing stock."

Betty had never seen this side of him. Tears welled up, spilling down her cheeks. "I'm so sorry, Roy. Please forgive me."

Roy misunderstood her words and thought she was apologizing for giving the ring back and for hurting him. "Of course I will forgive you," he said. He stepped closer and reached out to take her into his arms.

Betty took a step back. "Goodbye, Roy," she said. Her words had a gentle finality that hit him like a sledgehammer. She turned to walk away.

Roy reached out, grabbed her by the arm and spun her around. Her face winced in pain. "Roy, you're hurting me!" The desk clerk looked up again and began to walk around the counter.

Roy pulled Betty closer and moved his face to hers. "You're mine!" he whispered through clenched teeth. "I won't let you go. I won you, and you're mine."

"Excuse me, miss," said the clerk, "is everything all right?" He was about halfway to reaching the couple.

Betty wrenched her arm free and stepped back. "Yes, everything is fine!" she said while keeping her eyes riveted on Roy. She looked at her former fiancé with rage in her eyes. "You … won me? Was I some sort of bet? A prize?"

Roy realized what he had said. He took a step closer to her. "Oh, no, Betty, my love. I didn't mean—"

The clerk was now within an arm's length of the two. "Hey, fella, is there a problem?" he said.

"Get lost!" Roy yelled back.

"Goodbye, Roy," said Betty. She hurried toward the stairs and disappeared.

Roy made a move to follow her, but the clerk stepped in front of him. "I'm going to have to ask you to leave, sir," he said.

"I told you to get lost!" He shoved the clerk out of the way, causing the man to stumble over a nearby chair. The clerk extended his arm to break his fall, knocking it against the edge of a mahogany table. He cried out in pain and lay on the floor, holding his right arm. A second clerk saw the fray and dialed the police.

"You'll be back!" Roy yelled after Betty, oblivious as to what he had just done. "I played whatever part you wanted me to play. I won you, and you'll be back. And next time, I won't be so forgiving."

A few early-risers in the lobby began helping the clerk over to the couch. They turned and looked at the man who was yelling at no one. Roy turned to them and smiled. "She'll be back, you'll see," he said as if they were old acquaintances. He took one more look at the diamond ring he held in his right hand, and then placed it into his pocket. *I need a good breakfast,* he thought. He picked up his suit coat and headed for the dining room.

Five minutes later, Roy was being escorted, in handcuffs, out of the hotel and into a police cruiser. He proclaimed his innocence all the way.

Chapter 46

The Chase

September 20, 1975, 6:40 AM

Betty could still hear the shouts from Roy as she walked down the corridor. *Oh, God, forgive me,* she prayed. *How I have played the fool. Whatever happens now, I will trust You.* She said the mental prayer with more confidence than she felt.

Again, she found herself standing in front of the door numbered 241. She breathed in deeply, released the breath, and knocked. There was no response. *He must be asleep*, she thought. She knocked louder, and waited. *He knows it's me and won't answer. Oh, God, make him answer!* Her next knock was without caution. "Jeremy, it's Betty!" she called out, unaware of how loudly she had spoken the plea. "Please open the door!"

"Betty, is everything okay?" said a voice.

Betty turned to see Jimmy, dressed in only his pajama bottoms, standing in the doorway across the hall. Donna stuck a head covered with trashcan-sized curlers out of the door and pulled her bathrobe tighter around her.

"I am so sorry to wake you," Betty apologized. "I need to speak with Jeremy again, and he's not answering." The pain on her face spoke volumes.

Jimmy stepped across the hall and knocked loudly on the door. "Jeremy!" he yelled. "We need to talk with you!"

The door to room 243 opened, and Lizzy stuck out her head. "What's up?" she said.

Carmen stepped past Lizzy and into the hallway. "Betty, are you okay?" she asked, tightening the bathrobe cord around her waist. Amy was close on her heels.

Jimmy looked at the door to room 241. "Wait here a minute," he said. He returned to his room, picked up the telephone and dialed the front desk.

"Front desk," the clerk answered. "How may I help you?"

"Can you tell me if a Jeremy Martel is still registered here?"

"No, sir, he is not. He checked out about, oh, twenty, twenty-five minutes ago."

Jimmy hung up without a thank you and hurried back to Betty. "He's checked out."

Betty stared at him. Her limbs felt numb, and she did not know what to do.

"Betty, where's the ring?" Carmen exclaimed, pointing down to Betty's left hand. Lizzy gave her a sharp blow to her shoulder. Everyone else had noticed the now-ringless finger, but they'd had the good sense to keep their mouths shut.

"Betty, we'll find him," said Jimmy. A thought came into his mind. "Wait a minute. I just remembered something." He stood for a moment as if lost in thought and said no more.

"Well, are you going to let the rest of us in on it?" Donna asked.

"I'll explain in the car," Jimmy said. He returned to his room to gather his wallet and keys from the night stand.

"But my hair," Donna complained. "And we're not dressed!"

"Woman, are you coming or not?" He began speedwalking down the corridor.

Woman? We'll definitely talk later. She filed this mental note and hurriedly got into step behind her husband. Jimmy led the five women—four of whom were dressed in pajamas, bathrobes, and slippers—down the stairs and out to the car.

The six piled into his Dodge sedan, with Betty squeezing into the front seat with a very pregnant Donna. Jimmy started the engine, put it into reverse, and backed out of his parking space. He cut the wheel too soon, and the front corner of his vehicle slammed into the car parked to his left. "We'll deal with that later," he said to Donna, who was ready to verbally crucify him. Betty noticed that the car—a black Corvette convertible—had just received a few thousand dollars' worth of damage.

Jimmy shifted into drive and pressed down on the gas pedal. The women, who had not yet buckled in, grabbed for the roof, the door handles, each other, and anything else they could find to keep from being tossed around.

Jimmy took the turn out of the parking lot exit almost on two wheels. "Slow down!" Donna pleaded. "I'm not ready to go into labor!" Several cars on the road skidded to avoid hitting him, their tires squealing as they braked to keep their fenders from getting creased. Betty heard several angry shouts from the drivers and saw arms extended out of windows with middle fingers raised.

"Is everyone still alive back there?" Donna asked the three back-seat passengers.

"Yeah, we're good … I think," Amy replied.

"Okay, dear husband, would you now please let the rest of us in on this master plan of yours?"

"Sure, it's simple …"

"Watch out!" Betty yelled. Jimmy swerved left, and then right. The five women turned and looked out the back window to see if any of the pedestrians in the crosswalk had been hurt as they jumped back onto the sidewalk. More angry shouts were heard and middle fingers were raised.

"As I was saying, it's simple …" Jimmy continued, pausing to slow and look left and right before running a red light. Donna and Betty gripped the dashboard. "The Sarge told me when I spoke to him on Thursday that he was heading for Canada.

"Canada?" said Betty. "How will we find him if he's on his way to Canada?"

"Well, to get to Canada, he has to start out from here and go north on Route 128. He's only got a … what, maybe twenty- to twenty-five-minute head start?"

Donna looked incredulously at her man. "That's your plan? To catch up with him on a highway that he *might* be on? You don't even know for sure if he is really heading for Canada."

"You got a better plan?"

There was no response.

"That's what I thought," Jimmy said victoriously. He glanced down at his watch as he turned onto the entrance ramp to Route 128. It was now 6:54 AM, and there was little traffic on the road this early on a Saturday morning. "Hang on, ladies. We've got some distance to make up!"

He pushed the gas pedal to the floor, and the speedometer climbed rapidly.

After leaving the Greystone Hotel, Jeremy turned onto Route 1 and drove a mile down the road toward Route 128. He noticed he was a little low on gas, so he turned into the first station he saw to top off the tank. He drove up to the pump and rolled down his window. An attendant saw him and stepped out of his booth.

"Yes, sir, what will it be today?" the attendant asked.

"Fill 'er up, will you? Regular. And check the oil, please."

"You got it."

The attendant started the pump and flipped the lever so it would run without him having to hold the handle. Jeremy pulled the release latch, and the attendant lifted the hood to check the oil. He removed the dipstick, looked at it, and then walked around to the driver's side window. "Looks like you need a quart," he said, holding it up for Jeremy to check. Jeremy nodded his approval. "Uh … I also noticed that you have a low front right tire. You might want to check the pressure."

"Thanks."

Jeremy paid for the gas and oil and pulled over to where the air pump was located. He checked the pressure on all four tires and filled each as needed. When he again got behind the wheel, his stomach quickly reminded him that he had not eaten since yesterday. He was in the mood for doughnuts and chocolate milk, so he parked his truck in a space near the front door of the convenience store and entered. A few minutes later, he exited with his breakfast in hand.

He munched on the doughnuts as he pulled away from the station and headed for Route 128. He looked at his watch as he entered the highway, which now read 6:53. He had toyed with the idea of driving by his grandmother's gravesite one last time, but he wanted to put as much distance between himself and his memories as fast as he could.

"Sorry, Grandma," he said aloud. "Maybe when I sort a few things out."

"Jimmy, do you know what Jeremy's truck looks like?" Lizzy asked from the back seat.

"Yeah, he drives a vintage black Ford pickup with an old slide-on camper on the bed."

"Oh, I saw that parked in the hotel parking lot yesterday."

"Do I need to know that, Lizzy?" Jimmy said a bit irritably.

"Well, I'm not real sure—it's kind of hard to see at this distance—but I believe there's a black truck with a camper down the road ahead of us." She pointed straight ahead to the vehicle she had seen. Silence fell as all eyes strained to look down the road.

"Jimmy, I think she's right," said Donna. He pressed the gas pedal further to the floor.

The flashing lights didn't catch Jimmy's attention in the rearview mirror until he heard the siren. Everybody else turned to look out the back window, then at each other and groaned. Jimmy had no choice but to pull over. Donna got the vehicle registration out of the glove box while Jimmy reached into his back pocket for his license.

Glancing into his side-view mirror, Jimmy watched the burly officer approach. "Let me do the talking," he said to the others.

"License and registration," the officer said when he had reached the driver's side window. Jimmy handed the documents to him. The officer quickly matched the picture on the license with the driver and then leaned over to scan the passengers inside the vehicle. He raised his eyebrows when he saw the pajama-and-bathrobe-clad women and Betty's stunning head of flaming red hair.

"Officer, I know I was going a bit fast," Jimmy said, "but I can explain."

The officer looked at Jimmy and noticed his bloodshot eyes from lack of sleep. "I'll bet you can," he said with little enthusiasm. It had been a long night. "Please step out of the vehicle, sir."

"But, officer, let me explain. There's been—"

"Step out of the car, sir." The tone in his voice told Jimmy that he shouldn't argue. Jimmy complied, his frustration rising. He knew that any chance of catching up to the black truck was rapidly slipping away.

"I am going to conduct a field sobriety test," the officer continued. "Spread your arms to the—"

"No-no-no-no! You can't do that! We're wasting time! You don't understand—"

"Sir, we can either do this here or at the station," the officer replied in a professional tone. It was obvious that he was not used to someone yelling *no* at him.

"Look, I'm sorry," Jimmy tried again, "but you don't understand, officer. There's been an accident."

The passengers in the car cast worried glances at each other. Betty wondered if they would be given any time off for good behavior.

The half-lie had an effect on the police officer. "Where?" he asked.

"Back at the Greystone Hotel." Jimmy pointed to the front left corner of his car. "We were hit by a truck—a black Ford pickup truck with a slide-on camper." The trooper took a step forward to examine the fender. Flecks of black paint were clearly visible in the damaged area. The women sank lower in their seats. "It was a hit-and-run, and we were following the driver when you pulled us over."

"Was anyone hurt?"

Jimmy looked back at the car. Betty had sunk down so low that he was no longer able to see her in the front seat. He looked back at the officer. "Yes! The driver knows it, but he just drove off anyway."

The five women had closed their eyes and were praying silently. "Oh, Lord," Donna whispered, "that man You gave me is going to burn in hell, and bring us right along with him."

"Wait here," the officer ordered. He walked over to his cruiser and picked up the mike to his radio. "Wainright, come in."

"Wainright here," said the voice on the receiver. "What's up, Carlos?"

"Are you still set up in the speed trap?"

"Sure am, buddy. Why?"

"Have you seen any black Ford trucks with slide-on campers go by recently?"

"Sure did. One just went by."

"Get out there and pull him over. He's suspected to be involved in a hit-and-run with physical injuries. I'll be there in one minute."

"You got it, good buddy."

Officer Carlos hung up the mike and walked back over to Jimmy. "Now, as for you, get into your vehicle and follow me."

The cruiser pulled out from around Jimmy and sped down the road. Jimmy kept pace. "Oh, Jimmy, I can't wait to see how you get out of this one," Donna said.

"Well, we got past phase one of the plan."

Donna looked at the other girls and shook her head. "My eternal optimist. And just what is phase two?"

"Don't know yet, but I didn't know what phase one was until it happened."

It did not take Officer Wainright long to catch up to the black Ford truck. He pulled behind Jeremy's vehicle and turned on his flashing lights and siren.

"You've got to be kidding me," Jeremy said as he pulled over to the breakdown lane. "Lord, I can't take much more."

The cruiser pulled in behind the truck. Jeremy sat with his hands on the steering wheel and waited for the officer to arrive. When he didn't immediately approach, he looked into his rearview mirror and saw the officer was standing behind his open cruiser door. He had drawn his revolver and was aiming it in Jeremy's direction.

"Get out of the vehicle and put your hands where I can see them!" yelled the officer.

Jeremy was stunned. "What the—"

"Now!"

Jeremy opened the door and got out as ordered.

"Put your hands behind your head and walk toward me."

Jeremy again did as ordered. "Officer," he said, "There has got to be some mistake."

"Now down on the ground and spread-eagle."

This guy means business, Jeremy thought. He laid down flat on the tarred surface and spread his arms and legs so he looked like an X. The officer straddled him and holstered his weapon. He pulled Jeremy's left arm behind his back and snapped a handcuff to his wrist. He did the same with the right wrist.

"Would it be too much to ask what I've done?" asked Jeremy.

Officer Carlos pulled up behind the first cruiser and quickly got out of the car. Jimmy pulled in behind Carlos's cruiser and also stepped out.

"You stay in your vehicle," Officer Carlos ordered.

"Officer, I need to explain something," Jimmy said, ignoring the order.

Jeremy could hear the voices, but he could not see who was speaking or make out what was being said. Officer Carlos frowned at Jimmy. He had a feeling that he would be taking this guy downtown.

Donna held her belly with her left hand and struggled to reach over Betty and push the passenger side door open. "Go to him, Betty," she said. Betty exited the car but hesitated to move forward. "Go!" the other girls encouraged.

Officer Carlos noticed she had stepped out of the car. "Ma'am, please stay in the vehicle," he said.

"Go," Donna counter-ordered.

"Uh, you're gonna find this a hoot," Jimmy began to explain, partly to distract Officer Carlos and partly because he really did need to explain.

"Just tell me one thing," said Officer Carlos. "Was there a hit-and-run?"

"A hit-and-run!" Jeremy shouted. By now he had completely lost his temper. "Is that why I'm in cuffs?!"

"Well ..." said Jimmy, "actually there was ... but, ah, not by him."

"How about the injured victim. Is there one?"

"Well, yes and no."

"Just what the devil does that mean?"

"Would you ... ah ... consider a broken heart to be an injury?"

Officer Carlos shook his head. "That does it. Wainright, take the cuffs off that fellow. This guy is going to the station with me." He removed a pair of handcuffs from his belt and placed them onto Jimmy's wrists.

Betty had moved forward enough so she could now see Jeremy, but he still could not see her from where he lay on the ground.

"Officer?" she said. Officer Wainright turned to look at her. "Would you mind leaving the handcuffs on him for a bit, but just help him to sit up?" The trooper looked over to Officer Carlos, who shrugged.

"Betty, is that you?" said Jeremy. His mind was spinning with questions.

Officer Wainright reached down, moved Jeremy into a sitting position, and leaned him up against the bumper of the cruiser. Jeremy looked up and saw Betty standing just a few feet away. She walked toward him, knelt, and deliberately folded her hands in front of her, the left over the right. Jeremy allowed his gaze to follow the movement.

"Do you love me?" she asked without any preamble.

Jeremy sighed deeply and looked straight into her eyes. His emotions had been wrung out, and he could no longer deny his true feelings. There would be no more lies. "Oh, Betty," he said, "I have never loved anyone else since the day I met you."

Betty's heart exploded. Her chin quivered, and tears of consummate joy began to fill her eyes and blur her vision. She smiled with a joy she had thought she would never feel again.

"I have never stepped on anyone else's toes since I stepped on yours," Jeremy continued. "I have never told any other girl that I am ... *fond* of her." That brought a chuckle from Betty. "I have never tricked anyone onto a roller coaster ride but you. Betty, I love you desperately."

Betty's voice quavered. "I … I need to know something else. What was in the black box?"

Jeremy laid his head back and rested it against the cruiser. "Unbutton my shirt."

"What? I don't understand."

"Unbutton my shirt."

Betty leaned forward and did as she was asked. Her hand shook as she noticed the leather pouch hanging around Jeremy's neck by the thin lanyard. "Open the pouch." She followed his instructions and tipped the contents into her hand. "That's what was in the black box."

Tears spilled as she looked down at the diamond. No words were spoken. None needed to be said.

"Now, ma'am?" Officer Wainright said as he held up the keys to the handcuffs. Betty nodded. The officer reached down and unlocked the cuffs.

Jeremy took the ring from Betty's hands. "Betty, I should have asked this seven years ago. Will you marry me?" He gently took her left hand and placed the ring on her finger.

Betty fell into his arms. "Oh, yes, my love," she whispered through trembling lips. "Yes, I will marry you."

Jeremy leaned back slightly to look into her face. "Are you absolutely certain? I can't promise you much." He motioned toward the camper. "That will be our home, at least for now. And … there's this." He pointed to the scar on his left cheek.

Betty reached up and tenderly touched the wound. "Don't worry, my love," she giggled. "You were never that good-looking anyway."

He pulled her to himself and kissed her lips.

Officers Wainright and Carlos exchanged glances. This was a situation that neither of them had ever encountered before, and they had no idea of how to handle it. It didn't help matters that the four other women had exited the sedan and were now standing around the couple, openly crying and hugging each other. One of the women looked as if she was ready to give birth.

Finally, Officer Carlos stepped over to Jimmy. "Well, as for you, Mr. Noonan, I think you've broken enough laws today. We really do need to take you downtown."

Jimmy shrugged and accepted the judgment. He would have paid any price to help the man who saved his life. He allowed Officer Carlos to slowly lead him toward the police cruiser.

"Semper fi, Sergeant Major," he said to Jeremy as he walked by.

Officer Carlos stopped short and looked at him. "What did you say?"

"When?"

"Just now, to that man."

"Oh, you mean 'Semper fi'? He was my sergeant major in 'Nam. This man saved my life."

"What year were you in 'Nam?"

"1970."

"Both Wainright and I were there in '69. I took one in the shoulder, and Wainright took one in the leg."

Jimmy moved his handcuffed hands to point to the scar that was visible on his bare stomach.

"That's not a gunshot wound," said Officer Carlos. "Bayonet?"

"Yup. And Sarge, over there, he was body bagged."

"No way!"

Jimmy raised his shackled hands as if he were being sworn in a courtroom before a judge. "Wouldn't lie to the State Police," he said.

Officer Carlos paused for a moment, and then turned to the other officer. "Hey, Wainright, you got any extra steaks?"

"Sure do, buddy."

Officer Carlos looked back at Jimmy. "Okay, here's the deal, Noonan. We can go downtown where I book you for—well, I haven't figured out yet how many laws you've broken—and you spend a few nights. Or you and all your friends can come to Wainright's house this afternoon for a barbecue, and we get to hear this tale. Your call."

Jimmy looked at Donna. His wife held up her hands in defeat, amazed that he had managed to get out of this one.

"Deal," said Jimmy.

Officer Carlos unlocked the cuffs and nodded in Carmen's direction. "And, uh, be sure to bring that blonde over there."

EPILOGUE

DECEMBER 18, 1976

The couple sat hand in hand on the California beach and buried their bare feet in the warm sand as they watched the moon-streaked tide inch closer to them. They had purchased the aluminum-framed fold-away chairs in which they now sat only yesterday, and they represented the newest and best furniture the couple had. Jeremy released Betty's hand and leaned forward to place another log on the dying campfire. Then, using a long piece of driftwood, he poked the embers, sending a spray of sparks shooting skyward as the fire came back to life.

"Jeremy, you've been awfully quiet this evening," said Betty. "Is anything wrong?"

Jeremy continued to poke at the embers. "No, nothing's wrong, hon. It's just that …"

"Just what?"

Jeremy dropped the stick into the sand and leaned back, taking Betty's hand again. "It's just that I've been doing some thinking."

Betty waited for him to continue, knowing her husband would share what was on his mind when he was ready.

Jeremy slid out of his chair, knelt in the sand in front of Betty, and placed his hands gently to her belly. The child kicked. "Did you feel that?" he exclaimed. "It's got to be a boy with a kick like that."

"What else would be the firstborn of a Marine?" She smiled at him.

He leaned forward and kissed her, and then stood up and took her by the hand. "Let's go for a walk."

They walked silently hand in hand along the edge of the water, allowing the incoming tide to wash over their feet. "Betty," Jeremy said, breaking the silence, "I've been thinking, quite a bit lately, about some of the more difficult situations that have come into my life. I remember Grandma and others commenting to me that God was 'sifting me as wheat.' I never really understood what they meant by that when I was younger. Now I realize that just as wheat is sifted to separate the better and useful seeds from the lesser unusable chaff, so does the Lord sift or test us, His people. His testing teaches and strengthens us, showing us what we need to let go of in life and also what to hold fast to. As God's Word says, His correction and testing isn't enjoyable at the time; but later, we can see the result—a quiet growth in grace and character. I feel God has taught me and grown me to be better able to be used by Him for His purposes. I am so grateful He hung on to me and didn't let me go during all those times I was angry with Him. I only regret that it took me so long to realize His love for me."

Betty loved how Jeremy shared his heart with her. She, too, was grateful for God's relentless pursuit of Jeremy and was thanking Him for just that as Jeremy spoke with her.

Jeremy squeezed Betty's hand lovingly as he continued his thoughts. "I also believe, my sweet wife, that I need to go back to college. We've prayed a long time about it, and I think I'm ready. And besides, I need to give you and our child more of a life than this. I mean, if it were just me, it would be one thing … but I've got a family now. We can't go on forever like this, with me dragging you around the country from job to job."

Betty sensed his feelings of unspoken guilt and reached up and held his face between her hands. "I love you dearly," she said. "And if that is what you want, then do it. But you need to know that I have never felt such contentment in my life now that I am with you. I would be willing to live in a cardboard box for the rest of my life, as long as you were there beside me."

"Well," Jeremy said, looking over at the truck and camper parked on the beach campsite, "considering what we have been living in, that might be an upgrade." They both laughed at the joke, and then continued on their walk.

"I don't know if Strickland State will even let me back in," Jeremy said. "And if they do, we would have to come up with the tuition. We've pretty much used up all of our savings, and we're penniless. I'm going to have to work nights and go to school during the day."

"But, I can—"

"No, you're not working. You'll be busy taking care of our baby. And we will need an apartment. They're not cheap, and—"

Betty stopped suddenly and turned to look into Jeremy's face. "Look, buster," she said, narrowing her eyes, "you can talk yourself right out of this decision if you want to do so, but have we ever gone one day hungry? Or gone one day without a home? Has one day gone by when God has not supplied our every need? God will provide, but He can't steer a vehicle unless it's moving."

Jeremy took a deep breath. "You're right," he said. "Let's go back to the camp. We can start to make plans. And I'll make you the best open-fire grilled-cheese sandwich you ever had."

"Double cheese with mustard?"

"Absolutely."

A half hour later, Jeremy placed the hot sandwiches on paper plates and set them aside to cool. He and Betty sat at the picnic table at the campsite, excitedly making plans by the light of their propane-fueled lantern.

The headlights from a vehicle driving straight toward them caught their attention. When it got close, they realized it was no ordinary beach-going vehicle but a stretch limousine. The driver, dressed in formal chauffeur's attire, parked next to the truck and stepped out. He opened the rear passenger door, and a black-suited, bow-tied little man stepped out. He picked up a leather briefcase from off the seat and approached the couple. The chauffeur folded his hands in front of him and remained by the open rear door. Whatever this was about, it was going to be a short visit.

"Mr. and Mrs. Martel?" the little man inquired as he approached.

Betty and Jeremy looked at each other, and then back at the strange guest. "Yes," they said together.

"I trust you'll pardon this intrusion. May I sit down?"

Betty and Jeremy again looked at each other. "Of course."

"I see I'm interrupting your meal. Please forgive me, but this won't take long." The little man pulled a white handkerchief from his lapel pocket and dusted some sand from one of the benches. He sat, placed the briefcase on the table, and reached across to shake the couple's hands. "My name is Connor Takesian. I am the executive vice president in charge of finance for Fenwick Pharmaceuticals. Have you heard of the company?"

"No, sir, I haven't," Jeremy said cautiously. Betty shook her head. Both of them were wondering where all this was leading.

"Well, I suspect you have, at least as far as our products are concerned." He rattled off a few well-known brands of drugs. Betty and Jeremy did, in fact, recognize some of the products, and even acknowledged using some of the over-the-counter brands on occasion.

"Excuse me, Mr. Takesian," said Betty, "but may I see some identification?"

Mr. Takesian smiled widely. "But of course." He reached into his inside suit coat pocket, pulled out his wallet, and flipped it open to his driver's license. "Very cautious of you, Mrs. Martel," he said, handing the wallet across the table. "It always amazes me how few people these days are appropriately cautious." Betty, satisfied, handed the wallet back to him.

Mr. Takesian proceeded to unsnap the locks on the briefcase and open it. "I have something for you to read, Mr. Martel." He reached inside and removed an envelope.

"Mr. Takesian," said Jeremy, "are you here to sell us something? Because if you are, you should know—"

The little man laughed heartily at the thought. "Oh, my goodness, no. As I said, I am one of the vice presidents of a well-established international pharmaceutical company. I can assure you my business here has nothing to do with selling anything. If you read this letter, it will explain everything." He handed the envelope to Jeremy.

Jeremy opened the envelope and removed a sheet of paper that had been typewritten front and back. He adjusted the lantern so Betty could see, and they read together in silence.

Dear Jeremy,

If you are reading this letter, then I am no longer on this earth. I have instructed Mr. Takesian to find you at my passing to conduct some final business. I want you to know that he has been a faithful employee of mine for many years and is totally trustworthy. He has a gift for you that I hope you will accept with my deepest gratitude.

As you may remember, we met once on a highway in Texas. Although our meeting was brief, it changed my life for all eternity. You fixed a flat tire for me, an old man no longer able to take care of such things for himself. More than that, you were gracious and showed selfless hospitality to me, a total stranger. You gave me a cup of cold water and served beans and a hot dog meal to me, a very hungry and thirsty stranger. You showed me what it meant to serve. Up to that point, that was something I had not done well in my ninety years on this earth.

If you remember, I offered you five dollars for your services. You refused it, but suggested I find a church and place it into the offering plate. I laughed at that when you drove away, thinking you a fool, and slipped it back into my wallet. You obviously could have used it.

At first, I had no intention of putting the money into any collection plate. I was raised in the church, but I had not been in one since my years in the Marines, where I had become very cynical. But—and this I cannot explain—as the days went by, I became more and more convicted that I needed to at least do that one thing in return for your kindness. I had already been diagnosed with cancer, and I knew I had little time left.

As I sat in a church for the first time in years, I heard again the words on which I was raised and once believed. They were truths I had known but rejected all these years. Jeremy, I am not ashamed to admit that this old man wept. And like Zacchaeus who came down from the Sycamore tree, I found salvation that day and knew I needed to correct my ways.

Now that I am in the hands of Almighty God, I am satisfied. My last gesture is the gift Mr. Takesian has for you. Receive it with my eternal gratitude. I have full faith that you will use it wisely.

Semper fi,
Harold Fenwick

Jeremy slowly put the letter down.

"Mr. Fenwick was a very brilliant but eccentric man, Mr. Martel," said Mr. Takesian. "He loved work and loved money even more, hoarding it like it was his life's blood. That may explain why he never married. Do you remember that old vehicle he was driving, the one you changed the flat tire for?"

Jeremy smiled at the memory, and nodded.

"As strange as it may seem for a man of his wealth, it was the only vehicle he drove—when he drove anyplace at all for himself. A new vehicle would have cost him some of his precious money. But, as you see from the letter, he changed in his last days, thanks to you."

Mr. Takesian reopened the briefcase and withdrew a second envelope. "This is yours, Mr. Martel," he said, handing it to Jeremy.

"What is it?" Jeremy asked.

"Open it." The accountant gave a wide smile and watched carefully, much as a parent would do in anticipation of the pleasure his child was about to receive as he opened a special Christmas gift.

Jeremy carefully tore the top off the envelope and removed the contents. His jaw quickly dropped. "I don't understand, Mr. Takesian," he said. "Why would Mr. Fenwick give me a check for $5,000?"

Betty grabbed the cashier's check from her husband's hands and looked at it closely. Mr. Takesian laughed again, more loudly than before.

"Jeremy," Betty said slowly, "it's not for $5,000." He took the check from her hands and stared at it again, and then looked up in shock at Mr. Takesian.

"Your wife is quite right," Mr. Takesian said. He reached across the table and pointed to the number. "I think you missed a few zeros."

"But … but … but … I … Betty, do you know what this means? We can finally buy that set of tires for the truck."

Mr. Takesian threw his head back and roared with laughter. "It's yours, all of it, to do with as you please." He stood and began to walk back to the limousine. "Oh, and Mr. Martel," he said, turning to give one last word before he entered, "All the taxes have been paid."

The driver closed the door for Mr. Takesian and then got behind the wheel. As the limousine drove away, all Betty and Jeremy could do was look at each other in stunned silence.

"Jeremy," Betty said at length, "twenty minutes ago, we had only the change in our pockets. Now we're millionaires. I'm afraid."

"Afraid? Afraid of what, sweetheart?"

"Afraid of what this sudden wealth will do to us."

Jeremy thought for a moment. "'The end of all things,' Betty. When we found out you were pregnant, do you remember what we did?"

"Yes," she nodded. "We prayed and thanked God for a joy we never thought would be. Then we gave our yet-to-born baby back to God, to use any way He chooses."

"That's right. And that's what we need to do with this." Jeremy laid the check on the table. They joined hands, bowed their heads, and, by the light of the lantern, prayed.

—THE END—

CPSIA information can be obtained at www.ICGtesting.com
Printed in the USA
BVOW04s1807241114

376522BV00004B/22/P

9 781632 690388